Whisked Away

Avery Morgan

Table of Contents

Chapter 1

The vanilla bean paste left a sticky trail across my wrist as I scraped the last precious drops from the jar. At twelve dollars for two ounces, I wasn't wasting a speck. The anniversary cake had to be perfect: a mirror-glaze masterpiece with hand-tempered chocolate decorations that had taken me three separate attempts to get right. Ten years together deserved something spectacular, even if the last few felt like we were running on autopilot.

"Just a bit more gold dust," I murmured, using a small dry brush to add shimmer to the chocolate pieces shaped like the Millennium Park Bean where Craig had first asked me out. The kitchen timer beeped, and I rushed to the oven, pulling out the roasted vegetables for Craig's favorite salmon dish. The timing was precise: dinner at seven, cake presentation at eight, and hopefully by nine, we'd be discussing our future instead of his upcoming business trip.

Our sleek Chicago apartment gleamed in the early evening light, all stainless steel, granite, and floor-to-ceiling windows showcasing a skyline I'd once found exhilarating but now barely noticed. Everything in its place, everything perfect. Just like Craig preferred.

I glanced at my phone. 5:47 PM. He'd be home in an hour, just enough time to change out of my flour-dusted clothes and into the new dress hanging on my closet door. I'd even splurged on the expensive perfume he once mentioned liking on a coworker.

My phone buzzed against the granite countertop. Craig's face appeared on the screen, the photo from our trip to Napa Valley three years ago, the last vacation we'd taken together. I smiled, wiping my hands on a kitchen towel before answering.

"Hey! Are you on your way?" I tucked the phone between my ear and shoulder, continuing to arrange the table, setting out the Waterford crystal glasses we received as a housewarming gift but rarely used.

"Maddy." His voice had that specific tone, the one that made my stomach instantly knot. I'd heard it so many times I could predict the next words before they came. "I'm still at the office. The Singapore client called with concerns about the proposal, and the whole team is staying late to revise it."

The sterling silver fork in my hand suddenly felt very heavy. "Tonight? But it's our anniversary."

"I know, I know. I'm sorry, but this account is worth millions. Jenkins is ordering dinner for everyone." He paused. "We can celebrate this weekend instead."

I set the fork down carefully, precisely aligned with the knife and spoon. We both knew what would happen. The celebration would be rescheduled, then rescheduled again, and again until it was forgotten entirely. Just like last year. And the year before that.

"We have theater tickets for Saturday. The ones we booked three months ago." My voice remained steady, reasonable. I was always reasonable.

"Right." The distraction in his voice was evident. Someone was talking to him in the background, a female voice, laughing. "Look, we'll figure it out. I've got to go...they need me in the conference room."

"Craig, I made your favorite... "

"Thanks for understanding, Mads. You're the best. I'll make it up to you."

The line went dead before I could respond. I stared at the elaborate table setting: the linen napkins folded into roses from a technique Gram had taught me, the candles waiting to be lit, the bottle of champagne already chilling. The apartment suddenly felt too quiet, the Chicago skyline outside our twenty-third-floor window just a blur of impersonal lights.

This wasn't the first time. Or the fifth. Or even the tenth. But something about this cancellation felt different — like the final ingredient in a recipe I'd been subconsciously assembling for months.

I moved to the oven and turned it off, covering the salmon with aluminum foil. My reflection in the stainless steel refrigerator door showed a woman in a flour-smudged apron, hair escaping from a messy bun, eyes a little too glossy with unshed tears. At twenty-eight, I'd spent my entire adult life building a world around a man who increasingly seemed to exist on the periphery of it.

An unbidden memory surfaced of a thirteen-year-old me, crying over my first heartbreak in the kitchen of Gram's bakery. She hadn't offered platitudes. Instead, she'd placed a mixing bowl in front of me, saying simply, "Knead the bread, Maddison. Put your feelings into the dough."

I wasn't going to cry. Not again.

Instead, I reached for the flour canister. When emotional upheaval threatened, I had one foolproof coping mechanism: I baked. The precision of measurements, the predictable chemistry of ingredients, the reliable transformation of raw components into something beautiful. It centered me in a way nothing else could.

Thirty minutes later, I had bread dough rising on the counter, two dozen lavender shortbread cookies cooling on a rack, and was in the process of separating eggs for a chiffon cake. A knock came from the door.

"It's open, Mrs. Gonzales," I called, knowing my elderly neighbor's knock by heart. She appeared in the doorway, immediately assessing the baking chaos with knowing eyes. At eighty-two, Mrs. Gonzales missed nothing.

"Anniversary didn't go as planned?" she asked, accepting the still-warm cookie I offered her.

"Craig had to work late." The words came out flatter than my failed soufflé from last week.

Mrs. Gonzales bit into the cookie and closed her eyes briefly in appreciation. "His loss. These are divine." She settled onto a barstool at my kitchen island, watching as I whisked egg whites. "You know, my Henry worked late a lot, too. Forty-three years we were married, and I can't count how many special dinners I wrapped up and put in the refrigerator."

I smiled despite myself. "At least you got forty-three years. That's impressive."

"It is. But if I could do it again, I'd have drawn some lines in the sand much earlier." She pointed her half-eaten cookie at me with a pointed look. "Henry missed our first anniversary because of work. I told myself it was dedication. By our fifth, I realized it was a choice. Your talent is wasted here, Maddison. These cookies alone should be sold, not just given away to lucky neighbors."

"Actually..." I hesitated, then set down my whisk. "I've been thinking about that."

"A bakery of your own? Like your grandmother had?"

I nodded, opening my laptop on the far end of the counter, away from the flour dust. "I've been researching spaces. Rent is astronomical, but there's a former café in Wicker Park that might work."

I turned the screen toward her, showing the real estate listing I'd bookmarked weeks ago. The space had original tin ceiling tiles, large front windows perfect for displaying pastries, and a small courtyard in back where I'd imagined customers enjoying coffee and scones on summer mornings. I'd already sketched layouts for the kitchen equipment and display cases, calculated startup costs, and drafted a business plan. The spreadsheets were hidden in a folder labeled 'Marketing Research,' the degree program Craig kept encouraging me to pursue.

Mrs. Gonzales leaned forward, adjusting her glasses. "When did you start looking?"

"About two months ago." I hadn't told anyone, not even Craig. Especially not Craig, who thought my baking was a 'cute hobby' that distracted from supporting his career. He'd been supportive when we first met in college, had even bragged about my cupcakes to his friends; but somewhere along the way, as his law career took off, my culinary ambitions had been relegated to 'something to do after we have kids and they're in school.'

"Your grandmother would be proud. She taught you well."

"She did."

Memories of Sugar Creek flooded back. The warm, yeasty scent of Gram's bakery on summer mornings, flour dust dancing in sunbeams through the front windows, the way she let me experiment with flavors when I was barely tall enough to reach the counter. "Gram's bakery was the heart of Sugar Creek. Everyone came there — not just for baked goods, but to connect."

I remembered the morning of my sixteenth birthday, when I'd arrived at the bakery before dawn to find Gram had set up a special workstation just for me with a brand-new set of professional pastry tools and an apron embroidered with "Maddy Cakes" in blue thread.

"You have the touch, Maddison. Some people can follow a recipe, but you understand the soul of baking." I had never forgotten when she told me those words.

"That's what makes a great bakery," Mrs. Gonzales said, pulling me back to the present. "Not just good food, but heart."

I clicked through more property listings, each one simultaneously exciting and terrifying. "Craig thinks I should focus on getting my marketing degree. He says if I want to work with food, I should aim for brand management at a major corporation."

Mrs. Gonzales's expression spoke volumes. "And what do you think?"

"I think..." I paused, surprised by the certainty in my voice. "I think I want flour on my hands, not a keyboard. I want to create recipes, not marketing campaigns."

The truth was, I'd been sleepwalking through my relationship with Craig for years. He was charming, ambitious, and had a clear vision for his future. I'd been drawn to his confidence, his ability to map out every step of his career.

My father died when I was twelve, leaving my mother adrift and our family in financial uncertainty, so Craig's stability had been irresistible.

And there had been good times: the summer we backpacked through Europe, the Christmas he surprised me with cooking classes from a famous pastry chef, the way he'd held my hand at a friend's memorial service when we returned to Sugar Creek during my sophomore year. But those memories were increasingly distant, preserved like the dried flowers I kept in my journal — still beautiful, but fragile and faded.

"Then perhaps — "

My phone rang, interrupting Mrs. Gonzales. I was met with a South Carolina number that I recognized as my grandparents landline.

"Maddy?" a somber male voice asked.

"Yes, Gramps. Yes, it's Maddy. Are you okay?"

"Oh, honey," he said, his voice quivering. "I'm sorry. Your Gram passed away this afternoon."

The world tilted sideways.

The whisk slipped from my fingers, clattering against the mixing bowl. Mrs. Gonzales must have seen my face because she was suddenly beside me, her small hand on my arm.

"There was no pain," he spoke gently. "She just never woke up from her nap this afternoon. I tried to wake her, but..."

Quiet sobs drifted through the phone line, and I gripped the counter edge. My chest felt hollow, as if someone had scooped out everything inside.

"I just spoke to her three days ago; she sounded fine."

"I know it's a shock. We've got the funeral. Your grandmother always handled these things, I don't know..."

Gram was gone.

The woman who taught me to fold whipped egg whites into batter with a gentle hand, who showed me how to tell when bread was ready by the sound it made when tapped, who mailed me care packages of her famous orange marmalade scones during college finals. The one who'd been more of a mother to me than my own had managed to be after Dad died.

My phone slipped slightly in my damp hand as I pressed it to my ear. "Maddy? Are you there?" came the voice on the other end.

"Yes," I choked, my throat tightening. "I'll come tonight if I can, or first thing tomorrow. I'll try to get a flight now."

The call ended, leaving a hollow silence in its wake. I stood frozen, the phone still in my hand, until Mrs. Gonzales gently guided me toward a chair.

"Your grandmother?" she asked softly, concern etching her features.

I nodded, unable to speak for a moment. The kitchen suddenly seemed too bright, too sterile. It was nothing like Gram's warm, lived-in bakery kitchen with worn wooden counters and mismatched measuring cups.

"I need to go to Sugar Creek. The funeral..." The reality was still sinking in. "I need to pack."

Mrs. Gonzales squeezed my hand. "Go. I'll take care of things here. Should I put the food away?"

"Yes, please. And if you could water the plants while I'm gone..." I was already mentally listing what needed to be done, using logistics to hold grief at bay.

"Of course. Now go pack."

An hour later, I had a flight booked for 7 AM and was throwing clothes into a suitcase when I heard Craig's key in the door. He entered our bedroom and loosened his tie, surprise evident on his handsome face. Even after a long day, he looked impeccable: not a wrinkle in his shirt, his dark hair perfectly styled.

"What's going on? Are you packing?"

I looked up from folding a black dress. "My grandmother died this afternoon. I'm flying to South Carolina tomorrow."

His expression softened. "Oh, Mads, I'm sorry." He came closer, resting his hands on my shoulders. There was genuine sympathy in his eyes, a glimpse of the Craig I'd fallen in love with. "When will you be back?"

The question punctured the moment.

It was not 'how are you feeling?' or 'what can I do?' or 'let me pack my overnight bag and call the office.'

No. *When will you be back?*

"I don't know yet. The funeral arrangements need to be made, and I'm sure there will be things to take care of with her house and... the bakery." My voice caught on the last word.

Craig frowned. "I thought the bakery was closed years ago."

"It was. But it's still there, still in her name." I hadn't thought about what would happen to it now.

"Well, you can't stay long. We have the Hendersons' dinner party next Wednesday, and you know how important they are to the firm."

I stared at him, really seeing him for the first time that evening — his perfectly pressed shirt, not a hair out of place despite his supposedly stressful day, the faint scent of unfamiliar perfume that definitely wasn't from the bottle I'd purchased. I wondered how many times I'd chosen not to notice these things, how many times I'd decided that asking questions would be too disruptive to the perfect life we'd constructed.

"My grandmother just died, Craig."

"And I'm very sorry about that," he scoffed, his tone suggesting he was being perfectly reasonable. "But life goes on. You can't just drop everything for an indefinite period."

"That's exactly what I'm doing." I zipped the suitcase with more force than necessary. "Gram was the most important person in my life. I'm going to Sugar Creek, and I'll stay as long as needed."

"But the Hendersons... "

"Can meet your other colleagues' partners." I moved past him to gather toiletries from the bathroom. "I already booked my flight."

Craig followed me, his reflection appearing in the bathroom mirror. "You didn't think to discuss this with me first?"

"The way you discussed canceling our anniversary dinner?" The words escaped before I could filter them.

His eyes narrowed. "That was work. This is... impulsive."

"No, this is necessary." I turned to face him directly. "I'm going, Craig. I've already made up my mind."

He ran a hand through his perfect hair, his expression shifting to the one he used when negotiating — calm, yet slightly patronizing. I had once found that expression reassuring; now it made me want to throw my moisturizer at the mirror.

"Look, I understand you're upset, but there's a major presentation on Monday that I need to prepare for this weekend. I can't just drop everything to fly to South Carolina."

I paused. "I didn't ask you to."

The words hung between us. In ten years together, through all the canceled dates and rescheduled plans, I'd never directly challenged him like this. I'd been the understanding girlfriend, the supportive partner. I'd built my life around his priorities, convincing myself it was what adults did. They compromised.

But standing there in our pristine bathroom, with the news of Gram's death still raw, I suddenly couldn't remember what I'd gained from all those compromises.

Craig's expression softened, shifting to the gentle persuasiveness that had resolved so many of our past disagreements.

"How about this: you go tomorrow, attend the funeral, and come back on Monday or Tuesday. I guess I'll make your excuses to the Hendersons. And maybe we can salvage our anniversary with a weekend to Napa. Or something."

Excuses? My grandmother was gone and he thought this was a negotiation. That my grief and obligation were things to be bargained down to fit his schedule, that a weekend in wine country could replace the anniversary he'd just missed. Our dinner now grew cold in the kitchen, alongside the ten years of gradually diminishing returns on my emotional investment.

"I'll come back when I'm ready to come back." I brushed past him, returning to the bedroom to finish packing.

"Maddy, be reasonable... "

"My flight leaves at seven tomorrow morning. I need to be up at four-thirty." I closed my suitcase and set it on the floor. "There's anniversary cake in the refrigerator if you want some."

Craig's phone buzzed. He glanced at it, then back at me. "We're not done discussing this."

"Yes, we are." I walked to my dresser, pulling out pajamas.

"Maddy..."

"You should answer that. Might be Singapore calling again."

He hesitated, clearly torn between continuing the argument and checking his message. Predictably, the phone won. He stepped into the hallway, his voice dropping to that special tone he used for important clients or people he wanted to impress. The tone he used to use with me.

I sank onto the edge of our bed, suddenly exhausted. On the nightstand sat a framed photo of Gram and me from my college graduation, her arm around my waist, both of us beaming. She'd driven eight hours to attend, bringing a car full of baked goods for my roommates.

"I'm coming, Gram," I promised solemnly, touching the edge of the frame.

My gaze drifted to the bakery listings still open on my laptop. For years, I'd been measuring my life in teaspoons of ambition, carefully rationed to fit into the space Craig allowed. But Gram had always measured with a generous hand — full cups of courage, heaping tablespoons of determination.

In the morning, I'd be on a plane to Sugar Creek, leaving behind an anniversary cake neither of us would touch and, quite possibly, a relationship that had been cooling in the refrigerator far longer than tonight's uneaten salmon.

The thought should have terrified me. Instead, beneath the grief, I felt something unexpected stirring; like yeast activating in warm water, the first bubbles of something new were rising.

Chapter 2

As a parting gift to myself, I commandeered a chunk of Craig's airline miles to get myself a ticket back to South Carolina.

Payment for services rendered, I thought as I clicked 'purchase.' It was the least he could do — if he hadn't been such a thoughtless jerk, I wouldn't have needed to get away from him so quickly. Same-week airline tickets are crazy expensive, and thanks to Craig's single-minded career quest, I'd had a succession of terrible jobs that paid almost nothing. A decent guy would realize the error of his ways and at least spring for the airline ticket. He always promised me he'd bring me back to Sugar Creek; I was just helping him make good.

Maybe I'd send him a thank you note on the back of a Maddy Cakes napkin or something.

As the plane descended toward Charleston International Airport, I pressed my forehead against the cool window, watching the landscape transform from abstract patterns to distinguishable features. The lush green canopy of trees, winding rivers, and sprawling coastal marshes were all so different from Chicago's grid of concrete and steel. My stomach fluttered with a mixture of nervousness and anticipation. This wasn't just another summer visit or holiday trip. This was my life now. I was coming home.

As the wheels touched down on the runway, I exhaled slowly, trying to release the tension that had built during the flight.

Sugar Creek.

I hadn't been back since Christmas two years ago, a brief forty-eight hour visit that had ended with Craig calling repeatedly about some work emergency, cutting my time with Gram short. Before that, it had been another rushed trip for Gramps' seventy-fifth birthday. The realization made my chest tighten with guilt. Why had I let so much time pass?

The airport was a blur of motion and noise as I collected my single suitcase and made my way toward the exit. I'd packed light: just enough clothes for the funeral and a few days after.

"Maddy Bell, as I live and breathe!"

I turned toward the familiar voice, my heart lifting at the sight of my best friend in the universe, Lacy Monroe, waving frantically from the arrivals area, her wild red curls bouncing as she jumped to make herself visible in the crowd. The tension in my shoulders eased slightly. Some things never changed, and Lacy's exuberance was one of them.

"Lacy!" I called back, quickening my pace.

She enveloped me in a fierce hug that smelled of vanilla perfume and something especially Lacy: a scent that instantly transported me back to sleepovers and secret-sharing sessions under blanket forts. For a moment, I was twelve again, and the weight of adulthood lifted from my shoulders.

"Let me look at you," she said, pulling back to hold me at arm's length. Her green eyes, bright with unshed tears, scanned my face. "You look exhausted, but still gorgeous. How do you do that?"

I laughed, the sound rusty from disuse. When was the last time I'd really laughed? "It's called crying for three hours straight on a plane. Very effective beauty regimen."

Her expression softened. "Oh, honey. I'm so sorry about Beatrice. She was one of a kind."

"She was," I agreed, my throat tightening. "I still can't believe she's gone."

Lacy linked her arm through mine and guided me toward the parking garage. "Come on. I've got cold brew coffee in the car and a shoulder that's perfect for crying on. You can do both while I drive us home."

Home. The word echoed strangely in my mind. Was Sugar Creek still home? Had it ever really been when I'd only spent summers and occasional holidays here? Yet something about the word felt right in a way that Chicago never had.

Lacy's new cherry-red Jeep Wrangler was exactly what I would have expected: bold, a little flashy, and unapologetically attention-grabbing, just like its owner. She tossed my suitcase in the back and handed me a mason jar of coffee as I climbed in.

"So," she said as we pulled out of the parking garage. "Tell me everything. How are you really doing? And when are you dumping that soul-sucking leech you called a boyfriend? I can't believe he didn't even come for the funeral."

The reminder stung like salt in a fresh wound. "He had a conflict," I began, the excuse sounding hollow even to my own ears.

"He *is* a conflict," she retorted, merging onto the highway with her usual confident recklessness.

Craig's dismissive reaction to my grandmother's funeral felt like it belonged to another lifetime, though it had been less than twenty-four hours ago.

"He's...Craig," I said, too emotionally wrung out to make a better argument. "You know how it is... inertia is a powerful force."

"Mhm," Lacy hummed, not sounding convinced. "That's not a good reason to stay in a relationship and you know it. What did he say about your Gram?"

I turned to look at her, surprised. "How did you..."

"Because I know Craig Beauregard," she interrupted. "He probably said something completely tone-deaf like 'that's too bad' and then immediately started talking about some work thing."

Her accuracy was startling. "Are you psychic now?"

"No, just observant. And I've watched him pull this crap for years, Maddy. Every time something important happened in your life, he found a way to make it about him." She glanced at me, her expression softening. "I'm just glad you're finally seeing it too."

Her words stung with truth. How many times have I rearranged my life to accommodate Craig's needs? How many important moments I missed because his career always took precedence?

"He didn't even *offer* to come to the funeral," I admitted, the hurt still fresh. "Said he had a big presentation that couldn't be rescheduled."

Lacy's knuckles whitened on the steering wheel. "Of course he didn't. God forbid he supports you during the hardest moment of your life."

The drive from Charleston to Sugar Creek had taken us along winding country roads flanked by ancient oak trees draped with Spanish moss that swayed gently in the breeze.

We fell into silence as the Jeep ate up the miles between the two towns. The landscape grew more rural, with sprawling farms giving way to dense woods. I sipped my coffee and watched familiar landmarks appear: the rusty water tower with SUGAR CREEK painted in fading blue letters, the old mill that had been converted into an arts center, the sign for Springer's Orchard where Gram used to take me apple picking every fall.

As we drove through town, a wave of nostalgia washed over me. The town's welcome sign with its faded lettering, the old-fashioned lampposts lining Main Street, the town square with its white gazebo where summer concerts were held. It all looked exactly as I remembered, as if preserved in amber while I'd been away.

"You haven't been back in a while," Lacy said finally, her tone carefully neutral.

I glanced at her profile, noting the slight tension in her jaw. "Not since Christmas before last."

"Two years," she nodded. "You missed the Spring Festival. And the Fourth of July picnic. And Founder's Day."

The accusation in her voice was subtle but unmistakable. I stared out the window, guilt washing over me in a fresh wave. "Craig always had something work-related those weekends."

"And you always chose him over coming home," she finished quietly.

The truth of her words hung between us, uncomfortable but undeniable. I had chosen Craig over and over again, prioritizing his needs and his schedule above my connections to Sugar Creek — to Gram, to Lacy, to the place that had given me my happiest childhood memories.

"I'm sorry," I said finally, meaning it. "I should have tried harder to visit."

Lacy sighed, reaching over to squeeze my hand. "I'm not trying to make you feel worse, Maddy. God knows you're going through enough right now. I just... missed you. We all did. Especially Beatrice."

My eyes burned with fresh tears. "Did she... did she talk about me?"

"All the time," Lacy assured me. "She kept everyone updated on your life in Chicago. She was so proud of you."

The lump in my throat grew. Had Gram really been proud of me? What had I accomplished that was worthy of pride? A series of dead-end jobs while I followed Craig from city to city? A relationship that had gradually drained the joy from my life? I hadn't even managed to visit her regularly in her final years.

As if reading my thoughts, Lacy added, "she understood why you didn't visit more. She never blamed you."

"Maybe she should have," I whispered.

Lacy shook her head firmly. "Beatrice wasn't like that. She just wanted you to be happy." She paused, then added more gently, "Were you? Are you? Happy with Craig, I mean."

The question hit me like a smack to the forehead. Was I happy? There had been good times, especially in the beginning. Craig's charm, his ambition, the way he'd made me feel safe after years of my mother's chaotic lifestyle. But when had that safety become a cage? When had his ambition begun to overshadow my own dreams?

"I thought I was," I said finally. "Or maybe I just convinced myself I was. It's hard to tell the difference sometimes. Less lately, though."

Lacy nodded, understanding in her eyes. "Well, for what it's worth, I'm glad you're here now. Sugar Creek hasn't been the same without you."

I sat up straighter, drinking in the sights of my childhood summers. Sugar Creek's main street looked like something from a Hallmark movie: historic storefronts with colorful awnings, hanging flower baskets bursting with summer blooms, old-fashioned lampposts lining the sidewalks. People strolled along the street, stopping to chat with neighbors or ducking into shops.

"What changed while I was gone?" I asked, drinking in the familiar sights. We passed the hardware shop, where Mr. Johnson had always slipped me a piece of candy when I was little, and Miss Ellie's Flower Shop, its window boxes overflowing with vibrant blooms.

"Sugar Creek? Change?" Lacy laughed. "The biggest news last year was when they repainted the bench outside the post office. Oh, and Mr. Finley's dog learned to skateboard. That was quite the sensation."

As we turned onto Main Street, my heart skipped a beat when I caught a glimpse of a faded storefront with peeling blue paint. *Maddy Cakes Bakery*. Gram's bakery. The windows were dusty, the CLOSED sign hanging crookedly in the door.

Someone had placed a small bouquet of flowers on the doorstep; a tribute to Gram, I realized with a pang.

It had been shuttered for nearly a year, since Gram's health had started to decline. I made a mental note to come back tomorrow and assess what needed to be done.

Just across the street, I noticed a well-maintained building with a sign reading 'Sugar Creek Veterinary Clinic.' A tall man in scrubs was just locking up, a stethoscope hanging around his neck.

"That's new," I remarked, nodding toward the clinic.

"Oh, yeah, Dr. O'Connor brought in a new vet about a year ago. Dr. Townsend. He's..." Lacy waggled her eyebrows suggestively. "Well, let's just say half the single women in town suddenly discovered their kitties needed frequent check-ups."

I rolled my eyes. "I don't have a pet, and I'm not interested."

"Sure, honey. Keep telling yourself that."

We pulled up to Lacy's charming bungalow on Magnolia Lane, just three blocks from Main Street. The house was painted a cheerful yellow with white trim, flower boxes overflowing with colorful blooms beneath each window. A porch swing swayed gently in the late afternoon breeze.

"Home sweet home," she announced, killing the engine.

"Your place?" I asked, surprised.

"You didn't think I'd let you stay alone in a hotel, did you?" She pulled into the driveway of a charming craftsman bungalow painted a cheerful yellow. "Mi casa es su casa, for as long as you need it."

Emotion welled up in my throat. Despite the years and distance between us, despite my neglect of our friendship, Lacy was still the same loyal, generous soul she'd always been.

"Thank you," I managed, blinking back tears.

She squeezed my hand. "That's what friends are for, Maddy. Now come on, let's get you settled. You've got about an hour before we need to head to the funeral home."

The funeral home. Reality crashed back over me like a cold wave. I was here to bury my grandmother, the woman who had been more of a mother to me than my own mother had ever managed to be. The thought made my chest ache with a pain so intense it felt physical.

"Don't worry, I'm not going to make you sleep on the pastry table in the bakery," she cracked, "sugar bag under your poor, weary head, a thousand cupcake wrappers to keep you warm... You're staying with me."

Inside, the house was exactly like Lacy: vibrant, a bit chaotic, and undeniably welcoming. Colorful throw pillows were scattered across a comfortable-looking sofa, handmade pottery adorned every surface, and the walls were covered with framed photographs, many featuring the two of us as kids. The air smelled of cinnamon and something floral, so different from the sterile, cologne-scented air of the Chicago apartment I'd shared with Craig.

"Let me show you your room," she said, leading me down a short hallway. She pushed open a door with a flourish. "Ta-da!"

Lacy's second bedroom was adorned with my favorite color, yellow, scattered throughout the room to make me feel at home. A sunshine-yellow quilt covered the bed, complemented by throw pillows in varying shades of gold and amber. A vase of fresh daisies sat on the nightstand, and she'd even found yellow-framed artwork for the walls. On the dresser was a framed photo of Gram and me from last summer, both of us covered in flour and laughing.

My throat tightened as I took it all in. When was the last time someone had put this much thought into making me feel welcome? Into what I might like? Craig had redecorated our bedroom last year without even asking for my input, replacing my colorful throw pillows with sleek, gray ones that 'better matched the aesthetic.'

"Lacy," I whispered, suddenly overwhelmed by the thoughtfulness of it all. "You did this for me?"

"Well, I wasn't going to make you sleep in a beige guest room like some hotel," she scoffed, but I could see the emotion in her eyes too. "Yellow is happy. And you deserve happy, Maddy."

I dropped my bags and hugged her again, blinking back tears. "Thank you."

"Don't get all sappy on me," she said, pulling away with a sniff. "Save the tears for when you see the bakery tomorrow. It's going to need some serious TLC."

Chapter 3

"I don't think I can do this," I whispered, panic rising in my throat.

Lacy's expression softened with understanding. "You can. And you will. Because Beatrice deserves a proper goodbye, and you're strong enough to give her that." She reached across to squeeze my hand. "Plus, I'll be right beside you the whole time."

Her confidence steadied me. With a deep breath, I nodded and opened the car door. One step at a time. That's how I would get through this... through the funeral arrangements, through the service, through whatever came next.

What I didn't realize then was that 'whatever came next' would be far more complicated than I could have imagined.

The funeral home was exactly what you'd expect in a small Southern town: dignified, traditional, with somber lighting and the faint scent of lilies hanging in the air. Grayden Whitfield, the funeral director, greeted us with the practiced compassion of someone who had guided countless families through their darkest days.

"Ms. Bell," he said, taking my hand between both of his. "I'm truly sorry for your loss. Your grandmother was a remarkable woman."

"Thank you," I replied automatically, the words feeling inadequate. "She was."

"Please, come this way," he gestured toward a private consultation room. "Your grandfather was here earlier, but we have a few last-minute matters to discuss."

Lacy squeezed my arm. "I'll wait out here. Take your time."

The consultation room was tastefully appointed with comfortable chairs and subtle decor clearly designed to put grieving families at ease. Mr. Whitfield settled behind a polished desk and opened a leather portfolio.

"Your grandmother was quite thorough in her arrangements," he began, his voice gentle but matter-of-fact. "She left specific instructions for everything from the music to the flowers, so there isn't much for you and your grandfather to take care of."

This didn't surprise me. Gram had always been meticulously organized, from her recipe filing system to her seasonal decorating schedule. Of course, she would have planned her own funeral with the same attention to detail.

"She requested a simple service at First Baptist, where she was a member for over fifty years," Mr. Whitfield continued. "Pastor Williams will officiate. She selected hymns and readings, and planned every detail."

My throat tightened. "Thank you."

"We've scheduled the service for this evening," Mr. Whitfield continued. "There will be a visitation hour beforehand, and a reception at the church fellowship hall afterward. The burial will be private, family only, at Meadowbrook Cemetery."

I nodded, trying to absorb the information through the fog of grief. "Thank you for handling all of this."

"Your grandmother made it easy," he said with a small smile. "She wanted to spare you the burden of these decisions during your time of mourning." He paused, then added, "She spoke of you often, you know. She was immensely proud of you."

The words, so similar to what Lacy had said, pierced my heart. Had Gram really been proud of me? What had I done to deserve that pride?

"I should have visited more," I confessed, the guilt overwhelming me. "I let work and... other things get in the way."

Mr. Whitfield's expression was kind. "Ms. Bell... may I call you Maddison?"

I nodded.

"Maddison, I've been in this profession for over thirty years. I've seen every kind of family dynamic, every shade of grief and regret. And I can tell you this with certainty: your grandmother understood. She never doubted your love."

His words were meant to comfort, but they only deepened my sense of unworthiness. What had I done to deserve such unconditional love and understanding?

After finalizing the remaining details, I rejoined Lacy in the waiting area. She took one look at my face and wrapped an arm around my shoulders.

"Come on," she said gently. "Let's go for a drive before we head back to my place. I think you need to see something."

We drove in silence through town, eventually turning onto Main Street. The afternoon sun cast a golden glow over the historic buildings, warming the red brick and making the hanging flower baskets seem to glow with color. Sugar Creek looked like a postcard version of small-town America: quaint and seemingly untouched by the passage of time.

I approached slowly, feeling like I was walking in a dream. Through the grimy windows, I could make out the shapes of the display cases and counter, the small tables where customers had once lingered over coffee and pastries. How many hours had I spent in this space, watching Gram work her magic with flour and sugar? How many secrets had she shared about the perfect pie crust or the ideal rise on a loaf of bread?

"Do you want to go inside?" Lacy asked softly. "I know where Beatrice kept the spare key."

I shook my head. "Not yet. I'm not ready."

As we stood there, I noticed two men in suits further down the street, heads bent in conversation. One gestured toward the bakery, his expression animated. I couldn't hear what they were saying, but something about their demeanor — calculating, assessing — made me uneasy.

"Who's that?" I asked Lacy, nodding toward the men.

She followed my gaze, her expression darkening slightly. "The taller one is Roland Pierce. He owns the real estate development company that's been buying up properties on Main Street. The other guy is probably one of his investors."

"What does he want with Main Street?"

Lacy shrugged, but her casual tone seemed forced. "He talks about 'revitalization' and 'bringing Sugar Creek into the 21st century.' Some people are on board with his vision. Others... not so much."

As if feeling our gaze, Roland Pierce looked up. His eyes met mine briefly, a flicker of curiosity crossing his face before he turned back to his companion. A chill ran down my spine, though I couldn't quite say what caused it.

"Come on," Lacy said, tugging gently at my arm. "We should get back. You need to rest before the gathering tonight."

The community gathering to honor Gram was held at the First Baptist Church fellowship hall, a spacious room that quickly filled with what seemed like half the town. I stood in a receiving line with Gramps, accepting condolences from a steady stream of people whose faces blurred together in my grief-fogged mind.

"Is my mom coming?" I whispered to Gramps.

"She said she can't do funerals, Cupcake" he replied quietly, hurt radiating from his face. "But she'll visit in a couple of weeks." Not exactly a shocker when it came to my mother, Clare. She wasn't exactly known for her ability to handle a crisis. She'd been running from them since my father passed.

"Maddison, honey, your grandmother was the finest woman I ever knew."

"Beatrice's coconut cake recipe saved my marriage. I'm not even joking."

"She talked about you all the time, dear. All the time."

Each comment, each memory shared, built a more complete picture of the woman I'd loved but perhaps never fully known. Gram hadn't just been my summer guardian, the person who taught me to bake and listened to my childhood woes. She'd been a pillar of this community, a friend to many, a confidante, a problem-solver, a creator of traditions.

"Maddy?" A gentle voice broke through my thoughts. I looked up to see an elderly woman with kind eyes and a plate of cookies in her hands. "I'm Mamie Rockwell. Your grandmother was one of my closest friends for over forty years."

"Ms. Mamie," I said, instantly recognizing her. "How are you holding up?"

She smiled at me weakly. "I'm as heartbroken as I know you are. Who am I going to talk garden club gossip with? "

She lowered her voice conspiratorially. "Though between you and me, your grandmother was much better at growing things. I mostly showed up for the lemonade and conversation."

I smiled, warming to her kind eyes. "She always said the best part of gardening was the excuse to sit in the shade afterward."

"Smart woman, your grandmother." Ms. Mamie patted my hand. "Now, I won't keep you long, but I wanted to give you these."

She handed me the plate of cookies. "They're snickerdoodles. Not as good as Beatrice's, mind you, but I did use her recipe. She shared it with me years ago, said they were one of your favorites."

The simple kindness brought tears to my eyes. "Thank you," I managed, accepting the plate. "They were one of my favorites. Still are."

"Well, you enjoy them, dear. And when you're ready...not now, but when the time is right, I have some things of Beatrice's I'd like to pass along. Letters, recipes, that sort of thing."

I nodded, a lump forming in my throat. "I'd like that very much."

Craig's parents, the Beauregards, were next to pay their respects, and Lacy spotted them coming before I did.

"Oh look, it's Great Aunt Margaret," she snickered as Craig's father took his mother's elbow and steered her our way.

I elbowed her in the ribs as they approached.

Craig's mother Genevieve wore a tasteful, solemn ensemble as always. The queen bee of the country club set in Sugar Creek, she'd never particularly warmed to me. I suspected she'd lined up a bevy of Charleston debutantes before Craig announced we were moving in together after college, but I never knew for certain.

"We're sorry for your loss Madeline," said Mr. Beauregard as he firmly clasped my hand.

"Maddison," Lacy corrected for the nine millionth time. Craig and I had only been together for ten years. Why bother learning my name?

"I know Craig wanted to be here with you," Genevieve said dramatically, dabbing her eye with a crisp cotton hankie. And louder still, "but he's so invaluable to his firm."

It was all I could do to keep from rolling my eyes. "Thank you for being here," I mumbled.

The Beauregards spent the next ten minutes working the room before making a swift departure. To be honest, I was relieved.

As the evening wore on, I found myself observing the interactions around me with growing fascination. Sugar Creek wasn't just a collection of buildings and streets; it was a living, breathing community with complex relationships and shared history. People moved between conversation groups with the easy familiarity of those who had known each other for decades. Inside jokes were referenced, old stories retold, connections reaffirmed. I felt simultaneously part of this world and separate from it. Connected through Gram but distanced by my years away. It was a strange, liminal space to occupy.

Lacy left my side to make a plate of food for me and find some water. Saying 'thank you' two hundred times in a row was more strenuous than you might imagine.

"You look like you could use some air," a voice said beside me. I turned to find a man about my age with kind eyes and a gentle smile. "I'm Les. I worked with Jimmy at the hardware store next to your grandmother's bakery."

"Maddy," I replied, though he clearly already knew who I was. "And yes, I think I could use a break."

He gestured toward the side door leading to a small garden. "It's quieter out there. Sometimes these things can get overwhelming."

I followed him outside, grateful for the cool evening air after the warmth of the crowded room. The garden was simple but lovely, with roses climbing a trellis and stone benches placed strategically along a winding path.

"Thank you," I said, settling onto one of the benches. "It was getting a bit..."

"Suffocating?" Les suggested with understanding. "That's Sugar Creek for you. We love hard, and we grieve hard too."

I nodded, finding comfort in his straightforward assessment. "Did you know my grandmother well?"

"As well as most folks, I suppose. Our shops shared a wall, so we saw each other daily. She'd bring over muffins sometimes, and I'd help her change light bulbs or fix the occasional leaky faucet." He smiled at the memory. "She was a force of nature, your grandmother. Strongest woman I ever met, in every way that matters."

"Yes, she was," I agreed, a fresh wave of grief washing over me. "I still can't believe she's gone."

Les was quiet for a moment, respecting my sorrow. Then he asked gently, "Will you be staying in Sugar Creek long?"

The question caught me off guard. How long would I stay? I hadn't thought beyond the funeral, beyond the immediate need to say goodbye to Gram. Chicago waited for me: my apartment, the life I'd built there. But was it really a life I wanted to return to?

"I'm not sure," I admitted. "I haven't made any plans yet."

Les nodded, not pressing further. "Well, whatever you decide, know that you've got friends here. Your grandmother made sure of that."

Before I could respond, the garden door opened, and Lacy poked her head out. "There you are! I've been looking everywhere. Mr. Patterson is here."

"The lawyer?" I asked, standing up as she handed me a small plate of tiny sandwiches, potato salad, and mini cupcakes.

"Yes, he says he needs to speak with you and your grandfather. Something about Beatrice's will."

I thanked Les for the momentary escape and followed Lacy back inside. Mr. Patterson, a silver-haired man in a meticulously pressed suit, was waiting near the entrance with Gramps. His expression was solemn but not unkind.

"Ms. Bell," he greeted me with a formal nod. "I apologize for the intrusion during this difficult time, but there are matters we need to discuss regarding your grandmother's estate. Perhaps we could find a more private setting?"

The pastor's study was offered for our use — a cozy room lined with bookshelves and dominated by a large oak desk. Mr. Patterson settled behind it with the air of a man accustomed to delivering important news, while Gramps and I took the chairs opposite him.

"As you know, I served as your grandmother's attorney for many years," Mr. Patterson began, opening a leather portfolio. "She was very specific about her wishes, particularly regarding the bakery."

My pulse quickened. The bakery? What did that have to do with me?

"Beatrice left the bakery to you, Maddison," he said directly, confirming my sudden suspicion. "Including the building, all equipment, and her recipe collection."

Though I'd half-expected it from his preamble, the news still hit me like a physical blow. "She left me the bakery? The whole thing?"

"Yes," he said. "However, there are conditions to this inheritance."

Of course there were. That was so like Gram — generous but strategic, never missing an opportunity to guide those she loved toward what she believed was best for them.

"What conditions?" I asked, my mind racing with possibilities.

Mr. Patterson adjusted his glasses and read from the document before him. "The property and business known as Maddy Cakes Bakery is bequeathed to my granddaughter, Maddison Bell, with the following stipulation: she must personally operate the bakery for a minimum period of one year before any decision to sell or lease the property may be considered."

The words hung in the air between us, their implication slowly sinking in. One year. Gram wanted me to run her bakery for at least a year before I could even think about selling it.

"But I... I live in Chicago," I stammered, though even as I said it, I realized I had no job tying me there, a mostly crappy relationship, an apartment filled with sleek, uncomfortable furniture I never liked, and some memories I was increasingly eager to escape.

"Your grandmother was aware of that," Mr. Patterson replied, his tone gentle but firm. "This stipulation was very important to her. She believed you needed time to truly understand what the bakery means to this community before making any permanent decisions about its future."

I glanced at Gramps, wondering if he'd known about this. His expression was unreadable, but there was a glint in his eye that suggested he wasn't entirely surprised.

"What happens if I can't accept these terms?" I asked, though something in me recoiled at the thought of refusing Gram's final wish. "I mean, if I'm unable to..."

"Then the property goes to the Sugar Creek Historical Society, with the provision that it be maintained as a historical site but never operated as a bakery again." Mr. Patterson's gaze was steady. "Your grandmother was quite clear that if Maddy Cakes couldn't continue under your guidance, she preferred it not continue at all."

The weight of the decision pressed down on me. Stay in Sugar Creek for a year and run a bakery I had no experience managing? Or walk away and let Gram's life's work become a museum piece, a relic of the past rather than a living business?

"I don't know the first thing about running a bakery," I protested weakly. "I can bake, yes, but business management? Finances? Employees? I've never done any of that."

"Your grandmother left detailed records and instructions," Mr. Patterson assured me. "And she arranged for mentorship from Eleanor Whitman, who ran a successful business on Main Street for thirty years before retiring. You wouldn't be without support."

My mind whirled with implications. A year in Sugar Creek. A year of early mornings and flour-dusted aprons. A year of building something that was both Gram's legacy and potentially my own future. It was terrifying. It was overwhelming.

It also, I realized with a start, was exactly what I needed.

"Can I have some time to think about it?" I asked, though I suspected my decision was already forming, like dough beginning to rise in a warm kitchen.

"Of course," Mr. Patterson agreed. "However, there are some time-sensitive matters regarding the property. The building has been sitting empty for several months, and there are maintenance issues that should be addressed promptly if you decide to accept the inheritance."

Gramps spoke up for the first time. "Maddy will have an answer for you tomorrow, after the service." He looked at me, his eyes gentle but knowing. "Won't you, Cupcake?"

The childhood nickname, spoken in his gruff voice, brought tears to my eyes. He knew — of course, he knew — what my decision would be. He'd watched me grow up in that bakery, had seen the joy it brought me even as a child. He understood what it meant to me, perhaps better than I did myself.

"Yes," I agreed, my voice steadier than I expected. "I'll have an answer tomorrow."

As Mr. Patterson gathered his papers, he paused, reaching into his briefcase for a small envelope. "One more thing. Your grandmother left this for you. She asked that I give it to you after discussing the bakery."

I accepted the envelope with trembling hands, recognizing Gram's handwriting immediately. Inside was a single key — old-fashioned and slightly tarnished — with a small tag attached.

Back door, it read in Gram's neat script. *Welcome home.*

The simple message broke something open inside me. Tears flowed freely down my cheeks as I clutched the key, this tangible connection to Gram and to a future I hadn't imagined for myself but that suddenly seemed inevitable.

Gramps wrapped an arm around my shoulders, his own eyes suspiciously bright. "She always knew you'd come back, Cupcake. She was just waiting for you to figure it out yourself."

"I love you, Gramps," I said, hugging him tightly.

"I love you too, Cupcake."

As we walked back to the gathering, the key warm in my palm, I felt a strange sense of clarity descending. The path ahead was uncertain, filled with challenges I couldn't yet imagine. But for the first time in years, it felt like my path, not one I was following because it was expected or convenient.

The bakery. Gram's bakery — no, *my* bakery now. Maddy Cakes, named for me all those years ago in a gesture that had been prophetic rather than merely sentimental.

I was going to stay in Sugar Creek. I was going to honor Gram's legacy. I was going to reclaim a part of myself I'd nearly forgotten existed.

And maybe, just maybe, I was going to find my way home in the process.

Chapter 4

"Turn off your phone," Lacy instructed. "Or he'll be blowing it up all night. And tonight is all about taking care of *you*, not him. For once."

"Yes ma'am," I replied, turning my phone off.

After we arrived back at Lacy's place and I got myself unpacked, we sank into her comfy couch, scarfing down Ms. Mamie's snickerdoodles, and clutching our glasses of wine. This had been the longest day I could remember. The familiar comfort of being with my oldest friend, the one person who knew me before and after my father's death, before and after my move to Chicago, felt like a balm to my soul. The couch cushions were soft and worn, molding to my body in a way that invited relaxation, so different from Craig's expensive, angular sofa that looked impressive but was never comfortable.

"Let's play a game," said Lacy.

"Oh God no," I sighed. "It's been a day, I'm too tired for games. I just want to lie on your couch until I die."

"No, not that kind of game. Let's play a game where it's a year from now. We'll call it *Future Maddy*. And in this awesome future life, you're the proud owner of Sugar Creek's favorite bakery, Maddy Cakes, and you finally dumped Craig's sorry ass, and now you're living your best life."

"What's your point?"

"I just want you to spend ten minutes thinking about how you'd design your own life if you *did* have an amazing opportunity right in front of you, and you didn't have the psychic albatross of Craig's twenty-four-hour care and feeding always weighing on you."

I allowed my mind to explore the myriad of possibilities. "Well, obviously, I'd be extremely successful with the bakery."

"Obviously," Lacy replied.

"And obviously, I'd be living in Sugar Creek two minutes away from my bestie. And my Gramps."

"In a super cute place with flower boxes outside. Check."

"And a dog."

"That's a no-brainer. Adorable dog."

"I'd be living in the only place I've ever been that felt like home..."

"Now you're getting it," she grinned.

"That life actually sounds pretty great..." I said, my thoughts wandering off in a dozen different directions.

We talked about a million possibilities, all the fun we would have together, fantasized briefly about Craig's life falling apart in some spectacular and mortifyingly public embarrassment, and the devastatingly handsome doctor-slash-entrepreneur-slash-philanthropist who worshipped the ground I walked on that my future self was sure to fall madly in love with.

"And unlike Craig, he'd never turn down a slice of peanut butter pie," Lacy interjected. "But *of course*, he still has the abs of an action hero."

"Well, of course! He *needs* the peanut butter to fuel his workouts," I giggle, and then Lacy joins in, and in seconds, the two of us were laughing so hard I was in danger of peeing my pants.

Lacy stood up to grab another bottle of wine, and refilled my glass.

"So, how long do you think before Craig calls you asking how to use the washing machine?" Lacy winked, tucking her feet underneath her.

A hearty belly laugh erupted without warning as I tried to picture Craig attempting to do his own laundry. "Probably about the same time he calls to ask me where I buy his stupid Paleo protein bars. I've really been starting to wonder – what have I been thinking, dating him for so long? How pathetic am I to keep following him around, working dead-end jobs, and making sure everything in his life was picture perfect? I don't think he even knows my favorite color. I don't think he knows what my favorite food is."

"That's easy, yellow and peanut butter pie," Lacy said, swirling her wine. "He doesn't know what your favorite food is because you've spent the last decade bending over backwards to accommodate his dumb Paleo diet, just so he won't end up looking like his Great Aunt Margaret when he turns 40 like every other man in that family." She snorted. "Remember when he made you hide your cookie jar when his law school friends came over?"

I winced at the memory. "He said it 'sent the wrong message' about our lifestyle."

"Maddy, you are not pathetic," Lacy said, her tone shifting to something softer. "You are the sweetest person I know, and Craig knew that. He is a narcissist who took advantage of you. I don't think Craig is capable of loving anyone but himself."

I took a long sip of wine, letting her words sink in. The rich, velvety cabernet coated my tongue, warming me from the inside. "C'mon he's not all bad. Sure, maybe I should have listened to you. And Gram. You both tried to tell me he wasn't the one. I think deep down I've always known he wasn't exactly supportive, but I keep thinking he'll be better once he's more settled in his career. Or who knows, maybe some part of me is afraid to face the world alone. Maybe I've been too busy fixing Craig's meals, doing the household chores, running errands, and packing and unpacking every time we moved to new places to notice."

"You know what I think?" Lacy said, picking through the remains of the snickerdoodles. "I think you spent so much time taking care of your mom after your dad died that you never learned how to put yourself first. You just transferred all that caretaking energy to Craig."

I blinked, startled by her insight. The memory of my mother, hollow-eyed and grief-stricken, barely able to get out of bed in those first months after Dad's accident, flashed through my mind. I'd been the one to make sure bills were paid, groceries were bought, meals were cooked. I'd been twelve years old.

"I never thought of it that way," I admitted quietly.

"Well, that's what best friends are for — to point out your psychological damage," she said cheerfully. "But seriously, Maddy, you deserve someone who takes care of you as much as you take care of them. Someone who supports your dreams the way you supported Craig's for a decade."

"I can't even think about what to do about Craig or relationships in general right now," I said firmly, though a small part of me wondered what that might be like, to be with someone who actually saw me, who valued what I wanted. "My focus is entirely on the bakery."

"Of course it is," Lacy said, her tone suspiciously innocent. "I'm just saying, when you are ready to dump his sorry butt, next time aim higher than Craig-the-human-leech."

I laughed, the wine making me feel warm and loose-limbed. "When did you get so wise?"

"I've always been wise. You were just too busy baking gluten-free, dairy-free, joy-free treats for Craig to notice."

Lacy raised her glass, "Well, here's to Future Maddy, putting your dreams first, just like you deserve."

After we took a sip, Lacy placed her wine glass down on the coffee table and went to the kitchen to rummage through a drawer. She returned with a piece of paper and a pen.

"Okay, let's celebrate. How about we jot down your Future Maddy bucket list?"

"Great idea! Opening a bakery, that's definitely number one." I grabbed the pen, feeling a little thrill as I wrote the words. For so long, it had been a distant dream, something I'd do 'someday.' Now, it was happening.

"Duh, Maddy, you have been talking about that since you were nine years old; of course that is number one."

I wrote at the top of the page:

Bucket List

1. Own a bakery

"What else?" Lacy prompted. "This is your chance to dream big. This is badass Future Maddy. No more playing small to fit into Craig's life."

The wine had loosened something in me, making it easier to imagine possibilities I'd long pushed aside.

"I'd love to witness a birth someday," I said, surprising myself with the admission. "Not necessarily have a baby right now, but maybe be there for a friend, you know? There's something magical about new life entering the world."

"Ooh, good one," Lacy said approvingly as I wrote it down. "I'm not planning on pushing out any babies anytime soon, but I'll let you know if I change my mind."

"Win an award," I added, the idea growing more concrete as I spoke it aloud. "Like, a real one. For my baking. Something that proves I'm not just playing at this."

"You will," Lacy said with such conviction that I almost believed her. "Your orange marmalade scones alone deserve a medal."

The list grew as we finished our first bottle of wine and opened a second. Some items were serious: get married, become a mom, others more whimsical: run a marathon, sommelier wine night, and some just for fun: get a tattoo, name a star.

"What would your tattoo be?" Lacy asked, her words slightly slurred.

"Something small. Maybe a little whisk or rolling pin," I said, giggling at the thought. "Definitely not a tramp stamp with Craig's name."

"Thank God for small mercies," Lacy snorted.

After another glass of wine, an hour later, and many, many laughs, we finalized the bucket list.

BUCKET LIST:

1. Own a bakery

2. Witness a birth

3. Win an award

4. Get married

5. Become a mom

6. Run a marathon

7. Sommelier Wine Night

8. Get a tattoo

9. Name a star

"Okay, nine is a boring number," Lacy remarked, "I am adding one more for you."

She snatched the pen from my hand and scribbled something at the bottom of the list. I leaned over to read what she'd written and nearly did a spit-take with my wine.

"No! Scratch that off! Right now!"

"Oh no, girl. It's staying on there," Lacy said, holding the paper out of my reach as I lunged for it. "Did you or did you not tell me that you always had to fake it with Craig?"

My face burned with embarrassment, the heat spreading from my cheeks down my neck. "Yes, but..."

"Every woman deserves a toe-curling orgasm. Multiple toe-curling orgasms."

"I know what an orgasm feels like, Lacy," I hissed, glancing around as if someone might overhear us in the empty house. "There are other ways than sex."

"Yes, that's true. But until you have had one during sex, it stays on the list."

I groaned, burying my face in a throw pillow. The soft fabric smelled faintly of lavender and Lacy's perfume. "Fine, not like that is happening anytime soon. If I do dump Craig, I'm swearing off men so I can focus on my bakery."

"Until your sexy new boyfriend, the pie-eater shows up in your life."

"Right," I rolled my eyes at her.

"Just so you know," she said matter-of-factly, "there's not a single item on your bucket list pertaining to Craig. Awesome *Future Maddy* apparently gets on just fine without him."

"That's not true," I protested, "it says 'get married' and 'become a mom'..."

"You've wanted those things since we were kids," she said. "Long before you ever met Craig. Besides, you didn't say, '*Marry Craig*,' '*Have Craig's baby*.' And I guarantee you'll *still* want to get married and have a baby when, at long last, you finally see the light and dump him."

Lacy put the bucket list on the refrigerator with a magnet shaped like a cupcake. The paper fluttered slightly in the breeze from the open window, as if alive with possibility.

BUCKET LIST:

1. Own a bakery

2. Witness a birth

3. Win an award

4. Get married

5. Become a mom

6. Run a marathon

7. Sommelier Wine Night

8. Get a tattoo

9. Name a star

10. Have an orgasm during sex

I took another sip of wine, hoping at least half of them came true. And even though I didn't mean to, suddenly I couldn't stop thinking about number 10. It had been so long since I'd felt that kind of desire. I mean, had I ever, really, with Craig? Maybe back in college. Our sex life had been as routine and bland as everything else in our relationship. I'd gone through the motions, said the right things, faked the right responses, all to maintain the peace and keep him happy.

But what would it be like to be with someone who actually paid attention to *my* needs? Someone who made me feel desired, who took the time to learn what I liked?

I shook my head, banishing the thought. No. If I dumped Craig, I was done with men. I had a bakery to run, a new life to build. Romance was the last thing I needed right now.

"You know," said Lacy. "If you move back to Sugar Creek you can stay here. At least until you decide whether you want to live above the bakery or get your own place."

I squeezed her tightly and kissed the top of her head. "You're the best friend in the world."

"Don't I know it!" Lacy joked.

As I drained the last of my wine, my eyes drifted back to number 10 on that list, and I couldn't quite suppress the tiny flutter of curiosity it stirred within me.

Tomorrow, I would see my bakery. Tomorrow, I would begin bringing Maddy Cakes back to life. Tomorrow, I would take the first real step toward building a future that was entirely my own.

But tonight, in the soft glow of Lacy's living room, with the taste of wine on my lips and the comfort of true friendship surrounding me, I allowed myself to imagine all the possibilities that might lie ahead... including, perhaps, the ones I wasn't quite ready to admit I wanted.

Chapter 5

The morning after Gram's funeral, I woke to sunlight dotted through the lace curtains of the guest bedroom in Lacy's house. For a moment, I couldn't remember where I was or why my eyes felt so swollen. Then it hit me. Gram was gone, and I was now the owner of her bakery, at least conditionally.

I reached for my phone, wincing at the screen full of missed calls and texts from Craig. I'd been so emotionally drained after the funeral and the meeting with Mr. Patterson that I'd forgotten to turn my phone back on and fallen into bed without even seeing Craig's increasingly irritated messages.

The latest one read: *Need to talk ASAP. Important firm dinner tomorrow night. When are you coming home?*

Home. The word stuck in my throat. Was our sterile Chicago apartment really home? Or was it just another temporary stop in Craig's carefully plotted career path? I scrolled back through my photo gallery, finding the images I'd saved just three weeks ago: listings for small commercial kitchen spaces in Chicago's Wicker Park neighborhood. I'd been researching bakery options for months, hiding the searches from Craig, knowing he'd dismiss them as impractical.

And now, I owned a bakery. Gram's bakery.

I dragged myself out of bed and padded to the kitchen, where Lacy was already brewing coffee, her wild red curls piled haphazardly on top of her head.

"Morning, sunshine," she said, sliding a steaming mug across the counter. "You look like hell warmed over."

"Thanks," I muttered, wrapping my hands around the mug. "Can always count on you for brutal honesty."

"Someone has to do it." She leaned against the counter, studying me. "So, bakery owner. That's a plot twist."

I took a long sip of coffee, letting the rich flavor ground me like flour on a pastry board: something solid and real in a world suddenly tilted on its axis. "I still can't believe it. I mean, I knew she'd leave me something, but the whole bakery? *With* conditions?"

"The one-year rule is classic Beatrice," Lacy said, grabbing a banana from the fruit bowl. "She always said you need to fully experience something before you can make a real decision about it."

"But what if I fail? What if I run the bakery into the ground in less than a year?" The doubts that had kept me tossing and turning all night came rushing back. "I don't know the first thing about running a business."

"Bullshit," Lacy said, pointing the banana at me. "You've been baking since you could reach the counter on a step stool. You have a business degree you never use because Craig convinced you to follow him around instead, and you've been dreaming about owning your own bakery since we were nine."

"Dreaming about it and doing it are two very different things," I countered, though her confidence in me was touching. "Besides, Craig and I have a life in Chicago. His internship at Harris and Harris is supposed to lead to an associate position."

Lacy rolled her eyes so hard I was surprised they didn't fall out of her head. "Right. What *life*? Because Craig's career is all that matters. What about your career, Maddy? What about your dreams?"

I stared into my coffee, remembering the night I'd shown Craig the listings for bakery spaces. He'd barely glanced at them before launching into a lecture about market instability and small business failure rates. "You're too talented to waste your time on a risky venture," he'd said, his tone gentle but patronizing. "Focus on something stable. Marketing, maybe. Once I make partner, you can do whatever you want."

Before I could respond, my phone buzzed. Craig's name flashed on the screen.

"Call him back later. Or never. Whatever. Twenty bucks says he's not calling to see how *you* are, and you certainly don't need to listen to his boring work drama after all the stress of Gram's funeral," whispered Lacy. She suddenly did an impromptu impression of Craig, standing up very straight, cocking her head to the side like a turkey, as she straightened an imaginary tie. "And then I whipped out Addendum B!!" she cackled in a vaguely familiar voice, like she'd just delivered a punchline.

I shook my head at her, hesitated, then answered.

"Hey," I said, stepping into the living room for privacy.

"Finally," Craig's voice was smooth but there was an edge of tension beneath. "I've been calling you for hours."

"I was at my grandmother's funeral service, Craig," I reminded him, keeping my voice level. "And then I went to bed."

"Of course, I understand," he said, his tone shifting to practiced sympathy. "I know this is a difficult time. That's why I think you should come home as soon as possible. The Hendersons' dinner is tomorrow night, and I need you there. Mr. Henderson specifically asked about you."

Something in his phrasing caught my attention. He needed me there. Not *wanted*. *Needed*. As if my primary function was to support his career goals. Had it always been this way?

"Craig, my grandmother just died. I just found out I inherited her bakery. I can't just rush back for a dinner party."

"What do you mean, you inherited her bakery?" His tone shifted from sympathy to confusion. "Like, the recipes?"

"No, the actual bakery. The building, the business, everything." I took a deep breath. "There's a condition, though. I have to run it myself for at least a year before I can sell or lease it."

There was a long pause. "You're not seriously considering this, are you?" Craig finally asked, his voice carefully controlled. "Maddy, we live in Chicago. My career is here. You can't just move to some backwater town to play baker."

The dismissiveness in his voice hit me like a slap. *Play baker.* As if my passion, my skill, my dream was just a childish game.

"I haven't decided anything yet," I said, surprised by the steadiness in my voice despite the anger building in my chest. "But this is important to me, Craig. It's my grandmother's legacy. Plus, you always promised we'd move back here."

"Look, I get that you're *emotional* right now," he said in that reasonable tone he used when he thought I was being irrational. "But be practical. We can go to court so you can sell the building, take the money, and come home. We'll use it for a down payment on a condo."

The casual way he dismissed something so precious to me — folding my inheritance and my grandmother's life's work into his own plans without a second thought — made something solidify in my chest.

"I need to go," I said abruptly. "I'll call you later."

I ended the call before he could respond, my hands shaking slightly. When I turned around, Lacy was standing in the doorway, arms crossed.

"Let me guess," she said. "Craig thinks you should sell the bakery and rush back to Chicago to play the supportive girlfriend at some boring work function."

I didn't answer, which was answer enough. Lacy's expression softened.

"Come on," she said, grabbing her car keys from the hook by the door. "Let's go check out your bakery."

Maddy Cakes Bakery stood silent and dark on Main Street, the morning sun reflecting off the windows. I hesitated on the sidewalk, key in hand, memories washing over me. How many summer mornings had I spent here, flour dusting my clothes, learning the secrets of perfect pastry at Gram's side?

"You going to open it, or just stare at it all day?" Lacy nudged me gently.

I took a deep breath and unlocked the door. The familiar bell jingled overhead as we stepped inside, the sound echoing in the empty space. The display cases stood bare, the tables waiting for customers who hadn't come in months. A fine layer of dust covered everything, but beneath it, the bakery was exactly as I remembered: the blue and white checkerboard floor, the vintage tin ceiling, the worn wooden counter where generations of Sugar Creek residents had placed their orders.

"It needs some TLC," Lacy observed, running a finger through the dust on a tabletop. "But the bones are good."

I moved behind the counter, my fingers trailing over the old cash register. The brass keys were cool beneath my touch, worn smooth from decades of use. "Gram refused to upgrade to a digital system. Said she could do math in her head just fine." The memory brought a smile to my face.

"Classic Beatrice," she agreed. "Remember how she used to quiz us on how to make change while we waited for cookies to bake?"

I nodded, throat tight with emotion, and pushed through the swinging door into the kitchen. Here, in the heart of the bakery, everything was immaculately clean. The scent of vanilla and cinnamon still lingered in the air, as if Gram had been baking just yesterday. The commercial mixer, ancient but reliable, stood ready for duty. The double ovens waited for trays of pastries. The marble-topped work island where I'd learned to roll pie crust gleamed in the light streaming through the windows.

I ran my hand over the cool marble, feeling the slight dip in the center where decades of rolling pins had worn a gentle valley. "She kept it ready," I whispered. "Like she knew someone would come back to it."

"She knew *you* would come back to it," Lacy corrected, squeezing my shoulder.

I wandered to the small office tucked in the back corner. Gram's desk was neat as always; her ledger books lined up precisely, and her fountain pen placed just so beside her blotter. A faint scent of lavender, her signature perfume, still hung in the air. I sank into her chair, the leather creaking familiarly beneath me.

"I don't even know where to start," I admitted, overwhelmed by the task before me.

"How about these?" she suggested, pulling a stack of folders from the bookshelf. "Might give you an idea of the business side."

For the next hour, we pored over Gram's meticulous records. Despite her old-fashioned methods, her business acumen was impressive. She'd kept detailed accounts of everything: expenses, income, inventory, even customer preferences tracked by season.

"Look at this," I said, pointing to a notation from three years ago. "She increased production of pumpkin muffins by 20% in October because the new dentist office opened down the street, and the staff kept ordering them for meetings."

"That's the kind of local knowledge that keeps small businesses alive," she nodded. "No algorithm can replace that."

I flipped through more pages, discovering Gram's system for tracking ingredient costs, her careful notes about which suppliers offered the best quality, and her seasonal promotions that kept customers coming back year after year. She'd built relationships with local farmers for fresh eggs and berries, negotiated favorable terms with her flour supplier, and created a calendar of community events that drove business from Little League bake sales to church fundraisers.

As I examined more recent records, I noticed a troubling trend.

"Business was declining in her last year," I observed, frowning at the numbers. "Revenue dropped almost 30%."

"She was sick," Lacy reminded me gently. "She started cutting back hours, then days. The last few months, she was only open three mornings a week."

I nodded, my chest tight with grief. What must it have cost Gram to see her beloved bakery gradually closing, to lose the daily connection with her community?

A file labeled 'Correspondence' caught my eye. Inside were dozens of letters, neatly organized by date. The most recent section held multiple letters from the same source: BAM Franchise Consulting.

"What's this?" I murmured, opening the first letter.

"Dear Beatrice," I read aloud. *"Thank you for meeting with us regarding the potential franchising of Maddy Cakes Bakery. As discussed, our proposal would allow your recipes and brand to reach a wider audience while providing you with a stable income stream..."*

I flipped through more letters, each offering increasingly generous terms. The most recent, dated just eight months ago, mentioned "strategic placement in high-traffic locations throughout the Southeast" and "maintaining the authentic charm that makes Maddy Cakes unique."

"Gram was considering franchising?" I looked up at Lacy, surprised.

"Not exactly," came a voice from the doorway.

I jumped, startled to see an elderly woman standing there, her silver hair pulled back in a neat bun, her eyes sharp despite her advanced years. She wore a crisp blue dress with a hand-embroidered apron over it, the kind no one makes anymore.

"Mrs. Whitman!" Lacy exclaimed. "You scared us half to death."

"Door was open," Mrs. Whitman said unapologetically, making her way into the office with the help of a polished wooden cane. "Saw the lights on. Thought I'd see who was disturbing Beatrice's peace."

"I'm her granddaughter, Maddison," I said, standing to offer her my chair.

She waved me off. "I know who you are, girl. Got your grandmother's eyes. And apparently her bakery now." She peered at the letters in my hand. "Those vultures have been circling for years."

"Vultures?" I repeated, confused.

"BAM Consulting," she said, the name coming out like a curse. "Started showing up about five years ago. Every few months, like clockwork. Two men in fancy suits, Davis and Potter. Always the same pitch, just wrapped in prettier paper each time." She tapped the folder with her cane. "Your grandmother wasn't fooled for a minute."

"But why would she even meet with them if she wasn't interested?" I asked, puzzled.

Mrs. Whitman's eyes twinkled with mischief. "Know thy enemy, child. Beatrice wanted to understand what they were really after. First meeting, she served them her worst coffee and day-old muffins. Said if they couldn't tell the difference between fresh-baked and stale, they had no business talking about her recipes."

I couldn't help but smile, picturing Gram's subtle test. "These terms look pretty good, though," I said, gesturing to the latest offer.

Mrs. Whitman snorted. "Terms always look good on paper. It's what's between the lines that matters. Keep reading. You'll find Beatrice's replies. She kept copies of everything."

Sure enough, at the back of the folder were carbon copies of Gram's responses, each more firmly worded than the last. The final one, dated just six months ago, was particularly blunt:

Dear Mr. Davis and Mr. Potter,

As I have stated in our previous correspondence, I have no interest in franchising Maddy Cakes Bakery. The recipes and methods developed in this establishment are not for mass production. They require care, attention, and a personal touch that cannot be replicated in a franchise model.

Furthermore, I have reason to believe your interest in my property extends beyond my recipes. Let me be perfectly clear: This building, this business, and these recipes will remain in my family. They are not now, nor will they ever be, for sale to BAM Consulting or any affiliated entities.

Please do not contact me again on this matter.

Sincerely,

Beatrice Prescott

"Gram knew something about BAM," I said, looking up from the letter. "Something that made her suspicious of their motives."

"Smart woman, your grandmother," Mrs. Whitman said, settling herself on a small sofa in the corner. "Always could see through people's pretenses. Those BAM fellows, they don't care about pastries. They care about prime real estate on Main Street."

"For what?" I asked.

Mrs. Whitman's mouth tightened. "Hard to say for certain. But they've approached every independent business on this block. The hardware store, the bookshop, even my little fabric store before I sold it to the Delberts." She leaned forward, lowering her voice conspiratorially. "Your grandmother did some digging. Found out BAM is connected to a development company that specializes in turning small-town main streets into what they call 'curated shopping experiences.' Generic chain stores dressed up to look quaint."

My stomach clenched at the thought. "They want to turn Sugar Creek into a tourist trap?"

"Some folks call it progress," Mrs. Whitman said with a sniff. "Your grandmother called it the death of community."

Before I could ask more questions, my stomach growled loudly, reminding me we hadn't eaten since early morning.

"Let's grab lunch at the diner," Lacy suggested. "We can continue this investigation after food."

Mrs. Whitman insisted on locking up the bakery herself, her gnarled fingers surprisingly deft with the keys. "Been helping Beatrice close up for forty years," she explained. "Old habits die hard."

As she turned the key in the lock, she fixed me with a penetrating gaze. "What are you planning to do with the place, girl? Your grandmother had high hopes for you."

The directness of the question caught me off guard. "I'm not sure yet," I admitted. "I only found out about the inheritance yesterday."

Mrs. Whitman studied me for a long moment, then nodded once, as if coming to a decision. "You come see me when you're ready to talk recipes. I've got some of Beatrice's original formulas, the ones she didn't write down. She'd want you to have them."

With that, she turned and walked away, her cane tapping a steady rhythm on the sidewalk.

"Did that just happen?" I asked Lacy, watching Mrs. Whitman's retreating figure.

"Eleanor Whitman doesn't waste time on people she doesn't think are worth it," Lacy replied. "I'd say you just received the Sugar Creek equivalent of a royal blessing."

The Sugar Creek Diner was a local institution, its chrome-and-red-vinyl interior unchanged since the 1950s. The lunch rush was in full swing when we arrived, every booth filled with locals catching up over meatloaf specials and cherry pie. The familiar scent of coffee and grilled onions wrapped around me like a hug.

"Maddy Bell! Look at you, all grown up!" Doris, the head waitress for as long as I could remember, enveloped me in a hug that smelled of coffee and hairspray. "Heard you inherited Beatrice's place. About time we got some decent pastries around here again."

She led us to a small table by the window, efficiently taking our orders before hurrying off to greet more customers. I was just taking my first sip of sweet tea when a shadow fell across our table.

"Well, well. If it isn't Sugar Creek's newest business owner."

I looked up to see a tall, impeccably dressed man in his late forties standing beside our table. His silver-streaked dark hair was expensively cut, his smile practiced and professional. Something about him immediately put me on edge, like a soufflé that *looks* perfect when it comes out of the oven but you know will collapse at the slightest touch.

"Roland Pierce," he introduced himself, extending a manicured hand. "Pierce Development. I don't believe we've had the pleasure."

I shook his hand briefly, noting his firm grip. "Maddison Bell."

"Of course. Beatrice's granddaughter." His smile didn't quite reach his eyes. "My condolences on your loss. Your grandmother was... quite a character."

The way he hesitated made it clear this wasn't entirely a compliment.

"Thank you," I said neutrally. "She certainly was."

"Mind if I join you ladies for a moment?" Without waiting for an answer, he pulled up a chair from a nearby table. "I've been hoping to speak with you about your plans for the bakery."

Lacy shot me a warning look, but I kept my expression polite. "I've only just arrived in town, Mr. Pierce. I'm still getting my bearings."

"Of course, of course." He waved a dismissive hand. "But it's never too early to consider options. That building of yours... prime location, historic charm. But the business itself..." He trailed off and made a sympathetic face. "Well, small-town bakeries are hardly profit centers in today's economy."

"Maddy Cakes did just fine for fifty years," Lacy interjected, her tone frosty.

Pierce's smile tightened. "Times change, Miss...?"

"Monroe. Lacy Monroe."

"Ah, the Monroe family. Your father still on the town council?" When Lacy smiled stiffly, Pierce turned his attention back to me. "The point is, Miss Bell, that building is worth far more than the business it houses. I'd be happy to make you a very generous offer. No rush, of course. Just something to consider while you're... getting your bearings."

There was something predatory in his gaze that made me sit up straighter, like a hawk eyeing a mouse. I'd seen that look before, in the eyes of developers who'd approached my mother about selling our family home after my father died. They'd smelled vulnerability and moved in for the kill.

"Mr. Pierce, my grandmother's will stipulates that I must operate the bakery myself for at least a year before any sale can be considered."

His expression flickered briefly, a flash of irritation quickly masked, before smoothing back into practiced charm. "A year is a long time to put your life on hold, especially for someone used to city living. Chicago, isn't it?"

The fact that he knew where I lived sent a chill down my spine. "I haven't made any decisions yet," I said, keeping my voice even. "But I appreciate your interest."

"Of course." He stood, straightening his already immaculate suit jacket. "Here's my card. When you're ready to discuss options, any options, give me a call." He placed a heavy cream-colored business card on the table. "Enjoy your lunch, ladies."

As he walked away, I noticed him stopping at another table, where two men in similar expensive suits sat hunched in conversation. One of them glanced my way, then quickly looked away when he saw me watching.

"Well, that was subtle as a sledgehammer," Lacy said, leaning forward. "Roland Pierce has been trying to buy up half of Main Street for years. Wants to turn Sugar Creek into a 'destination shopping experience,' whatever that means."

I picked up Pierce's card, turning it over in my fingers. The weight of the cardstock, the embossed lettering... everything about it screamed money and influence.

"He seemed very interested in Gram's building," I observed.

"Location, location, location," Lacy quipped. "Corner lot, original historic features, right in the heart of Main Street. Developers drool over properties like that."

"Those men he's talking to," I said quietly, nodding toward the table where Pierce had joined the suited men. "Any idea who they are?"

Lacy glanced over casually. "Never seen them before. Definitely not locals."

A suspicion formed in my mind. "I wonder if they're from BAM Consulting."

"Wouldn't surprise me," Lacy said. "Birds of a feather and all that."

Our food arrived, momentarily distracting us from Pierce and his associates, but as I bit into my grilled cheese, as perfectly golden and gooey as I remembered, I couldn't shake the feeling that I'd just met my first adversary in Sugar Creek. And something told me he wouldn't give up easily.

Chapter 6

Three days later, I was back in Chicago, packing up my life. The apartment Craig and I had shared for the past two years felt suddenly foreign, its sleek minimalist design reflecting his taste, not mine. How had I never noticed that before? The only space that felt truly mine was the kitchen, with its collection of mismatched baking tools and dog-eared cookbooks.

I was carefully wrapping Gram's hand-painted mixing bowls when I heard Craig's key in the lock. Steeling myself, I continued packing, my movements deliberate and calm despite the anxiety churning in my stomach like over-mixed batter.

"What the hell is this?" Craig demanded from the doorway, taking in the boxes stacked in the living room.

I looked up, noting his perfectly pressed suit, his carefully styled hair. Once, I'd found his polished appearance attractive. Now, it just seemed like another mask, hiding the real person beneath.

"I'm packing," I said simply.

"I can see that," he snapped, dropping his briefcase on the counter with more force than necessary. "Why are you packing? We have the Hendersons' dinner tonight."

"I'm not going to the dinner, Craig." I carefully placed the wrapped bowl in a box. "Or any dinner. I'm moving to Sugar Creek."

He stared at me as if I'd suddenly started speaking in tongues. "You're what?"

"Moving to Sugar Creek," I repeated, my voice steady despite my racing heart. "I'm going to reopen my grandmother's bakery."

Craig straightened his blazer, a rare gesture of genuine agitation. "Maddy, be reasonable. You can't just abandon your life here on some... some sentimental whim."

"It's not a whim." I stood, facing him directly. "I've been thinking about this for a long time. Even before Gram died, I was looking into opening my own bakery."

"What are you talking about? We never discussed this." His confusion seemed genuine.

"That's the problem, Craig. We never discuss *my* dreams. Only yours." The words came easily now, as if they'd been waiting just below the surface for years. "Your internship, your career path, your five-year plan. What about my plans? My career?"

"You have a job," he said, his tone softening to the one he used when explaining something obvious to a child. "And we've talked about your future. Once I make partner, we'll have the financial stability for you to explore options."

"That's exactly what I mean," I said, frustration building. "My future is always contingent on yours. It's always 'after Craig finishes law school' or 'after Craig makes partner.' When is it my turn?"

"That's not fair," he protested. "I've supported your baking. Remember those expensive pastry classes I got you for Christmas?"

"Classes that I never got to use because we moved to Chicago two weeks later for *your* internship," I reminded him. "And yes, you've 'supported' my baking as a hobby, but never as a career. Never as something that might compete with your plans."

Craig's expression hardened. "So this is what? Some kind of rebellion? You're throwing away everything we've built because you feel... what? Underappreciated?"

"No, Craig. I'm choosing my own path for once." I took a deep breath. "The truth is, we haven't built much together. We've built your career, your reputation, your future. I've just been along for the ride."

"That's not fair," he repeated, but there was a flicker of guilt in his eyes that told me he knew I was right.

"Isn't it? When was the last time you asked about my dreams? My goals? When was the last time you even tasted something I baked without checking your phone at the same time?"

Craig's jaw tightened. "This is about the bakery. Maddy, be practical. Small businesses fail all the time. You'll pour your heart and soul into that place, and for what? To barely scrape by in some backwater town?"

"That 'backwater town' is where I spent the happiest summers of my life," I said, anger finally seeping into my voice. "And yes, the bakery might fail. But at least I'll have tried. At least I'll have lived my own life instead of being a footnote in yours."

"You're being ridiculous," Craig scoffed. "What are you going to do? Throw away ten years over some... some sugar-coated fantasy?"

His dismissive words crystallized something I'd been feeling for months, maybe years: a growing realization that Craig saw my passion as childish, unworthy of serious consideration. To him, baking was just playing with food, not a craft requiring skill, knowledge, and creativity.

"It's not just about the bakery," I said quietly. "It's about us. About the fact that you can't even see how unhappy I've been. About the fact that when I told you I inherited my grandmother's bakery, your first thought wasn't 'Congratulations' or 'How do you feel about that?' but 'When are you coming back for my work dinner?'"

Craig's expression shifted from anger to calculation: the look he got when deep in negotiations on a settlement. "Look, I understand you're emotional right now. Your grandmother just died. But making major life decisions in grief isn't wise." His voice softened to the tone he used when he wanted something from me. "How about this: take a month in Sugar Creek, get the bakery sorted out, then we'll talk about next steps. Maybe we could even look into selling it to one of those franchise operations."

The casual way he dismissed my dream and my grandmother's legacy, crystallized everything I'd been feeling for years. This wasn't a partnership. It never had been.

"No, Craig," I said, surprising myself with the firmness in my voice. "I'm not taking a month. I'm moving there permanently. And we're not going to 'talk about next steps' because there is no 'we' anymore."

His face flushed with anger. "You're breaking up with me? Over a bakery?"

"No," I corrected him. "I'm breaking up with you because we want different things. Because I've spent ten years trying to fit myself into your life, and I don't fit. I never did."

"You're making a mistake," he warned, his voice cold. "When your little bakery fantasy crashes and burns, don't come crawling back."

I felt a strange calm settle over me, like the moment when a perfect meringue forms stiff, glossy peaks. "I won't," I promised. "Because even if the bakery fails, I'll still have chosen my own path. And that's worth more than security, or living some supporting role in someone else's story."

Craig stared at me for a long moment, as if seeing me for the first time. Then, without another word, he grabbed his briefcase and stormed out, the door slamming behind him.

In the sudden silence, I waited for the tears, the regret, the fear. But all I felt was a profound relief, as if I'd set down a weight I'd been carrying for years without realizing how heavy it had become.

I pulled out my phone and dialed Lacy's number.

"Hey," I said when she answered. "You were right. I just broke up with Craig. I'm coming home to Sugar Creek. For good."

Lacy's whoop of joy was so loud I had to hold the phone away from my ear. "Hot damn! It's about time! When do you arrive? Do you need help with moving? I can round up some guys with trucks."

I laughed, a genuine laugh that bubbled up from somewhere deep inside. "I'll be there by the weekend. And yes, I'll need all the help I can get." I looked around at the boxes, at the life I was leaving behind. "I'm coming home, Lace. I'm finally coming home."

"Sugar Creek won't know what hit it," she promised. "Maddy Bell, bakery owner and newly independent woman. Watch out, world."

As I hung up, my gaze fell on the business card Roland Pierce had given me, sitting on the counter where I'd tossed it earlier. I picked it up, remembering his predatory smile, his dismissive assessment of Gram's bakery.

Small-town bakeries are hardly profit centers in today's economy.

With a sudden decision, I tore the heavy cardstock in half, then in quarters, letting the pieces fall into the trash. Pierce, Craig, everyone who'd ever disregarded my dreams or tried to fit me into their plans. They were all part of a past I was leaving behind.

As I taped up another box, I realized something. For the first time in years, I felt like myself — not Craig's girlfriend, not the accommodating partner who molded herself to fit someone else's life, but Maddy Bell, baker and dreamer. The path ahead might be uncertain, filled with challenges I couldn't yet imagine, but it was *my* path.

I reached for my recipe journal, the one I'd kept hidden in my desk drawer, filled with ideas Craig had dismissed as impractical. Flipping through the pages, I smiled at the notes for cardamom morning buns, lavender shortbread, and the experimental sourdough I'd been developing in secret.

These would be the first things I'd bake in Gram's kitchen. No, in *my* kitchen. *My* recipes in *my* bakery in *my* town.

The future belonged to me now. And it smelled like possibility, freedom, and freshly baked bread.

Chapter 7

The moving truck rumbled to a stop in front of Maddy Cakes Bakery, its brakes releasing a tired hiss that seemed to echo my own exhaustion. I sat frozen in the passenger seat, my heart pounding against my ribs as I stared at the faded blue storefront. The storefront wore its age proudly: peeling paint, dusty windows edged with gold lettering reading *Maddy Cakes, Est. 1978,* and a wooden sign overhead that creaked gently in the spring breeze. My bakery now. The thought still sent a tremor of disbelief through me.

"You gonna sit there all day, or are we unloading this beast?" Lacy asked, yanking the keys from the ignition. She'd insisted on driving the twenty-foot truck herself, a decision I'd regretted approximately twelve seconds after we left the lot.

"Just... give me a minute," I whispered, unable to tear my eyes from the building. This wasn't just another move, another temporary stop like all those cities I'd followed Craig to. This was my destination. My choice. My future.

Lacy's expression softened. "Take all the time you need, sweetie. It's a big moment."

I closed my eyes, inhaling the sweet scent of honeysuckle that drifted through my open window. When I opened them again, I noticed a small crowd had gathered on the sidewalk, watching our arrival with undisguised curiosity. Word traveled faster than light in Sugar Creek.

"No more hiding," I murmured, pushing open the door and stepping down onto the sun-warmed pavement.

The crowd surged forward immediately, led by a tall, angular woman with steel-gray hair pulled back in a severe bun that looked physically painful.

"Maddison Bell," she announced, extending a bony hand. "I'm Eliza Montgomery, head of the Sugar Creek Business Association and owner of the Magnolia Inn. We've been waiting for you."

Her tone made it sound more like a judgment day than a welcome. I shook her hand, noting her firm grip and assessing gaze that reminded me of a particularly strict math teacher I'd had in seventh grade.

"Nice to meet you, Mrs. Montgomery. I'm looking forward to joining the business community."

Her thin lips curved into what might generously be called a smile. "Yes, well, we have standards in Sugar Creek. Your grandmother understood that. I trust you will too."

Before I could respond to this cryptic warning, a stylishly dressed man in his forties gently nudged her aside. "Don't mind Aunt Eliza, she considers intimidation a form of welcome." He extended his hand, his smile warm and genuine. "Trevor Montgomery, Bloom & Grow Florist, right next door. If you need anything at all, just knock on the wall. These old buildings, sound carries like you wouldn't believe."

"Especially when certain people play their show tunes at full volume at six in the morning," Eliza muttered, shooting her nephew a pointed look.

Trevor winked at me. "Lin-Manuel Miranda waits for no one, darling."

I couldn't help but smile, instantly warming to Trevor's easy manner. Before I could respond, others pressed forward, a flurry of introductions and handshakes that left my head spinning.

"Jimmy Cheng, Riverside Hardware," offered a friendly man about my age, with kind eyes behind stylish glasses. "I've got a spare key to your place. Your grandmother left it with us for emergencies. And we've been keeping an eye on things since she moved to assisted living last year."

"Ernestine Washington, Miss Ernestine's Soul Food," announced a regal elderly woman with cocoa skin and a brightly patterned caftan. "Your grandmother and I had an arrangement. She didn't sell sweet potato pie, I didn't sell cinnamon rolls. Hope we can continue that tradition."

I nodded eagerly. "Absolutely, Miss Ernestine."

"Josephine Carter, high school art teacher and Chamber of Commerce secretary," said a woman with paint-splattered jeans and a messy bun. "We're so glad to have Maddy Cakes reopening. The students have been bereft without Beatrice's cookies for their fundraisers."

The names and faces blurred together, each carrying expectations and memories of Gram that I wasn't sure I could live up to. These people had known her for decades, had built relationships and understandings I knew nothing about. The enormity of what I was taking on suddenly hit me like a fifty-pound bag of flour dropped from a high shelf.

"Alright, folks, let the girl breathe," Lacy intervened, sensing my overwhelm. "She's got a truck to unload and a bakery to set up. Plenty of time for proper introductions later."

The crowd dispersed reluctantly, though not before several people volunteered to help unload. Almost immediately, a human chain had formed, passing boxes from the truck up the narrow staircase to the apartment above the bakery. My new home. The efficiency of the operation was impressive. Clearly, this wasn't the first time Sugar Creek had welcomed a new resident this way.

As I directed traffic at the top of the stairs, I noticed an older man standing apart from the volunteers, watching the proceedings with calculating eyes. Unlike the others, he made no move to help, instead checking his expensive watch impatiently. When he caught me looking, he offered a thin smile that didn't reach his eyes.

"Roland Pierce," Trevor whispered, appearing at my elbow with a box labeled "KITCHEN/ FRAGILE." He gestured toward the man. "Local developer. Owns half the new construction on the edge of town. Been trying to buy this building for years."

My guard instantly went up. "We met last week."

Trevor raised an eyebrow. "He's got location lust. I mean, the corner lot on Main Street? Prime real estate. Plus, rumor has it he's working with some franchise outfit from Charleston. Wants to 'modernize' Sugar Creek, whatever that means."

Before I could ask more questions, Roland approached, hand extended. "Ms. Bell, congratulations. It looks like you've met the welcome committee."

His handshake was firm to the point of discomfort, his smile practiced and slightly predatory.

"Thank you," I replied, withdrawing my hand as quickly as politeness allowed. "Everyone's been very kind."

"Sugar Creek takes care of its own," he said, his gaze assessing me like a piece of property. "Of course, running a business in today's economy... well, it's not for everyone. If you need any advice about the challenges ahead, my door is always open. Small businesses face... unique obstacles these days."

The way he emphasized "unique obstacles" made it sound like a warning rather than an offer of help. Before I could respond, a loud crash from inside the kitchen drew my attention. I excused myself, grateful for the interruption.

By noon, the truck was empty, and the bakery was filled with stacked boxes. The volunteers departed with promises to check in later, leaving me and Lacy alone in the sudden quiet.

"Well, that was Sugar Creek for you," Lacy said, collapsing onto a couch still covered in Gram's plastic slipcovers. "Nosy as hell but they'll give you the shirt off their back."

The bakery's cozy office had Gram's touch everywhere. The floral wallpaper, the crocheted afghans draped over the desk chair, the collection of porcelain birds arranged on the windowsill. Pictures of me, my mom, and Gram and Grandpa were everywhere -- on the walls, on the desk, on the small bookcase. Her presence lingered in every corner, comforting and intimidating at the same time.

"Did you see how they all looked at me? Like they were assessing whether I'm worthy of taking over Gram's legacy."

"They're just protective," Lacy assured me, though her tone wasn't entirely convincing. "Beatrice was an institution around here. People want to know if you're going to maintain her standards or if you're some city newcomer who's going to turn their beloved bakery into a cupcake boutique with nine-dollar coffee."

"No pressure or anything. Can you believe that Pierce guy showed up?" I muttered, remembering his calculating gaze.

Lacy's expression darkened. "Roland Pierce is what happens when ambition meets opportunity and ethics take a holiday. He's been buying up properties all over town, tearing down historic buildings to put up condos and chain stores. Your grandmother couldn't stand him."

"He seemed very interested in the bakery."

"I bet he was." Lacy sat up straighter, suddenly serious. "Maddy, be careful with him. He's charming when he wants something, but there's always an angle. Always."

I mentally filed away the warning. "Come on," I said, hauling myself up from the couch. "Let's go check out my new business."

The bakery kitchen looked different in the harsh light of ownership. What had seemed charmingly vintage during my childhood summers now revealed itself as worryingly outdated. The commercial mixer, a hulking KitchenAid that had probably been state-of-the-art when disco was king, had a suspicious leak beneath it. The double ovens, while clean, showed signs of wear that made me question their reliability. The refrigeration unit hummed louder than it should, suggesting it was working overtime to maintain temperature.

I ran my fingers over the worn wooden countertop, feeling the thousands of indentations where Gram had kneaded dough, chopped nuts, and rolled pastry. The surface told a story of decades of use, each scratch and stain a memory of something delicious created there.

"This is going to need some serious updating," I said, opening the ancient refrigerator. The rubber gaskets around the door were cracked and brittle, barely maintaining a seal.

Lacy nodded grimly, opening cabinets to inspect their contents. "What's your budget looking like?"

I grimaced, pulling out a notebook where I'd been tracking my finances. "I've got about eighteen thousand from my savings, which isn't much after following Craig around the country for ten years. And Gram left a small insurance policy, but most of that will go toward initial inventory and operating costs until the bakery starts generating revenue."

I flipped through the pages, showing Lacy my calculations. "Essential repairs and upgrades will cost at least thirty-five thousand, by my estimate. And that's not including cosmetic improvements like fresh paint."

"What about a small business loan?" Lacy suggested. "The bank's always been supportive of local businesses."

"Worth a shot," I agreed, though the thought of taking on debt made my stomach clench. After years of watching Craig's student loans accumulate interest while he pursued his career dreams, the idea of owing money terrified me. "I've got a meeting with the manager on Monday."

We continued our inspection, making a list of necessary repairs and upgrades. The display cases needed new gaskets to seal properly. The front counter had a worrying crack running through it. The plumbing in the single bathroom was temperamental at best. The electrical system would need updating to handle modern equipment. By the time we finished, my list of "urgent" repairs was two pages long, and my initial enthusiasm had dampened considerably.

"Hey," Lacy said, noticing my fallen expression. "Don't get discouraged. Rome wasn't built in a day, and neither was Maddy Cakes. Your grandmother started with just an oven and a dream, remember?"

"I know," I sighed, running my hands through my hair. "It's just... I want to do this right. For Gram, for the community, for myself. But looking at this list, I'm not sure where to even start."

"You start with the basics," came a gravelly voice from the doorway.

We turned to see Mrs. Whitman standing there, a large wicker basket over one arm. Without waiting for an invitation, she shuffled into the kitchen, her cane tapping against the worn linoleum, and placed the basket on the counter.

"Brought you some essentials," she said, unpacking the contents with efficient movements. "Sourdough starter... descended from your grandmother's original. Some of my raspberry preserves. Coffee, tea, and a decent loaf of bread so you don't starve while you're getting set up."

"Thank you," I said, genuinely touched by her thoughtfulness. "That's incredibly kind." I might be the first person to ever tear up over sourdough starter.

Mrs. Whitman waved away my thanks with a gnarled hand. "Not kindness, practicality. Can't have Sugar Creek's only baker fainting from hunger." She glanced around the kitchen with a critical eye, taking in the worn equipment and my growing list. "What's the verdict?"

I showed her my list, watching as she nodded at some items and frowned at others. Her weathered fingers traced down the page with the confidence of someone who'd seen this all before.

"The mixer can be rebuilt," she said decisively. "My nephew Harold's a mechanical engineer. Fixed it for Beatrice three times already. The refrigerator needs a new compressor, not replacement. The ovens..." She pointed at the list with one crooked finger. "Those might be a problem. They're ancient."

"I was afraid of that," I admitted. "And they're the most expensive item to replace."

"Hmm." Mrs. Whitman's eyes narrowed in thought, and I could practically see the wheels turning behind them. "There might be a solution, but it'll take some doing. Let me make a few calls."

Before I could ask what she meant, the bell above the front door jingled.

I exchanged glances with Lacy, who grinned. "Customers already. Good sign."

I hurried toward the front of the bakery, calling towards the door, "We're not actually open yet, but — "

The words died in my throat as I pushed open the door with my hip, but to my surprise, it unexpectedly pushed back against me, catching me off guard as I struggled to maintain my balance. Suddenly I saw a man standing on the other side of the door, his white ARMY t-shirt freshly stained with the former contents of his crushed paper coffee cup. His tall, muscular frame commanded attention, and his piercing blue eyes held a mix of what looked like curiosity and mild annoyance. Mesmerized by their deep azure color for a split second, I scrambled to regain my composure.

"I am so sorry," I blurted out, my voice tinged with embarrassment as I took in the damage. Dark coffee dripped from the hem of his t-shirt, drawing my eyes downward, and I could see steam rising from what had clearly been a very hot beverage. "I didn't expect the door to push back. Here... let me clean this up right away."

The man was silent, his gaze fixed on me as he nearly ran his fingers through his short brown hair, stopping himself as he realized he had coffee all over his hands. Despite the coffee disaster, I couldn't help but notice how his presence seemed to fill the space around us, making the doorway feel suddenly smaller.

"I've got this," I called over my shoulder, dashing back into the bakery to grab towels.

When I returned, he was still standing there patiently, examining the coffee stain with what looked like mild amusement rather than irritation. He accepted the napkins I offered with a quiet "thanks," his movements deliberate and controlled. As I mopped up the floor, his expression softened slightly, a hint of amusement flickering in his eyes as he observed my frantic attempt to restore order.

A touch of self-consciousness crept in as I suddenly became acutely aware of my own disheveled appearance, from my old Northwestern t-shirt to my hair escaping from its messy bun and now the puddle of coffee at my feet.

Not exactly a great first impression.

As I glanced down to make sure I'd gotten all the liquid, a different kind of surprise awaited me. Slightly crushed under my foot, was something soft and squishy, a pre-packaged Cinnabon like the kind you get at gas stations, and definitely not the sort of treat worthy of a proper bakery.

"Is it customary for customers to bring their own coffee and pastries to a bakery?" I joked feebly, holding up the slightly mangled pastry.

"Isn't it?" he asked, deadpan, but I caught the hint of a smile tugging at the corner of his mouth.

I laughed nervously, heat rushing to my cheeks. "Well, uh... not exactly. You're kind of my first potential customer, and here you are with your own coffee and, uh... pastry... thing."

"That could be a great marketing plan for your bakery," he said, and now the smile was definitely there, transforming his whole face. "You could just run around town knocking hot coffee out of people's hands on their way to work..."

"Now hold on..." I started, then caught his teasing tone and relaxed slightly. I handed him back the sorry, plastic-wrapped excuse for a pastry, now considerably flattened. "I am so sorry. I think I ruined your breakfast."

"It wasn't much of a breakfast, but I've had to make do since your grandmother closed up shop. She's already missed in this town."

"Thank you," I said, glancing back toward the kitchen where Mrs. Whitman and Lacy were probably listening to every word, "I miss her too. I hope I can get the shop back open soon. We can't have you eating gas station pastries every day."

His eyes crinkled in a smile that made my knees suddenly wobbly.

"Hope? It's not just about turning on the lights then?"

I shook my head, "The equipment is... vintage."

"Vintage," he repeated, the smile returning. "That's a diplomatic way of saying ancient and possibly held together with prayer and duct tape?"

"You might not be wrong," I admitted. "I'm Maddy, by the way. Maddison Bell."

"Rex Townsend," he said, extending his hand. When our fingers touched, I felt an unexpected spark of electricity that made me quickly pull away. "I run the veterinary practice across the street."

Of course he did. The attractive, helpful man I'd just doused in coffee was my business neighbor. Perfect.

"Dr. Townsend," I said, trying to regain some professional composure. "I'm so sorry about your shirt. I'm happy to wash it for you. A quick vinegar soak and that stain will come right out."

"It's Rex, and that's not necessary," he said, but I was already heading back inside.

"Please, let me at least replace your coffee and whatever breakfast I destroyed. It absolutely is necessary. I can't have the local veterinarian thinking the new baker is a walking disaster."

"Trust me, what you destroyed wasn't worth mourning," Rex said. "When do you officially open?"

"Two weeks, if everything goes according to plan," I replied, then immediately regretted the qualifier. "Which it will. Definitely."

Rex's expression grew amused again. "Those vintage equipment issues?"

Before I could answer, Mrs. Whitman appeared in the doorway. "Dr. Townsend, perfect timing. We need a man with strong arms and actual tools. These cabinet doors are hanging crooked, and this girl doesn't own so much as a screwdriver. Yet."

I opened my mouth to protest being called "this girl," but Rex was already nodding. "Happy to help, Mrs. Whitman. Let me just grab my toolkit from the truck."

"Let me at least replace your shirt," I said, offering an extra-large Maddy Cakes t-shirt.

"Thanks, that's probably more comfortable than this *slightly* damp one," he smiled, gesturing at his t-shirt fully soaked through with the contents of one extra-large coffee.

He pulled his coffee-soaked shirt over his head in one deft move, revealing a strong chest and toned abs. It suddenly got twenty degrees hotter in the bakery as Lacy, Mrs. Whitman, and I stood there with our mouths agape. Fortunately, or unfortunately, the smoke show was over in seconds as he pulled the Maddy Cakes shirt on in its place.

"I'll grab my tools."

As he walked away, I noticed the confident way he moved and the easy smile he'd given Mrs. Whitman. There was something refreshing about someone who didn't hesitate to offer help to virtual strangers.

"That one's a keeper," Mrs. Whitman said quietly, watching Rex through the window. "Good with animals, good with his hands, and he looked at you like you're something special. Also, hubba hubba."

"Mrs. Whitman!" I protested, feeling my cheeks burn. "We just met. I literally spilled coffee on him two minutes ago."

"Best meet-cute story I've heard in years," she replied with a satisfied nod. "Much better than those dating apps all the youngins use."

Rex returned with a professional-looking toolbox, and for the next hour, I surreptitiously watched him work on the cabinet doors, the loose shelf, and a wobbly table. His movements were precise and efficient, and he explained what he was doing as he worked, treating me like an equal rather than someone who needed to be protected from sharp edges.

"The hinges just needed tightening," he said, demonstrating how the cabinet door now closed properly. "And this shelf was missing a bracket. Probably worked loose over time. Easy fix."

"You make it look easy," I said. "Where did you learn to do all this?"

"Military father," he replied, testing the stability of the table he'd just fixed. "Believed every man should know basic carpentry, plumbing, and electrical work. Turned out to be useful skills in veterinary practice too. You'd be amazed how many barn repairs I've done over the years."

The mention of barns made me curious about his practice, but before I could ask, a buzzing pop came from the display area. We both rushed toward the sound to find that the refrigerated display case was dark and no longer running.

"Well," I said, staring at what was sure to be an expensive and necessary repair, "that's not good."

Rex was already grabbing his toolbox. "Let's not panic just yet. It might just be the fuse. Let me see what I can figure out."

I winced. "Maybe. You don't have to clean up my disasters, Dr. Townsend."

"Rex," he corrected, not looking up from his work. "And yes, I do. Neighbors help neighbors in Sugar Creek. Besides," he glanced up with that disarming smile, "practically the whole town is counting on you bringing back your grandmother's cinnamon rolls. I'm investing in the future of my breakfast."

Something about the way he said 'future' made my heart skip a beat. As we finished cleaning up the glass, I found myself stealing glances at him: the way his hair fell across his forehead when he bent down, the competent way he handled the cleanup, the fact that he'd spent his morning helping a stranger without expecting anything in return.

"Thank you," I said as we headed towards the fuse box in the back of the shop. "For the help, for not being angry about the coffee, for... everything."

"Thank you for giving me something to look forward to. It's been a while since I had a reason to be excited about breakfast."

There was something in his tone, a hint of loneliness, maybe, that made me want to know more about him.

"Yep, that was it," he said, pointing to the blown fuse. "Might be a fluke, might be a problem. Let's see if we can at least get the case running again." He dug around in his toolbox, and pulled out a small box of fuses with a triumphant grin. "This should do it."

He replaced the burnt fuse, "Go ahead and take a look at the case to see if it's back on. I'll stay here, I want to see if it blows again."

I thanked him and headed up front. "It's on!" I yelled. "Thank you so much! I really can't handle another repair bill."

Rex emerged from the back room and inspected the case. "You'll want to keep an eye on that, but it seems like it's okay for now."

"Thank you again. At this point, I'm going to owe you free pastries for life," I smiled.

"I think I'm getting the better end of that deal," he grinned.

But before I could respond, his phone buzzed.

"Emergency call," he said, glancing at the screen. "I'm sorry to run off, but Mrs. Peterson's cat apparently got into something she shouldn't have. I've got to get back to the clinic, she's already there." He grabbed his toolbox from the back, headed for the door, then paused. "Will I see you around, Maddy?"

The way he said my name sent another flutter through my chest. "I'll be here for the next two weeks, trying to get this place ready. If you need a daily dose of chaos, you know where to find me."

"I might take you up on that," he said, and then he was gone, leaving me standing in my half-demolished bakery with a racing heart and the lingering scent of his cologne.

"That," said Mrs. Whitman, emerging from the kitchen where she'd been conspicuously absent during the cleanup, "is exactly what this place needed."

"A refrigerator disaster?" I asked, still staring at the door Rex had disappeared through.

"A man who doesn't run away when things get messy," she replied with a knowing smile. "Your Gram always liked him."

As I looked around at my disaster of a bakery — broken equipment, scattered boxes, a growing repair list — I realized Mrs. Whitman was right. Rex hadn't just stayed; he'd helped. Without being asked, without expecting anything in return, and without making me feel incompetent or overwhelmed.

I didn't feel...alone.

The bell above the door chimed again, and I looked up hopefully, but it was just Lacy returning with sandwiches from the deli down the street.

"Did I miss anything interesting?" she asked, taking in my slightly dazed expression. She whispered dramatically, "Did he take his shirt off again?"

"Thanks for lunch. Just the... beginning of something?" I said, unsure if I was talking about the bakery, my new life in Sugar Creek, or the way my pulse still hadn't quite returned to normal.

But as I bit into my sandwich and looked around at the work ahead of me, I realized I was excited rather than overwhelmed. This afternoon I'd start tackling that repair list. In two weeks, I'd open my doors to the community. And somewhere in between, I had a feeling Dr. Rex Townsend would be stopping by for coffee and conversation.

For the first time in years, uncertainty felt like possibility rather than fear.

Chapter 8

I arrived at the bakery at five-thirty in the morning to find my world shattered. Literally. Broken glass sparkled across the sidewalk like tears, and my grandmother's hand-painted "Maddy Cakes" sign lay in shards near the door. My hands trembled as I fumbled for my keys, my heart hammering against my ribs.

The front door hung slightly ajar, the lock mechanism damaged but not completely broken. I pushed it open cautiously, flipping on the lights with a shaking finger. Relief flooded through me as I surveyed the interior. Whoever had tried to break in hadn't made it past the front entrance. The display cases stood intact, the kitchen untouched. A small relief.

But that beautiful sign, the one my grandmother had painted by hand when she renamed the bakery for me all those years ago, was destroyed. I knelt on the sidewalk, gathering the larger pieces, blinking back tears. This felt like more than vandalism, it felt personal. So personal.

Who would do such a thing? And why? My grandmother was beloved in Sugar Creek. Was this about me? Rowdy teenagers? Some kind of threat? An accident?

My mind spun with hurt and fear, anger and sadness, and a thousand questions about *who* could have done this, and *why*.

"Maddy? What happened here?"

I looked up to find Rex jogging toward me, his morning run apparently interrupted by the sight of me crouched among broken glass in my pajamas and hastily thrown-on coat. His hair was slightly damp with sweat, and concern etched deep lines around his eyes.

"Someone tried to break in," I managed, holding up a piece of the sign with my grandmother's delicate brushwork still visible. "They didn't get inside, but they destroyed this."

Rex immediately knelt beside me, his presence warm and reassuring in the pre-dawn chill. "Did you call the police?"

I shook my head. "I just got here. I haven't... I don't even know what to do first."

"Police first, then cleanup," he said decisively, pulling out his phone. "You shouldn't be handling this alone."

As Rex made the call, I continued collecting sign fragments, feeling overwhelmed by the violation of this space that meant everything to me. When he finished, he gently took my hands, still clutching broken pieces.

"Let me help," he said simply.

The police arrived within ten minutes, the benefits of small-town service, and took a brief report.

"Who would do this?" I asked the officer, trying my best to be strong but knowing I'd cry my heart out the second I was alone. "Is this someone angry about me reopening the bakery?"

Officer Martinez, a kind woman in her forties, assured me, "most likely not. This was likely just random vandalism. Possibly teenagers."

"Are you sure?"

"Maddy Cakes was closed a long time. The vandals might have assumed the bakery was still vacant."

That made sense. It sucked, but it made sense.

The security of knowing it wasn't targeted didn't ease the sting of seeing my grand-mother's art destroyed.

"We'll check with the businesses nearby to see if anyone has a camera that caught your vandal. Most of the shops here don't bother, but it's always a possibility."

After the police left, Rex rolled up his sleeves. "What do you need to happen before the bakery opens today?"

"I can't open with the front door like this," I said, examining the damaged lock mech-anism. "And the sign..." I gestured helplessly at the pile of broken wood and glass.

"Lock's an easy fix," Rex said, getting closer to examine the damage. "I've got tools in my truck. The sign will take more time, but we can secure everything else."

"You don't have to — "

"Maddy." He placed his hands on my shoulders, his blue eyes serious. "Let me help."

Something in his tone, the quiet certainty, made me nod. "Okay."

Rex was comfortable with his tools, his strong hands repairing the broken door. Within an hour, he'd installed a temporary lock and helped me sweep up the glass. I watched him work, noting the careful way he handled my grandmother's broken sign pieces, setting them aside with reverence rather than just discarding them.

"You're good at this," I observed, as he tested the new lock mechanism.

"Growing up, if something broke at our house, you learned to fix it yourself or did without," he said simply.

I was about to ask more about his background when the bell above the door chimed. A young woman with short brown hair and bright, eager eyes stepped inside, carrying a large portfolio case.

"Oh! I'm sorry, are you open? I saw the lights..." She trailed off, taking in the temporary repairs and remaining glass fragments. "Oh no!"

"We're not quite open yet," I said, but something about her earnest expression made me pause. "Can I help you with something?"

"I'm Allison Carmichael," she said, extending her hand. "I just graduated from the Culinary Institute, and I was hoping to speak with you about a position."

Rex and I exchanged glances. "I'm not really hiring right now," I began, but Allison's face lit up with such hope that I felt terrible crushing it.

"I know you probably get a lot of applicants," she said quickly, "but I have a special connection to this place. My great-grandmother used to work for Mrs. Prescott when the bakery first opened. She always told me stories about the recipes and the care that went into every item. I've been dreaming of working here since I was a little girl."

That stopped me cold. "Your great-grandmother worked here?"

"Eleanor Barkley. She helped Mrs. Prescott develop the recipe for her famous pecan pies. My family still makes them at Christmas using her notes."

I looked at Rex, who raised his eyebrows. The universe seemed to be sending me help whether I'd asked for it or not.

"I can't pay much," I said honestly. "Actually, I can't pay anything until the bakery's profitable. I'm barely scraping by as it is."

Allison's smile didn't dim. Not even a little. "I understand. Could I work for experience? And maybe... trade? I could help with the morning prep, learn your methods, and in exchange, you could teach me the business side? I'm good with social media, bookkeeping, customer service..."

Before I could respond, another voice interrupted. "My goodness, Maddy, what happened here?"

Roland Pierce stood in the doorway, immaculately dressed despite the early hour, his expression a picture of concerned sympathy that somehow felt calculated.

"Break-in attempt," I said carefully. "Nothing serious."

"How terrible." He stepped inside, surveying the scene with sharp eyes. "You know, this is exactly the kind of thing I worry about with these old buildings. The security systems are outdated, the neighborhood watch is practically non-existent..."

Rex straightened beside me, and I sensed tension radiating from him.

"Mr. Pierce," Rex said evenly. "Kind of early to be checking on local businesses, isn't it?"

Roland's smile was smooth as silk. "I was driving by on my way to a breakfast meeting in Charleston. When I saw the police car earlier, I made a mental note to circle back and check on our newest entrepreneur." His gaze settled on me with what felt like predatory interest. "These kinds of incidents really highlight the vulnerabilities of running an independent operation."

"What do you mean?" I asked, though something in his tone set my nerves on edge.

"Well, when you're part of a larger organization, you have resources. Security systems, insurance protections, and corporate backing when things go wrong. Independent businesses..." He gestured around the damaged entrance. "They're so exposed."

"The bakery is fine," I said firmly. "This was just random vandalism."

"Of course, of course." Roland raised his hands peacefully. "I'm just saying, if you ever want to discuss options that could provide more *security*, more *stability*... Well, I know people who specialize in helping small businesses transition to more sustainable models."

Rex moved closer to me, a subtle but unmistakable positioning that made Roland's eyes narrow.

"That's very kind," I said. "But I'm committed to running this as an independent business."

"Admirable," Roland said, though his tone suggested he found it naive rather than impressive. "Well, if you change your mind, you know where to find me. Sometimes the universe has a way of showing us when we need help."

After he left, an uncomfortable silence settled over us.

"I really don't like that guy," Rex said bluntly.

"Maybe he was trying to help," I said, though I didn't entirely believe it myself.

"He was pushing an agenda." Rex began packing up his tools. "Just... be careful with him, okay?"

Allison had been quietly observing this exchange, and now she cleared her throat. "If it helps, I could work early shifts. Extra eyes on the place, you know? My great-grandmother always said this bakery was the heart of Sugar Creek. I'd hate to see anything happen to it."

Looking at her earnest face, then at Rex's concerned expression, I felt a warmth that had nothing to do with the rising sun. Maybe I didn't have to face all these challenges alone.

"You know what?" I said to Allison. "Let's talk. But first, help me figure out where I'm going to find a replacement sign."

Rex paused in his packing. "Actually, I might know someone who does hand-painted signs. Local artist. She's good."

"Really?"

"Really. And Maddy?" He touched my arm gently. "You're going to be okay. The bakery's going to be okay."

As I watched him walk away, and turned back to find Allison beaming at me, I almost believed him.

Later that morning, while Allison helped me get the bakery in shape before our opening, I was cleaning behind the damaged display case when my fingers found something unexpected: a small wooden box wedged into a gap between the case and the wall. I worked it free, finding it was an old recipe box I'd never seen before.

Inside were cards written in my grandmother's familiar handwriting, but these weren't typical recipes. They were notes, observations, warnings. And at the bottom of the stack, a card that made my blood run cold:

Remember, the legacy is about more than recipes. Some people will try to buy what cannot be bought. The heart of this place lives in its independence. Protect it always. - B.P.

On the back, in different ink: *Roland Pierce, 1995. Franchise International, 1998. Sweet Dreams Corp, 2003. All refused. Stand firm.*

I stared at the card, my grandmother's final message, and realized that my morning's challenges were just the beginning.

Chapter 9

The rhythmic whirring that had been my morning soundtrack for the past two weeks suddenly transformed into an ominous grinding sound, like metal teeth trying to chew through concrete. I looked up from the batch of cinnamon rolls I was preparing, my heart sinking as the ancient KitchenAid mixer shuddered to a stop mid-knead.

"No, no, no," I whispered, rushing to the machine that had been Gram's faithful companion for over thirty years. The dough hung limply from the hook, half-mixed and useless. I pressed the power button repeatedly, but the mixer remained stubbornly silent except for an occasional mechanical wheeze that sounded like its dying breath.

The grand opening was in exactly nine days. Nine days to establish Maddy Cakes as a legitimate business, and my most essential piece of equipment had just surrendered the fight.

I pulled out my phone and dialed the repair service, already knowing what they'd tell me. After a fifteen-minute hold punctuated by cheerful elevator music that made me want to scream, a gravelly voice confirmed my worst fears.

"Ma'am, that model's been discontinued for twenty years. Parts are nearly impossible to find, and even if I could locate them, you're looking at more than the machine's worth. My honest recommendation? It's time for a replacement."

The number he quoted made my stomach drop. Three thousand dollars for a decent commercial mixer — money I'd already mentally allocated to oven repairs and ingredient inventory. I thanked him and hung up, staring at the silent machine that represented just one more obstacle in my increasingly precarious path to opening day.

"Think, Maddy," I muttered, rolling up my sleeves. I'd watched Gram coax this mixer through countless tantrums over the years; maybe I could perform one more miracle.

Two hours later, I was elbow-deep in mechanical components I didn't understand, my apron stained with grease and my confidence thoroughly shattered. The mixer sat in pieces on my prep table like a patient that had died during surgery.

The bell above the front door chimed, and I looked up to see Rex's familiar silhouette through the window between the kitchen and main dining area. My pulse quickened... not just from attraction, though I couldn't deny the way my heart did a little flutter when I saw him, but from embarrassment. I was supposed to be a competent business owner, not a woman surrounded by mechanical carnage at eight in the morning.

"Maddy?" His voice carried concern as he approached the kitchen. "I saw the lights on and thought I'd check on you. Everything okay?"

I gestured helplessly at the disassembled mixer. "Define okay. If you mean 'is my essential equipment completely dead nine days before my grand opening,' then yes, everything's fantastic."

Rex stepped around the prep table, his trained eyes taking in the scattered parts. "Mind if I take a look?"

"Are you secretly a mixer repairman in addition to being a veterinarian?"

He smiled, that easy grin that always seemed to calm my nerves. "I'm pretty handy."

I stepped aside, grateful for any help but trying not to get my hopes up. "The repair guy said it's beyond saving."

Rex crouched beside the mixer's motor housing, his hands moving with the same careful precision I'd watched him use with animals. "Those guys make money selling new equipment. Sometimes they're right, but sometimes..." he paused, "Hand me that flashlight?"

For the next hour, I watched Rex work with quiet concentration, his competent hands bringing order to the mechanical chaos I'd created. He explained each step as he worked, his voice patient and reassuring. When he asked me to hold a component or shine the light at a specific angle, our fingers would brush, sending small electric shocks up my arm that had nothing to do with the equipment we were repairing.

"There," he finally said, wiping his hands on a shop towel. "Try it now."

I held my breath and pressed the power button. The mixer sprang to life with its familiar whir, steady and strong. Relief flooded through me so suddenly that my knees felt weak.

"Rex, you're amazing. How did you — "

"The motor mount had come loose and was causing the grinding. Simple fix once you know what to look for." He studied my face with those perceptive blue eyes. "But this is just a temporary solution, Maddy. This mixer is on borrowed time."

The relief evaporated as quickly as it had come. "How long do you think I have?"

"Maybe a few months if you're lucky. But you should start planning for a replacement."

Three thousand dollars I didn't have. I forced a smile, not wanting Rex to see how much this setback affected me. "Well, at least I can get through the grand opening. Thank you so much for saving my morning."

"It's what neighbors do," he said, but there was something in his tone that suggested he meant more than just physical proximity.

I wondered why he was helping me so much. Not that I minded, of course. He was pretty handy, not to mention pretty easy on the eyes. (Although he did make it very hard to focus sometimes.) It was no mystery why he'd become one of the ladies of Sugar Creek's most popular attractions. I mean, who doesn't love a vet? Especially a tall one with mischievous eyes.

Reopening Maddy Cakes was the toughest thing I'd ever done after losing my dad, and I needed all the help I could get. But it was interesting, how he always appeared just at the right time.

I was probably reading too much into it.

Maybe it was just a bit of culture shock, being back in a small town after living in a big city. Three hours later, I sat in the sterile office of Sugar Creek Community Bank, facing loan officer Penny Williams across a desk that seemed designed to intimidate borrowers. Her sympathetic smile didn't quite reach her eyes as she slid my loan application back across the polished surface.

"I'm sorry, Miss Bell, but given your current lack of income and the seasonal nature of bakery businesses, we can't approve additional funding at this time." She folded her hands, the gesture somehow managing to be both apologetic and final. "If you could provide additional collateral or a co-signer with established income..."

"What about the property value?" I asked, grasping for any possibility. "The bakery building has to be worth something as collateral."

"The building is certainly valuable, but it's tied up in your inheritance terms. Until you've operated the business successfully for the required year, we can't consider it as loan security."

I left the bank feeling like I'd been punched in the stomach. Three thousand dollars for a mixer. Nearly every piece of equipment on its last legs. Another thousand for the initial inventory I'd need for opening week. My emergency savings account, already depleted from earlier renovations, couldn't cover everything.

But I had to make it work. The alternative, giving up on Gram's bakery after coming this far, wasn't an option I could accept.

I trudged back to the bakery, the loan officer's words echoing in my mind. No additional funding. No collateral. No co-signer. Just a whole lot of problems and not nearly enough solutions.

The afternoon sun streamed through the dusty front windows as I unlocked the door, illuminating the half-finished space that represented both my dream and my biggest challenge. Dust motes danced in the sunbeams, making the emptiness of the bakery seem almost magical. But I couldn't afford to be enchanted by dust particles when I had a business to launch.

I slumped onto one of the newly refurbished chairs, forcing myself to take a deep breath. Getting overwhelmed wouldn't solve anything. Gram always said that when your hands are shaking from worry, the best thing to do is put them to work. And there was still plenty of work to be done.

The paint cans I'd purchased last week sat untouched in the corner. The walls needed a fresh coat, something to cover the faded yellow that had seen at least two decades of bakery life. I'd chosen the color ages ago, just waiting for the perfect place.

Painting would be the perfect mindless activity to process my disappointment. I pried open the first can with a screwdriver, the smell of fresh paint filling my nostrils as I stirred the thick liquid into a smooth consistency.

As I taped along the baseboards and trim, memories of another painting project surfaced. Craig had been buried in law school textbooks, and I was determined to keep my baking dream alive, even if it was just theoretical planning at that point. I'd spread color swatches across our dining table, already picturing my future bakery.

"What's all this?" Craig had asked, seemingly annoyed I was taking up space on our dining table, and barely looking up from his constitutional law casebook.

"Just planning for my future bakery," I'd replied, excitement bubbling in my voice. "I've always imagined blue walls with bright yellow accents. This one is perfect." I'd held up the Resolute Blue, the one that reminded me of Gram's eyes.

Craig had given the swatch a cursory glance. "You should go with Manitou Blue," he'd said, pointing to a completely different shade. "Superior undertones."

I'd stared at him, taken aback by his dismissive tone. "I really love this one," I had insisted. "It's peaceful. And it's the same color as Gram's eyes."

"Do whatever you want," he'd said with a shrug, turning back to his book. "But Manitou Blue is objectively better."

I'd folded up my swatches and put them away, the joy of planning momentarily dimmed. It was such a small thing, but looking back, it was one of the countless moments where Craig had subtly diminished my choices, my joy, my vision.

Rolling the first streak of Resolute Blue onto the wall felt like a declaration of independence. This was my bakery, my dream, and I would paint it whatever damn color I wanted.

Two hours and one wall later, I stepped back to admire my work. The blue transformed the space, making it feel both larger and more intimate at the same time. It was exactly what I'd envisioned all those years ago.

I kept painting, losing myself in the rhythm of the work. The repetitive motion was meditative, allowing my mind to wander. Despite the bank's rejection, I wasn't going to give up. There had to be a solution to my financial challenges. Maybe I could phase in equipment purchases, starting with only the essentials. Or perhaps I could find used equipment in better condition than what Gram had left behind.

By late afternoon, I'd finished three walls and made considerable progress on my mental state as well. The panic had subsided, replaced by a stubborn determination. I would make this work, one way or another.

I set down my roller and stretched my stiff shoulders, realizing I'd been painting for hours without a break. Stepping outside for some fresh air seemed like a good idea. Plus, I needed to check on another project I'd been thinking about.

The sidewalk in front of the bakery was quiet at this hour, most of Main Street's shops already closed for the day. I retrieved the stainless steel dog bowl I'd purchased from the hardware store, filled it with fresh water from a jug, and placed it strategically near the small bench outside my shop. With the veterinary clinic directly across the street, I figured offering water for the four-legged patients might be a nice gesture... and maybe bring in some two-legged customers as well.

I was adjusting the bowl's position when I heard footsteps approaching.

"Planning a pet-friendly establishment?" Rex's voice sent an unexpected flutter through my chest.

I looked up to find him in his green scrubs, white coat thrown over his shoulder, the late afternoon sun catching gold highlights in his hair. His smile was warm if a bit tired around the edges.

"Just being neighborly," I replied, straightening up. "You've got the pet clientele cornered, so I thought I might as well cater to them too."

"Smart business move," he said, crouching down to examine my handiwork. A small furrow appeared between his eyebrows. "Although, community water bowls can sometimes be vectors for parasites and bacteria."

I felt my face fall a little, and he quickly added, "I know you mean well. Maybe just make sure to change the water every hour or so and wash the bowl with soap. Your heart's in the right place."

"Noted, Dr. Townsend," I said, trying to keep my tone light even as I mentally added 'wash dog bowl hourly' to my ever-growing list of daily tasks.

He straightened, his eyes catching on something over my shoulder. "You've been painting?"

I turned to follow his gaze. Through the window, the fresh blue walls were clearly visible in the slanting evening light.

"Yeah, trying to breathe some new life into the place." I gestured to the small spots of blue paint that had somehow found their way onto my forearms despite my careful rolling.

"It looks good," he said, his eyes moving from the walls back to my face. "The color suits you." He reached forward and gently brushed a fleck of paint from my cheek with his thumb leaving a trail of tingles. Something in the way he said it made me feel warm all over. It wasn't just a casual compliment; there was a note of genuine appreciation in his voice that Craig had never once managed in ten years of the relationship.

"Thanks," I said, suddenly shy. "It's actually a color I picked out years ago. Resolute Blue."

"Resolute," Rex repeated, a slight smile playing at the corners of his lips. "That fits too."

Before I could respond, the town hall clock chimed six, its resonant tones carrying down Main Street.

"The council meeting," I said, remembering with a start. "I need to get over there."

The Sugar Creek Town Council was voting tonight on a historic preservation ordinance that would affect all the Main Street businesses, including my bakery. I'd planned to attend but lost track of time with all the painting.

"I'm heading that way myself," Rex offered. "Want to walk together?"

I hesitated for just a moment, glancing down at my paint-spattered clothes. "I'm a mess."

Rex's eyes swept over me, lingering in a way that made my pulse quicken. "You look fine to me. Besides, showing up with a little paint on your clothes just proves you're a working business owner, not someone who just talks about it."

His words bolstered my confidence. "Alright then," I said, quickly locking the bakery door. "Let's go represent the small business contingent."

We fell into step together, the evening air cool on my skin after the warmth of the bakery. The town hall was only a few blocks away, an elegant brick building with white columns that housed both municipal offices and community meeting spaces.

"So," Rex said after a comfortable moment of silence. "How are the bakery preparations coming along? Besides the painting, which looks fantastic."

I considered giving him the polite answer, the one where everything was on track and under control, but something about his genuine interest made me opt for honesty instead.

"Honestly? I'm facing some challenges," I admitted. "Equipment issues mainly. The mixer you fixed this morning? That's just the beginning. I need to replace several key pieces before opening, but the bank turned down my loan application today."

I hadn't planned to share that last part, but it slipped out anyway. Rex's expression grew thoughtful.

"That's tough," he said. "Banks can be short-sighted, especially with new businesses. But from what I've seen, you're resourceful. You'll figure it out."

His confidence in me, stated so matter-of-factly, felt like a warm blanket on a cold day.

"What about you?" I asked, eager to shift the conversation away from my problems. "What brings you to the council meeting?"

"The historic preservation ordinance," he said. "If it passes, it'll protect buildings like yours and mine from developers who'd rather tear down and rebuild than preserve what makes Sugar Creek special."

"You own your building?" I asked, surprised.

"Bought it last year when Dr. O'Connor decided to semi-retire. She still comes in for special cases, but the practice is mine now." There was unmistakable pride in his voice, the kind that comes from building something meaningful.

"That's impressive," I said, and meant it. "So we're both invested in keeping Sugar Creek's character intact."

"Exactly," he said with a smile that crinkled the corners of his eyes. "Though I suspect Roland Pierce will be there arguing the opposite. He's intent on buying practically all of Main Street."

"He's already approached me," I said, remembering the conversation that had left me feeling vaguely unsettled. "Very smooth talker, but something about him seems..."

"Off?" Rex supplied. "Trust that instinct. Roland's idea of progress usually involves bulldozers and franchise agreements."

We reached the town hall steps, the building's windows glowing invitingly in the deepening twilight. Rex paused, turning to face me.

"Listen, Maddy," he said, his voice taking on a more serious tone. "About the equipment issues... I might know someone who could help. An old college buddy runs a restaurant supply company in Charleston. They often have refurbished equipment at decent prices. I could put in a word."

I blinked, caught off guard by his offer. "That would be... really helpful, actually. Thank you."

"Don't thank me yet," he said with a slight grin. "His stuff isn't fancy, but it's reliable. Kind of like me."

The self-deprecating joke made me laugh, easing the tension that had built up during our conversation. As we climbed the steps side by side, I felt a growing certainty that Rex Townsend was becoming more than just a helpful neighbor or potential friend. The way my body seemed attuned to his every movement, the comfort I felt in his presence despite having known him for such a short time — these weren't casual reactions.

And that was terrifying. I'd come to Sugar Creek to rebuild my life and launch my business, not to dive into another relationship.

Yet as we entered the crowded meeting room together, his hand lightly touching the small of my back to guide me through the throng of people, I couldn't deny the spark between us. For now, I told myself, I would focus on the bakery and the council meeting. The rest wasn't helping matters.

The room was packed, every folding chair occupied and people standing along the walls. Clearly, the historic preservation ordinance was a hot topic. Mayor Whitman sat at the center of the council table, her silver hair pulled back in a no-nonsense bun. I recognized several other shop owners from Main Street scattered throughout the audience.

And there, in the front row with a portfolio of documents on his lap, sat Roland Pierce, his expensive suit making him look out of place among the casual attire of most Sugar Creek residents.

Rex and I found standing room near the back just as Mayor Whitman called the meeting to order. As the discussion began, I listened intently, trying to understand the nuances of the proposed ordinance. It would require maintaining the historic facades of buildings in the designated district, limit signage size and style, and establish a review process for major renovations.

For property owners like me who wanted to preserve their buildings' character, the ordinance seemed like a blessing, but I could see why developers like Roland might oppose it.

When the mayor opened the floor for public comments, Roland was the first to approach the microphone. His voice was smooth and confident as he outlined his concerns about 'stifling economic growth' and 'preventing necessary modernization.' He painted a picture of a dying town center that needed revitalization through new development. Development he was eager to provide.

Several people spoke after him, most in favor of the preservation ordinance.

"These restrictions will kill business development," argued a man I didn't recognize, his expensive suit marking him as someone from outside Sugar Creek. "You can't preserve your way to prosperity."

"And you can't destroy character for the sake of profit," shot back Jimmy from the hardware store. "We've seen what happens when chain stores move in. Local businesses disappear, and communities lose their souls."

I hadn't planned to speak, but as I listened, I felt an unexpected surge of conviction. This wasn't just about my bakery; it was about what kind of community Sugar Creek would be.

Before I could talk myself out of it, I was moving toward the front of the room. Rex gave me an encouraging nod as I passed by.

"I'm Maddison Bell," I said, my voice carrying farther than expected in the suddenly quiet room. "I recently reopened my grandmother's bakery on Main Street, and I wanted to share why these preservation measures matter to someone starting a business here."

My hands trembled slightly, but I pressed on. "I inherited Maddy Cakes about a week ago. And what drew me back to Sugar Creek wasn't just the building. It was the character of this place. The way neighbors help each other, the way businesses serve the community rather than just extracting profit from it."

I caught Rex's eyes, his encouraging nod giving me confidence to continue.

"The preservation ordinances won't prevent progress," I said, finding my rhythm. "They'll ensure that progress respects what makes Sugar Creek worth preserving. My bakery benefits from being part of a historic district that draws visitors who value authenticity. We need to protect what makes us unique, not homogenize ourselves in pursuit of generic growth."

The applause that followed was warm and genuine, and I felt a sense of belonging I hadn't experienced since childhood summers with Gram. As I returned to my seat, several people offered quiet words of support.

I felt *legitimate.*

"Well said," murmured the woman beside me. "We need more young business owners who understand what this town means."

After the meeting, I lingered outside the community center, still processing the evening's discussions. The preservation measures had passed by a comfortable margin, but the underlying tensions about Sugar Creek's future were clearly far from resolved.

"That was quite a speech," said a familiar voice behind me.

I turned to find Roland Pierce approaching, his smile friendly but somehow calculating. "Mr. Pierce."

"Fascinating to see how passionate people get about maintaining the status quo," he said smoothly.

Something in his tone set me on edge. "I'd hardly call protecting our community character 'status quo.'"

"Oh, I agree completely," he said, his voice taking on a more earnest quality. "Historical preservation is crucial. But so is ensuring that businesses can actually survive and thrive within those preserved facades." He studied my face carefully. "Speaking of which, how are the renovations progressing? I imagine you're discovering all sorts of *unexpected* expenses."

The accuracy of his observation made me uncomfortable. "Things are going well, thank you."

"I'm glad to hear it. Though I have to say, from a business perspective, I admire your courage in taking on such a challenging venture. Independent food service has notoriously thin margins, especially in a seasonal tourism market like ours."

"Many businesses face challenges," I replied carefully, wondering where this conversation was heading.

"Absolutely. Which is why I've been so impressed by some of the innovative approaches I've seen recently." He reached into his jacket and pulled out an elegant business card. "I've been working with a company that specializes in helping independent establishments maintain their local character while accessing the resources they need to truly succeed."

I accepted the card reluctantly; BAM, the company everyone had been warning me about.

"They're not like the typical franchise operations," Roland continued, his voice taking on the smooth cadence of a practiced sales pitch. "They focus specifically on preserving local traditions while providing the business support that makes the difference between struggling and thriving. Given your obvious commitment to quality and community values, I think you'd find their approach very compelling."

My grip tightened on the card. "I'm not interested in franchising."

"Of course, not...not in the traditional sense. But what if you could maintain complete control over your recipes and operations while accessing professional marketing support, proven business systems, and,most importantly, the financial backing to handle any unexpected equipment needs or expansion opportunities?"

The mention of equipment needs felt too coincidental to be casual. "How do you know about my equipment situation?"

His smile never wavered. "Sugar Creek is a small town, Miss Bell. Word travels. I simply notice when a promising new business faces the kinds of challenges that could benefit from the right kind of support."

"And you just happen to have connections with a franchise company that specializes in exactly the kind of support I might need?"

"I believe in bringing solutions to problems," he said simply. "The representative from BAM will be in Sugar Creek next week. No obligation, of course, but they'd love to meet with you and explain how their partnership model works. You might be surprised by how closely their values align with yours."

"Think about it, Miss Bell. Sometimes the best way to preserve independence is to ensure you have the resources to maintain it."

After he walked away, I stood under the streetlight examining the card. The cynic in me recognized a perfectly timed sales pitch, but the part of me that had spent the morning surrounded by mixer components and the afternoon being rejected by the bank couldn't quite dismiss the possibility he was offering.

Three thousand dollars for a mixer. More equipment failures were inevitable. The constant pressure of operating on such thin margins that any setback could destroy everything I was working to build.

I slipped the cards into my pocket and headed home, but Roland Pierce's words echoed in my mind: 'Sometimes the best way to preserve independence is to ensure you have the resources to maintain it.'

The worst part was some small part of me was beginning to wonder if he might be right.

Chapter 10

I'd been awake since 3 AM, standing in the bakery kitchen with flour up to my elbows, a sheen of sweat on my forehead despite the pre-dawn chill. The soft opening of Maddy Cakes Bakery was less than four hours away, and terror gripped me like a vise.

"What if nobody comes?" I whispered to the empty room, my voice bouncing off stainless steel mixers and industrial ovens. "What if they come but hate everything?"

I squinted at the recipe card in my grandmother's precise handwriting, a recipe I'd made a hundred times before, but suddenly I couldn't remember if I'd added the baking powder or if I was supposed to fold or beat the egg whites. My hands trembled slightly as I wiped them on my apron.

The industrial oven, the same one my grandmother had used for decades, made a concerning grinding noise before settling into its familiar hum. The sound sent a flash of panic through me. *Not today. Please not today.*

Focusing on the tasks at hand, I methodically filled trays with croissants, danishes, and my signature orange scones, arranging them in the still-working display cases. Every surface gleamed, every detail perfect. I'd been cleaning for days.

"It's just baking," I reminded myself. "You know how to bake."

But this wasn't just baking anymore. This was my livelihood, my dream, my second chance. This was the culmination of everything I'd walked away from Chicago for. Everything I'd walked away from Craig for.

The bell above the door jingled, and I nearly dropped the tray I was holding.

"Whoa, you look like you've seen a ghost," Allison said, slipping off her raincoat. "How long have you been here?"

I glanced at the clock. "Three hours... give or take."

Allison's eyes widened. "Maddy, you need to pace yourself. This is a marathon, not a sprint."

"I know, I know," I said, but my voice lacked conviction. "I just... I want everything to be perfect."

"Perfect is overrated," Allison replied, tying an apron around her waist. "Let's aim for 'amazing but sustainable.'"

I laughed despite my nerves, once again grateful that I'd hired her. In the weeks since she'd started, Allison had proven herself not just capable but essential: her culinary school training complementing my self-taught techniques. More importantly, she had a calm steadiness I desperately needed on days like today.

"The health department gave us final approval yesterday, right?" she asked, washing her hands at the sink.

"Yes, thank god. Everything passed inspection." I didn't mention how close it had been, or how many last-minute fixes we'd needed after discovering the refrigeration unit wasn't maintaining temperature correctly. That was yesterday's crisis. Today had enough of its own.

By 6:30 AM, the bakery was filled with the intoxicating scents of butter, sugar, and freshly baked bread. The cases were stocked, coffee was brewing, and the handwritten chalkboard menu displayed today's specials. The morning light was just beginning to filter through the freshly washed windows, casting a golden glow on the polished countertops. The gorgeous blue walls made the space feel both nostalgic and fresh.

"Allison, would you mind finishing the specials display while I check the register one more time?" I asked, my stomach fluttering with nerves.

"On it," she replied with an easy confidence I envied. Allison moved with practiced efficiency, arranging pastries on tiered stands while I counted the float money and made sure the credit card system was working properly.

At 6:55 AM, we stood side by side, surveying our work. The bakery looked beautiful — better than I'd imagined during those long Chicago nights when dreaming of this moment was all that kept me going.

"We did it," I whispered, half to Allison and half to myself.

She squeezed my hand. "No, Maddy. You did it. Now let's see what Sugar Creek thinks of your grandmother's legacy."

The next minutes seemed to stretch into hours as we waited for our first customer. My heartbeat synced with the methodical ticking of the wall clock, a cherished heirloom salvaged from my grandmother's kitchen. Each passing moment heightened my anxiety. Had I made a terrible mistake? Would anyone care that Maddy Cakes Bakery had reopened?

At precisely 7:00 AM, the bell above the door chimed, signaling our first customer. My heart leaped into my throat as I looked up from arranging the display case.

Rex Townsend stood in the doorway, the early morning sunlight creating a golden outline around his tall frame. He was dressed casually in jeans and a button-down with rolled-up sleeves, looking unfairly handsome for this hour of the morning.

"Looks like I'm your first customer," he said with that easy smile that did absurd things to my pulse. "Couldn't wait to see what all the fuss was about."

I straightened my shoulders, suddenly conscious of the flour probably dusting my nose and the loose strands of hair escaping my hasty ponytail. "Welcome to Maddy Cakes," I said, trying to sound professional despite the inexplicable jumpiness in my stomach.

Rex approached the counter, his eyes scanning the freshly stocked display case. "Everything looks amazing," he remarked, his gaze lingering on the orange scones. "What would you recommend?"

"The orange marmalade scones are my personal favorite," I admitted. "Made with my grandmother's recipe, but I add a bit of fresh ginger to enhance the citrus."

"Sold," he said. "And a black coffee, please."

As I prepared his order, the bell chimed again. I looked up to see an elderly man in a navy cardigan stepping inside, pausing to inhale deeply.

"Well now," he said, his wrinkled face breaking into a smile, "smells just like Beatrice never left."

My throat tightened. "Mr. Daniels?" I recognized him from my childhood summers. He'd come every morning for coffee and Gram's bran muffins.

"The very same," he replied, approaching the counter. "Hoped I'd be your first customer, just like I was for your grandmother forty-seven years ago." His gaze shifted to Rex, and he chuckled. "But it seems the good doctor beat me to it."

I placed Rex's scone and coffee on the counter. "This is on the house," I told him. "After all the help you've given me with repairs, it's the least I can do."

Rex's eyebrow arched slightly. "I appreciate the gesture, but I insist." He placed a five-dollar bill on the counter, then turned to greet Mr. Daniels. "Good morning, sir. How's that hip doing?"

As the men exchanged pleasantries, I turned my attention to Mr. Daniels. "What can I get for you today?"

"Coffee, black. And one of those bran muffins if you've kept your grandmother's recipe," he replied, setting exact change on the counter.

My hands trembled slightly as I wrapped the muffin. "I haven't changed a thing about that recipe, sir."

He nodded approvingly. "I'll be the judge of that."

As I handed him his order, Mr. Daniels leaned in conspiratorially. "See that dollar taped to the register?" He pointed to the framed bill hanging on the wall behind me. "First dollar I ever spent here. Your grandmother said it was good luck to keep your first dollar. Looks like she kept it all these years."

I glanced at the faded bill, the date on it marking a time long before I was born. "I had no idea that was from you."

Mr. Daniels smiled, his eyes crinkling at the corners. "Your grandmother would be proud, Maddison. This town needs its heartbeat back."

Rex took his coffee and scone to a small table by the window, and I forced myself to focus on other customers as they began arriving, rather than stealing glances at him. I mostly failed at this endeavor.

When the morning rush finally subsided, I spotted Rex's five-dollar bill still on the counter where I'd been too busy to put it away. Picking it up, I noticed something written on the edge in neat, precise handwriting:

YOUR FIRST DAY.

-RT

I felt a smile spread across my face as I carefully placed the bill in the register. Maybe I'd frame it.

The morning continued to flow with a steady rhythm of customers, and I was just beginning to feel a sense of accomplishment when I heard it — an ominous mechanical gurgle followed by a hiss from the espresso machine.

"Uh, Maddy?" Allison called, a note of concern in her voice. "Something's wrong with... "

The espresso machine gave a final dramatic sputter before going completely silent. My stomach dropped. The morning rush was just hitting its stride, and at least half our customers were ordering coffee.

"Keep taking orders," I instructed Allison quietly. "I'll see if I can fix it."

I hurried to the machine, trying to project calm confidence while internally panicking. The pressure gauge was fluctuating wildly, and steam was escaping from a valve that definitely shouldn't be leaking. I'd watched a maintenance worker repair it during my training with Gram years ago, but I couldn't remember the specifics.

"Trouble?" a deep voice asked near my ear. I turned to find Rex standing closer than expected, his coffee cup empty.

"Just a minor technical glitch," I said, trying to sound casual as I fiddled with the machine's knobs.

"Mind if I take a look?" he offered.

I hesitated only briefly. Pride wasn't worth losing customers. "Be my guest."

Rex set down his cup and studied the machine with the same focused attention I'd seen him give the mixer earlier. His hands moved confidently over the various components, checking connections and adjusting pressure valves. There was something undeniably attractive about his competence.

"The pressure release valve is stuck," he diagnosed. "Do you have a small wrench?"

I grabbed my brand new toolkit from beneath the counter, and Rex selected the appropriate wrench. Within minutes, he had the machine humming properly again. "We need some machine oil to keep this running properly, I'll swing by the hardware store later and see if Jimmy has something."

"You're a lifesaver," I whispered gratefully as he washed his hands at the sink.

"Just returning the favor," he replied. "That scone was possibly the best thing I've ever tasted."

The compliment warmed me more than it should have. "Really?"

"Really." His voice was low, just between us despite the crowded bakery. "You're talented, Maddy. Don't let anyone tell you otherwise."

Our eyes locked for a moment that stretched beyond professional courtesy. Something electric passed between us before the bell chimed again, breaking the spell.

"I should get to the clinic," Rex said, glancing at his watch. "But I'll be back."

"Is that a promise or a warning?" I asked.

"You pick," he grinned. "But save a cookie for me later, would you?"

"Anything for my favorite volunteer repairman."

He winked at me and waved as he headed towards the front door.

The lunch rush hit harder than I anticipated, with many morning customers returning and bringing friends. By 2 PM, we'd sold out of nearly everything except a few cookies and muffins. My feet ached, my back was stiff, but I'd never been happier.

Allison and I worked side by side, serving the final customers before our scheduled closing time. As the last patron left, she flipped the sign to CLOSED and we both collapsed onto stools.

We were sold out.

"That," she declared, "was amazing."

I grinned, too exhausted to speak but glowing with pride. We'd done it, actually pulled off our first day with only minor hiccups.

"So...Dr. Townsend made a big save today. Who knew the good doctor was so handy with a wrench?" Allison laughed. Of course, it will just add to the Sugar Creek mystique."

"What's that?" I laughed.

"The whole town is just drooling over him. I swear my cousin keeps adopting hamsters just so she has an excuse to go see him."

"So he's single?" I asked overly-casually and then immediately felt my skin flush. *What was I doing?*

"He's in between casual relationships right now," she grinned, like she was letting me in on a state secret.

"What do you mean?"

"Let's just say he's very popular with the ladies, but he never sticks around long enough for it to get serious. Everyone says he's a gentleman. But..."

"But what?" I asked, a little too interested.

"But then, poof! He's left with a trail of disappointed gals who feel like they just met the one who got away."

I mentally packed that away as we finished wiping down the counters.

"Go home and rest," I told Allison after we'd cleaned up. "You were incredible today."

"You too, boss," she replied with a grin. "See you bright and early tomorrow?"

"I'll be here," I promised. After Allison left, I sat at the counter with the day's receipts, calculating our sales with growing excitement. We'd made almost double what I'd projected for the soft opening.

I was just finishing the count when a knock sounded at the door. Rex stood outside, holding what appeared to be a small toolbox.

I unlocked the door, acutely aware of my disheveled appearance after a long day. "We're officially closed, but I might make an exception."

"Not here as a customer," he said, holding up the box. "Thought you might want a more permanent fix for that espresso machine before tomorrow."

"You don't have to do that," I protested, but stepped aside to let him in.

"Consider it an investment in my future coffee drinking," he replied, already heading toward the machine.

I watched as he worked, explaining each step of the repair as he lubricated the pressure release valve. There was something comforting about his presence... steady and unpretentious despite his obvious intelligence.

"Craig would have just told me to buy a new one," I said without thinking, then immediately regretted mentioning my ex.

Rex glanced up, his expression unreadable. "Sometimes the things worth keeping require a little TLC." He tightened a final component and wiped his hands on a shop towel. "There. That should hold for a good long while."

"Thank you," I said, meaning it deeply. "Not just for this, but for earlier, too. You saved the day."

"You would have figured it out," he replied with unexpected conviction. "But I'm happy to help when I can." He hesitated, then added, "The bakery's going to be a success, Maddy. Your grandmother would be proud."

Something about his certainty made my throat tight and my eyes burn. Coming from him, it didn't feel like empty reassurance.

"I hope so," I managed.

"I know so," he countered.

I pulled a box from behind the counter, "Your cookies."

"I could get used to this," he smiled, digging into the box immediately. He took a big bite of a chocolate chunk cookie, his pleasure evident all over his face. "Mmmm that's good. I'm going to have to run an extra mile a day to burn off my new Maddy Cakes habit."

I beamed.

"Maddy, there's something you should probably be aware of."

"What's that?" I asked, suddenly anxious again.

"Roland Pierce was watching the bakery all morning from across the street."

"What a creeper. No means no, buddy."

"He's persistent but mostly harmless," Rex said, his tone darkening. "Just... be careful with any offers that seem too good to be true."

Before I could ask what he meant, Rex's phone buzzed. He checked it and grimaced. "Emergency at the clinic. I've got to run."

"Of course," I said, following him to the door. "Thanks again for everything."

"Anytime," he replied, and I had the distinct impression he meant it. "By the way," he added, pausing at the threshold, "save me an orange scone tomorrow?"

I found myself smiling. "I'll set one aside."

After locking the door behind him, I leaned against it for a moment, processing the day. The bakery had been well-received, the finances looked promising, and I'd even managed to handle a crisis without falling apart. It felt like a solid start.

The bakery's grand opening was the day after tomorrow, only one day away--and for the first time since I stepped inside the bakery a few weeks ago, it felt like I might actually pull it off.

Chapter 11

When I got back to Lacy's bungalow after the bakery's first successful day, I collapsed onto the bed without even kicking off my flour-dusted sneakers.

I'd been so busy opening the bakery, I hadn't had a moment to set up my apartment. And after so much time apart over the last few years, Lacy and I were in no rush to split up our ongoing slumber party.

Every muscle ached from hours of standing, baking, and greeting customers with my brightest smile. But beneath the physical exhaustion was a bone-deep satisfaction. I'd done it, opened my own bakery, served my first paying customers, taken the first real step toward the life I'd always dreamed of.

I woke to the sound of Lacy bursting into my bedroom, flipping on the lights with dramatic flair. The digital clock on the nightstand read 7:30 PM.

"Up and at 'em, sleeping beauty! Let's go out for drinks and celebrate your big day," she announced, yanking open my closet doors and rifling through my clothes.

I groaned, burying my face in the pillow. "Can't we just order pizza and watch a movie? I'm exhausted."

"Absolutely not," Lacy declared, pulling out a dress I hadn't worn in years. "This is a momentous occasion. You've officially broken free from Craig's soul-sucking orbit, opened your dream bakery, and served your first paying customers. That calls for proper celebration, not sweatpants and Netflix."

An hour later, after Lacy had practically forced me into a form-fitting black dress and heels that made me at least five inches taller, we headed out of the apartment. I wobbled slightly, unused to walking in anything higher than the sensible shoes I wore for baking.

"Wow, that's quite an outfit," Lacy said, nodding in approval as we waited for our rideshare. The black dress hugged my curves in ways my usual jeans and t-shirts never did, and the belt accentuated my waist.

"If this isn't a fuck-you Craig, showing the world you are better off without him, then I don't know what is," she joked.

I laughed, surprised to realize I hadn't really even missed Craig over these past few months. How was that even possible? My entire world had revolved around him for a decade, and now, it sometimes felt like he was never there at all. Like I'd wasted ten years of my life on a relationship that had left no lasting impression except the echo of his constant criticism.

"I'm not sure about these," I said, taking a few unsteady steps in the five-inch heels Lacy had insisted I wear. The last time I'd worn heels this high was at a firm dinner with Craig, where I'd spent the entire evening feeling like an impostor among the polished wives and girlfriends of his colleagues.

"You look amazing," Lacy assured me. "And they're the perfect height to look down on Craig if we happen to run into him."

"Funny," I rolled my eyes, checking my reflection one last time in the hallway mirror. The woman staring back at me looked confident, sexy even — someone I barely recognized. "It's not every day I get to let loose and trade my apron and sneakers in."

"You look like a new woman," Lacy said, her expression softening.

"Yeah, I do," I agreed, kissing her on the cheek as we headed out the door.

We arrived at the Sugar Creek Country Club just a short time later. The Club was the epitome of elegance in Sugar Creek; the go-to venue for major events like weddings, parties, and school dances.

Lacy's family were long-time members, but my grandparents had never been the country club type. Gram always said she preferred flour on her hands to white gloves, and Gramps claimed golf was "just an excuse for men to escape their wives for five hours."

"You were right about this place," I remarked to Lacy as I took in the classic, timeless surroundings. "It's a nice change from the honky tonks we usually visit."

Lacy scanned the surroundings appreciatively. "You are a businesswoman now, it's only fitting to celebrate here. Look at those plush, deep-red armchairs. That's a nice upgrade since the last time I was here."

"Have you seen the Beauregards since Gram's service?" she asked.

"No, and I'm really hoping we don't see Craig's parents tonight."

"It's a small town, so you're bound to run into them, but thankfully they're not at their usual table," Lacy whispered.

Heading towards the bar stools, I couldn't help but appreciate the sophisticated ambiance: the gentle, muted gold walls and the grand crystal chandelier suspended from above, bathing the space in a cozy, golden radiance. Behind the bar, the bartender was expertly mixing drinks, the sound of ice clinking against glass filling the air. The bar was well-stocked with top-shelf liquor and fine wines, displayed on gleaming glass shelves that lined the walls.

As we made our way to the vacant bar stools, I noticed the other patrons. There were well-dressed businessmen sipping scotch and discussing deals, couples sharing romantic moments over glasses of champagne, and a group of friends laughing and chatting while enjoying colorful cocktails. It was a far cry from my usual environment of flour-covered countertops and the comforting scent of vanilla extract.

We were greeted warmly by the bartender, a middle-aged man with salt-and-pepper hair and a friendly smile. I ordered an espresso martini, craving something that would both celebrate the occasion and keep me alert after my long day, while Lacy opted for a gin and tonic.

"Cheers to finally opening your bakery," Lacy said, raising her glass to clink against mine.

"And to the single life and having fun," I added, taking a sip of my martini. The rich coffee flavor mixed with the sharp bite of vodka sent a pleasant warmth through my chest.

"The single life has treated me well," Lacy said, stirring her drink with the small plastic straw. "But just because I think Craig never deserved you, doesn't mean you have to be single forever. You can have both, Maddy, your dream job and your dream guy."

"I am not ready to jump into anything else, anyway," I responded honestly. "Truth is, I think I relied on Craig more than I care to admit. I never allowed myself to truly evolve into the person I wanted to be, settling instead for a mediocre relationship. I guess I was afraid of failing and taking risks by myself. Moving around constantly with him and working dead-end jobs left me feeling unstable and incapable of venturing out on my own. Now, here I am with way more responsibility than I ever had before..."

"Bullshit, Maddy," Lacy interjected, her voice sharp with conviction. "You always had the talent and strength. Maybe there was a part of you that used Craig as an excuse to not take the risk and go after your own dreams. But he always made you feel like you weren't good enough, too. And it's hard to muster up your bravery to go for your dreams when the person who's supposed to love you is constantly cutting your legs out from under you. Remember when he said that you could never compete with the real bakeries in Chicago? I wanted to fly up there and punch him right in the face."

I winced at the memory. Craig had said that after I'd spent an entire weekend perfecting a new recipe, only to have him dismiss it with a casual "It's fine, but it's not like you're going to be the next Dominique Ansel or anything." I remembered how I'd smiled and pretended it didn't hurt, then quietly thrown away the recipe I'd been so proud of. I'd never tried it again.

"Deep down, I think I always knew the truth... Craig was controlling and manipulative, making me believe that sacrificing so much for him was the right thing to do." I took another sip of my martini, the alcohol warming my veins and loosening my tongue. "He was pursuing his career, and he made me feel selfish if I tried to put energy into my dreams. Honestly, Lacy, I am so over him. But now really putting myself out there with the bakery is terrifying. What if Sugar Creek doesn't like it, or me? It's such a tight-knit community."

The melody of a piano playing in the background caught my attention, a soft jazz tune that seemed to float through the air, wrapping around us like a comforting blanket.

"Maddy, everyone will love you just like they loved your Grams," Lacy said, her voice softening. "You are kind, giving, and really make some amazing frigging scrumptious goodies. I believe in you."

And so did Grams.

It was time I believed in myself. I took a sip of my martini and scanned the room. The air was alive with the chatter of old friends, the clink of glasses, and the warm glow of soft lighting. Despite the comforting atmosphere, I couldn't help but feel like an outsider. I had grown up in the city, surrounded by the hustle and bustle, but it never felt like home to me. I hoped Lacy was right, and the town would welcome me, so I could make this place my true home.

In my mind's eye, I pictured a space that was warm and inviting, filled with all the sights, sounds, and textures that brought joy to my heart. The smell of freshly-baked cookies wafting through the air, the sound of laughter ringing in my ears, the feel of soft, plush furnishings beneath my fingertips. All these things and more contributed to the sense of comfort and relaxation that I so desperately craved.

"Earth to Maddy," I heard Lacy's voice as I saw her hand wave in front of me. "Did you hear me? Let's do a shot!"

"You're going to kill me. We've only been here ten minutes."

"We're celebrating, and you'll survive."

Something about my best friend sparked a sense of adventure within me, a desire to throw caution to the wind and embrace the night. She leaned over the counter and signaled for two more drinks.

As I sipped my second martini, feeling the alcohol's warmth spreading through my veins, Lacy surprised me with a unique shot.

"Two Pink Starburst shots, please," she told the bartender. "It's Vanilla Vodka, Sweet and Sour, Watermelon Pucker, and Sprite. I saw it on a viral video and it looked good."

"To new adventures," I said, raising my shot glass. Lacy clinked her glass with mine, and we both downed the sweet concoction. To my delight, the shot tasted exactly like the candy it was named after.

"Speaking of adventures, where is your mom these days?" Lacy asked, aware that my mom hardly stayed in one place for long.

I shrugged, the bitterness rising in my throat like a noxious fume. "I think she's in Belize with boyfriend number six, or sixty-eight, getting inspiration for her next art project."

My mother, Clare Bell, had never been the same after my father died. While I'd clung to stability and routine, she'd gone in the opposite direction, embracing a nomadic lifestyle that took her around the world with a series of increasingly younger boyfriends. Her paintings sold well enough to fund her wanderlust, but not well enough to help with my college tuition or to visit more than once every couple of years.

"Clare," Lacy laughed, taking a sip of her second gin and tonic. "At least she's living the life she wants to live."

"You make a point," I conceded. "She does live life on her own terms. But I still wished sometimes she would settle down and do normal stuff, like I don't know, have a holiday meal with me or at least come see my bakery. Or show up for Gram's funeral like a normal person."

Lacy leaned back in her chair, as if she were considering her words carefully. "Maddy, you can't change your mom. She's a free spirit, and trying to fit her into a 'normal' mold won't work. You'll build an amazing life here. Focus on the people who truly appreciate you. Your mom may not show up in the traditional way, but she loves you in her own way. She went through a very tragic experience at a young age, losing your dad."

As I sipped my second martini, feeling the alcohol's warmth spreading through my veins, I changed the subject. "Okay, enough heavy talk. Dish on the guy I spotted making a sneaky exit from your room this morning."

Lacy grinned mischievously. "Let's just say if I had my own bucket list, I would've needed to check off item number ten multiple times after last night."

10. Have an orgasm during sex.

"Well, there is a reason it's number ten on my list, it may never happen," I said, feeling my cheeks flush. "Is that why you can barely sit on the bar stool tonight?"

"I consider that an accomplishment, in case you were wondering," she winked, shifting in her seat with exaggerated discomfort.

Just as I finished my martini, the bartender set two glasses of champagne in front of us.

"We didn't order those." I informed him, puzzled.

The bartender's finger led my gaze to the end of the bar, where a man sat in solitude. As soon as I recognized him, my heart began to race, and a feeling of gratitude overcame me.

Rex was here.

He looked even better than he had this morning, if that was possible. His blue collared shirt brought out the color of his eyes, and his hair was slightly tousled, as if he'd just run his fingers through it. The soft lighting of the bar cast shadows that accentuated the strong line of his jaw and the breadth of his shoulders. He lifted his glass in a subtle toast when our eyes met, and I felt a flutter in my stomach that had nothing to do with alcohol.

I mouthed a thank you to which he nodded in response. But Lacy's voice brought me back to reality.

"Go talk to him!" she urged, nudging me with her elbow.

I knew she was right, but my nerves got the best of me. Rex was sitting up straight on a barstool, looking confident and composed. He had a tight grip on his tumbler, and I couldn't help but notice how his forearms flexed as he lifted it to his lips. A single drop of condensation trailed down the side of the glass, and I found myself following its path with my eyes, suddenly parched.

"No way, this is a girls' night," I told Lacy, purposely leaving out the part where talking to Rex would be venturing into dangerous territory. I'd only been single for a few weeks after a decade with Craig. The last thing I needed was to jump into something with a man who, according to town gossip, wasn't exactly the commitment type.

"Rex Townsend is the definition of sexy. I fully support you talking to that delicious man even if it is girls' night," Lacy gave a mischievous smile, causing me to roll my eyes. "Girls' night does not mean you have to be a nun all night."

"Sure, he's good looking, but he definitely knows it too. I'll bet he has no problem getting the ladies in this town to drop their panties for him."

"Ooh! *Salty*! Hello — with a face and body like that, I'd drop mine too."

Sometimes, I wished I could be as carefree as Lacy. But years with Craig had made me cautious, always second-guessing myself, always weighing the potential consequences of every action.

"Allison already filled me in on Dr. Rex over there."

"Yeah? What's the local gossip say about our sexy vet?" She took another long sip from her drink. "What's the scoop on Sexy Rexy?"

"Oh gawd, do not call him that."

"Who? Sexy Rexy? Or maybe Doctor Sexy Rexy? I can't decide. It's been my sworn duty as your BFF to nickname all your boyfriends since grade school, and I will not shirk my duties. I'm not a shirker, you know that."

"Right, not a shirker..." I rolled my eyes. "So, apparently, according to Allison, Rex has become quite the local heartthrob since moving here a few years back. He has a bit of a playboy reputation, and a trail of broken hearts." I chuckled, feeling a bit guilty for indulging in all the juicy details with Allison, but a part of me couldn't resist hearing everything she was willing to dish out.

"Oh Maddy, that is just small-town gossip. I am sure there is some truth to it, but I also heard he volunteers with the local animal shelter and is heavily involved with some philanthropies. Don't believe all the gossip. If you did, you'd think I slept with Machine Gun Kelly when he came through town, but all I did was snag a selfie with him. And, if you won't go for Sexy Rexy, maybe I'll ditch my tattooed bad boys and give him a shot myself."

I knew Lacy well enough to understand her playful nature, but my stomach still churned at the thought of Lacy going home with Rex.

What was that about?

I'd be Lacy's wingwoman any day, but when it came to Rex, he felt... off-limits. Was I just protecting her? Or was I trying to protect myself?

Lacy teased, "You know what they say about getting over someone, you have to get under... "

I quickly cut her off, not wanting to entertain that idea. "Lacy, you know I don't do one-night stands. Plus, I'm a thousand percent over Craig. I don't need another man to help with that, thank you very much," I asserted, perhaps a bit too defensively.

"Well, Maddy-who-doesn't-do-one-night-stands, just because you're swearing off re-lationships doesn't mean you have to swear off men altogether. Having some fun and enjoying yourself doesn't make you a tramp. It's perfect for you. No strings attached."

"I'm not going home with Rex," I said, more firmly than I anticipated. Not sure if I was trying to convince myself or Lacy. "I've been single for literally five minutes."

"He hasn't stopped staring at you with those ridiculously deep blue eyes," she nudged me playfully.

As I turned my gaze towards Rex, his eyes locked with mine, and a subtle smile formed at the corner of his lips. The way he looked me over made me feel more than just an attractive woman in a little black dress. Something in his eyes seemed curious, almost searching. Maybe he wanted to get to know me, or maybe he was just picturing me naked right now. It had been a long time since a man looked at me that way — like I was something precious and rare, something to be savored.

I realized I liked it.

Despite my very rational thoughts urging me not to approach him, I could sense my own body betraying me. My heart raced, my palms grew damp, and a warmth spread through me that had nothing to do with the martinis.

"Alright, fine," I muttered, giving in to the inexplicable pull. "I'll go over, but *just* to be polite and thank him for the drinks."

"It *is* the polite thing to do," Lacy said, batting her eyelashes over the top of her martini glass.

It seemed like a harmless enough gesture, but deep down, I knew there was more to it than mere politeness. My heart fluttered traitorously in my chest as I approached him.

"Thanks for the champagne," I said, as I approached the empty space next to him, clenching my glass tighter so it would not slip from my now damp palms. What was this? Seventh grade at the school dance?

The bar was bustling with activity around us, so he leaned in closer to be heard over the noise. My body reacted by sending shivers down my spine as I caught the scent of his cologne, something woodsy with hints of citrus and spice.

It must have been the champagne.

"I just wanted to congratulate you. I hear the mayor is coming for the official rib-bon-cutting ceremony. Looks like your soft launch is going well; most of my patients couldn't stop talking about you in the office today," Rex complimented, leaning in a little closer.

As he spoke, I could feel his breath on my neck, stirring a hint of unexpected sensation. My heartbeat quickened, and suddenly I wanted to change the subject, to steer the conversation away from the electrifying undercurrents.

"Did you ever get the stain out of your shirt?" I asked him, hoping the presoak trick I suggested had worked.

Rex let out a chuckle, the sound rich and warm. "I did, the vinegar worked wonders," he replied, flashing his perfectly straight smile. "You're a woman of many talents."

"When you come back to the bakery, I promise I will try not to spill anything else on you."

Rex shifted his body towards me, and I felt a rush of excitement. "Is that a promise you can keep?" I caught his eyes scanning my body from head to toe, and I was suddenly grateful I wore this dress. Despite my nerves, I found myself so drawn to him.

"Oh, and I think you will be happy to know, I took your advice. Instead of the dog bowl, I now have pup cups, well, compostable bowls. Each dog gets their own individual water."

I knew I had to make an impression on Rex, and not just because he was the town's veterinarian, or because his business was right across the street from mine. It was something about the way he looked at me. I couldn't resist it. I had to see more.

"That's a great solution," he smiled. "I'm sure they'll appreciate it. And I am glad to hear my shirts will be safe because I planned to stop in tomorrow. I couldn't stop thinking about those orange scones all day."

I felt a spark ignite in my gut at the mention of my scones, awakening some dormant desire within. I pictured Rex with his lips parted, savoring each bite of my delectable creation. Satisfaction on his face as he savored every last crumb, his tongue darting out to lick his lips in anticipation of the next bite.

"I'll have one waiting for you," I replied, trying to keep my composure. The truth was, I couldn't stop thinking about Rex. I found myself drawn to him, more than just a customer. Rex was craving my scones, and I was starting to crave Rex. Was I flirting with him? No, of course not. I was just being friendly to a work neighbor. And I could use another friend, since the only two I had at the moment were Lacy and Allison.

Okay fine. Maybe I was flirting a little.

I felt conflicting urges to retreat to the safety of my bar stool. But something kept pulling me closer to Rex. Whatever it was, I couldn't resist it.

The bar had started to fill up with more people. Lacy was off to the side laughing at some man's apparent jokes. As I tried to navigate the increasingly crowded space, a lady bumped into me, causing my leg to end up between Rex's legs. Surprised by the contact, neither of us moved.

"Sorry," she said quickly before continuing on her way.

I glanced over at Rex, hoping he didn't notice the red hue spreading up my cheeks. Or if he did, that he'd at least have the courtesy to blame it on the alcohol. But his eyes darkened slightly, and I could feel the heat radiating from him, the solid muscle of his thigh against mine.

"Excuse me a moment," Rex said, getting up from his stool. His voice sounded rougher than before.

I tossed back my champagne, finishing it in one swig. Lacy hurried over.

"You and Rex are looking cozy," she teased.

"No, he is just a fan of my scones. And I am being polite."

"Whatever you say, Maddy Girl. I have to go, Rich just bought me another drink."

She disappeared, leaving me alone with an empty bar stool beside me. Suddenly, a 30-year-old clearly trying to relive his frat boy years stumbled over and claimed the spot, slurring his words as he tried to start a conversation with me.

"Hey there, beautiful," said Frat Boy, flashing a lopsided grin. "What's a pretty thing like you doing all alone?"

I gave him a polite, forced smile, hoping to discourage him. Lacy would have kneed him in the balls and told him to get lost.

"Just having a drink. I'm not really in the mood for company."

He leaned in closer, his breath hot against my ear and reeking of whiskey. "Come on, don't be like that. Let me buy you another drink."

I shook my head, pulling away from him. The guy persisted, his hand landing on my thigh.

"Come on, just one more. I promise I'll make it worth your while."

My jaw clenched. I grabbed his hand, taking note of the ring on his left hand. He was clearly ignoring my cues.

"I said — " I was just about to lose my patience when a tall figure appeared next to me.

"Hey, man, I think it's time for you to go," Rex said to Frat Boy, his voice firm and commanding. With one hand on the guy's shoulder, Rex guided him off the stool and towards the exit. I felt a wave of relief wash over me.

"Thanks, Rex. I think that is my cue to leave."

The crowded atmosphere of the bar was wearing on me, so I walked over to Lacy and let her know I was calling a rideshare and heading home.

"The night's just getting started, Madd. Are you sure you want to leave now?" Lacy implored, not wanting me to go alone.

"It's been a long day at the bakery, and a nice bubble bath sounds great right now. I'll grab an Uber. You are officially released from Girls' Night."

"Fine," Lacy grumbled, "I can go with you. I don't want you heading home with a stranger."

"It's Uber."

Unbeknownst to me, Rex had been nearby and overheard our conversation. "I can give you a ride home if Lacy wants to stay," he offered generously. I declined, shooting Lacy a playful glare as I noticed her nodding in agreement with Rex.

"Thanks, but seriously, I'll be fine."

"Well, if you won't let me take you home and you prefer an Uber, how about I ride in the Uber with you to your place?" Rex suggested. "Just to make sure you get home safe," he added quickly, confirming that it wasn't some pick-up line to take me home.

Lacy chimed in, "See? It's all good. Stay safe, and text me when you get home." With Lacy's approval, I felt more at ease. I accepted his offer, and a few moments later we found ourselves getting into the rideshare.

"So, is it a habit of yours to hop into cars with guys you meet at the bar?" Rex teased, flashing that gorgeous smile again.

I playfully nudged his side, realizing that my elbow encountered nothing but solid muscle. "Well, technically, I met you at my bakery," I retorted, "but I must admit, I prefer this interaction a bit more. At least I didn't spill a drink on you this time."

Rex and I had a light-hearted conversation on the short ride to my apartment. As we arrived, he exited the car first and opened the door for me.

"Thanks for making sure I got home safe, Rex."

We stood there for a moment, a beat longer than I expected, neither of us speaking. The night air was cool against my skin, and I could smell the faint scent of his cologne – something woodsy and masculine that made my heart race.

"Goodnight, Maddy," he finally said. "Don't worry – I'll wait until you're safely inside the door."

"Thanks," I said over my shoulder as I unlocked the door. Once inside, I was just about to take off my heels when a sudden knock at the door startled me. Peeking through the peephole, I saw Rex fidgeting with something in his hands.

"You forgot your phone in the Uber," he explained, holding out my familiar blue iPhone with the cupcake-decorated phone holder. Relief washed over me.

"Oh my gosh, thank you Rex! Lacy would have killed me if I didn't text her right away. She probably would have sent the SWAT team," I said, taking the phone from his hand. But as our fingers brushed, a jolt of electricity shot through my body. "Do you want to come in for a drink?" I blurted out, surprised by my own words. "I promise not to spill it on you."

Rex laughed and a smile spread across his face. "Um...sure," he said, accepting the unexpected invitation.

Rex cancelled the Uber driver while I sent a quick text to Lacy letting her know that I got home safe. I cracked open a couple of beers and handed one to Rex.

"I'll be right back," I said, hoping he didn't notice my voice trembling. "I'm going to get out of these heels." In truth, I needed a moment to gather myself. There was a man alone with me in Lacy's house. Rex was in the house.

Okay, get it together, I told myself. There was no need for things to be awkward. We were two new friends, getting to know each other. Plus, I wanted to impress the business owners on Main Street if I needed to be taken seriously as a business owner myself. Quickly, I changed into a comfy pair of slippers, and headed back to the kitchen where I found Rex standing by my refrigerator, engrossed in something.

"When did you write this?" Rex pointed to something on my refrigerator, turning towards me.

Confused, I walked closer, forgetting what I had placed there, and then it hit me like a semi-truck. Oh, no. Rex had stumbled upon my bucket list. How could I have forgotten it was right there for anyone to see? I took a sip of my drink, desperately trying to wash down the lump that had formed in my throat.

"Umm, that's not mine," I stammered, my face starting to heat.

Rex let out a chuckle, telling me he must have read all of it.

"Oh yeah?" he teased. "Lacy also wants to open a bakery?" he quipped, catching me off guard. He had seen at least the first item on the list. Panic washed over me. How much more had he seen? Trying to divert his attention, I quickly opened the refrigerator, pretending to search for something.

"I mean, it's not all mine. I wrote it with a friend. Anyway, do you want a cookie?" I blurted out, hoping for a change of subject.

Just as I handed a cookie to Rex, Lacy burst through the door. Thank God.

Lacy was staring at her boots as she unzipped them, oblivious to our presence in the kitchen. "Madddddyyyyyyyy, you won't believe what happened. Rich said he wanted to take me home, but I told him I had to go to my best friend to yell at her for not having a one-night-stand with the very hot — "

"Lacy!" I quickly interrupted her, as an amused smile spread across Rex's face. Her head snapped up at the sound of Rex clearing his throat, and her eyes darted between him and me.

"Oh, I was...just, ugh....leaving," she stumbled, her eyes wide with mortification.

Rex took a final swig of his beer and made his way towards the door. "Sounds like you two need some girl talk. I don't want to intrude. I'll catch you later, Maddy," he said, walking out the door before I could even respond.

As soon as Rex left, I let out the breath I had been holding.

"Oh my gosh, Maddy, I am so sorry. Did I just ruin your moment? You said you got home safe and didn't mention anything about Rex. I assumed you were alone," Lacy apologized, her face a picture of guilt.

"No, actually you arrived at the perfect time, BECAUSE HE JUST SAW THE BUCKET LIST YOU MADE ME WRITE..." I hissed, pointing frantically at the refrigerator.

"Soo..?" she trailed off, confused.

"Sooo...he saw number ten."

BUCKET LIST:

1. Own a bakery

2. Witness a birth

3. Win an award

4. Get married

5. Become a mom

6. Run a marathon

7. Sommelier Wine Night

8. Get a tattoo

9. Name a star

10. Have an orgasm during sex

Realization dawned on her face. "Oh.... that number ten." Lacy grinned and waggled her eyebrows in my direction. "Maybe Doctor Sexy Rexy was just here volunteering to assist with your list. Too bad I got here just in time to spoil it."

I groaned, collapsing onto the couch and burying my face in a throw pillow. "I'm never going to be able to look him in the eye again. He's going to think I'm some sort of sex-starved spinster."

"Or," Lacy countered, flopping down beside me. "He's going to think you're a woman who knows what she wants and isn't afraid to write it down. That's sexy, Maddy."

"There's nothing sexy about admitting to a virtual stranger that your ex-boyfriend couldn't satisfy you in bed for ten years," I moaned.

"First of all, it doesn't say 'have an orgasm during sex because Craig was a selfish lover who never bothered to learn what you liked.' It just says 'have an orgasm during sex.' For all Rex knows, you've never had sex."

"That's even worse!"

Lacy shrugged, kicking off her boots and tucking her feet beneath her. "Second of all, I think it's incredibly sexy to be honest about what you want. Most men would be thrilled to know exactly what a woman is looking for. Takes the guesswork out."

I peeked at her from behind the pillow. "You really think he's not completely freaked out?"

"Maddy, that man has been looking at you like you're a chocolate soufflé and he's been on a diet for years. Trust me, he's not freaked out. If anything, he's probably home right now, thinking about how he can help you check that item off your list."

The mental image her words conjured sent a rush of heat through my body. I tried to banish the thought of Rex's hands on me, his mouth on mine, but once the seed was planted, it was impossible to uproot.

"It doesn't matter anyway," I said, trying to sound more convinced than I felt. "I'm focusing on the bakery. I don't have time for... complications."

"Mmhmm," Lacy hummed skeptically. "And I'm sure the bakery is the only thing on your mind when Dr. Townsend comes in for his daily scone."

I threw the pillow at her, but she just laughed, ducking easily.

"Fine. He's attractive. I'm not blind. But that doesn't mean anything is going to happen," I insisted. "Besides, you heard Allison. He's not exactly the relationship type."

"And you heard me. Not every connection has to be a ten-year commitment. Sometimes it can just be fun." Lacy's expression softened. "When was the last time you had fun, Maddy? Real, uninhibited, 'I don't care what anyone thinks' kind of fun?"

I couldn't remember. With Craig, everything had been so measured, so controlled. Even our vacations had detailed itineraries, with little room for spontaneity or joy.

"Look," Lacy said, her tone gentler now, "I'm not saying you should jump into anything you're not ready for. But don't close yourself off to possibilities just because you're scared. You're not the same person who left here a decade ago. You're stronger, wiser, and a hell of a lot more deserving of happiness than you give yourself credit for."

I sighed, knowing she was right. "When did you get so wise?"

"I've always been wise. It's just hard to recognize wisdom when it's packaged with this much fabulousness," she grinned, gesturing to herself.

I laughed, feeling the tension drain from my shoulders. "Thanks, Lace. For everything."

"You're welcome. Now, tell me everything about your little ride home with Rex. Did he smell as good as he looks? Did he try to kiss you? Did you want him to?"

As I recounted the details of my evening, carefully editing out the parts where my heart had raced at his proximity, I couldn't help but wonder what Rex was thinking now. Was he laughing at my bucket list? Was he intrigued? Disgusted? Or was Lacy right? Was he thinking about how he could help me check off item number ten?

The thought sent a shiver down my spine, a mixture of embarrassment and anticipation that I wasn't quite ready to analyze. For now, I'd focus on the bakery, on building my new life in Sugar Creek. If Rex Townsend happened to be a part of that life, well... I'd cross that bridge when I came to it.

But as I lay in bed later that night, my mind kept drifting back to the way his eyes had lingered on me at the bar, the electricity I'd felt when our fingers touched, the subtle scent of his cologne that still clung to my memory. For the first time in years, I felt a stirring of desire, a longing for something I'd almost forgotten existed.

Sleep eluded me as I tossed and turned, my thoughts a jumbled mess of bakery plans, bucket lists, and blue eyes that seemed to see right through me. When I finally drifted off, my dreams were filled with strong hands, gentle touches, and a pair of lips that tasted like orange marmalade scones.

And tomorrow, I'd be making those scones again, just for him.

Chapter 12

I 'd finally gotten myself mostly moved out of Lacy's place and sort of settled into the apartment above the bakery.

The gentle buzz of my alarm pierced the 4:30 AM quiet. I groaned, rolling over to silence it before it could escalate to its full-volume wail. After the chaos of yesterday's soft opening, I wanted nothing more than to burrow back under my covers and hibernate for a week, but the grand opening was tomorrow, and there was still so much to do.

I shuffled to the bathroom, catching my reflection in the mirror. Dark circles had taken up residence under my eyes: welcome to business ownership. Splashing cold water on my face, I reminded myself that Gram had done this for decades. If she could handle it, so could I.

Forty-five minutes later, I was unlocking the bakery's front door, breathing in the lingering scents of yesterday's offerings: cinnamon, butter, and the subtle tang of sourdough. The space felt different in the pre-dawn darkness, almost reverent. This was my favorite time in the bakery, when it was just me and the possibilities of the day ahead.

I flipped on the lights and headed straight for the kitchen, mentally running through my to-do list. The health inspection yesterday had gone well, with only a few minor suggestions for improvement. Today I needed to bake double our usual inventory to prepare for tomorrow's official grand opening. The marketing had paid off; all signs pointed to a busy day ahead.

I had just finished mixing the first batch of dough when a sharp knock at the front door made me jump. Who could that be at.. I glanced at the clock...5:45 AM? Through the glass, I could make out the silhouette of a woman holding what looked like a clipboard.

My stomach dropped. I recognized that clipboard. Health inspector.

I wiped my hands on my apron and made my way to the door, pasting on my most welcoming smile as I unlocked it.

"Good morning," I said, holding the door open. "Can I help you?"

"Stella Rodgers, South Carolina Department of Health." The woman was middle-aged with a severe bob and glasses perched on the end of her nose. She held out a badge. "I'm here for an inspection."

I blinked in confusion. "Sorry, we just had our inspection two days ago. We passed with only minor suggestions."

"Yes, I have that on file," she said, her tone brisk and official. "However, we received an anonymous complaint about possible health code violations. I'm required to follow up immediately."

"A complaint?" My voice came out higher than I intended. "We've only been open for one day!"

She simply raised an eyebrow, clipboard clutched to her chest like armor. "May I come in, Ms. Bell?"

I stepped aside, mind racing. Who would file a complaint after just one day? We hadn't even had time to develop enemies yet — well, except for Roland Pierce, who'd made it clear he wanted this property. But would he stoop so low?

"I'll need to see all food storage areas, preparation surfaces, employee handwashing stations, and your refrigeration units," Ms. Rodgers said, clicking her pen. "Let's begin."

What followed was the most excruciating forty-five minutes of my life. The inspector who came two days ago was rigorous, but pretty easygoing. Ms. Rodgers, however, examined every inch of my kitchen with a thoroughness that bordered on obsession. She opened every container, checked every temperature, measured every clearance space. And with each notation on her clipboard, my anxiety ratcheted higher.

"Your refrigeration unit is running two degrees above the acceptable maximum," she said, making a note. "That's a violation that must be corrected immediately."

"But it was fine yesterday," I protested, peering at the thermometer. Sure enough, it read 42°F instead of the required 40°F or below. "It must have just started malfunctioning."

"Regardless, it needs to be fixed before you can serve food to the public." She moved on, examining the seals around our dishwasher.

"The seal on this dishwasher shows signs of wear, which could compromise sanitization. Another violation."

By the time she finished, she had identified six violations that needed immediate correction: the refrigerator temperature, the dishwasher seal, a small crack in one tile that could "harbor bacteria," insufficient sanitizer concentration in our cleaning solution, a hand soap dispenser that wasn't dispensing properly, and documentation issues with our employee health policy.

"I'll return tomorrow morning at 7 AM to re-inspect," Ms. Rodgers said, tearing off a copy of her report and handing it to me. "If these violations aren't corrected, I'll have no choice but to issue a closure order until they are addressed."

My hands trembled as I took the paper. "Tomorrow? It's our grand opening."

She adjusted her glasses. "I'm afraid health code regulations don't operate on your business schedule, Ms. Bell. Good day."

The bell over the door jingled cheerfully as she left, completely at odds with the disaster she'd just dropped in my lap. I stared at the report, the words blurring before my eyes.

"No, no, no," I whispered, sliding down against the wall until I was sitting on the floor. The grand opening — all the marketing, the special orders, the community anticipation — it would all be for nothing. And if word got out that we'd been shut down by the health department? The bakery might never recover from that kind of publicity.

I allowed myself exactly one minute of panic, then pushed to my feet. Crying wouldn't fix my refrigerator. I needed to take action, and fast.

I called Allison first, who was already on her way. Then Mrs. Whitman, who knew everyone in town and might have contacts who could help with repairs. And finally, almost without thinking, I found myself calling Rex.

He answered on the third ring, his voice rough with sleep. "Hello?"

"Rex? It's Maddy. I'm so, so sorry to call this early, but I have an emergency at the bakery."

There was a rustling sound, like he was sitting up. "What's wrong? Are you okay?"

The concern in his voice made my throat tighten. "I'm fine, but the health inspector just showed up due to an anonymous complaint. She found violations that weren't there two days ago, and if they're not fixed by tomorrow morning, she'll shut us down."

"What kind of violations?" His voice was fully alert now.

"Refrigerator running two degrees too warm, seal issues on the dishwasher, documentation problems... "

"I'll be there in twenty minutes," he said, cutting me off without hesitation. "Day off or not, I'd rather spend it helping you."

"Thank you," I said, relief washing through me. "Really, Rex, thank you."

"Hey," his voice softened, lingering in a way that made my chest tighten. "You don't have to thank me. I like being the one you call."

When the call ended, I set the phone down too quickly, as if that could quiet the flutter in my chest. *Rex was just being kind,* I told myself, but the way my skin tingled made it harder to believe the lie.

I immediately started on the problems I could fix myself. The sanitizer concentration was an easy adjustment, and I had extra hand soap dispensers in storage. The documentation issue just required updating and printing a form. That left the refrigerator, the dishwasher seal, and the cracked tile... all requiring professional help or parts.

By the time Allison arrived, I had worked myself into a productive frenzy, trying to catch up on my baking before the store opened after losing a valuable hour and a half this morning.

"Holy cow," she said, taking in the scene. "You weren't kidding about the inspection."

I handed her a copy of the report. "Can you start calling around for a dishwasher repair person? We need a new door seal ASAP."

Allison nodded, pulling out her phone. "My uncle's company does commercial kitchen repairs. He's like an hour away, but I'll see if he can squeeze us in today."

The bell jangled again, and Mrs. Whitman appeared, clutching her cane in one hand and a toolkit in the other. "Where's that cracked tile?" she demanded without preamble.

I blinked in surprise. "Over by the sink, but Mrs. Whitman, you don't need to — "

"Nonsense," she cut me off, marching toward the kitchen with surprising speed for someone her age. "I've been fixing things in this town since before you were born. Now, where's my light? I can't see a blessed thing with these old eyes."

Before I could protest further, Rex arrived, accompanied by a stocky man with a tool-belt who introduced himself as Harold, Mrs. Whitman's nephew, a mechanical engineer.

"Aunt Ellie said you've got temperature issues?" he asked, heading straight for our commercial refrigerator without waiting for an answer.

I watched in stunned silence as my bakery was suddenly filled with people working to solve my crisis. Allison caught my expression and grinned.

"Welcome to Sugar Creek," she said, squeezing my shoulder. "Where everybody knows everybody, and half of them are related."

I swallowed, caught somewhere between nerves and something else I couldn't name. "This is... I don't even know what to say."

"You don't need to say anything," Rex said, rolling up his sleeves, his gaze lingering on me a fraction too long. "Just tell me what still needs doing."

The door jingled. This time, it was Lacy. "I figured you could use some extra hands since you're opening in fifteen minutes."

I glanced back at Rex, and for a brief moment, our eyes met. There was a pulse there, quiet but undeniable, like a current running under the surface of ordinary words.

"You figured right," I said, giving her a quick hug. "Can you help me load the display case before we open? I've got to get the orange marmalade scones out of the oven."

"On it," she said, tying her hair back. "Oh, and just so you know, word's getting around about the 'anonymous complaint.' People aren't happy."

"Getting around?" Oh no. "How?" I asked, momentarily looking up from my paperwork.

Lacy smirked. "Mrs. Whitman called the town council, who called their children, who texted their friends... You know how it goes. Small town, big mouths."

I wasn't sure whether to be mortified or grateful. On one hand, having the whole town know about our health code violations wasn't ideal. On the other hand, the outpouring of support was overwhelming in the best possible way.

The bell rang yet again, and I looked up to see Jimmy from the hardware store carrying a toolbox. "Heard you might need some help," he said with a shy smile. "I'm pretty good with plumbing if you need anything fixed."

"Thank you, Jimmy. The plumbing seems fine for now, but if you could see if the mayor needs any help with the tile, that would be amazing."

Jimmy headed to the back, and the door opened again.

For the next two hours, my bakery looked more like a construction site than a food establishment. Harold discovered that someone had tampered with the refrigerator's thermostat settings; he fixed it with a few adjustments and declared it 'good as new.' Mrs. Whitman replaced the cracked tile with one she'd brought from home, claiming she'd been saving it for an emergency, while Allison's uncle arrived to replace the dishwasher seal, waving away my questions about payment with a gruff, 'first one's free for Beatrice's granddaughter.'

By mid-morning, we'd addressed four of the six violations. I was running the register and working on the documentation requirements when the door chimed again. This time it was Miss Ernestine from the soul food restaurant down the street, carrying a large cooler.

"Thought you all might need some lunch, working so hard," she said, setting it on an empty table. "Got fried chicken, potato salad, and my special sweet tea."

I felt tears prickling at the corners of my eyes. "Miss Ernestine, you didn't have to do that."

She waved a hand dismissively. "Child, when one of us is in trouble, all of us are in trouble. Besides, I can't have my favorite sweet tooth going hungry now, can I?"

As more people arrived to help or just buy their breakfasts — Trevor from the flower shop, Josephine from the bookstore, even the high school principal and his wife — I struggled to keep my emotions in check. This was more than neighborly assistance; it was a statement of acceptance. Sugar Creek was welcoming me, claiming me as one of their own.

Rex appeared at my side, wiping sweat from his brow. "You okay?" he asked, his voice low, almost cautious.

I nodded, not trusting my voice.

He didn't push, just stayed there a moment, eyes scanning me as if making sure I wasn't about to crumble. "The refrigerator's running at a perfect 38 degrees now," he said. "Harold thinks someone deliberately adjusted the settings: the access panel showed signs of tampering."

My head snapped up. "Deliberately? But who..." I stopped myself, the name Roland Pierce flashing unbidden in my mind.

Rex glanced at me, noticing the pause. "Don't let it worry you too much," he said gently. "We'll figure it out. And... if it's too much, you let me know. I'll handle whatever I can."

I caught the faint curve of his lips as he said it, the kind of look that made me forget I was supposed to be stressed about sabotage for a second.

Before I could say anything else, the door jingled, and Roland Pierce walked in, all polished charm and calculated ease. My stomach sank, and I felt Rex subtly shift closer, like a silent shield I hadn't asked for but couldn't ignore.

"My, my," he said, his gaze sweeping the room. "Quite the community effort you've inspired, Ms. Bell." His tone made it sound more like an accusation than a compliment.

I forced a small smile, my chest tightening. Rex's presence behind me felt grounding, like a quiet anchor I hadn't realized I was leaning on. He stayed close, but not crowding, just enough that his attention was clear.

"Mr. Pierce," I said, keeping my voice neutral. "What can I do for you?"

He smiled, but it didn't reach his eyes. "I heard about your unfortunate situation with the health department. Such a shame, especially right after your grand opening."

"Yes, well, as you can see, we have everything under control," I replied, gesturing to the people working around us.

"How fortunate for you," he said. "Though one does wonder how long this... enthusiasm will last. Running a business isn't about one-time fixes, Ms. Bell. It's about sustainable operations."

As Roland moved toward the fridge, Rex lightly rested a hand near my back, brushing my shoulder as he checked the settings again. Not necessary, but deliberate. I couldn't ignore the warmth of it, the way he seemed to silently say, *I've got you.*

Rex stepped forward, positioning himself slightly in front of me. "Was there something you needed, Roland? Or did you just come to make ominous statements?"

A flash of irritation crossed Roland's face before his smooth facade returned. "Always the knight in shining armor, aren't you, Townsend? I simply came to express my concern for our newest business owner and to remind her that my offer still stands. Sometimes accepting help is the wisest business decision."

"I appreciate your concern," I said, stepping around Rex to face Roland directly. "But as I've told you before, I'm not interested in selling or partnering."

Roland shrugged elegantly. "Pride before practicality. A common mistake among new entrepreneurs." He glanced around the bakery once more. "I'll leave you to your... community project. Do let me know when you're ready to discuss real business solutions."

He turned and left, the bell tinkling merrily in his wake.

Rex's jaw was tight as he watched Roland through the window. "That man has his fingers in half the commercial real estate deals in this county," he muttered. "And somehow they always end with the original owners getting squeezed out."

I noticed the way Rex's hand lingered near my shoulder for a fraction longer than necessary..

"You think he called in the complaint to the health department?" I asked.

His eyes flicked back to me, scanning for any sign that I was rattled. "The question is why he's so fixated on this property."

I caught the subtle tilt of his head, the way he paused to glance at me before moving on, and realized just how much attention he was paying—not the appliances, not the paperwork, but me.

Before I could respond, my phone rang, an unfamiliar number with a Charleston area code. "Maddy Cakes, this is Maddy," I answered.

"Ms. Bell? This is Marcus from Carolina Quality Foods. I'm calling about your delivery scheduled for tomorrow morning."

"Yes, of course," I said. "What can I do for you?"

"I'm afraid we have to cancel. Our delivery route has changed, and we no longer service Sugar Creek directly. You'll need to arrange pickup from our distribution center in Charleston or switch to a different supplier."

My stomach plummeted. "But we've had these deliveries planned for weeks! Our grand opening is tomorrow!"

"I understand your frustration, Ms. Bell, but this decision is final. If you'd like to arrange pickup..."

"Charleston is two hours away," I said, struggling to keep my voice level. "And I don't have time to drive four hours round trip the day before my bakery's official opening."

"I apologize for the inconvenience. Would you like me to recommend some alternative suppliers?"

I closed my eyes, counting to five before answering. "Yes, please."

When I hung up, my hand was trembling. Rex, who had been watching me the whole time, raised an eyebrow.

"Our egg supplier just canceled," I said, my voice hollow even to my own ears. "They apparently changed routes and won't come to Sugar Creek. The nearest alternatives either charge a fortune for last-minute delivery or won't arrive until after the weekend."

Rex pushed back from the counter, eyes narrowing thoughtfully. "I might have a solution," he said. "I service a small farm on the outskirts of town. They have fresh eggs. I can have several dozen delivered here within the hour if that helps."

I felt a flicker of hope, the tension in my shoulders easing slightly. "You... could really do that?"

Rex met my gaze, steady and unflinching. "I can. I know how important this is to you, and I won't let something like this derail it."

I chewed my lip, suddenly feeling exposed. "I... I don't want to drag you into this," I said quickly. "It's just eggs. I should be able to figure it out on my own."

Rex hesitated, then pulled up a chair to sit across from me, his eyes level with mine. "Maddy, look at me."

I raised my gaze to his, finding unexpected steadiness in his blue eyes.

"You have two options right now," he said, his voice calm and matter-of-fact. "You can either push back the grand opening, which is completely reasonable given these circumstances, or you can get creative with what you have." He gestured around the bakery. "You've already got half the town here helping. I'm betting there are some ingredients we can scrounge up locally."

I chewed my lip, considering. Postponing would be the safer choice, but it would mean Roland had succeeded in disrupting our launch. The thought made my spine stiffen with resolve.

"No," I said, pushing to my feet. "We're opening tomorrow as planned. We'll figure this out."

Rex grinned, and the genuine pride in his expression made my heart flutter. "That's what I thought you'd say. So, what's the plan?"

I took a deep breath, my mind already shifting into problem-solving mode. "First, inventory. We need to know exactly what we have and what we absolutely need. Then we'll figure out what we can substitute or do without." I turned toward the kitchen, calling out, "Allison! We need to do an emergency inventory check!"

Lacy joined our impromptu planning session. "Trevor at the flower shop has a cousin who delivers to the restaurant supply warehouse in Greenville. He might be willing to pick up some items for you."

Hope began to replace my panic. "That could work for the specialty items. But flour, sugar, butter... we need those in bulk."

"The community center is preparing for their big Fourth of July event next week," Mrs. Whitman piped up from her seat. "They've got more supplies than they'll need. I'll make some calls."

As everyone sprang into action, I felt a surge of gratitude so intense it was almost painful. These people barely knew me, yet they were going above and beyond to help save my bakery. It was humbling and inspiring all at once.

By closing time, we had managed to source almost everything we needed, though at a significantly higher cost than our normal supplier. I tried not to think about what this would do to our already tight profit margins as I tallied up the expenses.

We spent the next few hours moving through the kitchen, counting supplies, measuring flour and sugar, and checking every corner of the bakery. By late evening, the last customer had gone, and the helpers had trickled out. Everyone except Rex. I glanced at the clock: 8:30 PM. We'd been going nonstop for over fifteen hours.

"You should head home," I said, trying to stifle a yawn. "You've done more than enough."

Rex set down a tray of eggs and gave me a steady look. "You've done more than anyone could expect," he said softly. "I just... wanted to make sure you weren't carrying it all alone."

I swallowed hard, surprised by how much that acknowledgment touched me. Usually, I was the one helping others, the one keeping everyone else afloat. Having someone step in like this, it made me feel... fragile, in a good way, and a little off balance. "I... I'm not used to letting someone help me," I admitted, voice low. "I've always been the one everyone depends on."

He stepped closer, calm and unhurried. "You don't have to do it all alone, Maddy. You're allowed to let someone in, even for a little while."

I looked down, fiddling with the edge of a dish towel. "It's hard... letting someone see how much I actually worry, how much I'm juggling. I'm supposed to have it together."

Rex's hand hovered near mine, close enough that I could feel the warmth radiating off him without him touching me. "You don't always have to have it together," he said gently. "I see how hard you work. I see how much you care. But I also see you, Maddy. Not just the bakery, not just the tasks... you."

For a heartbeat, the air between us felt charged, the quiet of the empty bakery pressing in. My chest tightened, and I realized just how close we had come, physically and emotionally. I instinctively shifted back a fraction, suddenly aware of how exposed I felt under his steady gaze.

Rex's eyes flicked down for a moment, as if sensing the subtle retreat. When he spoke again, his voice was softer, measured. "I should... get going too," he said, though he made no move toward the door.

The day's events had left me emotionally raw, more vulnerable than I would typically allow myself to be. "Thank you for everything today," I said, my voice barely above a whisper. "I don't think I could have managed without you."

Rex nodded, a small, restrained smile tugging at his lips, as if he, too, felt the weight of the closeness but knew it wasn't the right moment to cross the line. He gave me a quiet, steady look before stepping back slightly, respecting the space between us. The pull of the moment lingered, unspoken, leaving both of us aware that something had shifted, even if neither of us was ready to name it.

"Yes, you could have," he said. "You're stronger than you give yourself credit for, Maddy.

I laughed softly, shaking my head. "I don't feel very strong right now."

"That's because you're exhausted," he said. His hand reached up, hesitating for just a moment before gently tucking a strand of hair behind my ear. The simple touch sent electricity racing across my skin. "But I've seen how you handle crises. You don't fall apart. You get focused and find solutions."

His words penetrated the fog of fatigue surrounding me, touching something deep inside that I hadn't realized needed reassurance. "I just can't fail, Rex." The confession slipped out before I could stop it. "Not with Gram's bakery."

His eyes softened with understanding. "You won't."

The certainty in his voice was like roots gripping the earth during a gale. Before I could second-guess myself, I stepped forward and wrapped my arms around him, burying my face against his chest. He stiffened momentarily in surprise, then his arms came around me, strong and secure.

We stood like that for several heartbeats, my ear pressed against his chest where I could hear the steady rhythm of his heart. It was the first moment of true peace I'd had all day.

Finally, reluctantly, I pulled back. "Sorry," I mumbled, suddenly self-conscious. "I'm not usually so... clingy."

Rex's arms loosened but didn't fully release me. "Don't apologize," he said, his voice lower than usual. "I've been wanting to do that since this morning."

My eyes flew to his, searching for any sign he was joking. What I found instead made my breath catch — there was hunger in his gaze, a heat that had nothing to do with the day's work and everything to do with me.

"Maddy," he whispered.

He leaned down slowly, giving me every chance to pull away. But retreating was the least of my intentions. As the gap between us lessened, my heart pounded with anticipation.

Just as his lips neared mine, the familiar surroundings swallowed by an unfamiliar warmth, a loud alarm erupted from the kitchen's back door. We jerked apart, both startled by the sudden interruption. Rex instinctively stepped back and immediately headed to the back of the bakery, his protective stance filling the space that moments ago held the promise of something more.

"Who's there?" he asked forcefully.

I began to trail behind him, but he turned to stop me. "Stay here," he said quietly, "in case it's not safe."

"Oh," was all I could manage, blinking out of the reverie. "I can go...thank you," I finally said, my heart still racing, my head filled with a whirlwind of emotions.

He disappeared into the back room and the alarm stopped. I could hear him opening the back door and re-closing it a minute later, and then he emerged from the back.

"Everything okay?"

His smile was reluctant but genuine. "Definitely. Kids maybe. Maybe not. I didn't see anybody back there and you're all locked up now."

He slowed, not coming any closer. "I'll be here first thing tomorrow. We should both probably get some sleep. You've got an exciting day tomorrow."

I nodded, not fully trusting my ability to speak coherently just yet. Rex collected his jacket and walked toward the door, but not before giving me one last glance, like an unfinished sentence.

"Maddy?"

"Yes?"

"Whatever happens tomorrow, you're not alone here." The simple statement held such earnest conviction that it brought a lump to my throat.

"Thank you," I managed.

After he left, I stood in the middle of my bakery, touched my lips with my fingertips, and allowed myself one full minute to replay that almost-kiss in my mind. Then I straightened my shoulders, locked up, and headed to my apartment upstairs. Tomorrow would be one of the most challenging days of my professional life, and I needed to be ready.

My mind raced between practical concerns about the opening and decidedly impractical thoughts about Rex Townsend. The memory of his lips so close to mine kept distracting me from my mental checklist of tasks for tomorrow.

I was so preoccupied as I looked out the window down to the street below that I almost missed the light-colored sedan parked across the street. Was that Roland Pierce behind the wheel? Suddenly, as though he was aware of my presence, he looked up at me and our eyes locked.

My blood ran cold. The message was clear: he knew where I was, and he was watching. Whatever game he was playing, it had just gotten more personal.

I pulled the drapes closed, and double-checked the lock on my door. Tomorrow was supposed to be a celebration, the culmination of weeks of hard work. Instead, it was shaping up to be a battle. And there was no way I was going to lose.

Chapter 13

The alarm on my phone buzzed persistently, but my eyes were already wide open, staring at the ceiling of my room. I reached over and silenced it, having been awake for nearly an hour already. Today wasn't just any day. Today was the official grand opening of Maddy Cakes Bakery.

After a quick shower, I dressed in the outfit I'd laid out the night before: dark jeans, comfortable shoes, and my new blouse, the exact shade of yellow as the accent color in the bakery. I'd decided against wearing my apron for the ribbon-cutting ceremony, but it was packed in my bag for the moment the real work began.

The streets of Sugar Creek were still dark when I pulled up to the bakery at 4:15 AM. My grandmother's sign, almost as good as new, hung above the door. I'd spent two days meticulously piecing it back together and freshening up the paint. Opening day wouldn't have been the same without it.

The streetlamps cast long shadows as I unlocked the front door, flipping on the lights to reveal my grandmother's legacy, now reborn as my own. The newly painted Resolute Blue walls seemed to glow softly in the early morning light, embracing the yellow-painted trim like an old friend.

The familiar rhythm of preparation settled over me as I moved through the kitchen, my hands finding their places without conscious thought. The heavy mixing bowls, the cool metal measuring cups, the specially sourced ingredients; each element had its place in this dance. I turned the ovens on to preheat, their gentle hum a comforting backdrop to my work.

As I kneaded dough for the morning's first batch of croissants, my mind drifted to how far I'd come since leaving Chicago and Craig. In just a few months, I'd transformed from a woman who arranged her entire life around someone else's dreams to a business owner following my own passion. The dough beneath my fingers was both a connection to my past and a bridge to my future.

By six o'clock, the display cases were filled with golden pastries, rich chocolate confections, and, of course, my signature orange marmalade scones. The coffee was brewing, filling the space with its rich aroma, mingling with the scents of butter, sugar, and vanilla. Outside the window, I could see the yellow ribbon stretched across the entrance, waiting for the official cutting ceremony at ten.

I stepped back, taking in the scene. Maddy Cakes was ready for its debut.

"Impressive," came a crisp voice from the doorway.

I startled, nearly dropping the tray of muffins I was arranging. Standing in the entrance was a middle-aged woman with a severe bob and rectangular glasses perched on her nose. She wore a navy pantsuit and carried a clipboard: the universal costume of someone with the power to ruin your day.

Health inspector.

"Stella Rodgers, County Health Department," she said, her voice all business. "Shall we get started?"

For the next forty minutes, Stella Rodgers examined every area that had failed inspection yesterday with the precision of a surgeon and the demeanor of a drill sergeant. She measured temperatures, checked seals, inspected my documentation, and examined surfaces with a bright flashlight seemingly designed to illuminate the slightest imperfection.

"Your refrigeration unit is at 38 degrees," she noted, making a mark on her clipboard.

"Yes, we keep it below 40 as required," I replied, trying to keep my voice steady despite the anxiety churning my stomach. "It turns out it wasn't malfunctioning yesterday, it had been...adjusted."

She raised an eyebrow over her glasses. "Interesting."

"We had it checked immediately after your visit yesterday," I explained, thinking about the panic it had caused. "And I've been monitoring it with a secondary thermometer since the readjustment with no issues."

Stella made another note, her expression giving nothing away.

When she finally turned her attention to the handwashing station, I held my breath.

"Soap dispenser is functioning properly," she murmured, dispensing a small amount into her palm. "Paper towels adequately stocked. Hot water reaches appropriate temperature within acceptable time frame."

I could have wept with relief.

Finally, after what felt like years, Stella closed her clipboard and removed her gloves.

"Congratulations, Ms. Bell," she said, her tone marginally warmer than before. "You've addressed all previous concerns. Your establishment meets county health standards."

A weight lifted from my shoulders so suddenly I felt light-headed. "Thank you," I managed, accepting the inspection report she handed me.

As she prepared to leave, Stella paused at the door. "For what it's worth, Ms. Bell, I'm impressed. Usually when we receive anonymous complaints about new establishments, we find at least *some* merit to them."

My happiness dimmed slightly. "Anonymous complaints?"

"Yes, someone called, concerned about your refrigeration units. Clearly unfounded, especially since you'd had a successful inspection the day before." Her eyes narrowed slightly. "Not everyone wants new businesses to succeed in small towns, Ms. Bell. Best remember that." With that cryptic warning, she left.

I didn't have time to dwell on her words. The clock showed 8:30, and I still had preparations to finish before the 10 AM ceremony and official grand opening.

By 9:45, a small crowd had gathered outside the bakery. I spotted Mayor Eleanor Whitman's silver hair gleaming in the morning sunlight, her tailored suit making her stand out from the more casual townspeople. Lacy was there too, directing people where to stand for the best view of the ribbon cutting.

At precisely 10 AM, Mayor Whitman stepped forward, scissors in hand.

"Citizens of Sugar Creek," she began, her voice carrying easily across the assembled crowd. "Today we celebrate not just the opening of a business, but the continuation of a legacy. Many of us remember Beatrice's bakery as the heart of this community for decades. Today, her granddaughter Maddison brings that heart back to life."

The mayor turned to me, her eyes warm. "Beatrice would be proud, my dear."

Fighting back tears, I stepped forward as she handed me the oversized scissors. With a deep breath, I cut the yellow ribbon stretched across the entrance to Maddy Cakes. The crowd applauded, and for a moment, I felt my grandmother's presence so strongly it took my breath away.

As people began to enter the bakery, Lacy appeared at my side, squeezing my hand. "You did it, Maddy," she whispered. "Look how many people came to support you."

The bakery filled quickly with curious and hungry people. I recognized faces from the funeral, from my previous soft opening, and many I didn't know at all. This was the true test: would Sugar Creek embrace Maddy Cakes as their own?

As I rang up sales and chatted with customers, I kept watching the door, hoping to see one particular face. But midmorning came and went with no sign of Rex. I tried to squash my disappointment. He was probably busy at the clinic. It's not like we had made specific plans for him to be here at a certain time.

By noon, we were running dangerously low on several items. The orange scones had sold out within the first hour, and the chocolate croissants weren't far behind. Allison had been baking continuously since the opening, trying to keep up with demand, but we were fighting a losing battle.

"What do we do?" Allison whispered as we passed in the kitchen, her face flushed from the heat of the ovens. "We're almost out of everything, and it's only lunchtime."

I took a deep breath, remembering my grandmother's advice for days when the line stretched out the door: When there's more demand than supply, you've done something right.

"We'll put up a sign," I decided. "First come, first served until we sell out. And we'll plan to make more tomorrow."

Allison nodded, already turning back to the mixer. "I'll get another batch of those cranberry muffins started. They seem to be a hit."

As the afternoon wore on, the initial rush gave way to a steady stream of customers. By four o'clock, our display cases were looking sadly depleted, but the cash register was satisfyingly full. Allison had proven herself invaluable, not just with her baking skills but with her easy way with customers and quick thinking during several mini-crises.

"Why don't you head home?" I suggested to her as the crowd finally thinned. "You've more than earned it today."

"Are you sure?" she asked, though I could see the fatigue in her eyes. "I can stay and help clean up."

"Go," I insisted. "Get some rest. Tomorrow will be busy too."

After Allison left, I began the closing routine, wiping down counters and putting away ingredients. As I stepped outside to bring in the chalkboard sign, something caught my eye: a new addition to the front of the bakery that definitely hadn't been there this morning.

Nestled beside the entrance was a beautifully crafted wooden doghouse, painted in the exact shade of Resolute Blue that colored my walls inside. The peaked roof had a hinged top, and when I curiously lifted it, I discovered a space perfectly sized for small dog bowls and treats. "Maddy Cakes" was painted on the front in the same script as my bakery sign, with a small silhouette of a dog beside it.

My heart did a little flip as I examined the craftsmanship, running my fingers over the smooth edges and perfect joinery. This was no store-bought item... someone had made this specifically for the bakery. And I had a pretty good idea who that someone was.

A small envelope was tucked inside the roof compartment. I pulled out the note inside:

This should provide plenty of shade for your four-legged patrons. Congrats on your grand opening. Be proud, this is your day. – Rex

I clutched the note to my chest, a ridiculous smile spreading across my face. It was such a thoughtful gift — practical but personal, showing he'd been paying attention to my ideas and concerns. The doghouse would solve my worry about providing water and shelter for the beloved pets of the community.

More than that, though, it was the exact shade of blue I'd chosen for my walls. The color I'd once told Rex reminded me of my grandmother's eyes. He'd remembered.

Back inside, I finished closing procedures and began counting the day's earnings. The numbers were good, better than I'd expected for an opening day. But as I factored in the costs of ingredients, utilities, and Allison's wages, the reality set in. We'd barely broken even, even with the exceptional turnout.

I sank into a chair, suddenly exhausted. The emotional high of the day faded, replaced by the sobering reality of small business ownership. If every day was as busy as today, we'd survive. But what about slow days? What about the off-season when tourists weren't swelling Sugar Creek's population?

The jingling of the bell over the door interrupted my calculations. I looked up, ready to inform the newcomers we were closed, when two men in matching charcoal suits entered. The taller one had salt-and-pepper hair and an easy smile, while his companion was shorter with wire-rimmed glasses and a more serious demeanor.

"I'm sorry, we're closed," I said, standing.

"Ms. Bell?" the taller man asked. "Maddison Bell?"

"Yes?" I said cautiously.

"Fred Potter," he said, extending his hand. "And this is my colleague, Larry Davis. We're with BAM Franchise Consulting."

I shook their hands automatically, my mind whirring. What would franchise consultants want with my tiny bakery on its first official day?

"Congratulations on your grand opening," Larry said, his tone warm and professional. "We happened to be in Sugar Creek for a meeting and couldn't resist stopping by when we saw your bakery. Roland Pierce mentioned you might be someone we should meet."

At the mention of Roland's name, my guard went up.

"We don't mean to intrude," Fred added, seeming to sense my hesitation. "We simply wanted to introduce ourselves and perhaps schedule a time to discuss some opportunities that might interest you."

"What kind of opportunities?" I asked, curiosity getting the better of me.

Fred exchanged a glance with Larry. "Opportunities that could solve all your financial concerns while preserving what makes Maddy Cakes special," he said smoothly. "Your grandmother created something wonderful here. We believe it deserves to be shared more widely."

Larry reached into his pocket and handed me a business card. The BAM logo was prominently displayed in the corner, the same logo I'd seen on letters in my grandmother's files. Letters she'd answered with rejections.

"We'll be in town for a few days," Fred said. "Perhaps we could meet for coffee and discuss how BAM Franchise Consulting might help Maddy Cakes reach its full potential."

I stared at the card in my hand, thinking of the slim profits from today's exceptional sales. "I'll think about it," I said finally.

As they left, I sank back into my chair, turning the business card over in my fingers. My grandmother had repeatedly rejected BAM's offers. But had she faced the same financial realities I was facing now? Had she had other options I didn't know about?

The doghouse outside caught my eye through the window, its Resolute Blue paint deepening in the evening light. What would Rex think if he knew I was even considering talking to franchise consultants? What would my grandmother think?

I tucked the card into my pocket. I didn't have to decide anything tonight. Today was for celebrating what I'd accomplished: a successful grand opening, a passed health inspection, and a bakery full of satisfied customers. I could worry about the future tomorrow.

Chapter 14

My grandfather had taken to stopping by the bakery every day with his chess buddies around 10 every morning since our grand opening, holding court at a large table near the window.

"It makes me feel closer to your Gram," he'd said, his grey eyes watery.

"Me too, Gramps," I hugged him.

We ran into each other just outside the bakery door as I was refilling the doghouse with treats I'd baked fresh this morning.

My heart swelled with emotion as I approached the doghouse. This wasn't just any gift — it was thoughtful, personal, and showed that Rex had been paying attention to the details that mattered to me. A man who didn't care about deeper connections wouldn't have gone to this trouble.

"Well, isn't that something," my grandfather said, admiring the doghouse beside me. "That veterinarian fellow must think highly of you."

I nodded, unable to find my voice for a moment. "He's... very thoughtful."

"Your grandmother always said you could tell a person's character by how they treat animals," Gramps mused, studying the doghouse with approval. "And by the care they put into the things they make with their own hands." He ran his weathered fingers over the smooth wood. "This is quality craftsmanship. Not rushed. Like your baking."

He looked at me, a knowing twinkle in his eye. "Seems like this young man passes your Gram's test with flying colors, Cupcake."

"We're just friends, Gramps," I said. "I'm focused on Maddy Cakes."

"We'll see," he replied with a smile.

It had been days since Rex read my bucket list and learned my deepest secret. I still couldn't stop thinking about it. Every time our paths crossed in town or when he stopped by the bakery, I wondered if he was thinking about it too... if he was picturing me with Craig, faking pleasure for a decade. The thought made me cringe.

I was mortified on the daily that he now knew I'd never experienced an orgasm during sex, but that was the truth. Craig never really cared about my pleasure, and I faked it so often that it became routine. I'd convinced myself that's just how things were supposed to be.

With a sigh, I pushed those thoughts aside as I pulled into my parking spot behind the bakery. It was still dark outside, the rain pouring down in sheets, turning the world into a hazy blur. I'd forgotten my umbrella, of course. Scanning the car for anything to shield me from the downpour, I spotted a canvas shopping tote in the backseat. Not much protection, but better than nothing.

Gripping the tote tightly over my head, I dashed toward the bakery entrance, the rain pelting me like tiny needles against my skin. By the time I made it inside, I was drenched and breathless, rainwater pooling at my feet on the tile floor. I flipped on the lights and surveyed my soggy state in the reflection of the stainless steel refrigerator. My hair clung to my face in wet tendrils, and my shirt was plastered to my skin.

"Perfect way to start the day," I muttered, wringing water from my hair.

A quick check of the weather forecast on my phone revealed that the storm should pass within a few hours. Thank goodness. With a sigh of relief, I hung up my raincoat and changed into the spare clothes I kept in my office. The familiar routine of prep work would calm my nerves.

The bakery felt different in these early morning hours: peaceful and full of possibility. This was my sanctuary, where I could lose myself in the simple pleasure of creating something delicious. Today, however, the storm outside matched the tumult inside me. I couldn't stop thinking about Rex and the way he made me feel whenever he was near.

As I measured flour for the morning's first batch of pastries, a loud banging noise startled me. The mixing bowl slipped from my hands, clattering to the floor and shattering into pieces. My heart pounded as thunder rolled in the distance.

I steadied my breath, bending down to pick up the broken pieces, when the banging sound echoed again. This time, it sounded clearer and closer. My pulse quickened as I realized it wasn't thunder at all.

Someone was banging on my door.

Oh no! Oh no! Oh no! Am I getting robbed? Vandals again?

Panic surged through me as I frantically searched for something to defend myself with. My eyes landed on a wooden rolling pin, and I gripped it tightly, my knuckles turning white. As I cautiously moved toward the front of the bakery, the rain intensified, ratcheting up my terror like the soundtrack of a horror movie. I tiptoed behind a large potted plant near the window, pulling the rolling pin back, ready to swing if necessary.

Peering through the rain-streaked glass, I caught sight of a tall figure standing on the other side of the door. Lightning flashed, illuminating his face for a brief second.

Rex.

A wave of relief washed over me, followed immediately by confusion. What was he doing here at four in the morning?

I moved to unlock the door, still clutching the rolling pin, chuckling at the realization that robbers don't typically knock on the front door.

"Rex, come in, come in," I urged, ushering him inside. "You're soaked to the bone!"

He eyed me clutching the rolling pin and entered slowly, hands raised in mock surrender. "Don't hit me over the head with that thing," he laughed, water dripping from his hair onto his face.

I swung the rolling pin around slowly, making lightsaber noises. "Maybe don't sneak up on people at 4 AM, then." I smiled, placing the rolling pin on a nearby table. "Sorry, I wasn't expecting anyone at my door at this hour."

Despite my teasing, a strange fluttering sensation filled my chest. I was genuinely glad to see him, even at the crack of dawn. There was something about Rex's presence that made me feel both excited and at ease, a contradiction I couldn't quite reconcile.

I offered him some napkins to dry off, but they disintegrated against his drenched form. He dabbed at his face, but it was a futile effort. I dashed back to the kitchen, snatched up a clean tea towel, and returned to find him attempting to wring water from his scrub top.

My eyes lingered on the damp fabric clinging to his muscled frame, outlining every contour of his chest and shoulders. I swallowed hard, my mouth suddenly dry. His biceps were...robust, like freshly baked bread. *Yummy.*

Focus, Maddy.

"Here," I said, thrusting the towel toward him, hoping he hadn't noticed me staring.

Rex wiped his face again, revealing his sharp jawline, and I felt a pang of something that felt dangerously like desire. "Come on back here. I have a shirt you can wear."

"Thanks, I'm starting a collection," he deadpanned.

He followed me to the back where I grabbed a clean Maddy Cakes Bakery shirt and tossed it to him, hoping to distract myself from my sudden burst of out-of-control attraction. Without hesitation, he lifted off his soaked scrub shirt, revealing taut abdominal muscles that made my breath catch in my throat.

"Hand me your scrub top, and I'll toss it in the dryer for you," I said, my pulse quickening as I brushed against his arm.

Yes, make it all about the laundry. You're not ogling your friendly neighborhood veterinarian; you're just concerned he'll catch a cold.

Which seemed like an awesome plan until he whipped his drenched shirt all the way off and handed it over to me.

Holy smokeshow.

My brain short-circuited for a brief second as I took in the sight of his bare torso, water droplets trailing down his skin. He quickly pulled on the blue and yellow Maddy Cakes t-shirt, and my twelve seconds of ogling bliss were over as quickly as they'd started.

"Your scrub pants are soaked too," I noted, trying to keep my voice steady. "Sorry I don't have any pants back here."

"It's okay, if you don't mind..." He looked down, seeming almost shy. "I've got basketball shorts underneath. I always do, just in case I need to change at the office."

Take your pants off in my kitchen? Don't mind if you do...

"No problem," I managed, turning toward the dryer to hide the blush creeping up my neck.

"Thanks," he said, quickly removing his scrub pants and handing them over. "And sorry again if I scared you. I saw the lights on and I..." His voice trailed off, and he looked as though he was suddenly deep in thought.

"It's okay," I said, my heart still racing, though no longer from fear. "At least I'd die in my kitchen, so there's some comfort in that."

"That doesn't exactly make me feel better about startling you," he joked, but his smile didn't quite reach his eyes.

"I was just surprised someone else was up this time of day," I replied, placing his clothes in the dryer. "Normally when I come to the bakery, the rest of the town is dark." Rex was the last person I was expecting to see before sunrise, but I couldn't deny the little thrill that ran through me in his presence.

"I'm not usually up at this hour," he admitted, leaning against the counter. "Unless you have a surprise inspection, of course." He smiled weakly.

His face was completely drained of color.

"What happened?"

"I had an emergency surgery. I haven't eaten in hours, and I was hoping you might have something." He paused, and for a second I thought he wanted to say more, but didn't.

As I turned to face him fully, I noticed the exhaustion etched on his face. His usually bright blue eyes were dull and bloodshot, and the tension in his shoulders betrayed his stress. I felt a pang of sympathy for him and wondered what had happened.

"Emergency surgery? Are you okay?" I asked softly, resisting the urge to reach out and touch him.

Rex nodded, his gaze fixed on the floor. We stood in silence for a moment, the weight of his unspoken burden settling between us. The only sounds were the rain pattering against the windows and the hum of the dryer. Then Rex's stomach growled loudly, breaking the tension.

"Let me whip you up some eggs," I offered, trying to lighten the mood. "Scrambled, okay?"

He looked up from the floor, meeting my gaze, "Thanks." His bloodshot eyes tugged at my heartstrings, making me want to ease whatever pain he was carrying.

I pulled out my cast iron pan and turned on the burner, dropping in a chunk of butter. The familiar motions of cooking grounded me, giving me something to focus on besides the distractingly handsome man in my kitchen.

I wanted to make everything better for him, even if it was just a plate of eggs at that moment. As I cracked the eggs into the mixing bowl, I felt his eyes on me, and I turned to face him.

"Do you want to talk about it?" I asked quietly.

He was silent for a long moment, and I wondered if he'd heard me. Then, just as I was about to repeat myself, he spoke.

"Sometimes it's hard to save them all," he said, his voice soft and distant. "I did every-thing I could, but I lost Coco on the table."

His words tugged at my heart. Even as a seasoned veterinarian who likely saw animals pass away often, he still carried the emotional weight of each loss. It spoke volumes about the kind of man he was: one who cared deeply, who took his responsibilities seriously.

My heart ached for him as he looked away, his strong jaw clenched tight. I wanted to wrap my arms around him, to comfort him, and tell him that it would all be okay. I barely knew him, so why did I suddenly feel so protective?

Instead, I focused on the task at hand and mixed the eggs together, adding a pinch of salt and a dash of pepper. I poured them into the pan, the sizzle filling the silence between us.

"How'd you become a vet?" I asked, hoping to take his mind off things.

Rex shifted on his stool, his posture relaxing slightly at the change of subject. "Long story. I think I mentioned my dad was in the military, so we moved around a lot when I was a kid. I was eleven and had just started my eighth or ninth new school. I was still pretty small for my age back then, and I was getting bullied a lot."

"That must have been rough," I said, reaching out to gently touch his hand before I could stop myself. The brief contact sent a jolt of electricity up my arm. It was hard to imagine someone as physically imposing as Rex ever being small or vulnerable.

"It's pretty common at schools outside the base," he continued. "You have a lot of kids traumatized from all the constant uprooting, and sometimes they go pretty rough on each other. I was pretty upset at having to leave my best friend at my old school, and I hadn't really met any new friends yet — just the welcoming committee that decided to knock me around on the playground every chance they got."

His mouth twisted into a half-smile that didn't reach his eyes. "But I had a dog, a great dog. A beagle named Bailey, who was a dirty sock thief and the best dog a kid could have. Especially a kid like me."

My heart sank, fearing where his story was headed.

"Bailey started acting strangely," Rex continued, his voice becoming softer. "She stopped eating, didn't want to play, spent all day and night sleeping on my bed with her head on my pillow. By the time we took her to the vet, it was too late to save her. She had lymphoma. The vet said he couldn't do anything; the cancer had spread too much."

"Oh, Rex," I whispered, my chest tightening at the thought of an eleven-year-old boy losing his only friend. "That must have been devastating."

"I was so angry," he admitted, running a hand through his damp hair. "Bailey was basically my only friend at that point, and I was distraught that the vet couldn't do anything to save her. The week after she passed, I told my mom and dad that I would not be going to West Point, as my father had always wanted, and that I was going to be a vet because I never wanted any other kid to lose his pet. I was going to save them all."

"Like a superhero," I said softly. "Except with milkbones."

He laughed, a genuine sound that made his shoulders relax. "Something like that."

"What did your parents say?" I asked, hoping his trauma hadn't been compounded by their response.

"My dad said I could do both," Rex replied, a hint of bitterness in his tone. "And from that moment, I knew I wanted to be a military vet." His eyes were still full of emotion, the passion in them palpable. "The call of military life always had a hold on me. The sense of duty to serve our country was ingrained in me from the day I was born," he explained, running a hand through his thick hair.

"That's really admirable," I said, plating the eggs. "And pretty heartbreaking." The thought of young Rex, determined to save every animal, made my chest tighten with emotion.

He sighed deeply, as though the weight of his memories was pressing down on him. "What can I do for you?" I asked gently, placing the plate in front of him.

"Honestly, making me breakfast is about the kindest thing anyone could do for me right now," he said, offering me a tired smile. "I really appreciate it."

I fussed over the eggs, gently breaking them up with the wooden spoon. "If you ever need someone to talk to, I'm here."

He nodded and took a bite of the eggs. I watched him eat, taking in every movement of his jaw, every swallow. *Jeez Louise, how was that so sexy?*

He stood up from the stool and leaned his back against the counter, his tall frame towering over me. Suddenly there was a tension in the room, an electricity that hadn't been there before.

He looked so sad, so vulnerable that it made my heart ache.

"Her chance of survival was very low," he said in a low voice. "But still, it's hard anytime I lose an animal, someone's pet, on the table. A little piece of me goes with them to the rainbow bridge." I realized that Rex might have a tough exterior, but there was more to him than met the eye. "I've been taking care of Coco since she was a puppy," he continued. "I was just as devastated as her owners when I discovered the tumor on the x-ray."

He turned away from me and placed his elbows on the counter, bringing his hands up to his forehead. I wanted nothing more than to go over to him, wrap my arms around him, and try to comfort him. But I stopped myself, not sure if that would be welcome.

"It's my job to protect and care for the animals, and sometimes when owners disagree with me, it makes it even harder to do. The tumor was large and likely already spreading. I told the owners it would be in Coco's best interest to euthanize. She was already showing signs of distress, not eating. Difficulty breathing." He exhaled loudly, and I saw the pain etched on his face. "Euthanizing her would have allowed her to go in a humane way, reducing pain and distress. But they insisted on the surgery."

He sighed deeply. "I understand why they did. It's nearly impossible to let go of someone or something you love so much."

He put his hands on top of his head and stretched backward. "And while completely understandable, they made the wrong decision. But ultimately, it was their decision, not mine, to make." He moved his hands back to his legs, rubbing up and down his thighs. "I knew I had to give it my all for Coco to have a fighting chance. Once I got in there, I realized it was going to be a long night. I was making progress, but ultimately, her body just couldn't handle the anesthesia."

My heart broke for him as he blinked hard, tears pooling in his eyes. He sat back down on the stool, resting his arm on the counter beside him. I reached out and placed my hand over his, feeling the warmth of his skin.

"I am so sorry," I said softly, hoping to offer some comfort. He turned his hand over, giving mine a squeeze that sent a flutter through my chest.

We sat in silence for a moment. The rain against the windows and the hum of the dryer were the only sounds. Rex finished his eggs, scraping the plate clean with his fork.

"Thank you for breakfast," he said, his voice stronger now. "It was delicious, and I appreciate it more than you know."

"I was just getting ready to make those orange scones you like," I said, the words tumbling out before I could stop them. I hadn't actually planned on making those today, but I really wanted to cheer him up. I scurried around the kitchen gathering ingredients, trying to ignore the way my heart sped up when he smiled at me.

As I grabbed the mixing bowl, I noticed he was fiddling with a whisk on the counter. "Do you want to help?" I asked, hoping the activity might take his mind off his sadness.

A funny look crossed his face, like a child being offered the chance to lick brownie batter from the spoon. It was endearing to see this playful side of him emerge from beneath the sadness.

I walked to the oven to preheat it, grabbing the parchment paper for the baking sheets. As I gathered the flour and sugar from the cabinet, I glanced behind me and saw him still staring at the whisk, turning it over in his hands as if it were a foreign object.

"Do you know how to whisk?" I asked, a smile tugging at my lips.

A slight grin spread across his face, and seeing it made me smile too. There was something deeply satisfying about being the person who could make him smile after such a difficult night.

I showed him how to mix the flour, sugar, baking powder, and orange peel while he worked the whisk with surprising dexterity. "You're a natural," I said, enjoying the sight of his muscles rippling under the borrowed shirt as he worked.

As he stirred, I prepared the butter, pressing it into small pea-sized bits with the pastry blender. A comfortable silence fell between us, broken only by the soft patter of rain against the windows and the rhythmic sound of the whisk against the bowl.

There was something intimate about baking with someone in the early morning hours, sharing the quiet sanctuary of my kitchen. I started to feel a sense of ease wash over me, a contentment I hadn't experienced in a long time.

Together, we added the marmalade, milk, and egg, and then I handed him the Danish dough whisk. "This will work better for creating the dough," I explained, our fingers brushing as I passed it to him.

"It was your grandmother who taught you to love baking?" he asked, his voice softer than before.

I walked over to the counter and sprinkled flour to prepare the dough for kneading, smiling at the memories that flooded my mind. "She taught me everything I know. We would spend every summer together, and she would show me the secrets of the kitchen."

I demonstrated how to knead the dough, placing my hands over his to guide him. His fingers intertwined with mine, and I felt a jolt of electricity at the contact. The rhythm of our hands guided the sticky dough into a soft consistency. As we worked together, I felt a connection growing between us, like the ingredients in our hands transforming into something new.

It was starting to feel intense, and I realized I had to pull back before this went any further. I gently withdrew my hands, pretending to need something from the other counter.

"I grew up in Chicago with my mom," I continued, trying to keep my voice steady, "but coming to stay with my grandparents every summer was the highlight of my year. I fell in love with Sugar Creek and with baking."

I showed him how to roll the dough into round circles. "You want them to be about an inch thick," I instructed, trying not to notice how close he was standing. As he rolled them, I started to cut them into wedges and pull them apart slightly. I could feel his eyes on me as I sprinkled sugar over the scones.

"You have such a talent for this," he remarked. "It's obvious how much baking means to you." His observation touched me. Even someone I barely knew like Rex Townsend could recognize my passion for baking when Craig never seemed to notice. "Your grandmother must be so proud."

I beamed at him, warmth spreading through my chest. "I hope so."

He was staring at me with a look of fascination that made my cheeks flush. I clumsily knocked over a bowl in response, flour dusting the counter. *Ever the professional, Maddy.* But he stood there looking at me like I was some rare celestial event... not just a baker who was prone to constantly knocking over bowls.

"I'd like to think she would be proud of me," I admitted, sweeping the flour into a neat pile. "When she left me this bakery, I knew immediately it was where I was meant to be."

"Sometimes the universe has a way of leading us where we're meant to go," he said, his voice low and intimate. I felt a delicious tingle down my spine at his words.

"I used to wonder if baking would end up just a hobby, a passion that I would keep to myself," I confessed. "But something about my grandmother's kitchen, the warmth and love in this space, made me believe I could do more. And after she passed, a big piece of me was missing." I met his gaze, surprised by my own honesty. "I'm starting to find that piece again here."

I placed the scones in the oven and set the timer. Gathering more ingredients, I poured flour, sugar, and baking powder into a spacious bowl. Adding a hint of salt, I handed it to Rex to whisk. In another bowl, I carefully blended egg, milk, and vanilla extract.

I tried to focus on the task at hand, acutely aware of his eyes tracing my every move-ment. The intensity of his gaze made my hands tremble slightly as I worked.

"She believed in me, more than I believed in myself," I continued, needing to fill the charged silence between us. "And that's when I realized that dreams can become reality if you have the courage to pursue them." I took a deep breath and glanced over at him. "What about you? How did you end up in Sugar Creek?"

"It's kind of a long story," he said, setting down the whisk.

"Well, we have twenty minutes until your scones are ready," I reminded him with a smile.

He leaned against the counter, crossing his arms. "After college I followed my father's footsteps and enlisted in the Army, and that's where I met Andrina," he said. I noticed how his tone changed when he mentioned his father, making the word seem difficult to articulate.

"Your mom and dad must be very proud of you," I said. "Especially following in his footsteps and going into the military. Are your parents still together?"

"Yeah, they've been married for over thirty years," he replied, his expression unreadable. "They were really proud of me."

Rex's voice became heavy with resignation as he leaned against the counter. I extended my hand to take the bowl, absentmindedly stirring the mixture with gentle, soothing motions.

"At eighteen, I discovered my hero, my dad, wasn't as flawless as I'd believed. It made me reevaluate life," he said, a shadow crossing his face. I began to butter the muffin tin, curious about what had happened but not wanting to push him. "That's a story for some other time. I usually don't share these things... I must be really tired." As I watched Rex's expression, it was clear something significant had shaped him, leaving scars that were still tender.

"I'm sorry," I said softly, sensing his discomfort. "And Andrina? You mentioned meeting her in the Army?"

"Oh, sorry..." he said, seeming to collect himself. "Andrina, Dr. O'Connor, she owned the clinic across the street. We were both stationed at Fort McPherson. She was a reservist and my mentor for the Health Professional Scholarship, which allowed me to go to vet school for free."

I nodded, piecing it together. "So, you went to vet school in the Army and then came to Sugar Creek?"

"Yep. After a few years on active duty, I went into the reserve. Andrina offered me a job, and I moved here." He shrugged, as if it were that simple, but I sensed there was more to the story than he was sharing.

"Must have been a big change from military life," I commented, trying to imagine the transition from the structured environment of the Army to the quiet pace of Sugar Creek.

"It was," he admitted, "but I get to focus on what I truly love, caring for animals."

"Could you ever be deployed?" I asked, the thought of Rex being called into active duty sending an unexpected pang of worry through me.

"It's unlikely," he said, his tone reassuring. "Being in combat isn't typically a part of a veterinarian's role, but there's always a risk, especially during unexpected attacks. My job when I was active duty was mainly to take care of military working dogs and horses, and the pets of military families. I also worked with a team to prevent the spread of animal-borne diseases."

Relief washed over me, but I still needed to know more. "But would you ever have to go into combat?" I pressed. "I mean, is it dangerous?"

"It depends," he said, his expression guarded. "Danger isn't completely off the table for most jobs in the military." I got the distinct sense that he was downplaying the danger for my benefit.

A feeling of admiration swelled within me. He was so brave and selfless, putting himself in harm's way for his country and the animals he loved. I could only imagine how his loved ones must have felt when he was away. I took a sip of water, trying to shake off the heaviness that settled over me.

"It must have been tough for your mother when you were away," I said, my voice soft.

A somber look crossed Rex's face. "Yes, it was. But she was always supportive of me, even when she didn't understand."

"Will you stay in Sugar Creek now, permanently?" I asked, surprised by how much I wanted the answer to be yes.

"I plan to," he said, his expression softening. "Military life was hard as a kid constantly moving around. Bailey was always there. She was my constant, my anchor. Just when I felt like a place might become a home, we moved again." His voice became quieter, more reflective. "I've always wanted to put down roots somewhere. But I never seem to."

I got the feeling he was revealing a part of himself that he'd never shared before. The image of Rex as a little boy with his dog Bailey, the way his eyes lit up talking about her, made my heart skip a beat.

"Having a loyal companion like that makes all the difference," I murmured, feeling the bond between man and dog in his words.

"I'm sure making lasting friendships is tough when you're constantly moving around," I added, grateful for my own lifelong friendship with Lacy and how we'd navigated life's awkward stages together.

"I didn't intend to ramble," he said, appearing a bit self-conscious. "I don't usually talk about this stuff."

"I loved hearing about your childhood and how much you loved Bailey," I assured him, touched that he'd shared something so personal with me.

It made perfect sense that he became a vet — a man whose best friend growing up was a dog, who understood the profound bond between animals and their people.

I tried to lighten the mood, hoping to ease the vulnerability that had settled between us. "You know, they say that kitchens are the best places to share secrets, and bakers make the best listeners." I smiled at him, wanting him to know that he could confide in me, that I was here for him.

I reached up to grab a pan from an overhead cabinet, but it slipped from my grasp and clattered to the floor. We both reached for it at the same time, our fingers brushing as we collided. A shockwave of desire surged through my body at the contact. I caught my breath as Rex picked up the pan, my heart pounding in my chest. A shiver ran through me as his arm brushed against mine, his touch igniting a spark deep within me.

Suddenly, laughter bubbled up from within me, the tension of the moment breaking. The oven timer went off, and I opened the door to check on the scones. One tray needed a few more minutes, but the other was perfectly golden brown.

I pulled the tray out of the oven and placed the scones on the cooling rack, adding another minute and a half on the oven timer for the other tray.

Rex's eyes lit up as he took in the sight of the freshly baked scones, their aroma filling the kitchen. "Ooh! Can I have one of those?" he asked, his earlier sadness momentarily forgotten.

"You can," I replied, "but you might want to give them a few minutes to cool down so you don't burn your lips off."

He grinned, the expression transforming his face. "I'm like a stray dog. If you keep feeding me, I'll keep coming back for more."

"I don't mind feeding you," I said, trying to hide the blush creeping up my neck. That sounded smuttier than I'd intended, but Rex's eyes darkened slightly at my words, and I knew he'd caught the unintentional double entendre.

I realized with a start that in just a few short weeks, Rex had become an important part of my new life here. He wasn't just the handsome vet from across the street anymore; he was someone I looked forward to seeing, someone who made my day brighter just by being in it.

"I'm sorry again I wasn't able to make it to your official grand opening ceremony the other day," he said apologetically, breaking into my thoughts.

"We missed you of course," I said, touched by his thoughtfulness. "But I can't thank you enough for everything you did to help me open this place. And the dog house is incredible! I can't believe you made that for me. It's perfect. It's Resolute Blue! Honestly, I think it's one of the most thoughtful gifts anyone has ever given me."

"You're very welcome." Rex approached me, and my heart started to race. He reached his hand toward my face, and I found myself suddenly anticipating a kiss. But instead, he brushed a speck of powder from my nose. I felt a shiver run through me at his touch, and my heart pounded with even more intensity.

"You had some flour on your nose," he explained, his voice low and husky.

"Thanks," I managed, hyperaware of how close he was standing.

We locked eyes, and I could feel the heat between us, a magnetic attraction that neither of us could ignore. We stared at each other for a long moment, caught in a web of tension and desire.

As he leaned in closer, I instinctively moved toward him, licking my lips. Our mouths were so close that I could feel Rex's breath on my skin, warm and inviting. My palms grew slick with sweat as anticipation built within me. I wanted nothing more than to close the gap between us and feel his lips on mine.

And then the oven timer went off again, shattering the moment.

Chapter 15

I couldn't remember the last time I'd slept past five in the morning. My body had become so accustomed to pre-dawn bakery hours that even on my first day off in three weeks, my eyes had fluttered open at 6:30 AM, practically late by my standards. I'd promised Allison I wouldn't set foot in Maddy Cakes today. "The bakery won't burn down without you for one day," she'd insisted, practically shoving me out the door yesterday afternoon.

But as the morning stretched on, restlessness crawled under my skin like an itch I couldn't scratch. I tried reading the steamy romance novel that had been collecting dust on my nightstand, but the words blurred together as my mind drifted to tomorrow's inventory order and whether we had enough vanilla beans for the week ahead.

By noon, I'd reorganized my sock drawer, scrubbed the bathroom until it sparkled, and made a list of new flavor combinations to try next week. Clearly, relaxation wasn't in my new, business owner skill set.

"That's it," I muttered to myself, tossing aside the notebook where I'd been scribbling recipe ideas. "I need to get out of this place."

Twenty minutes later, I was jogging down my favorite trail, the rhythmic pounding of my feet against the packed earth matching the Taylor Swift anthem pumping through my earbuds. The path wound through a dense forest on one side with glimpses of a sun-dappled lake on the other. The perfect blend of shade and scenery.

With each stride, the knots in my shoulders loosened. This was exactly what I needed: fresh air, movement, and space to think about something other than proofing times and profit margins.

My mind drifted to the notes I'd discovered in Gram's old files: correspondence from the businessmen in Charleston who'd been interested in franchising her bakery. Why had she never mentioned it to me? Had she been considering it? Or had she dismissed the idea outright? I couldn't help but wonder if expanding Maddy Cakes was something I should be thinking about too.

And then, like he always seemed to do lately, Rex Townsend slipped into my thoughts. Our early morning encounter at the bakery last week had left me... unsettled. The way he'd opened up about losing a patient, the vulnerability in those striking blue eyes, the electricity when we'd almost...

I shook my head, as if I could physically dislodge thoughts of Rex from my mind. The last thing I needed was another complication in my life, especially one as potent and unpredictable as Rex.

A full week of working in the bakery had taught me that Rex was the subject of a whole lot of gossip and speculation when it came to his love life. I'd heard the Breakfast Club, a group of five retired teachers who started meeting for breakfast a couple of times a week, call Rex a "heartbreaker" on a regular basis and "veterinary Valentino" at least once.

As the trail curved around a bend, a small clearing appeared with wooden benches overlooking the lake. I slowed to a walk, my breath coming in quick puffs as I made my way to the nearest bench and sank down onto it. Closing my eyes, I tilted my face toward the flecks of sunlight filtering through the leaves, letting the gentle rustle of the trees and distant lapping of water against the shore wash over me.

For the first time that day, maybe that week, my mind quieted.

The peaceful moment was shattered as something massive barreled toward me. My eyes flew open just in time to see an enormous dog charging in my direction, tongue lolling, paws thundering against the ground.

"Oh my g — " was all I managed before the Great Dane launched itself at me, knocking me clean off the bench. I landed on my back with an ungraceful "oof" as the dog proceeded to thoroughly wash my face with enthusiastic licks.

"Chloe! Heel!" a familiar voice called out. "Chloe, no!"

The dog, apparently named Chloe, gave my cheek one final slobbery kiss before obediently sitting back, looking entirely too pleased with herself. I pushed up onto my elbows, wiping dog saliva from my face with the back of my hand, and looked up to see none other than Rex Townsend jogging toward us.

Shirtless Rex Townsend.

My brain short-circuited.

If I'd thought he looked good in scrubs or a t-shirt, it was nothing compared to how he looked now: all rippling muscles and sun-kissed skin glistening with sweat. A drop slid tantalizingly down his chest, tracing the contours of his abs before disappearing into the waistband of his running shorts. I swallowed hard, my mouth suddenly dry.

Heel, Maddy.

"I am so sorry," Rex said, reaching me and extending his hand. "Chloe gets overexcited when she sees new people. Are you okay?"

I took his hand, warm and strong with a slight roughness, and let him pull me to my feet. The simple contact sent a jolt of awareness through me that had nothing to do with the dog's enthusiastic greeting.

"I'm fine," I managed, brushing leaves and dirt from my leggings. "Just wasn't expecting to be tackled on my morning run."

Rex's mouth quirked up in that half-smile that did funny things to my insides. "She's in training to be a therapy dog, believe it or not. Still working on the 'gentle greeting' part."

I laughed, genuinely amused despite my embarrassment. "Well, she certainly made an impression." I bent down to scratch behind Chloe's ears, and she leaned into my touch with shameless pleasure. "Is she yours?"

"No, she belongs to — "

"Rex!" A female voice called from down the path. "Did you find her?"

I glanced up to see a woman jogging awkwardly toward us, her ponytail bouncing with each step. She was stunning: tall and lean, with sharp cheekbones and startling blue eyes. Something tightened in my chest as she approached.

Rex walked over to meet her, and they spoke in hushed tones, their heads bent close together. The woman laughed at something he said, playfully swatting his arm. The easy familiarity between them made my stomach knot uncomfortably.

I shouldn't care. I barely knew Rex. Yes, there was... something... between us, but it wasn't like we were dating. He was free to run around shirtless with whomever he pleased.

So why did watching them together make me want to turn and sprint in the opposite direction?

I was just about to make my excuses and leave when Rex turned, beckoning me over. "Maddy, this is Della. Chloe's owner."

I approached cautiously, extending my hand. "Nice to meet you."

The woman, Della, rolled her eyes dramatically at Rex. "This is how you introduce me?" She turned to me with a warm smile. "I'm Della, Rex's half-sister."

Sister. Half-sister. Relief washed through me with embarrassing intensity.

Della looked about ten years younger than Rex, and something in his expression — a flicker of discomfort, maybe even shame — made me curious about their story. Rex had mentioned his parents had been married for thirty years. How did a half-sister fit into that picture?

As if reading my confusion, Della clarified, "We share the same father, but didn't grow up together. I was a 'fling' baby." She nudged Rex's arm playfully, but I caught the flash of something darker in his eyes.

Suddenly, a comment Rex had made during our early morning bakery encounter clicked into place: *At 18, I discovered my hero, my dad, wasn't as flawless as I'd believed. It made me reevaluate life.*

Finding out your father had a child from an affair would certainly qualify as life-reevaluating.

"Rex is helping me train Chloe," Della continued, seemingly oblivious to the undercurrent of tension. "Great Danes can be a handful, but they're the sweetest dogs. So affectionate and loyal."

"Like owner, like dog," Rex said, his expression softening as he looked at his sister.

"This is Maddy," Rex told Della. "She owns the bakery across from my clinic."

"Wait, are you the Maddy Cakes Maddy? You're making my birthday cake for next weekend!" Della's eyes widened with recognition. "O.M.G, you have the best chocolate croissants! Rex hasn't stopped talking about you." She turned to her brother with a mischievous grin. "Right, Rex?"

A hint of color touched Rex's cheeks, and I felt a flutter of pleasure at the thought of him talking about me.

I searched my mental catalog of orders. "Happy Birthday, Della... vanilla cake with raspberry filling?"

"That's the one! I'm impressed you remember the details! You must get tons of orders."

In truth, hers was my only custom order for next weekend, but I wasn't about to admit that. "I try to keep track of all my special orders," I said instead.

"My fiancé ordered it for me," Della explained. "We have plenty of bakeries in Charleston, but after Rex wouldn't shut up about your pastries, I had to try them myself. Once I did, I told Jason my cake absolutely had to come from Maddy Cakes."

I felt my cheeks warm at the compliment. "That's very kind of you."

"Oh my god, you have to come to my birthday party!" Della said suddenly, her eyes lighting up. "We're taking Jason's yacht out for the day. It's in Charleston, so it's a bit of a drive, but it'll be so much fun!"

Before I could respond, Rex interjected, "D, I'm sure she's busy. She doesn't want to hang out on a yacht with a bunch of strangers."

Um, yes I do. Who wouldn't want to go to a yacht party?

Besides, I could meet more potential customers.

And spend more time with Rex outside of Sugar Creek.

"What are you talking about? Everyone loves a yacht party," Della said, elbowing her brother. "Plus, you'll be there, Rexy, and you two clearly know each other." She winked at me. "Maddy, you're welcome to bring a plus one too. My friend Vanessa is single...she could be your date, Rex."

Something in my chest tightened at the thought of Rex with another woman, which was ridiculous. We weren't together. He could date whoever he wanted.

"I'd love to come," I said, pushing the unwelcome feeling aside. "Thank you for the invitation."

"See?" Della said triumphantly to Rex. "Everybody loves a yacht party."

She glanced at her watch and groaned. "I've got to run... literally. I'm supposed to be at rehearsal in an hour." She gave Rex a quick hug and flashed me a bright smile. "Rex will give you all the details. Maddy, I'm so glad we met! See you next weekend!"

With that, she jogged off, Chloe trotting obediently at her side, leaving Rex and me alone on the trail.

Rex pulled a small towel from his pocket and wiped the sweat from his face. "Sorry about that. Della can be... a lot."

"I like her," I said honestly. "She seems fun."

"She is. Great Danes and their owners often share personality traits, you know. They're loyal, affectionate, a bit clumsy sometimes, but generally well-intentioned."

"What do you mean?" I asked, as a cyclist whizzed by, forcing us to step closer together to make room on the path. Rex's proximity sent a wave of awareness through me — the clean scent of his skin beneath the sweat, the heat radiating from his body.

"If you're not busy, I was heading down to grab a coffee. I can tell you all about it," he offered. "Just need to stop at my car for a shirt first."

My eyes involuntarily dipped to his chest again, and when I looked up, I caught him watching me with a knowing glint in his eye. Heat flooded my cheeks.

Busted.

My heart was already racing from our run-in, and if I'm honest, from the view, so caffeine was the last thing I needed. But I found myself nodding anyway. "Coffee sounds good."

As we walked toward the parking lot, Rex continued his explanation about dog breeds and personality types. "Great Danes are gentle giants. Big, sometimes unaware of their size, but incredibly sweet. They love being around people and want to please their owners. Della was like that as a little girl, always eager to please my father... our father."

Something in his voice changed on those last words, a subtle tightening that spoke volumes. I wanted to ask more, to understand the pain I glimpsed behind his easy smile, but it felt too intrusive. We'd only just started... whatever this was between us.

Instead, I asked, "What kind of dog would I be?"

"Border Collie," he answered without hesitation, as if he'd already considered the question.

"A Border Collie?" I repeated, unsure if I should be flattered or offended.

"They're incredibly intelligent, hardworking, and loyal," Rex explained. "But also a bit guarded sometimes. They need to trust you before they let you in."

Guarded? Me?

"Yeah, well, if you were a bakery item, you'd be a molten lava cake," I retorted. "Hard outer shell with a gooey center."

And delicious to taste.

Where did *that* thought come from? I walked a bit faster, trying to put some distance between us before he noticed the blush creeping up my neck.

"What the fuck does that mean?" Rex asked, his voice caught somewhere between amusement and confusion.

"I don't know," I admitted. "But you called me a Border Collie. And guarded. Couldn't I have been something more elegant, like a poodle?"

Rex laughed, the sound rich and warm. "Border Collies happen to be my favorite breed. And the most intelligent. I didn't mean it as an insult. Quite the opposite. You have this focused energy that's... captivating. But you do keep people at a distance. I've noticed."

Had he been watching me that closely? The thought sent a little thrill through me, followed quickly by defensiveness.

"I'm not guarded," I insisted. "At least, I try not to be. I'm just... cautious. New town, new business. I need to establish myself."

Even as I said it, I wondered if it was true. Had ten years with Craig, constantly walking on eggshells and adjusting myself to his expectations, made me build walls without realizing it?

"Being guarded isn't always a bad thing," Rex said, his gaze fixed on the horizon. "It means you understand that trust has to be earned. That not everyone deserves access to your inner world."

Something in his tone made me think he wasn't just talking about me anymore.

"I don't know," I said softly. "Sometimes being too guarded is just a way to avoid commitment. To keep people at arm's length so you don't have to risk getting hurt."

Rex's eyes met mine, something unreadable flickering in their blue depths. "Maybe. Or maybe it's just being smart. Protecting yourself."

A warning bell sounded in the back of my mind. Was he trying to tell me something?

I changed the subject. "Are you and Della close? You seem to have a good relationship."

Rex's shoulders relaxed slightly. "More so lately. We didn't grow up together. I didn't even meet her until she was ten and I was eighteen."

I couldn't imagine discovering I had a sibling after so many years. "That must have been... complicated."

"That's one word for it," Rex said with a humorless laugh. "Finding out your father had a whole other family tends to rearrange your worldview a bit."

"I can imagine," I said softly. "My Grams always said we should be true to our feelings. No one could blame you for *whatever* you felt when you found out."

"I gained a sister that day," Rex said, his voice low. "But I lost my father. The man I'd hero-worshipped my entire life wasn't who I thought he was. We didn't speak for a long time after that."

Despite the years that had clearly passed, I could hear the raw pain still lingering in his voice. It made me want to reach out, to offer some comfort, but his body language had changed: his strides longer, his posture more rigid, as if he'd suddenly remembered he was sharing too much.

He was walking ahead of me now, putting physical distance between us just as he'd started to open up emotionally.

And he thought I was the guarded one?

As we approached the coffee shop at the end of the trail, I found myself wondering what else lay beneath Rex Townsend's charming exterior. What other wounds had shaped him into the man who seemed to keep everyone at a careful distance, even as he drew them in with those magnetic blue eyes?

And more dangerously, why did I suddenly want so badly to be the one he'd let past those walls?

Chapter 16

The next week was weird. Rex showed up at the bakery for his scone every morning.

He was nice, he was polite, and he was a ghost.

When we'd run into each other at the park last week, Rex had invited me for coffee, and then bailed as we arrived, claiming he had to go back to the clinic. At the time, I didn't think much of it; but except for the few minutes I saw him every morning, we'd barely spoken all week. Even Allison and Lacy had started wondering out loud where he'd disappeared to.

I hoped the yacht party wouldn't be awkward. Maybe he'd just been really busy. Or maybe he was avoiding me. I could barely even bring myself to wonder why. Just when he was starting to open up, he'd retreated behind that wall of his.

And now, despite the fact that I'd been determined to focus all my energy on Maddy Cakes, I'd gotten myself sidetracked — swooning like a high-schooler over a guy who clearly didn't want anything more than the occasional flirtation over a pastry counter.

After the two-hour drive to the coastline, Lacy and I finally arrived in Charleston. The view was spectacular, a stark contrast to the waters in Chicago. While Chicago's waters were characterized by the vastness of Lake Michigan and its urban surroundings, Charleston's coastline boasted pristine beaches and charming coastal scenery that left me breathless.

"Don't make us late," I teased Lacy, checking my watch. "I don't want to have to swim out to the boat with a cake strapped to my back."

"Just making sure we have everything," she replied, rummaging through her bag one last time. "You look great, obviously I look great. Phone, lip gloss, shoes, seasickness patches, Della's birthday gift. Okay, we're all set."

"You're sure we're not under-dressed?" I asked, smoothing down my navy linen sundress. The last thing I wanted was to embarrass myself in front of Rex and his sister.

"Her invitation said dressy daytime casual. On a yacht, that means nautical-inspired; linen, silk, or cotton; bright colors, structured or flowy pieces. You look perfect." Lacy gave me a reassuring once-over.

"Thank god for your country club upbringing."

Lacy grinned, a hint of pride in her smile. "My mother always did love a good yacht party." She carried our handbags from the car to the dock, while I carefully managed the massive cake I'd decorated with tiny tone-on-tone waves as a nod to the party's setting.

We stepped onto the yacht where guests were already mingling, champagne flutes in hand. A woman in a crisp white chef's toque quickly approached us.

"Maddy?"

"Yes!" I said, relieved to see her. "Are you Julie, the caterer? Where would you like us to drop off the cake?"

"Yes, I am! I'll go ahead and take the cake below." Her eyes widened as she examined my handiwork. "This is gorgeous work!"

"Thank you so much!" I replied, warmth spreading through my chest. Having a professional caterer complement my work felt like validation I didn't know I needed. Julie carefully took the cake from me and headed down a narrow hallway.

"Let's hit the bar," said Lacy, already scanning the deck. "I'm ready to get this party started."

The sun beat down on us, casting diamonds of light across the water's surface. The smell of salt air filled my lungs, mingling with the scent of expensive perfume and freshly polished teak. I closed my eyes for a moment, savoring it all.

"This boat is amazing!" Lacy exclaimed, gesturing broadly. The yacht was a sleek, white vessel with three levels, easily large enough to fit the entire population of Sugar Creek. "Please feel free to invite me to be your plus-one for all future yacht parties. This is a lifestyle I could get used to."

"Me too," I laughed, as a waiter appeared with a silver tray of champagne flutes.

"Thank you," we said in unison, our synchronicity reminiscent of our childhood days. We clinked glasses and took a sip, the bubbles dancing on my tongue.

Lacy's eyes suddenly widened, and she leaned in close. "Don't make it obvious," she whispered, "but you need to turn around and see how insanely good looking Sexy Rexy looks on a yacht."

I casually glanced over my shoulder, trying to appear nonchalant, but my breath caught in my throat. Rex stood near the bow, his arms crossed over his chest, gaze fixed on the horizon. He wore a fitted white polo shirt that showcased his toned biceps and navy shorts that hugged his muscular thighs in all the right places. His tousled hair was swept back from his forehead, and aviator sunglasses shaded his eyes from the bright sun. He looked effortlessly handsome, like he'd stepped straight out of a Kennedy family photo. The boat hadn't even left the dock yet, and my stomach was already in knots.

"Stop staring," Lacy whispered, though her grin told me she was enjoying my reaction.

"I'm not staring," I insisted, immediately turning away. "I'm just... observing."

"Uh-huh. And I'm just *observing* the way your cheeks get all flushed when you *observe* him."

As Lacy and I made our way toward the front of the yacht, I felt the weight of Rex's gaze on me. My skin tingled with awareness, but before I could meet his eyes, he turned away, his attention back on the ocean. I shook my head, trying to clear the cobwebs from my mind. I couldn't let myself get carried away with thoughts of Rex. First, I wasn't even sure if he was actually interested in me. Second, I'd made a pact with myself to steer clear of relationships until I'd gotten my bakery off the ground.

I had learned my lesson with Craig, jumping into a relationship and making it the center of my universe. It had been so easy to lose myself, to gradually replace my dreams with his until I could barely remember what I had wanted in the first place. I couldn't afford that now, not when Maddy Cakes was just finding its footing.

But damn it, Rex Townsend made that whole plan a lot harder than it should have been. I kept inching closer, like I hadn't been burned before.

"Maddy! I'm so glad you came!" Della's voice pulled me from my thoughts as she approached with a tall, handsome man at her side. "This is my fiancé, Jason."

I hugged her and shook hands with Jason, thanking them for inviting us.

"This is my friend Lacy," I said, gesturing to my best friend who was already charming Jason with her smile.

"I love your dress," Della said, and then leaned closer to whisper in my ear. "Looks like I'm not the only one who noticed how cute you look." She raised an eyebrow toward her half-brother, who appeared to be studying the water with unusual intensity. "Don't be fooled by his sudden interest in the sea," she added with a conspiratorial nod. "He's had an eye on you since the second you and Lacy arrived."

"No..." I started to say, feeling heat rush to my cheeks.

"Don't look!" she whispered, putting a hand on my arm. "Okay, look now."

I felt a flutter in my stomach as I glanced toward Rex. His eyes flickered over me for a moment before turning away once he caught my gaze. The brief connection sent electricity racing down my spine.

Della raised her eyebrows as if to say, 'I told you so.' "See?"

I *wanted* him to want me.

But it sure would be a lot easier to keep my focus if he didn't.

After some friendly chit-chat, Lacy and I made our way upstairs with the other guests to watch the boat leave the dock. The engines hummed to life beneath us, and the massive yacht began to ease away from the shore.

"Maddy, isn't this amazing?" Lacy exclaimed as she twirled, her dress flowing around her like water. "I can't believe we're at the hot vet's half-sister's yacht party. Speaking of which, he's totally got it bad for you."

I rolled my eyes and took a long sip of my drink. "Lacy, please. Don't start with that. You know I'm not going there."

"Oh, come on, Maddy. I've seen the way you look at him. And he's definitely looking at you." She stared at me over her glass, and then her eyes traveled to where Rex was standing. A wicked grin spread across her face. "Busted, buddy."

"Lacy, you don't know that."

"Uh, yes I do," she said, taking a long draw of her drink. "The man hasn't taken his eyes off you since we came aboard. Every time you look away, he looks at you. Every time you look at him, he pretends to be fascinated by seagulls."

"Am I even ready to pursue anything right now? Hard no." I shook my head firmly, as much to convince myself as her. "The bakery's barely getting on its feet. I've been single for like five minutes after ten years with Craig. And I'm still figuring out who I am without being someone's girlfriend."

"Don't worry," she said with a mischievous smile, "I get the very strong sense that Rex will be doing the pursuing."

Before I could respond, Della's voice rose above the chatter. "Everyone, come here! We're about to embark, and we need a toast!"

Lacy practically bounced her way to the back of the yacht, and I followed right behind. As we made our way through the crowd, I found myself scanning faces, looking for one in particular.

My heart sank when Rex was nowhere in sight.

Della greeted us with a bright smile. "There you are! I was wondering where you two went. Grab a glass of champagne and let's make a toast to my birthday!"

Lacy's eyes lit up with excitement as she took another glass from a passing server. "Thank you so much for inviting us, Della. This is amazing."

As we all clinked glasses and took sips of our champagne, the yacht began to pull away from the harbor. I gasped as I looked out over the water. The coast stretched out as far as the eye could see, and the sun cast a golden glow over everything, turning the waves into molten amber.

"Rex is looking at you pretty intensely," Lacy whispered, nudging me with her elbow. "Are you going to talk to him?"

My cheeks warmed at the mention of his name. Or maybe it was the second glass of champagne getting to me?

"I don't know, Lacy. He's hard to read. One moment he's pouring his heart out at the bakery, and the next he can't even bother to come over to say hello. He comes into the bakery, orders his usual orange scone, and leaves."

Lacy's eyebrows shot up. "Wait, did you say orange scone? You told me that was a specialty item. Only available on opening day, or as a special."

"Yeah, well, it's become a regular now," I said, trying to sound casual. "Easy to whip up and it's a crowd-pleaser. Everyone loves it."

Especially Rex.

"It sounds like you've made it a regular feature on the daily menu for a specific someone," she said, her voice teasing. "You really should go over there and thank him again for the dog house."

"I already thanked him. And sent over a basket of treats." I straightened my shoulders. "I have no intention of going over there. If Rex wants to talk to me, he's perfectly capable of approaching me himself."

Besides, I wanted to prove to myself that I could be in Rex's proximity without instantly gravitating toward him. However, with each passing moment, it was becoming increasingly challenging. Every stolen glance in his direction sent my heart racing.

My body was betraying me, and my brain couldn't wait to join in. *Traitors.*

As the yacht sailed further from shore, guests began to mingle more freely. I observed Rex from across the deck, sitting on a chair with a beer in his hand, his gaze fixed on the water below. I wished he were easier to read. His face seemed guarded, like a fortress protecting its secrets, leaving me wanting for the drawbridge to lower and reveal what was within.

I mingled with some of Della's friends, trying my best to be social and outgoing, yet my mind kept drifting back to Rex.

"Hey there, beautiful. I haven't met you before. I'm Carter, Jason's best friend."

I turned to see a handsome man with a flirtatious smile. He seemed harmless enough. "I'm Maddy. Nice to meet you."

Carter leaned in closer, and the scent of alcohol lingered in the air between us. "Want to head downstairs with me for a drink and some chit-chat?"

Although Carter wasn't my type, at least he was making an attempt, which was more than I could say for a certain veterinarian.

"Oh, Carter, you're wasting your time. Maddy's not interested." A striking woman with honey-blonde hair appeared at my side. "I'm Vanessa, by the way," she said to me. "Jason's cousin. Lucky me, I have been saving Carter from embarrassing himself since we were kids."

Carter looked crestfallen for a moment, but then shrugged and turned his attention to someone else. I shot Vanessa a grateful smile.

"Thank you for that."

"No problem. I can always tell when a girl isn't interested, and honey, you had the look." She laughed, a musical sound that made me instantly like her. "I wonder why it takes guys so long to figure that out?"

"Or why some guys are so hard to figure out if they are into you," I said without thinking, my gaze drifting toward Rex.

Vanessa followed my line of sight, and a knowing smile curved her lips. She grabbed a glass of champagne from a passing server. "Oh no! You always know when a guy is interested. You look for the three signs."

I raised an eyebrow, curious despite myself. "Three signs?"

"Number one, he initiates contact, whether it's a call, a text, or a simple 'hello.' Second, he makes an effort to spend time with you, even if it's just a few minutes. And three, he genuinely listens and remembers the little things you say, showing he cares."

Well, that clarified things. Clearly, Rex wasn't interested in me; he hadn't even greeted me yet.

But... he had built me a dog house using the exact paint shade matching my bakery. That had to count for something, right?

"You know, I met Rex through Della," Vanessa continued, her eyes fixed on my face.

My breath caught. "How well do you know Rex?"

She nodded, taking a casual sip of her drink. "We had a thing a while back," she said, as if discussing the weather. "But y'know, typical Rex. Three months and he was looking for the exit. That's his pattern. "

"Three months?" I echoed, trying to hide my disappointment.

"Like clockwork," Vanessa confirmed. "It's not that he's a player. He's actually a really good guy. But commitment? Long-term relationships? Not in his vocabulary. He has this whole speech about it, too. Something about moving every two years as a kid because of his dad's military career, never being able to put down roots." She shrugged. "Plus he's still in the reserves. Could be deployed or transferred anytime. He uses that as his get-out-of-relationship-free card."

A whirlpool of emotions churned within me. Disappointment coursed through my veins as the realization settled in: Rex might not be wired for serious relationships. It was a disheartening thought, one that made me question whether investing any feelings was worth it.

But could there be a sliver of a chance that I was different to him? It was a dangerous line of thought that tugged at the edges of my better judgment.

Why on earth was I even contemplating this? And how many other women had wondered the very same thing right before they got Rex's patented 'time to ship out' speech?

I wasn't on the lookout for a serious relationship. At least, not consciously.

But then again, maybe I was deceiving myself. Rex, with his easy charm and elusive nature, represented a challenge to my own rules. Maybe that's what intrigued me the most — the idea of breaking away from my usual mold, embracing something more spontaneous, unattached, and carefree.

Could I be the kind of person who could handle a fling? The question lingered in the back of my mind, urging me to reconsider everything I thought I knew about myself and what I wanted.

"Let me introduce you to some people," Vanessa offered. "Come on, I'll grab you a refill."

The next hour passed in a blur of dancing and cocktails. Despite enjoying my new friends' company, there lingered a tinge of disappointment at Rex's continued absence. My heart skipped a beat when he finally reappeared, only to find him engrossed in a lively football game with Carter, Noah, and a group of guys on the beach. Shirt off, sexy as hell. It was hardly fair.

"Maddy, Lacy, come swim with me," Della called, waving from the water's edge.

Normally, I'd be the type to lounge on the sand with a book, but something about today made me bolder. Maybe it was the two glasses of champagne, or maybe it was the knowledge that I had nothing to prove to anyone here. I slipped out of my cover-up, revealing the emerald bikini I'd chosen with more care than I'd admit to anyone but Lacy.

Just then, I noticed Rex's gaze on me, his eyes darkening as they traveled slowly down my body. The intensity in his stare sent heat rushing through me, settling low between my thighs. I'd never been looked at like that before, like I was something to be devoured.

Craig barely ever looked up from his phone. The attention from Rex was intoxicating. It felt...*powerful.*

A thrill raced through me as I walked toward the water, feeling his eyes follow my every move. I tested the water with my toes before wading in with confident strides, acutely aware of the picture I presented. I was definitely not the same woman who'd followed Craig around for a decade, carefully avoiding anything that might draw attention to herself and take the shine off him for even a second.

I playfully splashed water at Della as she dove under the sparkling surface of the water. When I glanced back at the shore, Rex's gaze remained fixed on me, intense and hungry.

Something wild and reckless fluttered inside me. I wanted to make him as unsettled as he made me.

"Hey Carter, come in! The water's great!" I called out, making sure my voice carried. My eyes flickered to Rex, who snapped his head toward me, his expression darkening.

His brows furrowed, and something that looked like jealousy flashed across his face. *Bingo.*

But I glanced down when our eyes connected across the water, suddenly feeling like I'd gone too far. Playing games wasn't really my style; it was something Craig would have done. The realization doused my momentary satisfaction like cold water.

"You look like a sea goddess, Maddy," Carter said as he splashed into the water beside me and Lacy.

"Just what a lady likes to hear," laughs Lacy.

After a few minutes of swimming, I started to feel the effects of the cocktails I'd consumed. Deciding it was time for a break, I headed back to shore. Della returned to shore with me while Lacy and Carter continued to splash around in the water. As Della handed me a towel, her sudden gasp caught my attention.

"Oh my god, Maddy, you're bleeding!"

I looked down to see blood trickling from my finger. A jagged seashell had sliced across my skin, leaving a deep cut. I grimaced, plucking the offending shard from my finger. The pain hit a moment later, sharp and throbbing.

"Rex!" Della called out, waving frantically. "Maddy's hurt!"

Rex rushed over, his face a mask of concern. My heart pounded as he took my hand in his, examining the cut with gentle fingers.

"It's deep," he noted, his voice dropping to that professional tone doctors use.

A small laugh escaped me.

"What?" Rex looked puzzled.

"Oh, nothing," I replied, biting my lip.

I knew he was referring to the cut, but for some reason, my mind had wandered to item number ten on my bucket list. What was wrong with me?

"Come with me," he said, wrapping a towel around my shoulders. "We need to clean this properly."

I tried to downplay it, uncomfortable with the attention. "I'm fine, really."

"There's bacteria in the water," he insisted, his tone brooking no argument. "We need to clean it and get it wrapped up to avoid infection."

We walked back to the yacht, now eerily quiet without the party guests. The contrast was stark: no music, no laughter, no clinking glasses.

Just Rex and me.

He led me down a set of stairs to the lower deck, where the white interior gleamed in the afternoon light. I was careful not to drip blood on the pristine surfaces as we moved through the space.

"In here," Rex said, guiding me into a small bedroom. "There should be a first aid kit."

I suddenly realized how isolated we were from the others, which sent my stomach into knots. The room was cozy, with a large window overlooking the sea and the gentle sound of waves lapping against the hull.

Rex rummaged through a cabinet while I perched on the edge of the bed, feeling the softness of the sheets beneath me. When I looked up, I caught him watching me, his eyes intense. My heart stuttered in my chest.

He brought the first aid kit over and sat beside me, so close that our knees touched. The air between us seemed to crackle with electricity. His woodsy aftershave filled my senses, and the masculine scent made my head swim.

I tried to keep my thoughts in check, reminding myself of all the reasons this was a bad idea. I needed to focus on anything other than the way his callused fingertips sent tingles up my arm as he gently examined my cut.

"Sorry I pulled you from the party," I said, searching for something to break the tension. "You looked like you were having fun earlier."

"You should be more careful, you know," he said, ignoring my question.

He dabbed a cotton ball with hydrogen peroxide and took my hand, pulling it under the running water from the small bathroom sink.

I flinched at the sting.

"Sorry," Rex murmured, his voice softening with concern. "I know it stings, but it's important to clean it thoroughly. Just a moment more, okay? You're doing great."

I'd had it with Rex's hot and cold behavior. One minute he's scolding me, the next he's tender and concerned.

"Look Rex, I didn't ask for your help. I appreciate it since you know more about this stuff than I do, but your mood swings are starting to give me a headache."

Rex looked at me and sighed, his shoulders dropping. "Look Maddy, I'm sorry. It's just that..." He seemed to want to say more but stopped himself.

He lifted my hand to his mouth and blew gently on the cut.

My heart dropped to my stomach at the intimate gesture.

I inhaled sharply, suddenly emboldened by the champagne and his touch. "So, you and Vanessa..."

"Vanessa was...a fling," Rex interrupted, his eyes meeting mine. "We had fun, but it wasn't serious." He paused, his gaze intensifying. "But with you...I don't know, Maddy. I feel like I can't get close to you without wanting more. And that's not fair to either of us."

Frustration built inside me. "That's not fair, Rex. You can't just pull me in and then push me away. You opened up to me at the bakery, and then you pushed me away."

Rex's expression grew serious. "I don't do long-term, Maddy. Never have."

"What does that mean, exactly?" I challenged.

He ran a hand through his hair, a gesture I was beginning to recognize as a sign of discomfort. "It means I'm a three-month guy. When things get too real, I'm gone. Ask anyone in Sugar Creek who's known me longer than you have." His voice dropped lower.

"The reserves could call me up anytime. I could be gone tomorrow or next year. I've seen what that uncertainty does to relationships."

I felt tears welling up in my eyes and tried to blink them back. I told myself it was just the pain from the cut, but deep down, I knew better. "So why are you even..."

"Why am I what? Helping you with your cut? Being a decent human being?" His tone held a defensive edge.

"No," I said, frustration making my voice sharper than I intended. "Why are you looking at me the way you do? Building me a doghouse? Coming to the bakery every morning? If you're so determined to keep your distance, then keep it. Stop..."

"Stop what?"

"Stop making me want you," I whispered, the words escaping before I could hold them back.

Rex's gaze shifted upward as he noticed a tear trailing down my cheek. With a gentle motion, he wiped it away, his touch feather-light. "Are you okay?"

"It hurts," I said. We both knew I wasn't talking about my finger.

He lifted my finger to his mouth again, blowing softly. The sensation sent a tingle straight through my body.

"I've watched my father uproot our family every two years," he said quietly. "Just when we'd settle in somewhere, just when I'd make friends, we'd move again. New school, new house, start all over. The only constant I had was Bailey. And when I lost her..." His voice trailed off. "I promised myself I wouldn't do that to someone I cared about. I wouldn't build something just to tear it down."

"So you tear it down before it's even built?" I asked.

His eyes met mine, and I saw vulnerability there that made my heart ache. "It's easier that way."

"For who?"

"For everyone."

"That's bullshit, Rex. You're just scared."

His jaw tightened. "Maybe I am. But you should be too. You just got out of a ten-year relationship. You're building your business. The last thing you need is to jump into something with a guy who has one foot out the door."

"Don't tell me what I need," I said, my voice low but firm. "I spent ten years with someone who thought he knew better than me what I needed, what I wanted. I'm done with that."

"What do you want, then, Maddy?" His voice was husky, his eyes intense.

I swallowed hard, gathering my courage. "Right now? I want to stop overthinking everything. I spent a decade planning every step, considering every consequence, putting everyone else first. Maybe for once I just want to do something impulsive." I paused, my heart hammering. "Maybe I want you to kiss me, Rex."

For a moment, he seemed caught off guard, as if my unexpected suggestion had startled him into speechlessness. His gaze shifted from my eyes to my lips and back, his features betraying a complex mix of emotions: confusion, desire, and something deeper, something hungrier.

"Maybe you should go back to the party," he said, his voice strained.

His words hit me like a physical blow. I'd put myself out there, and he'd rejected me. The party suddenly seemed a million miles away, and none of the people there could distract me from the overwhelming humiliation I felt. I turned toward the stairs, my steps leaden with disappointment.

As I reached the second step, I heard movement behind me and turned around, colliding with Rex's solid chest.

There was a heartbeat of hesitation before his hands came up to frame my face. Without warning, he leaned forward and pressed his lips against mine. The kiss started slow and tender, our mouths meeting with hesitant exploration. But as the seconds ticked by, something ignited between us, and the passion flared into an inferno.

I wrapped my arms around his neck, pulling him closer as the kiss deepened. Our tongues tangled together in a feverish dance, exploring and tasting. I could feel the hard planes of his chest pressed against me, his hands sliding down to the small of my back, drawing me tighter against him.

It was a kiss unlike any I'd experienced: raw, hungry, and filled with a desperation that matched my own. Rex's tongue traced the seam of my lips before delving deeper, and I moaned softly against him, lost in the taste of him: a hint of beer, a touch of salt, and something all Rex that I couldn't get enough of.

We broke apart, both panting for breath, but the intensity between us only grew stronger.

I was going to have sex with Rex Townsend.

Right now, right here on this boat.

And I didn't care that it would probably only last three months, or that I should be focusing on my bakery, or that I was usually the type of girl who needed a relationship before intimacy.

For once in my life, I wanted to do something reckless, something selfish, something that was just for me.

The room was alive with the sound of ocean waves crashing against the windows, providing the perfect soundtrack for our passionate encounter. Rex pressed me against the wall, his body a delicious weight against mine. I could feel him hardening against my thigh, and the realization that he wanted me as much as I wanted him sent a fresh wave of desire coursing through me.

His lips found my neck, trailing hot kisses down to my collarbone. My hands explored the broad expanse of his back, feeling the muscles ripple beneath my fingertips. When his thigh pressed between my legs, I gasped at the exquisite pressure exactly where I needed it most.

"Maddy — " he breathed against my skin.

"Maddy! Is your finger okay?" Lacy's voice called down from the top of the stairs, shattering the moment like glass.

Rex broke the kiss, staring down at me with eyes dark with desire while I tried to wrap my mind around what had just happened. He sprang up from where he had me pressed against the wall as I stumbled to my feet, calling out to Lacy, "I'm okay! Be right up!" My voice sounded breathless and strange to my own ears.

By the time Lacy appeared at the bottom of the stairs, Rex had already disappeared into the bathroom. My mind was still reeling from the passion that had coursed through my body moments before.

"They're about to slice into the cake and honor the chef," Lacy said, tugging at my arm. "You don't want to miss it."

I followed her back up the stairs, my heart still racing, lips still tingling from Rex's kiss. As we rejoined the party, I couldn't help but wonder what would have happened if Lacy hadn't interrupted us.

The worst part was, we'd already gone too far. Item ten on my bucket list would remain unchecked for now, but my carefully constructed walls against getting involved with Rex had already crumbled. I was in trouble, and I knew it.

The rest of the party passed in a blur. I found myself going through the motions — smiling, chatting, clapping during speeches — while my mind kept replaying that kiss over and over. Rex and I barely spoke again, though I caught him watching me several times, his expression a mixture of desire and regret.

What had I done? I knew better than to get involved with someone like Rex, someone who had already told me point-blank that he didn't do relationships, that he had a three-month expiration date. I'd just escaped one bad relationship; the last thing I needed was to dive headfirst into another doomed situation.

But that kiss. That mind-blowing, earth-shattering kiss that made every kiss I'd shared with Craig pale in comparison. How was I supposed to forget that?

As the yacht made its way back to the dock, I stood at the railing, sipping water and watching the shoreline grow closer. I was waiting for Lacy to finish her conversation with Vanessa's brother so we could leave when I felt a presence beside me.

"Do you have plans tomorrow?" Rex asked, his voice low and intimate. "There is something I want to show you."

I was taken aback by the sudden question. Sunday was my day off, and my only plans had been to relax and process the day's events with Lacy while binge-watching old episodes of Gilmore Girls.

"No plans," I replied, trying to sound casual despite the butterflies taking flight in my stomach.

"I'll pick you up at noon," Rex said, his hand briefly touching mine before he walked away.

Rex had just asked me out on a date.

I think.

And despite all my reservations, all my promises to myself about focusing on the bakery, despite knowing that Rex Townsend was the very definition of temporary, I *wanted* to see what tomorrow would bring.

Sometimes the things we know we shouldn't want are exactly the things we need the most.

Chapter 17

I woke to sunlight blasting me in the face and the lingering heat of a sex dream so vivid it left me breathless. In my dream, Rex and I had never been interrupted on that yacht. Instead, his strong hands had explored every inch of my body while his lips had claimed mine with an urgency that set my blood on fire. I could still feel the phantom pressure of his weight above me, the way his mouth had traveled down my neck to my collarbone, the dirty promises he'd whispered against my skin.

With a groan, I buried my face in my pillow. This was ridiculous. I was having explicit dreams about a man who'd made it clear he didn't do long-term relationships, and yet I couldn't stop thinking about him. About that kiss that was *so close* to turning into so much more.

I stumbled to the kitchen, trying to shake off the lingering sensations of my dream. As I carefully measured coffee grounds and poured steaming water over them, my phone chimed. My heart skipped when I saw Rex's name on the screen.

Good morning. Are you still free today? I want to show you something

My pulse quickened, and it wasn't from the caffeine. I'd only taken a single sip.

Yes, I'm free. What do you want to show me?

My mind instantly sprang to this morning's dream. *Okay, simmer down, Maddy.*

He texted back immediately: *I'll be there in an hour. You should wear something comfortable. Yoga pants would work.*

An audible giggle escaped me. The idea of Rex thinking about what I should wear sent my mind wandering back to my dream once again. I finished my coffee quickly and headed for the shower, where I deliberately turned the temperature to cool.

As the water sluiced over my body, I tried to make sense of my conflicting emotions. Yesterday on the yacht had been... intense. That kiss had awakened something in me I hadn't known existed... a hunger, a craving I'd never experienced with Craig. But Rex had also been honest about his three-month dating limit. About his inability to commit long-term.

Was I setting myself up for heartbreak by pursuing this attraction? Probably.

Did I care? The jury was still out on that one.

I was an adult woman who'd spent most of my twenties in a relationship that had slowly drained the color from my world. Rex made me feel vibrant again. Maybe that was worth the risk of eventual pain.

I absently wondered if the clock had already started, or if his three-month limit started after we'd had sex. I hoped it was the latter. I mean, if I was going to actually go through with this.

I slipped into black yoga pants and a fitted turquoise top that brought out my eyes. A glance in the mirror confirmed what I already knew: the pants showcased the results of all those hours baking, lifting heavy bags of flour, and moving equipment. My curved hips and toned legs looked damn good, if I did say so myself, despite the fact that I hadn't been near a gym in months. Running a bakery prone to disasters was the most effective workout plan I'd ever had.

The decisive knock at my door sent a flutter through my stomach. Craig had always texted "here" from the car, expecting me to come to him. These small acts of consideration from Rex: picking me up at my door, the dog house, and remembering my preferences highlighted all the ways I'd accepted less than I deserved for years.

When I opened the door, the appreciation in Rex's eyes as he took in my appearance was impossible to miss. His gaze traveled slowly from my face down to my toes and back again, lingering in places that made heat bloom across my skin.

"Wow," he said simply. "You look incredible."

His voice had dropped half an octave, taking on that husky quality that made my knees weaken. I took a moment to appreciate him too: faded jeans that hugged his muscular thighs, a simple gray t-shirt that stretched across his broad chest, and a weekend scruff that made me want to run my fingers along his jaw.

"Thank you," I managed, reaching for my purse. "Not so bad yourself, Doc."

The drive out of town was both relaxing and exhilarating. We fell into easy conversation, the kind that flows naturally between two people who genuinely enjoy each other's company. I found myself sharing stories about growing up in Chicago that I'd never told anyone — not even Craig.

"For being such a big city, it often felt lonely," I admitted, watching the urban landscape give way to rolling countryside. "The schools were huge, the noises constant. My mother was always working or... distracted. I started running because it gave me something to do, somewhere to go."

Rex listened with genuine interest, asking questions that showed he wasn't just waiting for his turn to speak. When I fell silent, he didn't rush to fill the space with his own stories. Instead, he let the quiet settle comfortably between us, reaching across to squeeze my hand briefly before returning his to the wheel.

That simple touch sent electricity shooting up my arm. The memory of his hands on my waist, in my hair, cupping my face as he kissed me yesterday... it all came rushing back with startling clarity. I cranked down the window, needing fresh air to clear my head.

"So where are we going?" I asked, desperate for distraction from the vivid images playing in my mind.

"It's a surprise," he replied with a secretive smile. "But I think you'll like it."

"Oh yeah? What if I hate it?" I teased.

"Then I'll have learned something important about you, and we'll go do something else." His answer was so simple, so accommodating, yet so different from what I was used to. Craig would have been annoyed if I hadn't appreciated his plans; Rex seemed to care more about my enjoyment than being right.

As we traveled further from town, the landscape opened up into vast fields dotted with farmhouses and barns. When Rex turned down a dusty dirt road with no houses in sight, my curiosity piqued.

"Are you taking me somewhere remote to murder me?" I joked. "Because several people know I'm with you."

Rex laughed, the sound warm and genuine. "If I were planning to murder you, I wouldn't have worn my favorite jeans."

"So you dressed up for me?" I asked, not bothering to hide my pleasure at the thought.

He glanced over at me, his eyes briefly leaving the road to meet mine. "Maybe I did."

"Good call. Those are now officially my favorite jeans too." I blushed as I said it but I didn't care.

The air between us seemed to thicken with unspoken words and lingering questions. What were we doing? Where was this going? Did yesterday's kiss change things between us? Neither of us seemed ready to break the delicate balance by asking directly.

After another mile down the winding dirt road, a massive metal arch appeared, bearing the name "ROBERTSON RANCH" in imposing letters. Beyond it lay a sprawling two-story log home surrounded by outbuildings, a large stable, and pastures where cows grazed peacefully in the morning sun.

As we pulled up to the main house, I turned to Rex with wide eyes. "Please tell me we're not mucking out stables on our first date." The word "date" slipped out before I could stop it, hanging in the air between us.

Rex cut the engine but didn't immediately move to get out. Instead, he turned to face me, his expression serious. "Is that what this is? A date?"

My heart hammered against my ribs. Was I reading too much into this? "I... I don't know. What would you call it?"

His eyes dropped briefly to my lips before meeting my gaze again. "I'd call it something I've been looking forward to since I left you yesterday."

The simple honesty in his words made my breath catch. Before I could respond, a majestic peacock strutted in front of the truck, breaking the moment.

Rex cleared his throat and opened his door. "Come on. I believe there's an item on your bucket list we might be able to check off today."

I felt my face flame with embarrassment. The bucket list. Of course he'd seen number ten, but he was referring to...

"Number two, you perv," Rex said, grabbing a bag from behind his seat. "Witness a birth."

My embarrassment gave way to excitement. "Wait... Really? That's why we're here?"

A smile playing at the corners of his mouth. "One of the mares is ready to foal any day now. They called me last night because she's showing signs of labor."

As we approached the barn, a tall, weathered man with silver-streaked black hair came to meet us. Dressed in jeans, cowboy boots, and a classic cowboy hat, he looked like he'd stepped straight out of a western.

"Rexford," he greeted, shaking Rex's hand with easy familiarity.

"Tom, this is Maddison Bell," Rex introduced. "Maddy, this is Thomas Robertson, the owner of this ranch."

Tom's handshake was firm, his palm calloused from years of work. "Pleased to meet you, Maddison. I'd introduce you to my wife, but she's at our niece's baby shower today." His eyes crinkled with amusement. "I believe the cake at that shower came from your bakery."

Pride swelled in my chest. "I hope she enjoys it."

"Sugar Creek's been waiting for Beatrice's granddaughter to reopen that bakery since she closed it last year," Tom said. "Your grandmother was a special woman."

"She was," I agreed, touched by his words. "Thank you."

Tom led us to the barn, where the sweet smell of hay mingled with the earthier scents of animals and leather. We passed stall after stall of beautiful horses, each poking their heads out curiously as we walked by.

"Stormy's in the last stall," Tom said, stopping at the end of the row. "I'll leave you to it, Rex. You know where everything is."

Inside the stall, a stunning chestnut mare stood in a thick bed of straw, her sides visibly swollen with the weight of her unborn foal. She shifted restlessly, letting out occasional soft nickering sounds.

"Hi, Stormy," Rex murmured, approaching her with confident ease. He ran his hand along her neck, speaking to her in soothing tones. "Easy, big girl. You're going to be a mama soon."

Watching him with the horse, seeing his gentleness and skill, stirred something deep inside me. His hands moved with practiced precision as he examined her, his voice remaining calm and steady though he moved with efficiency that suggested urgency.

"We need to prepare," he said, turning to me. "I think this is happening sooner rather than later."

"What do you need me to do?" I asked, suddenly nervous about witnessing something so momentous.

"Just stay close and hand me things if I ask for them." His eyes softened as he must have noticed my anxiety. "Don't worry. Birth is the most natural thing in the world, and Stormy's done all the hard work. We're just here to make sure everything goes smoothly."

He began setting up equipment: clean towels, disinfectant, gloves, and various instruments I didn't recognize. His movements were precise and practiced, but I could see the excitement in his eyes.

"Have you done this many times?" I asked, watching him work.

"Hundreds, maybe thousands," he replied. "But it never gets old. Witnessing new life coming into the world..." He paused, searching for words. "It changes you, every time."

There was such sincerity in his voice, such genuine wonder, that I felt my heart expand in my chest. This man...this complex, frustrating, beautiful man, continued to surprise me with the depth of his passion and the gentleness he kept hidden beneath his guarded exterior.

"Thank you for bringing me here," I said softly. "But why?"

He looked up from his preparations, confusion creasing his brow. "You wanted to witness a birth, right? It's on your bucket list."

I nodded.

"I just figured," he continued, misinterpreting my embarrassment, "that since I could help with this one, I should. I didn't mean to overstep."

That's not the only item on my bucket list he could help with...

"No," I hurried to reassure him. "It's not that. I'm touched that you remembered. I'm just not used to someone paying such close attention to what I want."

Something flickered in Rex's eyes. Anger, perhaps, on my behalf? It was gone before I could be sure.

"Well," he said, his voice gentler than before. "Get used to it."

Chapter 18

S tormy let out a low groan, drawing our attention back to her.

"It's starting," Rex said.

The solid wooden gate of the horse stall creaked as Rex pushed it open, gesturing for me to follow him inside. Stormy's restless movements and heavy breathing filled the space with a palpable tension. The rich scent of hay, leather, and animals surrounded us as we stepped into the dimly lit enclosure where the mare paced uncomfortably.

"Talk to her," Rex suggested, his voice lowered to a gentle murmur. "It'll help keep her calm while I check her progress."

I moved toward Stormy's head while Rex positioned himself at her rear, pulling on elbow-length gloves. Witnessing birth had been on my bucket list for years, but now that the moment was here, I felt a strange mixture of excitement and trepidation. This wasn't the sanitized hospital scene I'd imagined: it was raw and real and slightly intimidating.

"Hey there, beautiful girl," I whispered, stroking Stormy's neck as she tossed her head nervously. Her coat was damp with sweat, her dark eyes wide and anxious. "You're doing great. I know it's scary, but Rex is going to help you."

Rex worked quickly but calmly, his movements confident and practiced. "She's definitely in active labor," he confirmed after a moment. "Fully dilated. The foal is positioned correctly, which is good news."

"How long until..." I gestured vaguely, unsure of the proper terminology.

"Could be minutes, could be an hour," Rex replied. "First-time mothers sometimes take longer, but Stormy's making good progress."

As if responding to his words, Stormy let out a low wicker and shifted her weight, her sides heaving with increased intensity.

"Actually," Rex amended, a new urgency in his voice, "I think we're closer than I thought. Maddy, stay by her head and keep talking to her. This is happening now."

The next twenty minutes passed in a blur of focused intensity. I murmured encouragement to Stormy as she labored, amazed by the primal power of what I was witnessing. When two tiny hooves first appeared, my breath caught in my throat.

"Oh my God," I whispered, torn between watching the miracle unfolding at Stormy's rear and maintaining my position at her head.

"You're doing great, Stormy," Rex said, his voice steady and reassuring despite the intensity of the moment. "And you too, Maddy. Keep talking to her."

I stared in wonder as more of the foal emerged with each of Stormy's powerful contractions. First the delicate hooves, then a nose, and gradually the rest of its head and body. The foal slid into the world in a rush of fluid and movement, its coat slick and dark with moisture. Rex moved with practiced efficiency, clearing the newborn's nostrils and making sure the umbilical cord was intact.

Tears pricked at my eyes, and I blinked them away, not wanting to miss a second of this miracle. I'd baked countless new creations, but nothing compared to the raw wonder of witnessing new life enter the world.

"It's a colt," Rex announced, a rare, unguarded smile lighting up his face as the newborn foal lay in the straw. "A healthy boy."

Stormy turned her head, her eyes now focused on her newborn as maternal instinct took over. Within minutes, the foal was attempting to rise on wobbly legs that seemed impossibly long for his small body, falling and trying again with determination that made me laugh through my tears.

"He's perfect," I whispered, overcome with emotion.

Rex continued his work, ensuring the afterbirth was delivered properly and checking both mother and baby for any complications. His hands moved with gentle confidence, his focus absolute, yet he still found time to explain each step to me.

"This is actually my favorite part of being a vet," he admitted as we watched the foal successfully stand on shaking legs. "Helping bring new life into the world never gets old."

"I can see why," I replied, mesmerized by the foal's first tentative steps. "Thank you for sharing this with me."

After ensuring mother and baby were doing well, Rex finally stepped back, pulling off his gloves. The pride and joy on his face made him look younger, more open — as if the miracle we'd just witnessed had temporarily removed the guarded expression he usually wore.

"We should let them bond," he said, his voice soft with reverence. "Come on, let's wash up."

At the large sink in the barn's utility area, we scrubbed our hands side by side, the adrenaline of the birth slowly giving way to a comfortable silence. Without thinking, I turned and threw my arms around Rex, overwhelmed by the experience we'd just shared.

"Thank you," I said, my voice muffled against his chest. "That was incredible."

His arms tightened around me, and for a moment, we just stood there, the connection between us deepening in the aftermath of something so profound. When we finally stepped apart, his eyes remained on mine, a new warmth in their blue depths.

I couldn't stop smiling. "That was... I don't even have words. Thank you for letting me be part of this."

"Thank you for coming," he said, his voice husky with emotion. "Not everyone appreciates these moments the way you did."

We stood side by side outside the stall, watching the new mother and baby bond, neither of us wanting to break the spell of the moment. When Rex's hand found mine, his fingers lacing through mine felt as natural as breathing. We didn't speak. We didn't need to. Something intense had shifted between us in that barn, watching new life enter the world.

I didn't know what the future held for us. I didn't know if Rex would still adhere to his three-month limit or if I could protect my heart if he did. But standing there, his hand warm in mine, I knew one thing with absolute certainty: whatever happened next, I was going to embrace it fully — the joy and the risk, the sweetness and the possible pain.

Some experiences were worth the price of admission.

Rex gathered up his equipment and we headed towards the exit.

Tom met us as we emerged from the barn, his weathered face breaking into a wide smile when Rex confirmed that mother and foal were doing well.

"That's fine news," he said, clapping Rex on the shoulder. "Lynn will be pleased. She's been fretting all day about that mare."

As we prepared to leave, Tom suddenly turned to me. "Maddy, there's one more thing before you go," he said. "If you'd like to, you can name the foal."

"Really?" I asked, surprised and touched by the offer.

Tom smiled. "You helped bring him into this world. It's only right."

The name came to me instantly, as if it had been waiting. "Asher," I said without hesitation.

Tom's eyebrows rose slightly, but he nodded his approval. "Asher it is, then. I'll put it in the registry."

As we climbed into Rex's truck and began the drive down the long gravel driveway, Rex glanced over at me. "Asher, huh? That's not a name you hear every day."

"It means 'happy one' or 'blessed,'" I explained, feeling a little self-conscious. "I've always loved the meaning. It seemed fitting for something so perfect and new."

"You know the meanings of names?" Rex asked, sounding genuinely curious.

I laughed. "I went through a phase in high school. I was fascinated by onomastics, the study of names. Do you know what 'Rex' means?"

"Rexford," he replied dryly. "After my grandfather."

"Well, technically, Rex means 'king,'" I informed him, enjoying the way his lips quirked upward at the corners. "Very regal, Your Majesty."

"And what does Maddison mean, oh wise one?" he asked, his tone light but his eyes intent on the road ahead.

I hesitated, always a little embarrassed by my name's meaning. "It means 'son of Matthew,' actually. Not very feminine. My dad's name was Matthew, and my mom thought she was being clever."

"I think you're wrong about that one," he grinned. "I'm pretty sure it means beautiful baker of scones."

I felt myself flush at the compliment.

Rex started to say something more, but his phone rang, interrupting our conversation. He glanced at the screen before answering. "Tom? Did we forget something?"

I watched as Rex's expression shifted from relaxed to concerned in an instant. His body tensed, and without explanation, he executed a sharp U-turn that had me grabbing the dashboard for support.

"What's happening?" I asked, alarm rising in my throat.

"Problem with the foal," Rex replied tersely, his jaw tight. "Tom says Asher is showing signs of distress."

My heart sank, a wave of dread washing over me. We'd just watched this perfect new life enter the world. The thought of something going wrong so quickly was unbearable.

When we pulled up to the barn, Rex turned to me, his expression grave. "Stay here, Maddy. If there's a serious issue, I need to focus without distractions."

"But... " I began.

"Please," Rex said, his voice softening slightly. "I promise I'll update you as soon as I can, but if something's wrong with Asher, every minute counts."

I reluctantly watched as he grabbed his medical bag from behind the seat and jogged into the barn, leaving me alone with my worry.

The waiting was excruciating. I paced beside the truck, alternating between staring at the barn door and checking my phone, though I knew barely fifteen minutes had passed. The sun was beginning to set, casting long shadows across the farmyard and painting the sky in shades of pink and gold that seemed almost offensively beautiful given my state of anxiety.

When a sleek white BMW pulled into the driveway, I straightened, momentarily distracted. A woman emerged, elegant with silver-streaked dark hair and the confident bearing of someone accustomed to managing difficult situations.

"You must be Maddy," she said as she approached, her smile warm despite the worry lines around her eyes. "I'm Lynn, Tom's wife. He called to let me know what was happening." She glanced toward the barn, then back at me. "You look like you could use a cup of tea. Why don't you come inside? Pacing won't make the time go any faster."

I hesitated, reluctant to move farther from where Rex was working, but the kindness in her eyes won me over. "Thank you."

Lynn's kitchen was exactly what you'd expect on a working ranch :spacious and practical with thoughtful touches. Copper pots hung from a rack over a large island, and a collection of blue and white pottery lined open shelves along one wall.

"Sit," Lynn instructed, gesturing to a comfortable chair at the kitchen table as she filled a kettle. "Rex is the best large animal vet in three counties. If anyone can help that foal, he can."

I nodded, unable to form words around the lump in my throat. The thought of losing Asher so soon after his birth was devastating enough. I couldn't imagine how Rex would feel if he couldn't save him.

Lynn placed a mug of fragrant tea in front of me, then took a seat across the table. "Tom tells me you're Beatrice's granddaughter. The baker who inherited Maddy Cakes?"

"Yes," I replied, surprised. "Did you know my grandmother?"

"Everyone in Sugar Creek knew Beatrice," Lynn said with a soft laugh. "She catered our wedding thirty-seven years ago. Made the most beautiful cake I've ever seen: four tiers with hand-painted wildflowers that looked exactly like the ones growing in the meadow where Tom proposed."

The image brought an unexpected smile to my face. "That sounds like Gram."

For the next hour, Lynn distracted me with stories about my grandmother and the early days of Maddy Cakes. Her kindness was a balm to my frayed nerves, though I still jumped at every sound, hoping it was news about Asher.

Finally, as twilight deepened into evening, the back door opened. Rex and Tom entered, both looking exhausted but relieved.

I rose to my feet. "Is he — "

"He's okay," Rex confirmed, and I felt my knees go weak with relief. "It was a meconium aspiration. He inhaled some amniotic fluid during birth. We had to clear his lungs and start him on antibiotics, but his breathing is much better now."

"Oh, thank goodness," I breathed.

"He's not completely out of the woods," Rex cautioned. "I need to stay overnight to monitor him."

"Thanks doc, you two can stay in the guest cabin," said Tom. "Or I can drive Maddy home if you'd like."

Rex ran a hand through his hair, looking suddenly uncertain. "I'm sorry about cutting our day short."

The thought of leaving made my chest tighten. "Actually, if it's okay, I'd prefer to stay." I looked to Tom and Lynn. "I'd like to see how Asher does through the night."

"Of course you're welcome to stay," Lynn said immediately. "The guest cabin is just past the orchard. It's small but comfortable."

Rex's expression softened, gratitude evident in his tired eyes. "Thank you," he mouthed silently.

Tom clapped his hands decisively. "Well then, I'll show you both to the cabin. Lynn, would you mind packing up some of that chicken pot pie for our guests? And Maddy will need something to sleep in. Maybe those flannel pajamas Hannah left last Christmas?"

As Tom led us out the back door and down a lantern-lit path, I felt a strange mix of emotions: concern for little Asher, but also a curious sense of rightness. This wasn't how I'd imagined our day ending, but somehow, helping Rex care for the foal we'd watched enter the world felt like exactly where I was meant to be.

The cabin came into view as we rounded a bend in the path: a charming one-room structure with a small porch and warm light glowing from the windows. I glanced at Rex, wondering if he felt the same nervous anticipation that was building in my chest at the thought of spending the night here. Together.

His expression gave nothing away, but as our eyes met in the lantern light, the intensity in his gaze made my heartbeat quicken. Whatever happened tonight, I knew with absolute certainty that something had fundamentally shifted between us today. Something that couldn't be undone — and that *I didn't want to undo*, even if I could.

Chapter 19

The glow of the lantern illuminated the rustic cabin as Tom led us inside. Despite the long, emotionally draining day, my senses felt unusually sharp. Every detail seemed heightened: the scent of pine from the wooden walls, the crackle of gravel beneath our boots as we crossed the threshold, the soft whirring of the ceiling fan stirring the air.

"It's not fancy," Tom said, gesturing around the single-room cabin with its kitchenette in one corner and a queen-sized bed taking up most of the space against the far wall. "But it's comfortable. Bathroom's through that door, and there are extra blankets in the trunk at the foot of the bed if you get cold."

The word 'bed' — singular — hung in the air between Rex and me, though neither of us acknowledged it aloud.

"This is perfect," I assured Tom. "Thank you for your hospitality."

Tom smiled as Rex set up and plugged in something that looked like a baby monitor on the kitchenette counter. "We can monitor Asher from here through the night," Rex said, pointing to the small screen. "See? We can see Stormy and the foal in real-time."

We. The casual way he included me in his vigil over Asher sent a quiet thrill through me.

"That's smart thinking. Beats sleeping in the barn." Tom continued, "Lynn's bringing over some food and necessities. The nights get cool out here, even in summer." He headed for the door, then paused. "Rex, you know where to find us if anything changes with the foal."

Rex nodded solemnly. "Thanks again, Tom."

After Tom left, a charged silence filled the cabin. I busied myself examining the space: the patchwork quilt on the bed, the small woodstove in the corner, the collection of well-worn paperbacks on a shelf above a rocking chair. Anything to avoid addressing the obvious issue of our sleeping arrangements.

"I should check on Asher one more time before we settle in," Rex said, breaking the silence. "The monitor's great, but I want to see him in person, check his vitals again, make sure his breathing is stable."

"I'll come with you."

The night air had cooled considerably as we walked the path back to the barn. Crickets chirped in the darkness, and somewhere in the distance, an owl hooted softly. Rex walked slightly ahead, his shoulders tense beneath his shirt. I could sense the weight of responsibility he carried for Asher's well-being.

In the barn, soft yellow light spilled from Stormy's stall. The mare stood protectively over her foal, who was curled in the straw, his small sides rising and falling with each breath. The sight of them together, mother and child, made my throat tighten with emotion.

Rex moved with quiet efficiency, checking Asher's vital signs and adjusting the small oxygen tank he'd rigged up near the foal's nose. His hands were gentle but confident as they moved over the newborn's body.

"His breathing's better," Rex murmured, more to himself than to me. "Still labored, but the antibiotic seems to be helping."

I hung back, not wanting to interfere with his work, but my eyes never left him. There was something profoundly moving about watching Rex in his element: the care with which he tended to the vulnerable creature, the soft words of encouragement he whispered to both mother and baby. This was a side of him I suspected few people got to see.

"Is he going to be okay?" I asked quietly when Rex finally straightened.

He ran a hand through his hair, a gesture I'd come to recognize as his way of processing complex emotions. "I think so. The next few hours are critical, but he's responding well to treatment."

"You're amazing with them," I said, stepping closer to the stall. "Stormy trusts you completely."

Rex's expression softened as he looked back at the mare and foal. "Animals know when you genuinely care. They can sense it." He glanced at me, and something in his gaze made my heart quicken. "People, too."

The weight of unspoken meaning hung between us as we made our way back to the cabin. By the time we returned, Lynn had delivered a basket of provisions: warm chicken pot pie, fresh bread, a bottle of wine, toiletries, and the promised flannel pajamas.

"I'm going to grab a quick shower," Rex said, reaching for the toiletry bag Lynn had provided. "It's been a long day."

I nodded, trying not to think about Rex under the shower spray, water cascading down his body. *Ahem.*

"I'll set up dinner."

While he disappeared into the bathroom, I busied myself arranging our late supper on the small table by the window. The homemade pot pie smelled heavenly, rich with chicken and vegetables in a creamy sauce. Lynn had thought of everything: plates, cloth napkins, a nice bottle of oaked Chardonnay, and even a small vase with wildflowers. As I poured the wine, it felt surreally domestic, like playing house in this secluded cabin with a man I'd known for mere weeks but who already occupied far too much space in my thoughts.

The bathroom door opened, and I turned automatically — then froze, my breath catching in my throat.

Rex stood in the doorway wearing nothing but a towel slung low around his hips. Water droplets clung to his broad shoulders and chest, tracing tantalizing paths down the defined muscles of his torso. His hair was damp and tousled, darker when wet, and a faint flush colored his skin from the hot shower.

"Sorry," he said, though the slight quirk of his lips suggested he wasn't entirely sorry to have caught me staring. "I forgot to grab the pajama bottoms Lynn sent over."

I swallowed hard, my mouth suddenly dry. "They're... " My voice came out as a squeak, and I cleared my throat. "They're on the chair."

He moved across the room, the muscles in his back rippling with each step, and I forced myself to look away, focusing intently on ladling pot pie onto our plates. *Get it together, Maddy.*

Rex slipped back into the bathroom. When I dared look up again, he'd mercifully put on the plaid pajama bottoms and a soft gray t-shirt he'd pulled from his bag. The casual intimacy of seeing him dressed for bed sent another flutter through my stomach.

"That smells incredible," he said, nodding toward the food.

We settled at the table, both suddenly ravenous after the day's events. For a few minutes, we ate in appreciative silence, the only sounds being the clink of utensils against plates and the occasional glance at the baby monitor to check on Asher.

"Lynn is an amazing cook," I said awkwardly, grateful for the safe topic. "I should get her recipe."

Rex refilled my wine glass and topped off his own.

"I can't believe Tom and Lynn just assumed we'd be comfortable staying together," I said finally, the wine loosening my tongue. "I mean, they just met me today."

Rex's mouth quirked into a half-smile. "Small towns. Everyone loves a good matchmaking opportunity."

"Is that what this is?" I asked, the question slipping out before I could stop it. "A matchmaking opportunity?"

His eyes met mine, serious despite his smile. "Would that be so bad?"

The directness of his question caught me off guard. I took another sip, buying time. "I don't know. Doesn't everybody in town already know you're just the three-month guy?"

I regretted the words as soon as they left my mouth. Rex's expression shuttered slightly, and he looked down at his plate.

"I'm sorry," I said quickly. "That wasn't fair."

Rex looked up slowly, his gaze intent on mine. "I dunno. Maybe they're looking at you and seeing the kind of woman who makes a guy long for the white picket fence."

My heart skipped.

"But, it's okay. It's true. I've never been good at..." He gestured vaguely. "This. Letting people get close."

"Why?" I asked softly.

Rex was quiet for a long moment, his eyes fixed on something I couldn't see. "When you grow up as an army brat, you learn not to put down roots. You learn that connections are temporary. It becomes a habit." He ran a hand through his still-damp hair. "And then when you find out that the person you trusted and admired most has been living a double life... it changes how you view relationships."

I reached across the table and laid my hand over his. "I can't imagine how hard that must have been."

"I was eighteen when I found out about Della," he continued, his voice low. "Old enough to understand what it meant that my father had another child, another family. It wasn't just the betrayal, though that was devastating. It was realizing that the man I'd modeled myself after, whose approval I'd sought my entire life, was capable of such deception. I felt like I didn't even know who he was."

"That would shake anyone's foundation," I said.

"I joined the Army right away. Partly because it had been my plan my whole life, I guess, but mostly to get away. To have some control over my own destiny." He looked up, meeting my gaze. "I swore I'd never do to someone what he did to my mother. That I'd never make promises I couldn't keep."

Understanding dawned. "So you just... don't make promises at all..."

"Better to be honest about limitations than to pretend they don't exist," he said. "At least, that's what I've always believed."

"Sounds lonely."

"It is. But it also feels more honorable than the alternative.

I processed his words slowly. "I understand that, I think. After watching my mother drift from relationship to relationship after my father died, I went in the opposite direction. I clung to stability with Craig, even when it meant sacrificing everything I really wanted."

"And what do you really want, Maddy?" Rex asked, his voice dropping to a near whisper.

The question hung between us, loaded with possibility. My heart hammered in my chest as I searched for the right words.

"I want..." I began, then paused, gathering my courage. "I want to stop being afraid. Of failure, of vulnerability, of taking risks. I want to build something meaningful with my bakery, to honor my grandmother's legacy. I want to feel truly seen by someone who values me for exactly who I am."

My eyes met his, and the intensity I found there took my breath away.

"I see you, Maddy," Rex said simply.

Those three words, spoken with such quiet conviction, undid me completely. No one had ever really seen me — not Craig, who'd viewed me as an accessory to his ambitions. Not my mother, too wrapped up in her own grief to notice mine. Sometimes, not even Lacy sometimes, who loved me fiercely, but didn't always understand my cautious nature.

But Rex saw me. And despite his self-proclaimed limitations, despite the walls he'd built around his heart, he was still here, still looking at me like I was something precious.

"I'm terrified of failing the bakery," I confessed, the words tumbling out now that the dam had broken. "Of letting down Gram, the town, myself. Some days I wake up paralyzed with doubt, wondering if I've made a huge mistake thinking I could do this."

"You haven't," Rex said immediately. "You're a natural, Maddy. The way you connect with people, the passion you bring to your baking... it's special. The whole town can see it."

"Even so, the responsibility is overwhelming sometimes," I admitted. "One bad health inspection, one economic downturn, one wrong decision, and it could all fall apart."

Rex nodded, understanding in his eyes. "I feel that same weight every time an animal's life is in my hands. Like with Asher today. You never get used to it, the knowledge that your actions can mean life or death."

"How do you handle it?" I asked.

"You focus on what you can control. You prepare for every contingency. And when things go wrong anyway, because sometimes they will, you try to forgive yourself and learn from it." His gaze was steady on mine. "And it helps to have someone who understands, someone you can talk to about the hard parts."

Someone like you, I thought, the unspoken words hovering between us.

We finished our meal in a comfortable silence, both lost in our own thoughts. When Rex stood to clear our plates, I rose too, and we moved around the small kitchenette in an easy rhythm, as if we'd done this a hundred times before.

"Thank you for today," I said as we finished cleaning up. "For letting me be part of Asher's birth, for sharing something so important with me."

Rex turned to face me, closer than I'd expected. "Watching you with Stormy and Asher..." he began, then shook his head, a smile playing at the corners of his mouth. "You were incredible. Most people would have been squeamish or uncomfortable, but you just... jumped right in. You talked to Stormy like you'd known her forever."

"It felt natural," I said. "Being there, helping. It was like nothing I've ever experienced."

Rex's expression became more serious. "When I saw how you connected with them, how invested you became in Asher's well-being... it made me wonder what it might be like to put down roots. To build something permanent."

My heart skipped a beat at his words. *Was he saying what I thought he was saying?*

"For the first time in a long time," he continued softly. "I found myself imagining a future that doesn't involve walking away."

He reached out, his fingers brushing a strand of hair from my face with exquisite gentleness. The touch sent electricity coursing through me, and I leaned into his palm as it came to rest against my cheek.

"Maddy," he whispered, his voice rough with emotion.

"Yes?" I breathed, my heart pounding so hard I was sure he could hear it.

"I don't know if I can be what you deserve. I don't know if I can give you forever. But a part of me wants to try. God, I want to try."

The raw honesty in his words moved me more than any practiced declaration could have. This wasn't a smooth line or an empty promise; this was Rex — guarded, cautious Rex — laying his fears bare, offering what he could with no guarantees.

"I'm not asking for forever," I said, my voice steadier than I'd expected. "I'm just asking for now. For tonight."

Rex's eyes darkened, and he stepped closer, one hand still cupping my face, the other coming to rest on my waist. "Are you sure?"

In answer, I rose onto my tiptoes and pressed my lips to his.

The kiss began softly, a gentle exploration that quickly deepened as Rex pulled me against him. His lips were warm and insistent, coaxing mine open, and I melted into him, my arms winding around his neck. Unlike our frantic kiss on the yacht, this one built slowly, a gradual crescendo of sensation that left me dizzy with want.

Rex's hands were everywhere, tangling in my hair, skimming down my sides, pulling me closer until there was no space left between us. I could feel the hard planes of his chest against mine, the beat of his heart matching my own frantic rhythm.

When we finally broke apart, both breathing heavily, Rex rested his forehead against mine. "You're making it very hard to be noble right now," he murmured.

I laughed softly, feeling reckless and alive. "Who asked you to be noble?"

He groaned, the sound sending heat pooling low in my belly. "Maddy, if we start this, I don't think I'll be able to stop."

"Good," I whispered against his lips. "I don't want you to stop."

Those words seemed to break the last of his restraint. Rex lifted me as if I weighed nothing, and I wrapped my legs around his waist as he carried me the few steps to the bed. He laid me down with a surprising gentleness, his eyes never leaving mine as he stretched out beside me.

"You're so beautiful," he said, his voice full of wonder as he traced the curve of my cheek, my jaw, my neck. "I've wanted to touch you like this since the first day I saw you."

"Even though I spilled coffee all over you?" I teased, trying to lighten the intensity of the moment.

He grinned, the expression transforming his face. "Especially then. You looked so adorably flustered."

His hand continued its exploration, skimming along my collarbone and down my arm, leaving goosebumps in its wake. When his fingers reached the hem of my shirt, he paused, looking at me for permission.

I nodded, and he slowly lifted the fabric, his breath catching as my skin was revealed inch by inch. When the shirt was gone, tossed somewhere on the floor, Rex sat back on his heels, his gaze traveling over me with such open appreciation that I felt beautiful despite my plain cotton bra.

"You have no idea how many times I've imagined this," he said, his voice husky with desire.

The admission thrilled me. I reached for him, pulling him down for another kiss, this one deeper and more urgent than before. My hands slipped beneath his t-shirt, exploring the warm skin and firm muscles of his back. When he groaned into my mouth, I grew bolder, tugging at the fabric until he helped me remove it altogether.

The sight of him shirtless, hovering above me in the soft lamplight, made my breath catch. He was all lean muscle and golden skin, with a sprinkling of dark hair across his chest that narrowed to a tantalizing trail disappearing beneath the waistband of his borrowed pajama bottoms.

"You're not so bad yourself, Doc," I murmured, running my hands over his shoulders and down his chest.

He laughed, the sound sending vibrations through his chest beneath my palm. "Such high praise."

His mouth returned to mine, the kiss deeper this time, more urgent. His hand slid beneath me to unhook my bra, and he pulled back just enough to watch as he slid the straps down my arms. When the garment fell away, Rex's breath audibly caught.

"Perfect," he whispered, cupping my breast reverently. His thumb brushed across my nipple, and I arched into his touch, a soft moan escaping me. "So responsive," he murmured against my skin as his mouth replaced his hand.

Every sensation was heightened: the gentle scrape of his stubble against my sensitive skin, the wet heat of his tongue, the weight of his body partially covering mine. I'd never felt so wanted, so worshipped. With Craig, sex had always been perfunctory, efficient, focused primarily on his pleasure. This was something else entirely. Rex seemed determined to discover every spot that made me gasp, every touch that made me tremble.

His mouth traveled lower, across my ribs and down to my navel, as his hands worked at the button of my jeans. He looked up, seeking confirmation once more, and I nodded again, lifting my hips to help him slide the denim down my legs.

When I was left in nothing but my underwear, Rex sat back again, his eyes dark with desire as they roamed over me. "I don't deserve this," he said, his voice rough. "But God, I want it. Want you."

"Then take me," I whispered, feeling bold and beautiful under his appreciative gaze.

He hooked his fingers in the waistband of my underwear, sliding them slowly down my legs until I lay completely bare before him. "So beautiful," he murmured, his hands stroking up my calves, my thighs, leaving fire in their wake.

When his fingers brushed against the most intimate part of me, I couldn't suppress a gasp. Rex watched my face intently as he explored, learning what made me writhe, what made me moan. When he slid one finger inside me, his thumb circling in a way that sent sparks shooting up my spine, I clutched at his shoulders, my nails digging into his skin.

"Rex," I breathed.

"I've got you," he promised, his voice a low rumble against my ear as he added another finger, curling them in a way that made my back arch off the bed. "Let go, Maddy. I want to watch you fall apart."

His words, combined with the exquisite pressure of his skilled fingers, pushed me toward a precipice I'd never quite reached before. The tension built, coiling tighter and tighter, until suddenly it snapped, sending waves of pleasure crashing through me. I cried out, my body shuddering as Rex continued his gentle ministrations, drawing out my climax until I was gasping, oversensitive.

As I lay there, trying to catch my breath, he pressed soft kisses to my neck, my cheek, the corner of my mouth. "You're incredible," he murmured. "The way you respond to my touch... it's intoxicating."

I reached for him, wanting to reciprocate, but he caught my wrist gently. "Not yet," he said with a wicked smile. "I'm not done with you."

Before I could process his words, he was moving down my body, settling between my thighs. The first touch of his mouth against me was so intense I nearly came off the bed. His hands held my hips steady as he explored with his tongue, and I wound my fingers into his hair, anchoring myself as another wave of pleasure began to build.

This time, my release came faster, more intense, leaving me trembling and incoherent. As I floated back to awareness, I felt Rex moving up the bed to lie beside me, his expression a mixture of pride and barely restrained desire.

"Come here," I said, tugging him toward me for a deep kiss. I could taste myself on his lips, and the intimacy of it sent another jolt of arousal through me. My hand slid down his chest, his stomach, until I reached the waistband of his pajama bottoms. He was hard beneath the thin fabric, and when I palmed him through the cotton, he groaned into my mouth.

"These need to go," I murmured, pushing at the offending garment. Rex helped me, kicking them off along with his boxers until he was gloriously naked beside me.

I took a moment to appreciate the sight of him: all lean muscle and golden skin, his arousal evident and impressive. When I wrapped my hand around him, Rex's eyes fluttered closed, his head tipping back slightly.

"Maddy," he groaned as I began to stroke him, learning what he liked by the sounds he made, the way his breath hitched. "If you keep that up, this will be over embarrassingly quickly."

I smiled, enjoying the power I had over him. "Then maybe we should move things along."

His eyes met mine, suddenly serious despite his arousal. "Are you sure about this? We can stop if..."

I silenced him with a kiss. "I've never been more sure of anything."

Rex kissed me back hungrily and reached for his bag. Retrieving his wallet, he extracted a condom from inside. The brief pause gave me a moment to catch my breath, to marvel at the unexpected turn this day had taken. When Rex returned to me, settling between my thighs, I felt a surge of anticipation mixed with the faintest trace of nervousness.

"Look at me," he said softly, and I met his gaze as he positioned himself at my entrance. "Stay with me."

The way he said it, like he wasn't just talking about this moment but something more, made my heart constrict in my chest. As he slowly pushed into me, stretching and filling me in the most exquisite way, I kept my eyes locked on his, watching the play of emotions across his face: pleasure, restraint, wonder.

When he was fully seated within me, he paused, giving me time to adjust to the sensation. "Okay?" he whispered, his voice strained with the effort of holding still.

"More than okay," I assured him, shifting my hips experimentally. The movement drew a groan from both of us.

Rex began to move, setting a gentle rhythm that quickly built in intensity as our bodies learned each other. His hands were everywhere: cupping my face, tangling in my hair, caressing my breasts, gripping my hips to pull me more firmly against him. All the while, his eyes stayed locked on mine, creating an intimacy that was almost overwhelming.

"You feel incredible," he murmured, his voice rough with passion. "So perfect."

The praise, combined with the increasingly urgent thrusts of his hips, pushed me toward the edge once more. When his hand slipped between us, finding that sensitive bundle of nerves, I shattered for the third time, crying out his name as waves of pleasure crashed over me.

My release triggered his own. With a groan that seemed torn from deep within him, Rex followed me over the edge, his body tensing above mine before collapsing gently to my side, careful not to crush me with his weight.

For several minutes, we lay there in silence, our breathing gradually slowing, our bodies cooling in the night air. Rex's arm was wrapped around me, my head tucked against his chest where I could hear the steady thump of his heart.

"Well," he said finally, his voice a rumble beneath my ear, "I think we can check item number ten off your bucket list."

I smacked his chest lightly, laughing despite my embarrassment. "I knew you saw that!"

"Hard to miss," he teased, pressing a kiss to the top of my head. "Though if I'd known it was on your agenda, I might have been more forward."

"You were plenty forward," I retorted, though there was no heat in my words. How could I possibly be annoyed when my body was still humming with satisfaction?

We fell silent again, the comfortable quiet broken only by the soft sounds from the baby monitor — Stormy's occasional movements, Asher's tiny snuffling breaths. There was something surreal about the moment, lying naked in Rex's arms in this cozy cabin, our bodies still flushed from lovemaking, while new life continued its miraculous journey just yards away in the barn.

"What are you thinking?" Rex asked softly, his fingers tracing lazy patterns on my bare shoulder.

I considered deflecting with humor, but the vulnerability we'd already shared tonight demanded honesty. "I'm thinking that I've never felt like this before," I admitted. "This... connected. This seen."

Rex's arm tightened around me. "I know what you mean."

"And I'm a little scared," I continued, the words barely audible. "Because this feels important. Significant. And I don't know what happens tomorrow."

Rex shifted, propping himself up on one elbow so he could look into my eyes. "I don't know either," he said, his expression serious. "I wish I could promise you forever, Maddy. I wish I could tell you with absolute certainty that I won't run when things get complicated, that I won't break your heart."

The honesty in his voice was both painful and precious. "I'm not asking for promises you can't keep," I said. "Just... be honest with me. Always. Even when it's hard."

"That I can do," he said, relief evident in his eyes. "And for what it's worth, I want to try. I want to see where this goes. You make me want things I thought I'd never want again: roots, stability, connection."

"But?" I prompted, hearing the unspoken qualification in his voice.

"But what if I'm not enough for you long-term? What if I can't give you everything you deserve?" The vulnerability in his question made my heart ache.

I reached up to cup his face, feeling the roughness of his stubble against my palm. "What if we just take it one day at a time? What if we stop worrying about what might go wrong and focus on what's going right?"

A slow smile spread across Rex's face. "That sounds suspiciously like good advice."

"I have my moments," I said, returning his smile.

He leaned down to kiss me, his lips gentle against mine. When he pulled back, the intensity in his eyes took my breath away. "For tonight, for now, I'm yours, Maddy. Whatever tomorrow brings, remember that."

As Rex gathered me back into his arms, I felt a peace settle over me that had nothing to do with physical satisfaction and everything to do with emotional connection. I didn't know what the future held for us — whether Rex would eventually retreat behind his walls, whether I would regret opening my heart so soon after Craig, whether the fragile trust we'd built tonight would withstand the pressures of real life.

But for now, in this moment, with the sound of Asher's breathing soft in the background and Rex's heartbeat steady beneath my ear, I allowed myself to hope. To imagine possibilities I hadn't dared consider before. To dream of a future where Rex Townsend and I might build something lasting, one day at a time.

The last thing I registered before sleep claimed me was Rex checking the baby monitor one more time, his protective instinct extending to the tiny life we'd helped bring into the world together. It was that, more than anything else, that made me think maybe, just maybe, he might be able to overcome his fear of putting down roots after all.

Chapter 20

Morning light snuck through the cabin's thin curtains, casting an ethereal glow across the rumpled sheets. I stirred slowly, consciousness creeping in at the edges of a dream. The solid warmth pressed against my back registered before my eyes even opened. Rex's arm draped protectively over my waist, his breath soft against my neck. For a moment, I kept perfectly still, savoring the unfamiliar but exquisite sensation of waking up next to someone who made me feel both safe and alive.

The baby monitor on the nightstand emitted a soft nicker as Stormy shifted positions in her stall. The sound seemed to penetrate Rex's sleep as well. I felt him stir behind me, his arm tightening briefly around my waist before he realized I was awake.

"Morning," he murmured, his voice rough with sleep. His lips pressed a gentle kiss to my shoulder, sending a pleasant shiver down my spine.

I rolled over to face him, suddenly shy despite our intimacy the night before. "Morning."

Rex looked impossibly handsome in the soft dawn light, his hair tousled, stubble darkening his jaw. His eyes, still heavy-lidded with sleep, regarded me with a warmth that made my heart skip.

"How's Asher?" I asked, glancing toward the monitor.

"Let me check." Rex reached for the small screen, studying it intently. His expression softened with relief. "Looking good. His breathing seems much easier."

"Should we go see him?"

Rex brushed a strand of hair from my face with gentle fingers. "In a minute." He leaned forward, pressing his lips to mine in a soft kiss that quickly deepened, his hand sliding along my bare hip beneath the sheets.

"Rex," I murmured against his mouth, though I made no move to stop him. "We should check on Asher."

He sighed dramatically, pulling back with obvious reluctance. "You're right. Responsibility calls." His smile turned mischievous. "But we're definitely continuing this discussion later."

We dressed quickly, exchanging shy glances and occasional touches that promised more. The domesticity of it all — brushing teeth side by side at the tiny sink, Rex helping me make the bed, sharing the last of Lynn's bread for a quick breakfast — felt both strange and incredibly right.

The morning air was crisp as we walked the path to the barn, dew still clinging to the grass. Rex's hand found mine, our fingers intertwining naturally. I couldn't remember the last time I'd felt this light, this hopeful.

Inside the barn, Asher had improved dramatically overnight. The little foal was standing steadily on his spindly legs, nursing from Stormy with enthusiastic little tail swishes. The oxygen tank Rex had rigged stood unused in the corner of the stall.

"Look at that," Rex said, pride evident in his voice. "He's definitely feeling better."

I squeezed his hand. "Aw. You saved him."

Rex shook his head, his eyes never leaving the foal. "He's a fighter. I just gave him a little help."

Tom appeared at the barn entrance, his weathered face breaking into a smile when he saw us. "Morning, you two. Our little fighter's looking good today."

"His breathing is much better," Rex confirmed, his hand still holding mine. "I'd like to keep the antibiotics going for another day or two, but I think he's out of the danger zone."

Tom nodded, his gaze dropping briefly to our joined hands before returning to Asher. If he noticed the change in our relationship, he had the good grace not to comment directly. "That's great news. Lynn's got breakfast ready in the house if you're hungry."

Over a hearty breakfast of eggs, bacon, and Lynn's incredible homemade biscuits, we discussed Asher's care going forward. The conversation flowed easily, and I found myself relaxing into the gentle rhythm of ranch life. Lynn kept our coffee cups filled, her knowing smile warming me almost as much as the hot liquid.

"You know," she said, refilling my cup for the third time, "Beatrice used to come out here regularly. She'd bring pastries, and we'd talk recipes over coffee while the men pretended to discuss ranch business."

The mention of Gram brought both warmth and a pang of longing. "I had no idea she visited the ranch."

Lynn's eyes sparkled as she settled back in her chair. "Oh yes. She was quite the horsewoman in her younger days. Even rode in the Sugar Creek Summer Festival parade until her knees got too bad." She glanced at Tom with gentle affection. "Remember that chocolate cake she made for our thirtieth anniversary? With the little sugar horses on top?"

Tom's eyes crinkled at the corners. "Best cake I ever tasted. Triple chocolate with that filling that melted in your mouth."

"Chocolate ganache," I supplied automatically. "Gram always said a good ganache was worth its weight in gold."

"That's it!" Lynn beamed. "You have her touch, you know. I can taste it in your pastries."

The casual way they spoke about Gram, as if she might walk through the door at any moment with fresh pastries in hand, made my throat tighten. It was a reminder of how deeply she'd been woven into the fabric of this community, and how I was now taking up those threads, continuing the pattern she'd begun.

By mid-morning, Rex had checked Asher one final time and pronounced him stable enough for us to leave. Tom promised to follow Rex's care instructions to the letter, and Lynn pressed a container of leftover biscuits into my hands as we said our goodbyes.

"You come back anytime," she said, hugging me warmly. "Both of you," she added with a meaningful glance at Rex that made me blush.

The drive back to Sugar Creek was comfortably quiet, both of us lost in our own thoughts. Rex's hand rested on my knee, a casual touch that felt both tinglingly new and familiar at the same time. The scent of his aftershave mingled with the earthy smell of the ranch that still clung to our clothes, creating a combination I already associated with comfort and desire.

"Thank you for yesterday," I said finally, breaking the silence. "For sharing Asher's birth with me, for everything."

Rex glanced at me, his expression softening as he teased, "Well, it was on your bucket list."

I felt a blush creeping up my cheeks as I recalled the other bucket list item I'd crossed off last night. Particularly item number ten. A smile tugged at my lips just thinking about it.

"Besides," he continued more seriously. "It felt important to me that you were there. That you understood that part of my life."

The weight of his words settled over me. For a man who carefully guarded his emotions, who kept everyone at arm's length, sharing something so central to his identity was significant.

"So..." I ventured, suddenly nervous. "What happens now? With us, I mean."

Rex's hand squeezed my knee gently. "Well, I was thinking I'd come by the bakery more often. Maybe bring you lunch sometimes. Take you to dinner when you're not too exhausted from baking all day." He glanced at me, a hint of vulnerability in his expression. "If that sounds good to you."

The simplicity of his answer, free from grand declarations or complex negotiations, made me smile. "That sounds perfect."

The next few weeks passed in a whirlwind of work and stolen moments with Rex. Maddy Cakes was busier than ever, with summer tourists swelling our regular crowd of locals. Allison proved herself invaluable, taking on more responsibility as I struggled to keep up with demand. The morning rush often stretched until eleven, followed by a brief lull before the afternoon crowd descended.

True to his word, Rex appeared regularly, sometimes with coffee when he knew I'd been up since 3 AM, other times with takeout from the diner when I forgot to eat lunch. He'd slip into the kitchen for a quick kiss, help unload a delivery, or simply sit at the counter for fifteen minutes, his steady presence a calm in the storm of my workday.

"You're spoiling me," I told him one afternoon as he helped me count inventory in the storeroom, his organizational skills making quick work of a task I'd been dreading.

"That's the plan," he replied with that half-smile that still made my heart flip. "Get you addicted to having me around so you can't get rid of me."

I glanced up from my clipboard, a bag of flour in my other hand. "Sneaky but effective. I already look forward to your visits way too much."

Rex stepped closer, his fingers trailing along my arm. "The feeling's mutual." He leaned down, capturing my lips in a kiss that made me forget about inventory entirely.

Lacy, naturally, had figured out the change in our relationship approximately thirty seconds after seeing us together.

"Well, well, well," she'd said, cornering me in the kitchen the day after our night at the ranch. "Somebody's getting her bucket list checked, aren't they?"

My scarlet cheeks had confirmed her suspicions, leading to an hour-long interrogation that left me both embarrassed and oddly proud.

"Told you he wanted to help with item number ten," she'd crowed triumphantly. "And? Details, please. Was it everything you'd hoped for? Multiple times? Did he... "

"Lacy!" I'd hissed, glancing nervously toward the front where customers were still milling about. "I am not discussing this here."

"Fine," she'd relented with a dramatic sigh. "But I want all the juicy details later. I'll bring the wine. Lots of wine."

Despite the teasing, Lacy was genuinely happy for me. "Just promise me you won't lose yourself in this relationship like you did with Craig," she'd said, her expression turning serious for a moment. "You've worked too hard to build this new life."

I'd promised, but as the weeks went on, I sometimes struggled to maintain the balance. The bakery demanded so much of my time and energy, and I found myself torn between my commitment to making Maddy Cakes succeed and my desire to nurture this fragile new relationship with Rex.

My days fell into an exhausting rhythm: up at 3 AM, baking until opening, serving customers until closing, then inventory, planning, and bookkeeping until I collapsed into bed, often too tired to do more than exchange sleepy texts with Rex. Some nights he'd come over, and we'd fall asleep together, his arms around me providing the only real rest I got.

One bright spot: we'd checked off another bucket list item together. On a rare Sunday afternoon off, Rex had surprised me with a wine tasting at a small vineyard in the neighboring county. Item number seven, Sommelier Wine Night, was officially complete, though I'd had to ask the sommelier to slow down his explanations when Rex's hand kept wandering to my thigh under the table.

Despite the fatigue, the bakery was thriving. We'd developed a loyal customer base, and word was spreading beyond Sugar Creek. A food blogger from Charleston had written a glowing review of our orange marmalade scones, bringing in tourists who were willing to drive an hour just to try them.

But success came with its own challenges. As summer stretched on, the ancient air conditioning system in the bakery began to struggle against the South Carolina heat. The temperamental refrigerated display case required daily adjustments. And most worryingly, the larger of our two commercial ovens had started making an ominous clicking sound that grew louder each day.

The sound haunted my dreams, a metallic ticking like a time bomb counting down to disaster. Each morning, I'd hold my breath as I fired it up, silently pleading, *Not today. Please, not today.*

I was just closing up one Wednesday evening, mentally calculating whether we had enough in the emergency fund to replace the air conditioning, when I heard the clicking transform into a grinding noise, followed by an alarming pop and the acrid smell of electrical burning.

"No, no, no," I muttered, rushing to the oven and switching it off. Smoke seeped from behind the control panel, confirming my worst fears. The smell of melted wiring filled the kitchen: a nauseating blend of burning plastic and metal that sent me back to childhood memories of the time our ancient Christmas lights shorted out on our tree and almost caught the living room on fire.

I grabbed my phone, dialing the repair service with shaking fingers. After a brief conversation that involved a lot of technical terms I didn't understand and some impromptu testing, I received a grim verdict: the control board was fried, the heating elements were failing, and the cost of all the repairs would be nearly as much as a new oven.

"How soon can you replace it?" I asked, mentally reviewing our upcoming orders. The weekend was always our busiest time, and without the larger oven, we'd struggle to keep up with the fifteen specialty cake orders and standard daily items.

"Parts are backordered," the repairman said apologetically. "Best case scenario, two weeks."

"Two weeks?" I echoed, panic rising in my throat. "That's not possible. We can't operate at half capacity for two weeks!"

"I'm sorry, ma'am. That's the earliest we can get the parts."

After hanging up, I sank onto a stool, my mind racing. The smaller oven could handle basic items, but not in the volume we needed. We'd have to cut our menu, reduce orders, maybe even close early on busy days. The loss in revenue would be significant, and with our razor-thin profit margins, potentially devastating.

I was still sitting there, staring at the broken oven, when the bell above the door jingled. I looked up to see Rex entering, a paper bag from the Chinese restaurant in one hand, his expression lighting up when he saw me.

"I thought you might want dinner. You mentioned you'd be inventory counting tonight, so I figured..." His voice trailed off as he took in my expression. "What's wrong?"

"The oven," I said, gesturing helplessly at the metal beast. "It's dead. And repairs will take at least two weeks, if not longer."

Rex set down the food and crossed to me, his strong arms enveloping me in a comforting embrace. I buried my face against his chest, inhaling the familiar scent of his cologne mingled with the antiseptic smell that always clung to him after a day at the clinic.

"Let me take a look," he offered, pulling back to examine the oven with a critical eye.

"It's not a dog with a thorn in its paw," I said, though I appreciated his instinct to help. "It needs professional repair. Parts that are backordered."

"How much will it cost?" he asked, his tone carefully neutral.

I named the figure the repairman had quoted, and Rex winced slightly. "That's steep. Have you considered a replacement instead?"

"New ones cost even more," I said, pulling away to pace the kitchen. My hands kneaded an invisible ball of dough, a nervous habit I'd developed over years of baking. "And we'd still have the same timeline issue. I've been saving for equipment upgrades, but we're not there yet." I ran a hand through my hair, frustration mounting. "We can't operate at half capacity for two weeks, Rex. We'll lose customers, momentum..."

"What about a used one?" Rex suggested. "Commercial kitchens close down all the time. There might be something available locally."

"Maybe," I said, though I didn't hold out much hope. "I'll make some calls tomorrow." I shook my head, trying to clear the fog of panic. "I'm sorry. You brought dinner and I'm having a meltdown over an oven."

"Hey," Rex said, catching my hand as I paced past him. "This is your business, your livelihood. It's a big deal." His voice was steady, reassuring. "We'll figure it out."

We. Such a small word, but it made my chest constrict with emotion. Rex had somehow become part of my "we" without me even noticing the shift.

We ate the now-lukewarm Chinese food at the small table in my office, Rex listening patiently as I ran through various scenarios: reducing the menu, renting commercial kitchen space elsewhere, even temporarily moving operations to the church kitchen. The walls of the tiny office seemed to close in as each solution revealed new problems.

"I'll have to call all our weekend special orders," I said, picking at my lo mein. The noodles had become sticky and cold, but I hardly noticed. "See if they can reschedule or if they want to cancel." I sighed, setting down my fork. "Which will give me a reputation for being completely undependable. The Mitchells have that big anniversary party Saturday, and Mrs. Weatherson's daughter's wedding cake is due Sunday..."

"Let's not panic yet," Rex said, his voice calm. "There might be options we haven't thought of."

By the time we locked up and headed to my place, I was emotionally exhausted but grateful for Rex's steady presence. He didn't try to minimize my concerns or offer platitudes about how everything would work out. Instead, he listened, offered practical suggestions, and held me when words weren't enough.

That night, as we lay in bed, Rex's arm a comforting weight around my waist, I found myself thinking about Gram. How had she handled crises like this during her decades running the bakery? Had she ever faced equipment failures, financial setbacks, moments of doubt?

Of course she had. And somehow, she'd always found a way through.

"What are you thinking about?" Rex murmured, his breath warm against my ear.

"Gram," I admitted. "Wondering how she handled emergencies like this."

Rex's arms tightened around me. "She adapted. Like you will."

With that reassurance echoing in my mind, I finally drifted into a fitful sleep.

The next morning brought no miracle solutions. I spent hours on the phone, calling every restaurant supply company within a hundred-mile radius, but used commercial ovens in good condition were apparently as rare as unicorns in South Carolina.

"Nothing before next month," said the seventh supplier I called, his voice apologetic. "These supply chain issues are affecting everyone."

I hung up, staring blankly at the small wall calendar above my desk. The weekend loomed large. Fifteen special orders, including three wedding cakes, plus our regular weekend rush. With only the small oven working, we'd need to bake around the clock just to meet half our commitments.

By mid-afternoon, I was fighting both exhaustion and despair. Allison had stepped up admirably, reworking our baking schedule to maximize the smaller oven's capacity, but we both knew it was a stopgap measure at best.

"We could prioritize the special orders," she suggested, pushing a strand of hair from her face, leaving a streak of flour across her forehead. "Cut down on the regular items for the weekend."

"But then our daily customers will be disappointed," I sighed, the impossible math of the situation weighing on me. "No matter what we do, someone loses."

The smell of vanilla and sugar that usually brought me comfort now felt cloying, almost suffocating. I stepped outside for a moment, hoping fresh air would clear my head. Main Street was bustling with afternoon activity: tourists browsing shop windows, locals going about their business. Across the street, I could see movement in Rex's clinic, a reminder of life continuing normally for everyone else while my world felt like it was crumbling.

I was just heading back inside when I spotted two familiar figures approaching: Fred Potter and Larry Davis, the BAM Franchise consultants who had visited after our grand opening. Their tailored suits and polished shoes stood out among the casual attire of Sugar Creek's typical visitors.

"Ms. Bell," Fred greeted me with a warm smile. "I hope we're not interrupting."

"It's not the best time," I admitted, my professional smile feeling strained as I held the bakery door open for them.

"That's exactly why we're here," Larry said, stepping inside and breathing deeply, as if savoring the bakery's aromas. "We understand you're facing some equipment challenges."

I blinked, surprised. "How did you know about that?"

Fred's smile never wavered. "Sugar Creek is a small town, Ms. Bell. News travels fast, especially when it involves a beloved local business."

That was true enough, though the speed with which they'd appeared after my oven failure seemed suspiciously convenient. The hair on the back of my neck stood up; something felt off about their timing.

"May we sit?" Fred gestured to a nearby table. "We believe we might have a solution to your current predicament."

Curiosity overcame my wariness, and I led them to the table farthest from the counter where Allison was serving the few afternoon customers. They moved with the smooth confidence of men accustomed to closing deals, their expressions sympathetic but eager.

"As we mentioned during our previous visit," Fred began once we were seated, "BAM Franchise Consulting specializes in helping independent establishments like yours access the resources they need to thrive while maintaining their unique character."

"And right now," Larry added, leaning forward slightly, "what you need is a new oven. Quickly."

I leaned forward slightly, the practical part of me desperate for a solution even as warning bells sounded in the back of my mind. "Go on."

Fred exchanged a glance with Larry before continuing. "We have a client interested in establishing a presence in Sugar Creek. They're particularly impressed with what you've accomplished here at Maddy Cakes, and they're prepared to offer immediate assistance."

"What kind of assistance?" I asked, suspicion creeping in despite my desperate situation.

"A new commercial oven," Larry said simply. "Top of the line, delivered and installed within 48 hours."

The mental image was almost too perfect: a gleaming new oven, twice the capacity of my old one, humming efficiently in time for the weekend rush. No disappointed customers, no canceled orders, no lost revenue.

"And what would they want in return?" I asked, my business degree finally coming in handy.

"Simply a conversation," Fred replied, his tone reasonable. "An opportunity to present their franchise model, which we believe would solve not just your current equipment crisis but also provide long-term stability and growth potential."

I thought of Gram's file drawer, her repeated rejections of franchise offers over the years. The memory of her handwriting, *Roland Pierce, 1995. Franchise International, 1998. Sweet Dreams Corp, 2003. All refused. Stand firm.* flashed in my mind.

But I also thought of the customers we'd disappoint this weekend, the revenue we'd lose over the next two weeks, the strain on our already tight finances. The weight of responsibility to my clients, to Allison, and to myself, pressed down heavily.

"This wouldn't obligate you in any way," Larry assured me, apparently reading my hesitation. "Consider it a show of good faith, an investment in a potential future partnership."

"Why would they buy me an expensive oven with no guarantee I'll accept their offer?" I asked, cutting through the salesmanship.

Fred smiled, appreciative of my direct question. "Because they believe once you hear what they can offer... the purchasing power, the marketing support, the operational systems that would free you to focus on what you do best... you'll recognize the value of the partnership." He leaned forward slightly. "But even if you ultimately decide it's not for you, the oven is yours to keep. No strings attached."

It sounded suspiciously like the business equivalent of a free puppy. Nothing is ever truly without strings.

"I'd need to think about it," I said cautiously. "And discuss it with my team."

"Of course," Fred said, sliding a sleek folder across the table. "All the details are in here, including specifications for the oven model we're proposing. Our client understands the time sensitivity of your situation, so we'd need your decision by tomorrow morning if you want the installation this weekend."

The pressure tactic wasn't lost on me, but neither was the reality of my situation. A new oven by the weekend would save us thousands in lost revenue and potentially preserve relationships with customers who might otherwise go elsewhere.

"I'll call you in the morning," I promised, accepting the folder.

After they left, I flipped through the materials they'd provided. The oven they were offering was indeed top-of-the-line — a model I'd drooled over in industry magazines but had never seriously considered given its astronomical price tag. Its specifications made my heart race with professional longing: perfect temperature distribution, multiple independent compartments, digital programming for precise baking times. It was the dream oven of every serious baker.

The franchise proposal itself was surprisingly tailored to my situation. Unlike the standard chain model that would transform Maddy Cakes into a cookie-cutter operation, this offered what they called a "partnership" approach. I would maintain creative control over recipes and local operations while gaining access to their supply chain, business systems, and marketing support. In exchange, they would receive a percentage of gross sales and require certain standardized elements to create brand recognition across all locations.

On paper, it looked almost reasonable. way to preserve the heart of what made Maddy Cakes special while eliminating many of the headaches of independent ownership. The financial projections showed substantial growth potential, with the possibility of opening additional locations in nearby towns.

The numbers made logical sense. My business degree brain recognized the value proposition: economies of scale, risk mitigation, and professional support systems.

So why did it make my stomach knot with unease?

I was still studying the materials when Rex arrived that evening, his expression brightening when he saw me, despite the obvious fatigue in his eyes. His clinic coat was slung over one arm, a coffee stain visible on his pale green shirt — evidence of his own long day.

"Any luck with the oven hunt?" he asked, leaning across the counter to kiss me quickly.

I hesitated, then pushed the BAM folder toward him. "Sort of."

Rex's brow furrowed as he flipped through the glossy pages. "BAM? The franchise consultants?"

"They came by this afternoon," I explained, watching his expression carefully. "Somehow they'd already heard about the oven situation."

His frown deepened. "That seems convenient."

"I thought the same thing," I admitted. "But they're offering a new oven, installed by this weekend. No strings attached, they say."

Rex looked skeptical, his blue eyes darkening with concern. "There are always strings, Maddy." He closed the folder, pushing it back toward me. "Especially when it involves Roland Pierce's associates."

"You think Roland is behind this?" The possibility hadn't occurred to me, though it made a certain sense given his persistent interest in my property.

"I'd bet my practice on it," Rex said grimly, his voice dropping so Allison wouldn't overhear from where she was wiping down tables. "This is exactly his playbook. Find a vulnerable business, swoop in with a too-good-to-refuse offer, and gradually take control."

I bristled slightly at the word "vulnerable," remembering all too well how Craig used to make me feel that way. "We're not vulnerable. We're just having an equipment issue."

Rex's expression softened immediately, regret crossing his features. "I didn't mean it like that. Your business is solid; that's why they want it. But they're opportunists, and right now, you have a pressing need they can exploit."

The clarification helped, but I still felt defensive. "So I should just say no? And do what instead? We can't operate at half capacity for two weeks, Rex."

"I understand that," he said, reaching for my hand across the counter. "I'm just saying be careful. Read the fine print. Make sure you understand exactly what you're agreeing to before you accept their help."

His concern was touching, but it also felt uncomfortably reminiscent of Craig's dismissive attitude toward my decisions. Craig had always thought he knew better than me what was best for my life, my career. But Rex wasn't Craig. He wasn't telling me what to do, just urging caution.

"I will," I said, squeezing his hand. "I'm not naive."

Rex's thumb traced patterns on my palm. "I never said you were. I'm just concerned because I... care about you. A lot." The admission seemed to cost him something, a rare vulnerability showing through his usual composure.

His words softened my defensiveness. "What does your gut tell you about their offer?" he asked, surprising me.

The question caught me off guard. Craig had never asked about my intuition or feelings; he'd only cared about logical arguments and bottom lines.

"Honestly? It makes me uneasy," I admitted. "But I'm not sure if that's because there's something actually wrong with the deal, or if I'm just being paranoid because of what happened with Craig."

Rex nodded thoughtfully. "Craig tried to control your decisions. I don't want to do that. This is your business, your call." He paused, his eyes never leaving mine. "But for what it's worth, I think your instincts are solid. You've built something special here, Maddy. Something that's uniquely yours."

His words eased the tension between us. "Thank you for that."

Rex glanced at his phone reluctantly. "Shoot. I have to head to the clinic for a bit. Emergency surgery. But I can come back after if you want to talk more about this."

"I'd like that," I said, feeling a surge of gratitude for his support, even when we disagreed. "Text me when you're done?"

"Will do." He leaned across the counter again, this time for a longer kiss that left me slightly breathless. "For what it's worth," he murmured against my lips, "I believe in you. Whatever you decide."

After Rex left, I found myself staring at the BAM proposal, my thoughts churning. The practical part of me recognized the undeniable benefits of their offer, not just the immediate solution to our oven crisis, but the long-term stability and growth potential they promised. Running an independent bakery was exhausting, and the constant financial tightrope walk was taking its toll.

But another part of me, the part that had finally broken free from Craig's controlling influence and claimed my independence, recoiled at the thought of giving away even a fraction of my autonomy. Gram had built this bakery from nothing and kept it fiercely independent for decades. Was I really considering selling out at the first major challenge?

But then again, times had changed. The business landscape was different now, more competitive, more complex. Maybe Gram would have made the same choice in my position. Maybe she would have seen the practical wisdom in adaptation.

As closing time approached, I found myself wandering to the small office in the back of the bakery. On a whim, I pulled open the drawer where I'd found Gram's hidden recipe box, the one with her notes about refused franchise offers.

The box was still there, tucked in the back corner. I lifted it out, running my fingers over the worn wood before opening it. Inside, nestled among the recipe cards and notes, was an envelope I hadn't noticed before. It was addressed simply: *For times of doubt.*

My hands trembled slightly as I opened it, unfolding a single sheet of paper covered in Gram's familiar handwriting:

My dearest Maddy,

If you're reading this, I'm gone, and you're facing a difficult decision about the bakery. Perhaps someone has offered to buy it, or to turn it into something bigger, more "efficient." They'll tell you it's progress, that it's the smart business move, that it's what's best for Sugar Creek.

They're wrong.

What makes Maddy Cakes special is the love baked into every loaf, the conversations shared over coffee, the recipes passed from generation to generation. It's knowing Mrs. Peterson needs her bread sliced extra thin, and that little Jimmy Garner's birthday cake must always have red balloons because they're his favorite.

Trust yourself, Maddy. I believe in you. Gramps believes in you.You have everything you need to face whatever challenges come your way. And if you ever doubt that, remember: you come from a long line of women who refused to be told what they couldn't do.

With all my love and faith in you,

Gram

Tears blurred my vision as I read the letter twice more, Gram's voice so clear in my mind I could almost hear her speaking the words. She'd known, somehow she'd known, I would face this moment of doubt. And like always, she was here for me.,

I gently folded the letter, pressing it to my chest as the scent of vanilla and cinnamon wrapped around me. For a moment, I could have sworn I felt Gram's presence in the small office, her hand on my shoulder, her soft voice in my ear: *You've got this, honey.*

I carefully refolded the letter, placing it back in its envelope. The answer seemed clear now, and yet...

The reality of our situation remained unchanged. We needed that oven, and we needed it quickly. Turning down BAM's offer meant potentially weeks of reduced operations, disappointed customers, and financial strain. Was I being impractical, clinging to Gram's ideals in a changing world?

The bell above the door jingled, pulling me from my thoughts. I emerged from the office to find Lacy standing at the counter, an expectant expression on her face.

"Rex texted me," she explained, slipping off her jacket. "Said you might need a sounding board for a big decision."

I couldn't help but smile at Rex's thoughtfulness, even as he was probably elbow-deep in emergency surgery. "He's right," I admitted. "I could use some Lacy wisdom right about now."

Over the next hour, as Allison finished cleaning the kitchen and headed home, I explained the situation to Lacy: the broken oven, BAM's too-perfect timing, their generous offer, and my conflicted feelings.

"So what's the alternative?" Lacy asked finally, stirring her tea with one of the mismatched spoons Gram had collected over the years. "If you say no to BAM, what's plan B?"

"That's just it," I sighed, running my finger along a scratch in the worn wooden tabletop. "I don't have a plan B yet. The repair parts are weeks away, and used ovens in good condition are apparently impossible to find."

"What about a short-term rental?" Lacy suggested. "Don't commercial kitchens sometimes lease equipment?"

"I've called everyone within a hundred miles," I said, defeat creeping into my voice. "Nothing available that would work for us."

Lacy's expression turned thoughtful. "What would Gram do?"

I smiled wryly, pulling out the letter from my pocket. "I think she made her opinion pretty clear."

Lacy read the letter, her eyebrows rising. "Damn. Beatrice coming in clutch with advice from beyond." She handed it back to me. "But you know, Maddy, Gram's not the one facing this situation. You are. And while her advice is always solid gold, times have changed."

"That's what I keep telling myself," I admitted. "Maybe it's foolish to turn down help when we need it so badly."

"Or maybe," Lacy said carefully, "there's another kind of help out there. Help that doesn't come with corporate strings attached."

"Like what?"

"I don't know exactly," she shrugged, her red curls bouncing with the movement. "But Sugar Creek takes care of its own, right? That's what Gram believed in, what you believe in. Maybe the answer isn't in that fancy franchise folder. Maybe it's right here, in this community."

Her words echoed what Gram had written, stirring something hopeful within me despite my exhaustion. Sugar Creek had already shown its support in countless ways since I'd reopened the bakery. Was it possible they might help with this crisis too?

But the practical voice in my head, the one that had spent years managing household budgets while Craig pursued his career, reminded me that community goodwill wouldn't magically produce a commercial oven by the weekend.

"I need to sleep on it," I decided. "Call BAM in the morning when I've had time to really think."

Lacy squeezed my hand. "Trust your gut, Maddy Girl. It hasn't steered you wrong yet."

After Lacy left, I locked up and headed upstairs to my apartment, still torn between practical necessity and instinctive caution. The BAM proposal sat on my kitchen counter, its glossy cover reflecting the overhead light as I moved around the small space, getting ready for bed.

Rex texted just as I was climbing under the covers:

Surgery went well. All finished up. Want me to come over?

I smiled at my phone, warmth spreading through my chest despite my troubled thoughts.

Yes, please. Door's unlocked.

Twenty minutes later, I heard him open the front door. A few seconds later, he appeared in my bedroom doorway, looking tired but relieved to see me. His shirt was rumpled, and a five o'clock shadow darkened his jaw, but the soft smile he gave me made my heart skip.

"Hey," he said softly, crossing to sit on the edge of the bed. "How are you doing?"

"Still undecided," I admitted, reaching for his hand. "Leaning toward no, but worried about the consequences."

Rex smiled warmly, understanding in his eyes. "It's not an easy choice."

"What would you do?" I asked, genuinely curious. "If it were your clinic facing a crisis?"

He considered the question seriously, his thumb tracing circles on my palm. "I'd start by asking for help from the community I'm part of," he said finally. "People who understand what my business means to Sugar Creek."

"And if that wasn't enough?"

"Then I'd do whatever I needed to keep going," he admitted. "But I'd be very, very careful about offers that seemed too good to be true."

His honesty was refreshing. "I found a letter from Gram," I said, reaching for it on my nightstand. "Almost like she knew this exact situation would come up."

Rex read it silently, his expression softening. "She was a wise woman."

"She was," I agreed. "But I still don't know if I can afford to follow her advice. Literally."

Rex set the letter down and began unlacing his boots. "Come here," he said, slipping under the covers beside me and pulling me into his arms. "Let's talk it through."

For the next hour, we weighed the pros and cons, examined all possible alternatives, and circled around the same essential conflict: practical need versus instinctive caution. Rex listened more than he spoke, asking thoughtful questions that helped clarify my thinking rather than pushing his own opinion.

"Whatever you decide," he said finally, his arms tightening around me, "I'm here. We'll figure it out together."

As I drifted toward sleep, safely enveloped in Rex's warmth, my mind continued to churn. The decision still loomed, urgent and unavoidable, but something had shifted. Instead of feeling trapped between two impossible choices, I began to wonder if there might be another path: one that honored both Gram's legacy and the practical realities of running a business in today's world.

The answer, when it finally came to me on the edge of sleep, was so obvious I almost laughed out loud. I didn't need to choose between corporate help and going it alone. I had something better than either option: I had a community.

I fell asleep with the beginnings of a plan forming in my mind, and for the first time since the oven died, I felt a flutter of genuine hope.

Morning brought clarity and renewed determination. I woke before Rex, slipping quietly from bed to make coffee and organize my thoughts. By the time he joined me in the kitchen, eyes still heavy with sleep and hair adorably mussed, I had filled three pages of my notebook with ideas.

"You look like a woman with a plan," he observed, accepting the mug I handed him.

"Maybe," I said, unable to suppress a smile as the rich scent of coffee filled the kitchen. "But I need your help. And Lacy's. And probably half the town."

Rex's eyebrows rose in interest. "I'm intrigued."

I explained my nascent idea, watching his expression shift from curiosity to enthusiasm.

"It's ambitious," he said when I finished. "But it just might work."

"We'll need to move fast," I warned. "And I'll have to say no to BAM this morning."

"I can make some calls right away," Rex offered, already reaching for his phone. "Start the ball rolling while you talk to the franchise guys."

An hour later, dressed and fortified with more coffee, I made the call to Fred Potter. His disappointment was palpable when I declined their offer, though he maintained his professional demeanor.

"May I ask why?" he inquired. "Perhaps there's an aspect of our proposal we could adjust to better meet your needs."

"It's not about the terms," I explained, twisting the phone cord around my finger as I stood in the bakery office. "It's about independence. Maddy Cakes has been family-owned and operated for over forty years. That's a legacy I intend to continue."

"I respect your decision," Fred said, though his tone suggested otherwise. "But please keep our number. When the realities of independent ownership become more... pressing, we'll be happy to revisit the conversation."

The condescension in his voice strengthened my resolve. "I'll manage just fine, Mr. Potter. But thank you for your interest."

After hanging up, I turned to Rex, who had been making calls of his own from my small kitchen table. "It's done."

"Good," he nodded, looking up from his notes. "Because Plan B is already coming together."

By mid-afternoon, what had started as a desperate idea had transformed into a community-wide effort. Lacy had rallied the Sugar Creek Business Association, Rex had tapped his extensive network of clients and colleagues, and I had swallowed my pride to ask directly for help.

The response was overwhelming.

The First Baptist Church offered the use of their commercial kitchen during off-hours. Miss Ernestine from the soul food restaurant rearranged her schedule to free up oven space during our busiest baking windows. A local family with an empanada food truck volunteered their equipment and time to help with smaller items.

Jimmy, who owned the hardware store, knew a guy who knew a guy with access to restaurant auctions in Atlanta. Mrs. Whitman had a nephew in the restaurant equipment supply business who thought he might be able to source parts more quickly than the official channels.

People I barely knew offered solutions, connections, and help without hesitation. Trevor from the flower shop next door volunteered his van for transporting baked goods. Josephine from the bookstore organized a phone tree to inform regular customers about our temporary limitations.

Even my chess-playing grandfather rallied his retirement community friends, several of whom had connections to restaurant suppliers or experience with commercial kitchens.

The bakery became command central, with people dropping by throughout the day to offer suggestions, make calls on our behalf, or simply provide moral support. Allison worked tirelessly, coordinating schedules and reorganizing production plans to make the most of our borrowed resources.

By closing time, we had cobbled together a workable solution: a combination of borrowed equipment, shared kitchen space, and a modified production schedule that would allow us to meet all of our obligations until our oven was repaired or replaced.

It wasn't perfect. It would mean longer hours over the next few weeks, some logistical gymnastics, and probably a few mistakes along the way. But it was a solution born of community support rather than corporate dependence, and that made all the difference.

As I stood behind the counter that evening, watching Rex and Allison finalize the complex scheduling spreadsheet we'd created, I felt a surge of gratitude so intense it brought tears to my eyes. In Chicago, equipment failure would have been a crisis faced alone. Here in Sugar Creek, it had become an opportunity for connection, for the community to demonstrate in tangible ways that Maddy Cakes mattered to them.

"We'll make this work," Allison promised, noting the emotion on my face. "It's actually kind of exciting... like a baking treasure hunt adventure."

"I just hope our customers see it that way," I said, still worried about the inevitable disruptions.

"They will," Rex assured me, looking up from the laptop. "Because they care about this place, about you. They want to see you succeed."

His confidence bolstered my own, but doubts still lingered. The next few weeks would be incredibly challenging. There was still a chance we'd lose customers, revenue, momentum. The practical concerns that had made BAM's offer so tempting hadn't disappeared.

That night, after everyone had left and I was alone in the bakery, I found myself standing in front of the broken oven, my hand resting on its cold metal surface. The future stretched before me, uncertain and daunting, full of both possibility and risk.

Had I made the right choice in turning down BAM's offer? Would our community-sourced solution be enough? Or would I look back on this moment as the beginning of the end for Maddy Cakes?

I slipped Gram's letter from my pocket, running my fingers over her familiar handwriting. *Trust yourself, Maddy. You have everything you need to face whatever challenges come your way.*

I was choosing independence over security, community over corporation. In doing so, I'd discovered that Sugar Creek was more than just a location for my bakery. It was a network of people who cared, who supported each other, who believed in preserving what made their town special.

As I locked up and headed upstairs to my apartment, I still couldn't shake the mixture of hope and anxiety churning in my stomach. I'd made a bold choice, but was it the right one? It was either the bravest decision of my life, or the dumbest.

Only time would tell.

<h1 style="text-align:center">Chapter 21</h1>

S leep became a distant memory in the week following the oven disaster. Every morning started earlier than the last, darkness still heavy outside the windows as I mixed dough in borrowed kitchens across town. Today was no different. 4 AM found me at First Baptist Church, the industrial-sized mixer humming as I prepared scones for the Saturday rush.

The fluorescent lights buzzed overhead, casting harsh shadows across the unfamiliar space. My shoulders ached from hauling ingredients between locations, and the constant mental math of timing everything across multiple venues had given me a permanent headache behind my right eye.

You're doing great, honey, I could almost hear Gram's voice in the quiet of the borrowed kitchen. *Just keep going.*

Was I, though? The cobbled-together solution had gotten us through the week, but barely. The church kitchen's ancient oven ran hot on one side, burning edges if I didn't rotate pans meticulously. Miss Ernestine's equipment could only be used during specific hours that didn't always align with optimal baking times. The food truck's limited space meant multiple small batches instead of efficient large ones.

Customers had been understanding, mostly. The regulars were sympathetic when told certain items were unavailable or limited. But I'd seen the disappointment in their eyes, felt the weight of their expectations. How long before understanding turned to frustration? How long before they found other bakeries with more reliable offerings?

I checked my watch: 4:35 AM. In twenty-five minutes, I needed to pull these scones, pack them for transport, clean this kitchen, and head to Miss Ernestine's to start the cakes before her restaurant opened at 11. Then back to Maddy Cakes to handle the morning rush. Then to the food truck to prepare specialty items for the afternoon.

My hands trembled slightly as I worked the dough, exhaustion seeping into my bones. Maybe I should have taken BAM's offer. Maybe this stubborn independence wasn't worth the cost.

Don't you dare give up, Gram's voice again, so clear I actually looked over my shoulder half-expecting to see her standing there in her flour-dusted apron. *Bell women don't quit when things get hard.*

"Easy for you to say," I muttered to the empty kitchen. "You're not the one running a bakery out of four different locations."

But I kept going. One batch after another, moving through the familiar motions that had sustained me through every crisis. The rhythm of baking had always been my solace, my meditation. Even now, exhausted and overwhelmed, I found comfort in the simple act of creation.

By 8 AM, I was back at Maddy Cakes, opening the doors to the usual Saturday crowd. Allison had arrived early to help, her face showing the same strain I knew was etched on mine. We'd been working split shifts to cover the extended hours, neither getting more than five hours of sleep a night.

"The display looks good," she said, arranging the last of the muffins we'd managed to bake. "You can hardly tell we're operating at half capacity."

It was a lie of kindness. The cases were noticeably emptier, and the selection was limited. We'd had to prioritize our most popular items and specialty orders, abandoning the variety that had been our hallmark.

"We'll make it work," I said, forcing confidence I didn't feel. "Just another week or two until the parts arrive."

The morning rush brought the usual faces: Gramps and his chess club, Mrs. Whitman and her church friends, the high school teachers grabbing coffee before weekend study sessions. They smiled, tipped even more generously than usual, and pretended not to notice when I told them we were out of their usual orders.

By 10:30, the initial rush had slowed to a steady trickle. I was boxing up an order when the bell jingled, announcing a customer I didn't recognize, a tall man in his forties with the impatient energy of someone accustomed to immediate service.

"Welcome to Maddy Cakes," I said, summoning my customer service smile. "What can I get for you today?"

"I called earlier this week," he said without preamble. "Ordered two dozen cupcakes for my wife's birthday. Red velvet with cream cheese frosting." His tone suggested I should already have them waiting.

My stomach dropped. With all the chaos, had something slipped through the cracks? I quickly checked our order book, finding his name, Martin Chambers, with the order noted for Saturday pickup. But the production schedule showed them assigned to the afternoon food truck session. They weren't ready yet.

"Mr. Chambers," I began carefully, "I'm so sorry, but there seems to have been a misunderstanding. Those cupcakes are scheduled for completion this afternoon. They're not quite ready yet."

His face darkened. "Not ready? The party is at noon. I specifically requested a morning pickup."

I checked the notes again. There it was, in small writing at the bottom: "Morning pickup preferred." Not required. Preferred. With everything going on, we'd scheduled based on our limited oven access, not his preference.

"I sincerely apologize for the inconvenience," I said, my customer service voice firmly in place. "We've been dealing with some equipment issues this week. I can offer you something else from our display case, or if you can wait until 1 PM, the cupcakes will be ready then."

"That's completely unacceptable," he said, his voice rising. "I placed this order days ago. My wife's entire family is coming. What am I supposed to serve them?"

The reasonable part of my brain recognized his frustration was valid. The exhausted part just wanted him to stop yelling.

"I understand you're disappointed," I said, fighting to keep my voice steady. "Let me see what I can do. Perhaps we could prepare something else for you right away — a cake or some pastry assortment."

"I don't want something else," he snapped, leaning across the counter. "I want what I ordered. What kind of business are you running here?"

The few remaining customers were watching now, conversations paused mid-sentence. Allison had emerged from the kitchen, sensing trouble.

"Sir, I'm doing the best I can under difficult circumstances," I said, hearing the slight tremor in my voice. "We've had a major equipment failure and... "

"That's not my problem," he interrupted, his face reddening. "Your incompetence isn't my problem. I need those cupcakes now."

The word "incompetence" hit like a physical blow, triggering a cascade of memories. Craig, standing in our kitchen, arms crossed as he looked at the burnt edges of the first anniversary dinner I'd prepared. "If you can't even handle this simple task, Maddy, how do you expect to run a bakery?" His voice, calm and reasonable on the surface but laced with that subtle disdain that made me feel two inches tall.

The familiar feeling of inadequacy washed over me, followed by the desperate need to placate, to fix, to make everything okay. My chest tightened, breaths coming quick and shallow. The bakery suddenly felt too small, the walls closing in as this stranger towered over the counter, his face flushed with the same righteous anger I'd seen on Craig's face so many times.

"Let me see what we have in the back," I said, backing away from the counter. "Maybe there's something I can... "

"No," he said, moving around the counter to follow me. "You're not going to pawn off some inferior substitute. I want what I paid for."

Alarm bells rang in my head as he breached the invisible boundary between customer and staff space. He was in my territory now, too close, his body language aggressive. The scent of his cologne, spicy and overpowering, filled my nostrils, reminding me of how Craig would stand too close when he was angry, using his physical presence to intimidate.

"Sir, you can't come back here," I said, instinctively backing up until I felt the edge of the prep table behind me.

"I'm not leaving without those cupcakes," he insisted, moving closer. I could see the beads of sweat forming at his hairline, the pulse jumping in his neck. "Do you know who I am? I could have this place shut down with one phone call."

My heart hammered against my ribs. This was supposed to be my safe space, my domain. But in this moment, with this angry man looming over me, I was back in Chicago, making myself small to avoid Craig's displeasure.

"I'm sorry," I whispered, hating the automatic apology but unable to stop it. My voice had gone high and thin, the way it always did when Craig's anger reached a certain point. "Please, let me try to make this right."

"Excuse me, sir." Allison's voice cut through my panic. She had positioned herself between us, a tray of scones held like a shield. "You need to step back and return to the customer area immediately."

Mr. Chambers turned his glare on her. "Stay out of this. This is between me and the owner."

"No, it's not," came another voice — Mrs. Whitman's, her tiny frame somehow imposing as she stood in the kitchen doorway. "It's between you and the entire Sugar Creek community, young man. And we don't tolerate this kind of behavior."

I realized then that the bakery had gone completely silent. Every customer was watching, many standing now. Gramps had moved to the counter, his chess buddies flanking him like an elderly honor guard.

"This is ridiculous," Mr. Chambers blustered, though he took a step back. "I just want what I paid for."

"What you paid for," said Mrs. Whitman crisply. "Was the privilege of being served by this establishment. A privilege you have now forfeited." She pointed to the door. "Leave. Now. Or I'll have Officer Martinez here faster than you can say 'red velvet.'"

For a moment, I thought he might argue further. But faced with the united front of Sugar Creek residents, his resolve crumbled. With a final muttered curse, he stormed out, the bell jangling violently in his wake.

The tension in the room deflated like a pricked balloon. I hadn't realized I was holding my breath until my lungs began to burn. My hands were shaking, and I could feel cold sweat beading at the back of my neck — the physical aftermath of adrenaline that had nowhere to go.

"Are you all right, dear?" Mrs. Whitman asked, her rheumy eyes sharp with concern.

"I'm fine," I said automatically, but my voice betrayed me, cracking on the second word. "I just need a minute."

I made it to the office before the tears came, hot and sudden. My hands shook as I gripped the edge of the desk, breathing in short, sharp gasps. The confrontation had triggered something primal, unearthing fears I thought I'd left behind in Chicago.

A soft knock at the door pulled me from the spiral of anxiety. "Maddy?" Allison called gently. "Can I come in?"

I wiped hastily at my cheeks. "Of course."

She slipped inside, closing the door behind her. Without a word, she pulled me into a hug, her embrace steady and grounding.

"I'm sorry," I began, embarrassed by my breakdown.

"Don't you dare apologize," she said fiercely. "That man was completely out of line."

"I should have handled it better," I said, pulling back to look at her. "I'm the owner. I should have stood my ground."

Allison shook her head. "You're also a human being who's been working herself to death trying to keep this place running with limited resources. Cut yourself some slack."

Her words were kind, but they couldn't erase the knowledge that I had reverted to old patterns at the first sign of conflict. All my progress, all my growth since leaving Craig, it felt suddenly fragile, illusory.

"I think we should close early today," Allison said, watching my face carefully. "We're both exhausted, and after what just happened..."

"We can't afford to close early," I protested, though the thought of facing more customers made my stomach clench. "We're already struggling to meet our weekly targets."

"Maddy," she said firmly. "We can't afford *not* to. You need rest. I need rest. The customers will understand."

The practical part of me wanted to argue, to push through like I always did. But the rest of me, the part that had been running on fumes for days, that had just been confronted by a hostile stranger in my own space, couldn't summon the energy to fight.

"Okay," I conceded, surprising myself. "Let's close at 1."

Allison's relief was visible. "I'll start letting people know. We'll just deliver any special orders that customers can't pick up by then."

Left alone in the office, I sank into Gram's old chair, feeling the worn leather cradle me. What would she think of me now? Would she be disappointed in my handling of the situation? In my failure to maintain the bakery's standards despite adversity?

"She'd tell you to take a nap and try again tomorrow," came a voice from the doorway.

I looked up to find Rex standing there, still in his clinic coat, concern etched on his features. Word traveled fast in Sugar Creek, apparently.

"Mrs. Whitman called you?" I guessed.

"Gramps, actually," he said, stepping inside without hesitation. "Told me some jackass threatened you. He thought you might need... more than just a friendly face."

The lump in my throat loosened at that, warmth flickering in my chest. "Not very subtle, is he?"

"Subtle isn't his strong suit," Rex said, his gaze steady, protective in a way that sent a ripple through me. He crossed the room and perched on the edge of the desk, close enough that I could catch the faint scent of cedar and soap clinging to him. "Talk to me, Maddy. What happened?"

I tried to keep it light, brushing off the man's aggression and my own shaken nerves. But as I spoke, Rex's jaw tightened, his arms folding like he was holding himself back from storming out to handle it himself. His eyes never left me, dark with anger on my behalf, but beneath it all, I saw something else. A quiet vow that he wouldn't let anyone hurt me.

"That's not just a difficult customer, Maddy," he said when I finished. "That's harassment, possibly assault. We should file a police report."

The suggestion caught me off guard. "Isn't that overreacting? Nothing really happened."

"A strange man cornered you in your workplace, invaded your personal space, and made threatening statements," Rex counted off on his fingers. "That's not nothing."

Put that way, it did sound more serious than I'd allowed myself to acknowledge. But the thought of making an official complaint, of dragging this out further, exhausted me.

"I just want to forget it happened," I admitted.

Rex studied me for a long moment. "Can I ask you something?" When I nodded, he continued, "When he got in your space like that, how did you feel?"

"Scared," I said automatically. "Trapped."

"What else?"

I looked away, uncomfortable with the question. "I don't know."

"Yes, you do," he pressed gently. "You're just not letting yourself feel it."

Something in his quiet certainty broke through my defenses. "Angry," I admitted, the word foreign on my tongue. "I was angry. This is my place. My bakery. He had no right to treat me that way, to make me feel unsafe in my own space."

Rex's expression softened, approval flickering in his eyes. "There it is."

I frowned slightly. "What?"

"The anger," he said simply. "It's not weakness, Maddy. It's strength. It means you know you're worth protecting—and you're right."

I hesitated. "Why does it matter so much to you that I admit it?"

He let out a slow breath, rubbing the back of his neck before meeting my eyes again. "Because you deserve to feel safe, Maddy. And because—" He stopped, his voice roughening slightly. "When Gramps called me, I swear my heart nearly stopped. The thought of someone cornering you, frightening you like that... I hated not being here."

My breath caught at the rawness in his words.

He shifted, almost restlessly, then reached for my hand, holding it gently but firmly. "I can't always protect you, I know that. But I wish I'd been there today. I wish he'd had to face me before he even thought about stepping toward you."

His thumb brushed over my knuckles, a subtle but steady anchor. "You matter too much to me to just shrug this off."

I'd spent so many years swallowing anger, smoothing over conflicts, making myself smaller to accommodate Craig's ego, that the emotion felt almost dangerous. But Rex was right. There was something cleansing in allowing myself to feel it, to acknowledge that my boundaries mattered.

"I used to just take it," I confessed. "With Craig. If he was upset, I'd apologize, try to fix things, even when I hadn't done anything wrong." The realization struck me with sudden clarity. "That's what I was doing with that customer. Falling back into old patterns."

"But you're not the same person you were then," Rex pointed out. "You've grown. You're stronger."

"Am I?" I wondered aloud. "I still froze. I still apologized."

"And then you let Allison and your community help you," he countered gently. "The old Maddy would've carried it alone, swallowed it whole. The new Maddy is learning she doesn't have to."

His words settled over me, warm and steady, like sunlight breaking through a storm. He was right. I hadn't handled everything perfectly, but I had let people in. That was something. That was new.

"So what now?" I asked, suddenly overwhelmed by the combination of the morning's events and the ongoing equipment crisis.

Rex's gaze softened as he pushed to his feet. He extended his hand, palm open, waiting. "Now," he said, his voice low and certain. "You let me take you to Lacy's for a proper meal and a nap. After that, we'll figure out a real plan for this oven mess."

"Lacy's?" I questioned. "But my apartment is right upstairs."

Rex's mouth quirked up in a half-smile. "Yeah, Lacy specifically said if you went to your own apartment, you'd just sneak back down to the bakery the minute I left. Her words were, 'That girl needs neutral territory where she can't hear the mixer calling her name.'"

A small laugh escaped me. Lacy was absolutely right. "That does sound like something I'd do."

"So," Rex continued, his expression softening, "will you let me take care of you for once?"

I placed my hand in his, allowing him to pull me to my feet. "Okay. But just for a few hours."

I awoke, momentarily disoriented. The digital clock read 6:37 PM; I'd slept for nearly six hours, longer than I'd managed in a single stretch all week. My body felt simultaneously lighter and heavier, that particular sensation of having finally caught up on desperately needed rest.

Rex's voice drifted from the kitchen, mingled with Lacy's distinctive laugh. The smell of something savory, pasta sauce with garlic and basil, wafted under the door, reminding me I hadn't eaten a proper meal in days.

I found them both in the kitchen, Rex stirring a pot while Lacy perched on the counter, wine glass in hand. The domestic scene made my heart twist with unexpected longing.

"She lives!" Lacy announced, raising her glass. "We were about to send in a search party."

"How long have you been here?" I asked, noting the way they moved comfortably around each other, like old friends rather than recent acquaintances.

"About an hour," Lacy replied. "Sexy Rexy here showed up with grocery bags and a mission. Said you needed real food and backup."

Rex rolled his eyes at the nickname but didn't contradict her. "Feeling better?" he asked, his gaze assessing as I joined them.

"Much," I admitted, accepting the glass of water he handed me. "Thank you for making me rest."

"What are..." He paused, seemingly caught between words. "Friends for?"

Friends. The hesitation told me he'd considered saying something else, something more significant, but had pulled back. I wondered if he was suddenly remembering his self-imposed relationship limits.

"Sit," he directed, gesturing to the table. "Dinner's almost ready."

The meal was simple but perfect: pasta with a rich garlic and herb sauce, crusty bread, and a salad that actually contained vegetables I hadn't seen in weeks. We ate in comfortable conversation, Lacy recounting neighborhood gossip while Rex occasionally interjected with dry commentary that made us both laugh.

It felt normal. Like family.

As Lacy launched into another story, Rex shifted closer on the bench, his arm sliding easily across the back of my chair until it rested against my shoulders. The weight of it was warm, grounding, and unmistakably his.

"So," Lacy said as we finished eating, topping off her wine, "are we going to talk about the oven situation, or just pretend everything's fine until Maddy collapses from exhaustion again?"

Leave it to Lacy to cut straight to the heart of the matter.

"We've been discussing options," Rex said, his thumb absently tracing a slow line against my shoulder. "I've made some calls, reached out to contacts."

"And?" I prompted.

"And I think we need to call a community meeting," he said. "Tonight, if possible."

I blinked in surprise. "A community meeting? For an oven?"

"For Maddy Cakes," he corrected. "Which, in case you haven't noticed, is kind of a big deal in Sugar Creek."

"He's right," Lacy agreed, surprising me with her seriousness. "This isn't just about your business, Maddy. It's about our town. That bakery has been the heart of Main Street for a generation."

"I thought we were already doing everything possible," I said, confused. "The borrowed kitchens, the adjusted schedules..."

"That was an emergency response," Rex explained. "But it's not sustainable, as today clearly demonstrated." His expression softened. "You're running yourself into the ground trying to make it work."

"So what's the alternative?" I asked, genuinely curious.

Rex glanced at Lacy, who nodded encouragement. "Let's get everyone together and figure that out. Tonight. The community center at 8?"

"I'll start making calls," Lacy said, already reaching for her phone. "Sugar Creek residents love nothing more than a crisis to solve and free cookies."

An hour later, I stood at the front of the community center's main room, astonished by the turnout. At least fifty people had squeezed into the space, filling every folding chair and lining the walls. Familiar faces from the bakery were interspersed with people I barely recognized, all united by their concern for Maddy Cakes.

Mayor Whitman had taken charge of the meeting, her authoritative presence bringing order to what could have been chaos. After explaining the specifics of the situation to those who hadn't heard, she opened the floor for suggestions.

What followed was both humbling and overwhelming. Ideas poured forth from all directions: some practical, some outlandish, all sincere. A retired contractor offered to examine any used ovens we were considering. The high school home economics teacher suggested a rotating schedule of student assistants to help with the logistics of borrowed kitchens. Lynn proposed a crowdfunding campaign to purchase a new oven outright.

"The bakery sustained me during my darkest days," Mrs. Peterson spoke up, her voice wavering with age. "When my Lewis passed, it was Beatrice's cinnamon rolls that got me out of bed each morning. I'd like to contribute to whatever solution we find."

"My grandson's wedding had Maddy's lemon cake," added Mr. Finley, his weathered face serious. "Best damn cake I ever tasted. Can't let a broken oven stop that beautiful tradition."

Each suggestion, each personal story reminded me that I wasn't facing this challenge alone. Each voice represented someone who valued what Maddy Cakes brought to their community, who wanted to see it succeed not just as a business but as a cornerstone of their shared experience.

"If I may," came a familiar voice from the back of the room. The crowd parted to reveal Jimmy Cheng, looking uncharacteristically nervous as he approached the front. "I have something that might help."

He pulled out his phone, scrolling to find something. "My cousin works for a restaurant supply company in Atlanta. He sent me this listing this afternoon." He handed me the phone, showing a commercial oven remarkably similar to our broken one. "It's used but refurbished. All the certifications are current. And he can have it delivered by Monday."

My heart leapt at the possibility. "That's amazing, Jimmy. But..." I hesitated, hating to bring up the obvious obstacle. "The cost..."

Jimmy's smile widened. "That's the thing. After we spoke this morning, I made some calls. Turns out several people in town were thinking the same thing." He gestured around the room. "We took up a collection."

Lynn yelled from the back, "Tom and I will contribute $100."

"A collection?" I echoed, not comprehending. The bridge club started digging in their purses.

Mrs. Whitman stepped forward. "What Jimmy means, dear, is that we've all chipped in. And I'm sure those who haven't had a chance yet will be more than happy to. The oven is pretty much paid for. I'm sure by the time we conclude tonight, we'll have all the funds we need. Consider it an investment in Sugar Creek's future."

I stared at her, then at Jimmy, then at the room full of faces watching me with varying degrees of pride, affection, and satisfaction. They had done this for me. For the bakery. Without being asked.

"I... I don't know what to say," I managed, my voice thick with emotion.

"Say you'll accept," Mrs. Whitman prompted. "And that you'll keep making those orange scones that my arthritis seems to find particularly therapeutic."

A ripple of laughter moved through the crowd. I smiled weakly, unable to speak around the lump in my throat.

"Well, isn't this touching," came a smooth voice from the doorway. Roland Pierce stepped into the room, impeccably dressed despite the late hour. "The town rallying around its struggling baker."

The atmosphere shifted instantly, a collective stiffening as all eyes turned to the newcomer. The temperature seemed to drop several degrees, the warmth of community solidarity replaced by wary attention.

"Mr. Pierce," Mayor Whitman acknowledged coolly. "This is a community meeting. Were you invited?"

"I heard there was a discussion about Maddy Cakes' future," he replied, unperturbed by the frosty reception. "As someone with a vested interest in Main Street's development, I thought I should participate."

His gaze found mine, his smile practiced and predatory. "I understand you declined BAM's generous offer, Ms. Bell. A decision that seems to have led to some... distressing circumstances." His eyes flicked meaningfully to where my hand still showed a slight tremor from the morning's confrontation. "I wonder if you might reconsider, given today's events."

The implication that he somehow knew about the difficult customer sent a chill down my spine. Had he been watching the bakery? Or was Sugar Creek's rumor mill simply that efficient?

Before I could respond, Jimmy stepped forward. "She hasn't reconsidered anything. We've found a solution that doesn't involve selling out to corporate interests."

Roland's eyebrows rose fractionally. "Ah yes, the community collection. Very charming." He reached into his suit jacket, withdrawing an envelope. "But I wonder if Ms. Bell might be interested in a more comprehensive solution. One that addresses not just the immediate crisis but the long-term stability of her business. And her personal safety."

The envelope he extended toward me might as well have been a snake, poised to strike. I knew what it contained — another offer, another attempt to get his hands on my property, on my grandmother's legacy. But the subtle reference to my safety felt like a threat, a reminder that he was watching, waiting for me to fail.

"I've seen this play out before," Roland continued, his voice carrying easily in the silent room. "A beloved local business struggles with infrastructure issues, the community rallies with heartwarming but ultimately inadequate support, and eventually, the harsh realities of modern commerce prevail." His smile never wavered. "I'm merely offering a more dignified exit strategy."

A week ago, exhausted and desperate, I might have been tempted. Even now, a small voice whispered that perhaps it would be simpler to accept his help, to let someone else shoulder the burden of keeping the bakery afloat.

But looking around the room at the faces that had become so dear to me in such a short time — Rex watching with quiet confidence, Lacy with fierce protectiveness, Allison with unwavering loyalty, Mrs. Whitman with dignified expectation — I knew there was only one answer I could give.

"Thank you, Mr. Pierce," I said, my voice stronger than I expected. "But as you can see, Sugar Creek takes care of its own. We don't need your kind of help."

"And we never will," added Mrs. Whitman, stepping to my side. "We've seen what happens to businesses that accept your 'help,' Mr. Pierce. They lose their soul, and then they lose their customers."

"The last three shops that sold to his development group are empty now," Mr. Finley called out. "Fancy signs, no substance."

A murmur of agreement rippled through the crowd. Roland's smile tightened almost imperceptibly.

"Your grandmother was equally stubborn," he observed, tucking the envelope back into his jacket. "I admired that about her, even as I recognized it as a business liability." His gaze swept the room. "Sentiment is a poor foundation for economic decisions, Ms. Bell. When you're ready to discuss more practical matters, you know where to find me."

I felt my fists clenching spontaneously; Roland's condescending tone reminding me of Craig's.

"My grandmother kept Maddy Cakes running for more than thirty years. And I plan to do the same. So you can just... keep your sketchy franchise offer and... and..." Roland looked up at me expectantly, a smug look plastered across his face.

Lacy nodded at me supportively and I felt the love of the entire community at my back.

"...kiss my cinnamon buns." I said defiantly.

The room roared with laughter.

With a slight nod to the crowd, Roland turned and left, his expensive shoes clicking on the linoleum floor. The sound lingered even after he was gone, like the echo of a threat not fully extinguished.

After he departed, the energy in the room shifted again, a collective exhale followed by renewed determination. The meeting continued, details hammered out for the oven delivery and installation. By the time we adjourned, a clear plan was in place. Not just for the immediate crisis but for supporting the bakery through the transition.

As people filtered out, stopping to offer encouragement or share memories of Gram, I found myself watching the interactions with a sense of wonder. This was what Gram had protected so fiercely. Not just a business, but a community hub, a place where lives intersected and relationships deepened.

"You okay?" Rex asked, appearing at my side as the last few stragglers departed. "That was quite a roller coaster."

"I'm better than okay," I said, surprising myself with the truth of it. "I'm home."

His eyes softened at the declaration, something vulnerable flashing across his features before he masked it with a smile. "Ready to head back? You could probably use another good night's sleep before tomorrow."

"Actually," I said, an idea forming, "there's somewhere I'd like to go first. Would you mind driving me?"

Darkness had settled over Meadowbrook Cemetery by the time we arrived. The ancient oaks cast long shadows across the neatly maintained grounds, their branches swaying gently in the evening breeze. A chorus of cicadas had begun their nightly serenade, the sound rising and falling like waves against a shore.

I led Rex along the gas-lit lamp path to Gram's grave, a simple granite marker beneath a flowering dogwood tree. The petals from the season's last blooms scattered across the grass like pale pink stars.

"I can wait by the car if you'd prefer some privacy," Rex offered, hanging back slightly.

"Stay," I said, reaching for his hand. "Please."

The small paper bag I'd brought from the bakery crinkled as I knelt beside the grave. Inside was a single orange marmalade scone. Not one of my best, given the makeshift kitchen conditions, but made with the same care Gram had always shown.

"Hey, Gram," I said softly, placing the scone at the base of the marker. "I brought your favorite."

Rex squeezed my hand gently, a silent show of support as I gathered my thoughts.

"You were right," I continued, addressing the stone as if Gram could hear me. "About everything. About Sugar Creek, about the bakery being more than just a business, about finding my own way." I traced the letters of her name, carved deep into the granite. "I think I finally understand what you were trying to teach me all those summers."

The breeze picked up, rustling the leaves overhead and carrying the sweet scent of honeysuckle from somewhere nearby. In the fading light, the cemetery felt less like a place of mourning and more like a quiet sanctuary, a connection between past and present.

"We're getting a new oven," I told her, smiling despite the tears that threatened. "The whole town pitched in. Can you believe that? They love the bakery as much as you did. As much as I do now."

I felt Rex shift beside me, his steady presence a comfort as I continued my one-sided conversation with Gram.

"I wish you could have seen it," I said, my voice catching. "The way everyone came together. It's exactly what you always said... a community is only as strong as the connections between its people." I paused, struggling to find the right words. "I think... I think I finally found where I belong. Who I belong with."

Rex's hand tightened around mine. When I glanced up at him, his eyes shimmered with emotion in the dusky light, fixed on me with an intensity that made my breath catch.

"Remember how you used to tell me that life isn't about checking boxes off a list?" I continued, turning back to the grave. "That it's about finding the things that make your soul sing? I think I'm starting to understand what you meant."

A memory surfaced — Gram in her kitchen, flour dusting her apron, looking up from her kneading to fix me with that knowing gaze. "Success isn't measured in dollars or achievements, Maddy-girl. It's measured in connections. In the people who'll show up for you on your darkest day."

"They showed up, Gram," I whispered, tears finally spilling over. "They all showed up."

I sat in silence for a moment, letting the tears flow freely. Rex remained beside me, his thumb tracing gentle circles on the back of my hand, offering comfort without words.

"I'm keeping your legacy alive," I promised, when I could speak again. "But I'm also building something of my own. Something that honors you but is uniquely mine." I stood, brushing grass from my knees. "I think you'd be proud of that."

As we walked back to the car, hand in hand through the deepening twilight, I felt a profound sense of peace settle over me. The challenges weren't gone. We still had a weekend of makeshift baking ahead, a new oven to install, a business to rebuild. Roland Pierce was still circling like a vulture, waiting for me to falter.

But for the first time since the crisis began, those challenges felt manageable. I had something Gram had always tried to teach me that was more valuable than any business plan or profit margin. I had a community. People who saw me, who valued what I brought to their lives, who would stand beside me when things got hard.

"Thank you," I said as Rex opened the car door for me. "For everything today. For making me rest, for bringing everyone together, for coming here with me."

Rex's expression was open, unguarded in the soft evening light. "Anytime," he said simply. Then, with a hint of his usual humor, "Besides, I have a vested interest in making sure those orange scones keep coming. I'm pretty much addicted at this point."

I laughed, the sound floating up toward the first stars appearing in the darkening sky. "Good thing I'm planning to bake them for a very long time."

"Promise?" he asked, something deeper than pastries in his question.

"Promise," I replied, making it a vow. To him, to Gram, to myself.

As we drove back toward town, I glanced at the picture of the bucket list Lacy had sent to my phone, the original now stuck to my fridge instead of hers. So many items already checked off. Not just the birth and experiences, but the deeper aspirations they represented. Finding my voice. Building something meaningful. Creating a home.

Sugar Creek's lights shone in the distance, warm and welcoming against the night sky. My town. My community. My home.

Gram had known all along what I was really searching for. Not just achievements to tick off a list, but a place to belong, people to love, work that mattered. She'd left me the bakery not just as a business but as a doorway into the life I was meant to live.

And I was finally walking through it, eyes wide open, heart ready for whatever came next.

Chapter 22

Six weeks had passed since the community meeting that had saved Maddy Cakes. Six weeks of transformation, of finding my footing, of finally feeling like I belonged. The bakery was thriving, not just surviving, with a steady stream of regular customers and special orders that kept us pleasantly busy without the frantic pace of those first chaotic months.

Even Craig's family's law firm had a standing order for a box of mixed pastries every Monday morning.

"I still can't believe someone brought a custom cake stand all the way from Charleston," I said, wiping down the counter as the afternoon sun streamed through the freshly cleaned windows. The new oven hummed contentedly behind me, its digital display showing a perfect 350 degrees.

"Mrs. Henderson says it's been in her family for generations," Allison replied, arranging fresh scones in the display case. "She wouldn't trust it with just anyone. Only 'Beatrice's girl' would do."

The compliment warmed me from the inside. Being known as "Beatrice's girl" no longer felt like a burden of expectations but a badge of honor, a connection to the woman who had shaped so much of who I was.

The bell above the door jingled, and I looked up to see Rex entering, right on schedule for his afternoon coffee break. My heart did the familiar little dance it always performed at the sight of him: a mixture of comfort and excitement that hadn't diminished despite the weeks we'd been together.

"There he is," Gramps called from his regular table, where he and his chess buddies were engaged in their daily tournament. "The man who dared to beat me at chess yesterday."

Rex grinned, stopping to clap my grandfather on the shoulder. "Pure luck, sir. I'm sure you'll reclaim your title today."

"Damn right I will," Gramps huffed, though his eyes twinkled with affection. "And none of this 'sir' business. Makes me feel ancient."

"You are ancient," said Mr. Peterson, moving his knight with deliberate precision. "And you're about to lose again if you don't pay attention to the board instead of gossiping."

Their good-natured bickering faded into the background as Rex made his way to the counter, leaning across it to plant a quick kiss on my lips. "Hey, beautiful. How's your day going?"

"Better now," I said, already reaching for a mug to pour his usual afternoon coffee. "How was the clinic?"

"Busy but good. Mrs. Thompson's retriever finally had her puppies — seven healthy little monsters who'll be terrorizing Sugar Creek in about eight weeks."

I handed him the coffee and an orange scone. Still his favorite after all these weeks.

Lacy appeared at Rex's elbow, stealing half his scone with practiced ease. "Are you two being disgustingly cute again? It's like watching a Hallmark movie, except with better pastries and occasional swearing."

"Thanks," I said, swatting her hand away as she reached for the rest of Rex's scone.

"Get your own," he protested, though he pushed the plate toward her with a resigned sigh.

"Delicious," Lacy declared, popping the last bite of scone into her mouth. "So when are you two making it official and moving in together? The constant back-and-forth between apartments is getting ridiculous."

I felt my cheeks heat. Lacy had a knack for asking the exact questions I'd been avoiding in my own mind. Rex and I had fallen into a comfortable routine of spending nights at each other's places, but we hadn't discussed anything more permanent. Part of me, the cautious part shaped by years with Craig, was afraid to push for more. The other part yearned for exactly what Lacy was suggesting.

Rex's expression was carefully neutral as he sipped his coffee. "We're taking things as they come," he said diplomatically.

"Mmm-hmm," Lacy hummed skeptically. "Well, when you decide to stop pretending you're not essentially living together already, I call dibs on helping decorate. Rex's townhouse looks like a veterinary textbook threw up in there, and Maddy's is still basically a storage unit with a bed."

"Thank you for that assessment," I said dryly, though I couldn't entirely disagree. Neither of our places really felt like a proper home — just spaces we happened to sleep in when we weren't at the bakery or the clinic.

"Just saying," Lacy shrugged, unrepentant. "Anyway, I'm off to meet the new art teacher at school. Rumor has it he's single, devastatingly handsome, and can quote both Shakespeare and Taylor Swift with equal enthusiasm."

"Your perfect man," Rex deadpanned.

"Perhaps," Lacy said with a dramatic flip of her hair. "Or perhaps just my next entertaining mistake. Either way, I plan to find out." She blew us both kisses as she sashayed toward the door. "Don't wait up!"

As the door closed behind her, Rex chuckled. "She's something else."

"She certainly is," I agreed, watching through the window as Lacy strutted down the sidewalk, heads turning in her wake. "But she's not entirely wrong about the living situation."

Rex's eyes met mine, something vulnerable flickering in their depths. "No, she's not."

Before we could continue the conversation, a young couple entered, looking slightly bewildered. "Hi, are you Maddison Bell?" the woman asked hesitantly. "We were told you make the best wedding cakes in three counties."

And just like that, the moment was gone, business taking precedence over personal revelations. Rex squeezed my hand once before returning to his usual table to finish his coffee, leaving me to handle the potential new clients.

The afternoon passed in a pleasant blur of customers, baking, and the comfortable rhythms we'd established. By closing time, I felt that particular satisfaction that comes from a productive day spent doing work you love surrounded by people you care about.

"I'll finish cleaning up," Allison offered as I checked the schedule for tomorrow's special orders. "You look like you could use an early night."

I glanced up, surprised by her perception. "Is it that obvious?"

"You've been yawning for the past hour," she said with a gentle smile. "And you were here at 4 AM. Go home. Rex is waiting outside anyway."

Sure enough, when I peered through the window, Rex was across the street, leaning against his parked truck and scrolling through his phone. The sight of him — solid, dependable, patient — filled me with a warmth that had become wonderfully familiar.

"Are you sure?" I asked Allison, already reaching for my purse. "There's still the... "

"Go," she interrupted firmly. "Before I change my mind."

I didn't need to be told twice. After a quick round of closing checks, I was out the door and crossing the street to where Rex waited.

"This is a nice surprise," I said, rising on tiptoes to kiss him. "I thought you had paperwork tonight."

"I did," he confirmed. "But then I decided I'd rather spend the evening with you." His smile turned playful. "I brought takeout from that Thai place you like. Thought we could have a quiet night in."

"That sounds perfect," I sighed. "I'm exhausted."

"Your place or mine?" he asked.

The question triggered Lacy's earlier comments about our living arrangements. "Mine? I'm starved, and I need fresh clothes for tomorrow anyway."

Rex grabbed the food from the front seat and locked the truck as we walked hand-in-hand towards my tiny apartment above the bakery. We settled into what had become our evening routine: sharing takeout while talking about our days, comfortable silences interspersed with easy conversation. Rex's presence in my space felt natural, as if he'd always belonged there.

Later, as we lay in bed, his arm draped protectively around my waist, I found myself thinking about Lacy's question again. We were practically living together already. Why not make it official?

"Rex?" I whispered, unsure if he was still awake.

"Hmm?" His voice was drowsy but attentive.

"What *would* you think about us finding a place together? Something that's ours, not just mine or yours?"

I felt him go still beside me, his breathing shifting from the slow rhythm of near-sleep to something more alert. For a heart-stopping moment, I feared I'd overstepped, pushed too far too fast.

"I'd like that," he said finally, his voice rough with emotion. "A lot, actually."

Relief washed through me. "Really?"

He shifted, propping himself up on one elbow to look down at me in the dim light filtering through the curtains. "Really. I've been thinking about it for weeks but wasn't sure if you were ready. It's a big step."

"I think I am," I admitted. "Lacy was right. This back-and-forth is a little chaotic. And... I like the idea of building something together. A real... home."

Rex's kiss was gentle but filled with promise. "Then let's do it. Start looking for a place. Something with a yard for a dog maybe."

The casual certainty in his voice, the way he was already envisioning our future together, made my heart swell. This was what I'd been missing with Craig: a relationship where both people moved forward together, making room for each other's dreams instead of subordinating one to the other.

"I love you," I whispered, the words slipping out naturally, without hesitation.

Rex went very still, his eyes wide in the darkness. We hadn't said those words yet, though I'd felt them building for weeks.

"I love you too," he replied, his voice hushed but certain. "More than I thought possible."

As we drifted to sleep, tangled together in my too-small bed, I felt a sense of rightness, of completion. Everything was finally falling into place. The bakery was thriving, I'd found my place in Sugar Creek, and I was building a life with a man who saw me, really saw me, and loved what he saw.

For the first time in my adult life, I felt truly at home.

The next morning brought a return to our usual routine of early alarm, quick breakfast together, then Rex heading to the clinic while I made my way to the bakery to start the day's baking. The conversation about moving in together hovered at the back of my mind, a warm promise of things to come.

Allison arrived just as I was pulling the first batch of muffins from the oven, the rich scent of blueberries and vanilla filling the kitchen.

"You look happier this morning," she observed, tying her apron around her waist. "I'm guessing the early night helped?"

"That and other things," I said, unable to suppress my smile. "Rex and I are thinking of finding a place together."

Allison's eyes widened with delight. "That's fantastic! Have you started looking yet? My cousin's a real estate agent. She could help you find something perfect."

"We just decided last night," I laughed, charmed by her enthusiasm. "But I'll definitely keep your cousin in mind when we're ready to start the search."

The morning passed in a blur of activity, the routine both soothing and satisfying. By mid-afternoon, I was boxing up a special order when Della burst through the door, her energetic presence immediately filling the space.

"Maddy!" she exclaimed, making a beeline for the counter. "Just the person I wanted to see!"

"Hey, Della," I greeted her, surprised but pleased. Since the yacht party, Rex's half-sister had become a semi-regular at the bakery, though she usually called ahead when she was making the drive from Charleston. "What brings you to Sugar Creek?"

"Jason had a meeting nearby, so I tagged along to see my favorite baker and do some shopping," she explained, hopping onto a stool at the counter.

"I'm sorry you missed Rex," I said, setting aside the order I'd been working on. "He had some kind of veterinary conference. He should be back this evening."

Della's brow furrowed slightly. "Hospital conference? Are you sure?"

Something in her tone set off a tiny alarm bell in my mind. "That's what he told me. Why?"

She hesitated, an uncharacteristic uncertainty crossing her features. "It's probably nothing. Just a mix-up."

"Della," I said firmly. "What's going on?"

She sighed, glancing around to ensure no one was within earshot. "Isn't today Rex's interview in New York at Cornell?"

"Interview?" I repeated, my stomach dropping. "In New York?"

Della's expression shifted from uncertainty to concern. "He didn't tell you?"

"No," I said, my voice sounding distant to my own ears. "He didn't mention anything about an interview. Or Cornell. Or New York."

"Oh, shit," Della muttered. "I'm sure there's an explanation. Maybe it's not what it sounds like. Or maybe he was planning to surprise you with the news after it was finalized."

But I barely heard her attempts at rationalization. My mind was racing, connecting dots I hadn't even realized existed. Rex's sudden 'conference' in Charleston. The way he'd been slightly distracted the past few days, checking his phone more frequently than usual. His reluctance to commit to plans for the coming weekend.

He really was a three-month man – and now, just as I thought we were getting more serious, he was planning to bolt. I never should have asked him about moving in together.

Or worse, told him I loved him. I'd just given him the perfect excuse to leave. And what was worse, I'd been warned.

"How long have you known about this?" I asked, trying to keep my voice steady.

Della shifted uncomfortably. "He mentioned something a few weeks ago about a prestigious position at Cornell's veterinary hospital. It would be a huge opportunity for his career... leading a department, pioneering new treatment protocols. But he was really conflicted about it because of... well, because of you."

"So he's been considering this for weeks," I clarified, the betrayal cutting deeper with each revelation. "And never thought to mention it to me. Even last night, when we were discussing moving in together."

I'd been so stupid. He'd warned me, and I'd just charged right ahead and served up my heart like a plateful of scones. And what did I do? Suggest moving in together and confess that I loved him as we were charging toward his usual relationship expiration date.

"What? That's great news! Maddy, I'm sure he had his reasons," Della began, but I cut her off with a raised hand.

"I'm sorry, I really need a minute," I said, turning toward the kitchen. "Allison, can you cover the front?"

Without waiting for a response, I retreated to the small office at the back of the bakery, closing the door behind me. My hands were shaking as I sank into the chair, breath coming in shallow gasps as the implications washed over me.

Rex was interviewing for a job in New York. A job that would take him hundreds of miles away from Sugar Creek. From me. And he hadn't said a word about it, even as we'd been making plans for our future together *last night*.

Was this just Craig all over again — the half-truths, the unilateral decisions, the expectation that I would simply adapt to whatever he decided was best? A sickly, familiar sensation of being an afterthought, a secondary consideration in someone else's life plan, settled over me like a suffocating blanket.

I pressed my palms against my eyes, trying to stem the tears that threatened. How could I have been so blind? How could I have convinced myself that Rex was different, that what we had was built on mutual respect and honesty?

The soft knock at the door barely registered. "Maddy?" Della called hesitantly. "Can I come in?"

"It's open," I replied, not trusting myself to say more.

She slipped inside, her expression a mixture of guilt and concern. "I'm so sorry. I honestly thought you knew."

"Not your fault," I managed. "Clearly, Rex didn't think it was important enough to mention."

Della perched on the edge of the desk, her usual vibrancy dimmed by the tension in the room. "That doesn't sound like him. Rex has always been almost painfully honest. Sometimes to the point of bluntness. There must be a reason he hasn't told you yet."

"There's always a reason," I said, bitterness seeping into my voice. "That's what Craig always said too. He had very good reasons for not including me in decisions that affected both our lives. They were just never reasons that considered my needs or feelings."

Understanding dawned in Della's eyes. "So... this isn't just about Rex, is it? It's also about your ex."

"It's about *me*," I corrected her. "About the pattern I apparently can't stop repeating. About falling for men who see me as an accessory to their lives rather than a partner in building something together."

Della shook her head firmly. "Rex isn't like that. I've known him my whole life, and he's never been more serious about anyone than he is about you."

"Serious enough to discuss a life-changing move with me? To include me in his decision-making process?" I challenged, anger finally breaking through the hurt. "If he's so serious about us, why am I hearing about this from you instead of him?"

Della had no answer for that, her silence more damning than any defense she might have offered.

"I should get back to work," I said finally, straightening my shoulders with effort. "We have orders to fill."

"Maddy — "

"It's fine," I interrupted, though we both knew it was a lie. "Thank you for telling me. At least now I know where things stand."

The rest of the afternoon passed in a blur of mechanical motions: mixing, baking, decorating, and serving customers with a smile I wasn't feeling plastered on my face. Allison kept shooting me concerned glances, but I avoided her questions, not ready to vocalize the betrayal that was still sinking in.

By closing time, my initial shock had crystallized into a cold, hard anger that sat like a stone in my chest. I went through the closing routine on autopilot, barely registering Allison's worried goodbye as she finally left for the day.

The bakery felt eerily quiet as I locked up, the silence amplifying the thoughts swirling in my head. I should have known better. I should have protected myself more carefully. I should have remembered that men like Rex — charming, handsome, talented — didn't put down roots, especially not for women like me.

The three-month limit. Wasn't that what Vanessa had warned me about on the yacht? Rex never stayed with anyone longer than three months. We were approaching that deadline now. Of course this job interview was just his convenient exit strategy, a way to end things on his self-imposed deadline without having to actually break up with me.

I was so lost in my spiraling thoughts that I almost didn't notice the truck parked outside my bakery as I closed up. Rex, leaning against the hood, looked up as I approached, his smile dying when he saw my expression.

"Hey," he said, pushing off the truck to meet me. "Everything okay?"

The casual question, as if this were just another evening, ignited something volatile within me. "You tell me," I replied, brushing past him to unlock my door. "How was your conference?"

A beat of silence told me everything I needed to know. When I turned to face him in the doorway, his expression had shifted from concern to wariness.

"It wasn't exactly a conference," he admitted, confirming my suspicions. "How did you..."

"Della stopped by the bakery," I cut him off, stepping inside without inviting him to follow. "You had an interview today?"

Rex closed his eyes briefly, a muscle working in his jaw. "I was going to tell you tonight."

"Were you?" I challenged, dropping my purse on the counter with more force than necessary. "Or were you going to wait until you had the offer in hand? That's a super convenient exit strategy for you and *right on schedule...*"

"Maddy..." he protested. "I don't have any intention of leaving you. I don't *want* to leave you."

"Maybe after we'd found a place together? Or were you thinking I'd just pack up and follow you to New York without question? Probably not, because that might have put us over your three-month relationship limit."

"Maddy, it's not like that," he said, stepping into the apartment and closing the door behind him. "I was struggling with how to bring it up because I'm not even sure I want the position."

"Then why interview at all?" I demanded, the hurt making my voice sharper than intended. "Why go through the process if you're not interested?"

Rex ran a hand through his hair, a gesture I'd come to recognize as a sign of his discomfort. "Because it's an incredible opportunity professionally. The kind that doesn't come along often in veterinary medicine. Dr. Wright approached me specifically; he's familiar with my work with military service animals, and she wants me to head up a new treatment program at Cornell."

"And when were you planning to include me in this decision-making process?" I asked, crossing my arms over my chest. "After you'd decided? After you'd accepted? Or were you just going to present it as a fait accompli and expect me to adapt?"

"I didn't think that far ahead," he admitted. "I've been conflicted about it from the beginning. On one hand, it's a dream job in many ways. On the other..." His eyes met mine, vulnerability evident in their depths. "On the other hand, it would mean leaving Sugar Creek. Leaving you. And that's the last thing I want."

"Yet you went to the interview anyway," I pointed out. "Without telling me. Without giving me a chance to be part of the conversation."

"I know," he acknowledged, his voice low. "I handled it badly. I was afraid — "

"Afraid of what?" I interrupted. "Afraid I'd be upset? Because I am upset, Rex. Not about the job opportunity, but about being kept in the dark. About making plans with you last night knowing nothing about this potentially huge change in our lives."

Rex took a step toward me, his expression pained. "I was afraid of losing you," he admitted. "Afraid that if I brought it up, you'd think I wasn't committed to us, to our future here. And then last night, when you talked about finding a place together..." He trailed off, shaking his head. "The timing felt impossible. I thought if I got through the interview, figured out how I really felt about the position, I'd be better equipped to discuss it with you."

"That's not how partnerships work," I said, the word sticking in my throat. "You don't make unilateral decisions and then present them as options. That's exactly what Craig used to do, and I promised myself I'd never accept that kind of treatment again."

At the mention of Craig, Rex's expression tightened, a flicker of something unreadable passing through his eyes. "Maddy... I'm not him. And this isn't the same. That isn't what's happening here," he murmured. "Not with us."

"Are you sure?" I challenged. "He made career decisions without consulting me too. He expected me to accommodate his choices, to fit myself into the spaces left over after he'd decided what our lives would look like." The parallels were becoming clearer with every word. "I spent ten years playing that role, Rex. I won't do it again. Not even for you."

"That's not what I'm asking," he insisted, frustration evident in his tone. "I'm not offering you leftover space in my life. I'm trying to figure out how to balance an unexpected opportunity with what matters most to me — which is us, our relationship, the life we're building here."

"But you didn't include me in that process," I pointed out, my voice breaking slightly. "You kept me completely in the dark while you explored options that would affect both our lives. How is that different from what Craig did?"

Rex opened his mouth to respond, then closed it again, the fight seeming to drain out of him as he recognized the truth in my words. "You're right," he said finally. "I should have told you from the beginning. I messed up, and I'm sorry."

The simple apology, delivered without excuses or qualifications, should have eased some of the hurt. Instead, it only highlighted the distance that had suddenly opened between us. Sorry didn't erase the fact that when faced with a significant decision, Rex's instinct had been to handle it alone rather than together.

"What happens now?" I asked, hating how small my voice sounded. "If they offer you the position, will you take it?"

Rex's hesitation was answer enough. "I don't know," he admitted. "Part of me wants to. It's the kind of work I've dreamed of doing. But a bigger part can't imagine leaving Sugar Creek. Leaving you."

"So I'm the obstacle to your dream job," I concluded, the realization settling like lead in my stomach. "The thing holding you back."

"That's not what I said," Rex protested. "You're not an obstacle, Maddy. You're the reason I'm questioning whether I even want this opportunity. Because what we have here... it matters more to me than any job."

"But you still went to the interview," I pointed out. "You're still considering it."

"Because I don't know what the right answer is," he admitted, spreading his hands in a helpless gesture. "I've never had roots before. I've never had someone I wanted to build a life with. I've never had to weigh professional opportunities against personal ones. I'm not good at this, Maddy. I'm trying, but I'm not good at it. My folks never had a conversation about where we wanted to live. My dad got orders, and we packed up our house and moved to the next military base. This...situation... is completely new to me."

The vulnerability in his confession struck a chord within me. He wasn't being malicious or manipulative like Craig. He was fumbling through unfamiliar emotional territory, making mistakes as he went. But understanding the reason for his actions didn't erase the hurt they'd caused.

"I need time to think," I said finally. "This is a lot to process."

Rex nodded, resignation settling over his features. "I understand. For what it's worth, I am sorry. Not just for not telling you, but for hurting you. That's the last thing I ever wanted to do."

As he turned to leave, a question escaped me before I could stop it: "What did you tell them? At the interview?"

Rex paused at the door, his back to me. "I told them I had serious reservations about relocating," he said softly. "That I had personal commitments in Sugar Creek that would make accepting the position difficult, regardless of the professional opportunities it presented."

With that, he was gone, the door closing quietly behind him. The apartment felt suddenly vast and empty, the silence ringing in my ears like an accusation.

I sank onto the couch, emotions warring within me: anger at being excluded from such an important decision, fear that history was repeating itself, grief at the potential loss of the future I'd begun to envision with Rex. But beneath it all, a quiet voice insisted: *You deserve better than what you settled for before. You deserve to be an equal partner in your own life.*

The thought carried me through a restless night of tossing and turning, memories of Craig's casual dismissal of my needs blending with Rex's earnest apology in a confusing swirl. By morning, I'd reached no resolution, just a bone-deep weariness and the certainty that I couldn't, *wouldn't,* compromise on being treated as an equal partner.

"He did what?" Lacy demanded, her green eyes flashing with indignation. We were sitting in her kitchen, mugs of cooling coffee forgotten on the table between us. I'd called her first thing in the morning, needing her particular brand of brutal honesty and unwavering support.

"Interviewed for a job in New York without telling me," I repeated, exhaustion weighing down each word. "Found out from Della yesterday."

"That absolute... dimwit," Lacy fumed, clearly substituting a milder word than she wanted to use. "After everything with Craig, he should know better."

"That's just it," I sighed, running a finger around the rim of my mug. "He's not Craig. He wasn't being manipulative or controlling. He was just... making a mistake. A big one, but still just a mistake."

Lacy's eyebrows rose skeptically. "You're defending him now?"

"No," I said quickly. "What he did was wrong. Full stop. But I don't think his intentions were the same as Craig's. Craig kept me out of decisions because he genuinely didn't value my input or consider my needs. Rex seems to have kept me out because he was afraid of hurting me or creating unnecessary conflict if the job wasn't even a real possibility."

"Still a crappy move," Lacy pointed out. "Intentions matter, but so do actions. And his actions show a fundamental lack of respect for *your* agency in this relationship."

Her blunt assessment resonated with the hurt still raw in my chest. "I know. That's why I'm so confused. Part of me wants to forgive him, to work through this. And part of me is terrified that I'm falling back into old patterns, making excuses for behavior I promised myself I'd never accept again."

Lacy reached across the table to squeeze my hand. "What does your gut tell you? Not your fears, not your past experiences with Craig, but your honest instincts about Rex?"

I considered the question carefully, trying to separate the tangled emotions. "My gut says he made a mistake. A big one. But not one that defines who he is or how he feels about me."

"And what about the job itself?" she pressed. "How would you feel if he took it? If he moved to New York?"

The thought sent a pang through my chest. "Devastated," I admitted. "I love him, Lacy. I love the life we've been building here. The thought of losing that..." My voice trailed off, unable to complete the sentence.

"Have you considered going with him?" she asked gently. "If he takes the job, I mean."

The question hit me like a physical blow. "No," I said, surprise coloring my tone as I realized the truth of it. "I haven't even considered that option."

"Why not?"

I blinked, momentarily thrown by the simple query. "Because... because I'm finally where I'm supposed to be. I've found my place, my purpose. Maddy Cakes isn't just a business to me. It's my connection to Gram, to this community, to the person I was always meant to be." The certainty in my voice grew with each word. "I spent ten years following

Craig, subordinating my dreams to his ambitions. I won't do that again. Not even for Rex."

Lacy grinned triumphantly, pride flashing in her eyes. "And that's your answer right there. You know what you want, what you need. The question now is whether Rex is willing to build a life around that reality, or if he needs something different."

"What if he chooses the job?" I whispered, giving voice to my deepest fear. "What if three months really is his limit, and this is just his exit strategy?"

Chapter 23

I'd been in the bakery kitchen since 3:30 AM, stress-baking my way through a tumult of emotions. Each recipe was one of Gram's comfort staples: sticky cinnamon rolls (aka "Kiss my Cinnamon Buns" to our customers,) buttery croissants, maple bars... foods that reminded me of simpler times when my biggest worry was whether the dough had risen properly. My hands moved automatically through the familiar motions while my mind churned with thoughts of Rex and our fight.

Even after a restless night, I still couldn't decide if I'd overreacted. Rex had kept a major job opportunity from me; that was undeniable. But his fumbling explanation, his clear remorse, and the fact he'd immediately admitted his mistake instead of making excuses all suggested this wasn't the calculated deception I'd initially interpreted it as.

Lacy's words from yesterday echoed in my head: "You know what you want, what you need. The question now is whether Rex is willing to build a life around that reality, or if he needs something different."

The timer dinged, pulling me from my thoughts. I pulled a tray of perfectly golden croissants from the now fully-functioning oven, their buttery aroma momentarily distracting me from my troubles. Baking had always been my therapy, my sanctuary. Even now, with my personal life in shambles, the precision and predictability of the kitchen offered some comfort.

I'd checked my phone at least a dozen times since arriving, hoping for a message from Rex. The last communication had been his simple text late last night: I'm sorry. When you're ready to talk, I'll be here. I'd read it over and over, typing and deleting responses until finally setting the phone aside, still unsure what I wanted to say.

By 7 AM, the bakery was bustling with the usual morning crowd. Allison had arrived at 6, taking one look at the mountain of baked goods I'd produced and wisely choosing not to comment. She'd simply tied on her apron and jumped in to help, her quiet efficiency more comforting than any words could have been.

"We're going to need more coffee," she noted, surveying the steadily filling tables.

"I'll start another pot."

The familiar rhythm of the morning rush kept me grounded: greeting regulars by name, boxing orders, making change. For brief moments, I could almost forget the ache in my chest, the uncertainty clouding my future.

The bell above the door chimed for what felt like the hundredth time that morning. I glanced up automatically, my customer service smile freezing on my face as I registered who had just walked in.

Craig.

Craig?

Craig.

He stood in the doorway, impeccably dressed in a tailored charcoal suit that probably cost more than a month's worth of bakery profits. His dirty blonde hair was perfectly styled, his clean-shaven face as handsome as ever, his posture radiating the same confidence that had once captivated me. In his hand was a bouquet of lilies. My favorite, at least they had been ten years ago.

The bakery seemed to go suddenly quiet, though logically I knew conversations hadn't actually stopped. Time felt suspended as my brain struggled to process his unexpected appearance.

Craig's eyes found mine across the room, and he smiled that practiced, polished smile I'd once found so charming. Now I could see the calculation behind it, the way it was designed to disarm rather than express genuine pleasure.

"Maddy," he said, approaching the counter as if it were perfectly normal for him to appear in my small-town bakery hundreds of miles from Chicago. "You look beautiful."

I became acutely aware of my flour-dusted apron, my hair hastily pulled back in a messy bun, the smudge of chocolate I'd noticed on my forearm earlier and hadn't bothered to wash off. Nothing about me qualified as "beautiful" at the moment, which only highlighted how empty his compliment was.

"Craig," I managed, finding my voice. "What are you doing here?"

His smile widened, revealing perfect teeth. "I had some business nearby and thought I'd surprise you." He held out the flowers. "These are for you. I remember how much you love lilies."

Mechanically, I accepted the bouquet, their heavy perfume suddenly cloying in the warm bakery air. "Thank you. That's... unexpected."

From the corner of my eye, I could see Allison watching the interaction with undisguised curiosity. Several regular customers had also taken notice, including Gramps and his chess club at their usual table by the window.

Craig was a hometown boy, but he certainly wasn't getting the hero's welcome.

"Your Gram's bakery looks wonderful," Craig continued, his gaze sweeping the space with the evaluating eye I recognized from our time together. "Very... uh, quaint. Just like you always wanted."

The slight pause before "quaint" told me everything about his true assessment. To Craig, "quaint" meant small-time, amateurish, unambitious, and beneath his professional standards.

I was more familiar with his polite insults than anyone, with only the exception of his mother Genevieve, who'd taught him everything he knew about insulting people with a smile.

"Would you like something to eat?" I asked, reverting to business mode to mask my discomfort. "The orange scones are particularly good today."

"Oh, no thank you," he replied quickly. "Still keeping paleo. You remember." He patted his flat stomach as if to emphasize his disciplined eating habits.

It took every impulse I had not to roll my eyes.

Allison appeared at my side, wiping her hands on a towel. "We have fruit if you'd prefer," she offered, her tone professionally polite but noticeably cooler than her usual friendly manner with customers. "Or would you rather stick with air and self-importance?"

I nearly choked, shooting her a warning glance. "Allison, this is Craig Beauregard, my ex from Chicago. Craig, this is Allison Carmichael, my right hand here at Maddy Cakes."

"Our families know each other," Allison said coolly.

Craig extended his hand, which Allison shook briefly before excusing herself to help another customer. His expression registered mild surprise at her frosty reception.

"She seems... dedicated," he observed. "I wouldn't have even recognized her... I haven't seen her since she was a kid.

"She *is* dedicated," I confirmed. "I'd be lost without her."

An awkward silence fell between us. I was acutely aware of the eyes watching our interaction — Gramps' chess buddies making no effort to hide their interest, Mrs. Whitman pausing her conversation with the bank manager to observe, even Jimmy Cheng lingering longer than necessary at the pastry case.

"Could we speak privately?" Craig asked, lowering his voice. "Just for a few minutes."

Every instinct told me to refuse, to keep this unexpected reunion firmly in the public sphere. But curiosity won out — what could possibly have brought Craig to Sugar Creek after all this time?

"Five minutes," I conceded. "I'll meet you in my office. It's through that door."

As Craig headed toward the back, I caught Allison's eye. "Could you handle things out here for a bit?"

"Are you sure you want to be alone with him?" she asked quietly, concern evident in her expression.

"It's fine," I assured her. "I just want to find out what he's doing here and then send him on his way."

She nodded, though her worried frown remained. "I'll be right out here if you need me."

I slipped into the office, finding Craig examining the framed photos on my desk: pictures of Gram, of Lacy and me, and one of Rex and me at a community picnic last month, both of us laughing as Chloe photobombed the shot.

"So," I said, closing the door partway but not completely. "What brings you back to Sugar Creek, Craig?"

He turned, setting down the photo he'd been studying. "Family visit," he said. "My parents still live here, remember?"

"Right." How could I forget? His family's law firm was just down the block near the courthouse, and Craig's parents lived on the wealthy outskirts of Sugar Creek, though they rarely ventured into town for social occasions, preferring Charleston's more upscale amenities. "And you just happened to stop by my bakery?"

"Not exactly a coincidence," he admitted, his expression shifting to something more serious. "I wanted to see you, Maddy. I've been doing a lot of thinking since you left."

I leaned against the edge of my desk, keeping physical distance between us. "It's been nearly five months, Craig. That's a lot of thinking."

"I know." He ran a hand through his perfectly styled hair, a gesture I once found endearing but now recognized as a calculated move to appear vulnerable. "I've been... reevaluating things. My priorities. What matters to me." He took a step closer. "I made mistakes, Maddy. I took you for granted. I didn't appreciate what we had until it was gone."

The words were right, but they felt rehearsed, like dialogue from a romantic movie rather than genuine reflection. "I see," I said neutrally. "And you came all this way to tell me that?"

"Partly," he acknowledged. "But also to share some news. I've been offered a partnership at Hargrove and Williams. It's one of the top firms in Charleston."

And there it was. The real reason for his appearance. Not to apologize, not to check on my well-being, but to boast about his latest professional achievement.

"Congratulations," I said, genuinely meaning it. Craig had always been talented and ambitious; his success wasn't surprising. "That's a big accomplishment."

"It is," he agreed, straightening slightly with pride. "And it changes things, Maddy. Charleston is just an hour away from here. We could make it work now. I could support your... hobby." He gestured vaguely toward the bakery beyond the door. "You wouldn't have to give up this place. I'd make sure of it."

My "hobby." Even now, after seeing every table packed out front, the thriving business I'd built, he couldn't bring himself to acknowledge it as a legitimate career, a true passion.

"Craig," I began carefully, "I'm glad things are working out for you professionally. But there is no 'we' anymore. That chapter of our lives is closed."

"Don't say that," he insisted, moving closer until he was standing directly in front of me. "We had ten years together, Maddy. That's not something to throw away lightly. I know I made mistakes, but I've changed. I see things differently now."

I studied his face, searching for evidence of this supposed transformation. His eyes held the same self-assured confidence they always had, his posture the same slight impatience, as if this conversation was taking longer than he'd scheduled for it.

"What things do you see differently?" I challenged gently.

"Well," he hesitated, clearly not having expected to elaborate. "I see that... balance is important. That relationships require compromise."

"Compromise," I repeated. "Like me compromising my dreams for your career for a decade?"

A flicker of annoyance crossed his features before he masked it with a conciliatory smile. "That's not fair, Maddy. I've always supported your interests. I just wanted you to be practical about them."

"No, you wanted me to keep them small enough not to interfere with your life plan," I corrected, the clarity of hindsight making the pattern obvious. "You were fine with me baking as long as it didn't take up too much space, too much time, or too much of my attention."

"That's not..." he began, but I held up a hand to stop him.

"It's okay, Craig. I'm not angry anymore. But I am done pretending that what we had was a partnership. It wasn't. It was me orbiting your life, trying to make myself small enough to fit into the tiny little nooks and crannies you left for me."

His expression hardened slightly, that familiar look of frustration when I wasn't following his script. "I think you're being unfair. I came all this way to offer an olive branch, to suggest we try again with a fresh perspective, and you're throwing the past in my face."

"I'm not throwing anything," I said calmly. "I'm just acknowledging reality. We want different things, Craig. We always did. I was just too afraid to admit it before. I didn't want to lose you. Now, I can barely remember why."

A knock at the door interrupted us. Allison peeked in, her expression apologetic but determined. "Sorry to interrupt, but we've got a situation with the delivery for the Henderson wedding. Apparently, there's confusion about the pickup time."

I knew immediately this was a rescue attempt; the Henderson wedding cake wasn't scheduled for delivery until next week. "I'll be right there," I assured her.

"Sounds like you're needed," Craig observed, unable to completely mask his irritation at the interruption. "But we should continue this conversation. Have dinner with me tonight. There's a nice place in Charleston I've been wanting to try."

The invitation caught me off guard. Despite everything I'd just said, Craig was proceeding as if my objections were merely a temporary obstacle to his plan. It was so familiar, his absolute certainty that he could eventually persuade me to his point of view, that I almost laughed.

But beneath my incredulity, I felt a strange curiosity. Was it possible Craig was actually different? Could one last dinner provide some closure for both of us?

I was just about to shut down Craig's dumb idea of driving all the way to Charleston for dinner, but the last thing I wanted was everybody in town gossiping about the two of us. Plus, a restaurant outside of town would substantially lower the odds of accidentally running into Rex.

"Alright," I heard myself say. "Dinner. But just to talk, Craig. Don't misinterpret this as anything more."

His smile was triumphant, as if he'd won an important negotiation. "Excellent. I'll pick you up at seven? Here, I assume?"

"I'll meet you there," I countered, unwilling to give him even that modicum of control. "Text me the details." No way was I going to be stuck in Charleston at Craig's whim.

As Craig left, breezing past Allison with a perfunctory nod, I caught the questioning look in her eyes. "Are you sure about this?" she asked once he was out of earshot.

"No," I admitted. "But we were together for ten years and I feel like I need to at least hear him out. Even if it's a total waste of time."

"If you say so," she replied dubiously. "But if you need an emergency phone call to escape, just text me 'recipe crisis' and I'll call with another fictional bakery emergency."

I laughed, grateful for her loyalty. "I might take you up on that."

The rest of the morning passed in a blur of customers and orders. Word of Craig's appearance spread through the Sugar Creek grapevine with predictable speed. By noon, Lacy burst through the door, eyes wide with indignation.

"Tell me I'm hearing things," she demanded, planting her hands on the counter. "You're having dinner with Craig? Craig 'Soul-Sucking Leech' Beauregard? What about Rex?"

"How on earth would you know that?"

"I just ran into his mother at the post office," she said. Small towns. Nothing is secret.

I sighed, setting aside the order form I'd been reviewing. "It's just dinner, Lacy. I think I need to put that relationship properly to rest."

"Can't you just run him over with your car instead?" She rolled her eyes dramatically. "You think dinner with him is the way to do that? While you and Rex are in the middle of your first real fight?"

"This has nothing to do with Rex," I insisted, though even to my own ears, the protest sounded weak.

"Bull," Lacy declared flatly. "This has everything to do with Rex. You're hurt and confused, and Craig shows up looking all polished and familiar, offering a version of your relationship that never actually existed."

Her blunt assessment hit uncomfortably close to home. "Maybe I just need the comparison," I suggested. "To remind myself why I left in the first place."

Lacy's expression softened slightly. "Honey, if you need a reminder of why Craig was wrong for you, I've got about eight hundred examples saved up. I don't think having dinner with the human equivalent of a cardboard cutout is going to provide any clarity you don't already have."

I couldn't help but smile at her description. "A cardboard cutout?"

"Yes!" she exclaimed. "He looks good from a distance, but there's no substance. No depth. He's a walking LinkedIn profile in expensive shoes."

My phone buzzed with a text message. Thinking it might be Craig with the restaurant details, I glanced down, my heart stuttering when I saw Rex's name instead.

I miss you. I made a mistake. Can we talk when you're ready?

The simple honesty of his message, so different from Craig's rehearsed speech and calculated gestures, made my throat tighten. Rex wasn't perfect; he'd messed up badly. But there was a genuineness to him that Craig had never possessed, a willingness to admit fault without qualification.

"That's Rex?" Lacy guessed, reading my expression.

I nodded, showing her the message.

"Well," she said after reading it, "at least one of the men in your life knows how to communicate like an actual human being."

"I'm still upset with him," I reminded her, though the sharp edge of my anger had dulled somewhat overnight.

"As you should be," Lacy agreed. "What he did was wrong. But wrong and unforgivable aren't the same thing, Maddy. Everyone makes mistakes. The question is whether this mistake is a dealbreaker for you."

Her words stayed with me throughout the afternoon as I prepared for my dinner with Craig. By the time I arrived at the upscale Charleston restaurant he'd selected, I felt oddly calm, as if I were observing the evening from a slight distance rather than actively participating in it.

Craig was already seated at a prime table, rising to greet me with a kiss on the cheek that I artfully dodged by pretending to adjust my purse. The restaurant was exactly what I would have expected from Craig — sleek, modern, with prices that made my small business owner heart clench. What did I care? He could afford it

"You look stunning," he said, his eyes appraising my simple navy dress with approval. "I've always loved you in that color."

"Thank you," I replied, taking my seat. "This place is beautiful."

"Only the best," he agreed, signaling the sommelier. "I took the liberty of ordering champagne to celebrate our reunion."

The phrasing made me cringe internally, but I kept my expression neutral as the sommelier approached with an ice bucket containing what I was sure was an absurdly expensive bottle.

"Actually," I interjected before Craig could speak, "I'd prefer just a glass of white wine. Sauvignon Blanc, if you have it."

The sommelier glanced at Craig, whose momentary flash of annoyance was quickly masked by a magnanimous smile. "Of course. A glass of your best Sauvignon Blanc for the lady, and I'll have a scotch, neat."

After our drinks arrived, Craig launched into a detailed account of his career trajectory since I'd left Chicago: the cases he'd won, the connections he'd made, the partnership track offer that had brought him to Charleston. I listened attentively, or at least created a convincing appearance of attentiveness, while my mind cataloged the familiar patterns in his conversation.

Everything was about him. His accomplishments. His challenges. His solutions. In the fifteen minutes he'd been speaking, he hadn't asked me a single question about my life, my business, or my experience since moving to Sugar Creek.

It was almost surreal, as though we'd just picked up where we left off five months ago.

"...and so when Harrison offered me the partnership, I knew it was the right move," Craig concluded, taking a self-satisfied sip of his scotch. "Charleston has all the culture and opportunities of a major city, but with better weather and a more relaxed pace of life."

"It sounds like things have worked out well for you," I said, genuinely glad that he'd found professional success. Craig had always been extremely ambitious and hardworking; he at least deserved his accomplishments. Even though they often came at the expense of my own dreams. Okay, yes, I was still maybe a bit salty over all that.

"They have," he agreed, his expression shifting to what I recognized as his 'serious discussion' face. "But something's been missing, Maddy. *Someone's* been missing."

And there it was — the pivot I'd been expecting. Craig had established his value through his professional achievements and was now moving to the personal proposition.

"Craig," I began gently, "I... "

"Let me finish," he interrupted, reaching across the table to take my hand. I allowed the contact, curious about my own reaction more than anything else. "I know things weren't perfect between us. I know I focused too much on my career, that I didn't always give our relationship the attention it deserved. But what we had was special, Maddy. Ten years of history isn't something you just walk away from."

I studied his face — the mock-earnest expression, the practiced sincerity in his eyes. There had been a time when this speech would have melted my resistance, when the mere suggestion that Craig Beauregard, rising star of the legal world, regretted losing me would have sent me scrambling to accommodate his needs and secure his affection.

But now was not that time.

All I felt was a strange detachment, as if I were watching a weird performance rather than participating in a genuine emotional exchange.

"What exactly are you proposing, Craig?" I asked, extracting my hand from his to take a sip of wine.

He seemed momentarily thrown by my directness but recovered quickly. "I'm suggesting we try again. With my position in Charleston and your... bakery project here, we could make it work. We have options now that we didn't have before."

"And what about long-term?" I pressed. "What does that look like in your mind?"

Craig's smile turned indulgent, as if I were asking about minor details rather than the foundation of a potential shared future. "Eventually, you could relocate to Charleston. There's a much bigger market for artisanal baking there. You could establish yourself in a real culinary scene, not just..." he waved vaguely, "...a small town with limited opportunities."

There it was: the assumption that my work, my passion, my dreams were secondary, adaptable to fit around his fixed priorities. Nothing had changed.

"I see," I said simply. "And it doesn't occur to you that I might not want to leave Sugar Creek? That I've built something meaningful there that can't just be transplanted to a new location?"

Craig's brow furrowed slightly, as if the question genuinely confused him. "But it's just a bakery, Maddy. You could open another one anywhere. It's not like you've established some multinational corporation with infrastructure that can't be moved."

"It's not just a bakery," I corrected, feeling a surge of pride in what I'd created. "It's a community hub, a space where people connect, a legacy passed down from my grandmother. It's woven into the fabric of Sugar Creek in ways you can't quantify on a balance sheet."

"That sounds lovely in theory," Craig said, his tone subtly patronizing, "but practically speaking, a business is a business. You provide a product, customers buy it. That *transaction* can happen anywhere. Why not a bigger marketplace?"

I took a deep breath, reminding myself that Craig wasn't being intentionally dismissive. He genuinely couldn't comprehend the value I placed on the intangible aspects of Maddy Cakes. We existed in different realities, with fundamentally incompatible worldviews.

"Let me tell you about last month," I said, setting down my wine glass. "A regular customer, Mrs. Thompson, eighty-three years old, didn't show up for her usual Tuesday morning muffin. By noon, Allison and I were worried enough to call her neighbor, who found her fallen in her bathroom, unable to reach her phone. That call probably saved her life."

Craig's expression registered polite interest, but I could tell he was waiting for the point of the story.

I leaned forward, warming to my subject. "Last week," I continued, "Gramps and his chess club organized a tournament that raised three thousand dollars for the elementary school music program. They planned the entire thing over coffee and scones at the corner table. The same table where the town council informally drafts most of their proposals before official meetings."

Craig's smile had become fixed, his eyes showing the glazed look he got when a conversation wasn't going in his preferred direction. "That's all very... community-minded," he managed.

"It's not just a bakery, Craig," I repeated firmly. "It's a vital part of a community. My community. I could no more transplant it to Charleston than you could practice law without passing the bar exam. The context, the relationships, the history... they're all essential components."

For a moment, genuine confusion crossed his features. "I didn't realize you'd become so... *invested* in small-town life," he said finally. "I thought this was a phase, a way to process your grandmother's death before moving on to something more substantial. I grew up in Sugar Creek, and I couldn't wait to get out of that place."

And there it was, the fundamental disconnect that had always existed between us. Craig saw my bakery, my passion, and my choices as temporary, less significant than his own career path. Not because he was intentionally cruel, but because he genuinely couldn't comprehend a definition of success that differed from his own.

"That *place* is the only place that's ever truly felt like home to me. It's not a phase," I said quietly. "This is my life now. The one I choose, every day."

Our entrees arrived, momentarily pausing the conversation. I realized I had no appetite despite the beautifully presented salmon before me. Craig, however, seemed eager for the interruption, quickly turning the discussion to more neutral topics: mutual acquaintances from Chicago, changes in the legal industry, and his parents' recent vacation to Italy.

I participated in the conversation on autopilot, my mind increasingly occupied with thoughts of Rex. His honest mistake, born of fear and inexperience with serious relationships, seemed so different from Craig's fundamental inability to see me as an equal partner with valid dreams of my own.

By the time dessert arrived, a deconstructed tiramisu that would have fascinated me under different circumstances, I had reached a clarity that surprised me with its certainty.

"Craig," I said, setting down my spoon, "I appreciate you reaching out, and I wish you every success with your new position in Charleston. But there's no future for us together. There never was, not really."

His expression shifted from surprise to disbelief. "You can't be serious. I'm offering you everything you wanted... support for your bakery, proximity, a fresh start. What more could you be looking for?"

"A partner who sees me," I said simply. "Who values what I value, not because it's important to him personally, but because it's important to me. Someone who thinks of us as equals building something together."

Craig's jaw tightened, that familiar tension that always appeared when negotiations weren't going his way. "This is about that veterinarian, isn't it? The one in the photo on your desk."

I shook my head. "No, Craig. This is about me. About who I've become, what I want, what I deserve. Rex is..." I paused, searching for the right words. "Rex is a separate question. But even if he weren't in the picture at all, you and I would still be wrong for each other. We always were. I just couldn't see it until I found the courage to leave."

"Courage?" he repeated, genuine bewilderment in his voice. "You think running away from what we had to make, I don't know, cookies or whatever, was *courageous*? Most people would call it self-sabotage."

"Most people aren't me," I said with a small smile. "And what we had was a relationship where one person's dreams always took precedence over the other's. That's not a partnership, or a relationship, Craig. That's just a bad arrangement. And I deserve more than that."

"Your bakery isn't exactly a resounding success," he said tersely. "My mother said the whole town had to pitch in to buy you a used oven. I don't know why you'd take charity when you could just take a bank loan."

"The fact that the whole town pitched in to buy Maddy Cakes a new oven isn't evidence that it is a failure. It's evidence that my bakery, Gram's bakery, *means something* to our community. They pitched in because a bank loan wasn't feasible because of the way Gram's will was structured, and I barely had any savings because I spent the last ten years taking crappy jobs in cities I didn't want to live in to support *your* career. I couldn't be prouder of what I've built."

For a long moment, he studied me, as if seeing me clearly for the first time. "You've changed," he said finally.

"I have," I agreed. "I've become the person I was always meant to be. And she doesn't cram herself into the spaces left over in someone else's big life. She builds her own big life."

I stood up, pulling the strap of my purse over my shoulder. "Thank you for dinner, Craig. Good luck with the rest of *your* life."

He remained seated at the table, shaking his head in disbelief.

I marched myself out to my car and sat shaking in the driver's seat for a moment, feeling more powerful than I ever had in my relationship with Craig.

My decision with regard to Rex suddenly crystallized with unexpected clarity. Rex had made a mistake — a significant one — but it wasn't unforgivable. It wasn't a reflection of fundamental disrespect or dismissal of my needs. It was a human error born of fear and inexperience, the kind of mistake that could be learned from, grown through.

Everyone deserved the chance to make mistakes and grow from them. Including Rex. Including me.

I pulled out my phone and quickly texted Rex: "I'm sorry too. I'm ready to talk when you are."

Chapter 24

The drive home from Charleston should have taken an hour. I made it in forty-five minutes, my foot heavy on the accelerator as Craig's dismissive words echoed in my mind. *Your bakery isn't exactly a resounding success... most people would call it self-sabotage.*

But instead of feeling hurt by his assessment, I felt... liberated. Sitting across from Craig tonight had been like looking at a photograph of my old life — flat, lifeless, confined to someone else's frame. The contrast with what I'd built in Sugar Creek was so stark it took my breath away.

I'd texted Rex an hour ago, but my phone had remained stubbornly silent. No response. No indication he'd even read the message.

By the time I pulled into my parking space behind the bakery, anxiety was gnawing at my stomach. What if Rex had taken my silence as a final answer? What if he'd already made his decision about the New York job and was done trying to work things out? What if I'd screwed this up?

I grabbed my phone and called Lacy.

"How was dinner with the stiff?" she answered without preamble.

"Clarifying," I said, climbing the stairs to my apartment. "Lacy, I was an idiot. About Rex, I mean. Craig just confirmed everything I already knew. Rex made a mistake, but he's nothing like Craig. Rex actually sees me and values what I've built here. What the hell was I thinking?"

"About damn time you realized that," Lacy said. "So what are you going to do about it?"

"I texted him an hour ago, but he hasn't responded. I'm thinking of just showing up at his place." I paused at my door, key in hand. "Is that crazy? Should I wait for him to text back?"

"Hell no, don't wait," Lacy declared. "Head over there and have an honest conversation like adults. Kiss. Have spectacular make-up sex. Rex is probably staring at his phone trying to figure out what to say back just like you were doing all day yesterday."

Her certainty bolstered my resolve. "You're right. I'm going over there."

"Good. Call me afterward and tell me how it goes. And Maddy? Don't let pride get in the way of happiness. You've both made mistakes, but that doesn't mean you can't fix them."

"What if I freaked him out by telling him I loved him and bringing up moving in together?" I wailed. "Rex is the one for me! I'm in love with him and… and what if I messed it all up?

"Maybe you did," Lacy responded thoughtfully, "but even if all of this ends in flames, it's still good."

"Are you crazy? Why would overreacting or acting like I'm trying to lock him down five minutes before his usual relationship escape be a *good* thing?"

"Because finally, finally, you said out loud what you wanted from your relationship. That's a huge step Maddy, even if it ends badly. Because you finally gave your needs as much importance as you did somebody else's. And chips fall where they may, you're standing up for yourself now. You've grown, Maddy. You're not the same person you were when you arrived in Sugar Creek. You're confident, you're excited about your life, and you're clear about what you really want. Gram would be so proud of you right now."

"Thanks," I said, trying to hold back my tears. "I want Maddy Cakes. I want Sugar Creek. And I want Rex."

"Then go get him," she laughed.

Ten minutes later, I was standing on Rex's front porch, my heart hammering against my ribs. His truck was gone, but there were lights on inside and another car in the driveway — a silver sedan I didn't recognize.

I knocked, and to my surprise, Della answered the door. Her face lit up when she saw me.

"Maddy! Thank God," she said, pulling me into an unexpected hug. "I was hoping you'd show up."

"Is Rex here?" I asked, confused by her enthusiastic welcome. "I sent him a text but haven't heard back."

Della's expression shifted to something like panic. "He left about twenty minutes ago for the Charleston airport." She ran a hand through her hair. "Maddy--he forgot his phone. There's no way to reach him."

My stomach dropped. "The airport? He's taking the job?"

"I don't know!" Della said, stepping back to let me inside. "He wouldn't talk to me about it. Just said he had something important to take care of in New York and that he'd be back tomorrow. But his interview was yesterday, so why would he need to go back unless..."

She didn't finish the sentence, but I could fill in the blanks. Unless he was accepting the position. Unless he'd decided Sugar Creek, and I, weren't enough to keep him here.

"What time is his flight?" I asked, already reaching for Rex's phone on the counter.

"Ten-thirty, I think? He was in such a rush, muttering about traffic and needing a rental car." Della watched as I checked his phone, seeing my own unanswered messages along with several missed calls from his clinic and what looked like work-related texts.

"Okay, it's nine-fifteen now," I said, my mind racing. "If I leave right now..."

"The airport's at least forty minutes away," Della pointed out. "And that's without traffic or having to park and get through security."

"Then I'd better hurry." I grabbed Rex's phone, ignoring Della's protests about the impossibility of the mission. "I'll tell him I'm returning this. At least then I can say goodbye properly."

"Maddy, wait!" Della called as I headed for the door. "Take my car. It's faster than yours."

She tossed me her keys as something from the counter caught my eye. "Are those macarons?"

"Yeah, why? Rex bought them earlier, said they were your favorites from that place in Charleston. I think he was planning to surprise you with them. Don't tell him I told you."

The gesture — Rex thinking of me even while dealing with his own career crisis — made my throat tight. I snatched the box of macarons and Della's keys, determination flooding through me.

"Thank you," I said, already moving toward her car.

"Go get him!" she called from the porch. "And drive safely!"

The drive to Charleston International Airport was a blur of speed limits pushed to their absolute maximum and increasingly frantic calculations of time versus distance. Della's car handled like a dream, but even so, I arrived at the airport at ten, with exactly five minutes until Rex's boarding time, which Della had texted to me as I drove like a speed demon to the airport.

I abandoned the car in short-term parking, grabbed Rex's phone and sprinted toward the terminal. The automated doors seemed to take forever to open. Once inside, I was faced with the overwhelming maze of departure gates and security checkpoints.

"Excuse me," I gasped to the nearest airline representative, a patient-looking woman in her fifties. "I need to reach someone before their flight takes off. Flight to New York?"

She glanced at her computer screen. "Ma'am, that flight is already boarding. You'd need a ticket to get past security, and... "

"Please," I interrupted, holding up Rex's phone. "He forgot this. I just need to give it to him."

The representative's expression softened. "I'm sorry, but I can't let you through without a ticket..."

"Okay, fine. I'll buy a ticket. What's the cheapest flight you have that gets me through security?"

"The purchase window has closed for that flight..."

"Any flight!" I say, frantically.

The agent continued, "However, I can call the gate and see if your friend is still there. What's the name?"

"Dr. Rexford Townsend," I panted.

She made the call while I stood there bouncing on my toes with nervous energy. After what felt like an eternity, she shook her head. "I'm sorry, but passenger Townsend isn't responding to the gate page. There's a weather delay, but it looks like the flight is boarding now."

My heart sank. I was too late.

"Please? Is there anything else we can do?" I pleaded. "It's not just about the phone, it's about...I made a mistake..."

"I'm so sorry," the agent patted my hand kindly. "How about some free drink tickets for the next time you fly with us?" she asked.

"Thank you anyway," I managed, crushed, trying to keep the tears from coming. I turned away from the counter with Rex's phone still clutched in my hand.

I was halfway back to the parking garage, feeling deflated and completely ridiculous and, emotionally, a lot like a sausage about to explode its casing. I briefly contemplated trying to sneak through the checkpoint or outrun airport security, but this wasn't *Love*

Actually and as my diet these days consisted primarily of scones and cupcakes, I thought better of it. This was not the time to start committing felonies. Devastated, I sat down on a hard bench next to the elevators, and unable to hold myself back any longer, I burst into tears.

I was digging through my purse looking for a receipt or a napkin or something to blow my nose on when I heard a familiar voice calling my name.

"Maddy? Maddy!"

I spun around to see Rex jogging toward me through the terminal, still sexy in his suit but looking thoroughly disheveled. His tie was loose, his hair mussed.

"Rex?" I stared at him in confusion. "I thought you were on the plane to New York."

"I was," he said, stopping in front of me, slightly out of breath. "But then they announced a two-hour delay due to weather, and I started thinking about what I was doing, why I was going, and..." He ran a hand through his already messy hair. "And I realized I was being an idiot."

"You're not taking the job?" I asked, afraid to hope.

"I was never taking the job," Rex said, his voice growing stronger. "Dr. Wright is someone I respect immensely. I was flying to New York to turn it down in person...I felt I owed her. But then I started second-guessing myself, wondering if I was making the right choice, if I was being fair to you..."

"Fair to me?" I interrupted, confusion evident in my voice.

"By staying," he explained, his eyes intense on mine. "By choosing Sugar Creek over, you know, a dream job. I didn't want *you* to feel responsible for holding me back from opportunities."

I stared at him, pieces clicking into place. "So you were going to turn down the job?"

"I was always going to turn it down," he confirmed. "From the moment Dr. Wright first contacted me, I was sure I didn't want to leave Sugar Creek. I just went through the interview process because I thought I owed it to myself to explore the option. And then I was too scared to tell you about it because I was afraid you'd think I wasn't serious about us, about staying. Or that you'd think I was *too serious*, to turn down this huge opportunity over a three-month relationship."

"Three months is sort of your thing though, isn't it?" I replied.

"Three months was never going to be enough time with you," he said quietly. "You're the type of woman that makes a man start thinking about forever."

Warmth, relief, and exasperation warred in my chest. "Rex, you absolute — " I stopped, registering something he'd said. "Wait. What made you decide not to get on the plane?"

A sheepish smile crossed his face. "I was sitting at the gate, feeling miserable about our fight and wishing I'd handled everything differently. And then this couple next to me started arguing about their trip. The guy apparently planned the whole itinerary and was insisting he knew what was best for both of them, not listening to a word she was saying." Rex's expression grew serious. "I realized that's exactly what I'd been doing with you. Making decisions about our future without including you in the conversation."

"So you're like a professional eavesdropper," I teased.

"Of course. I live in a small town," he replied nonchalantly.

"And you didn't get on the plane," I said softly.

"I didn't get on the plane," he confirmed. "I decided to drive back tonight instead of staying over in New York like I'd planned. I figured if I was going to grovel for forgiveness, I should do it properly and in person."

I held up his phone. "You forgot this. Della was worried when you didn't answer."

"Shit," Rex muttered, taking the phone and quickly scanning the missed messages and calls. His expression softened when he saw my texts. "Wait. You were ready to talk?"

"No, I just like to hang out at the airport," I replied. "I was ready to apologize. And to admit that I might have overreacted. *A little*."

"You didn't overreact," Rex said firmly. "I should have told you about the interview from the beginning. I should have trusted you with my doubts and fears instead of trying to protect you from them. I'm out of my depth with you Maddy. I want nothing more than to create a home with you, a life with you. But I swore I'd never subject someone I love to the uncertainty of military life...and even though I'm no longer on active duty, I still worry we'll create a life and a home together and I'll be pulled away and tear it all apart...and that's not fair to you."

"What's not fair to me is making a decision about what's fair to me without, you know, *checking* with me."

"You're right," he said, shaking his head. "You're right."

I took a step closer, closing some of the distance between us. "And I should have listened to your explanation instead of immediately comparing you to Craig. That wasn't fair either."

"Forgiven. Can we agree we both messed up and move forward?" Rex asked, hope evident in his voice.

"Yes. Please," I said, rushing into his embrace.

I stood on my tiptoes to kiss him. The kiss was soft, tentative at first, then deeper as relief and joy flooded through both of us.

When we broke apart, Rex rested his forehead against mine. "I love you, Maddy. I love how much you adore Sugar Creek. I love that it feels like I've known you all my life. I love that your hair always smells like sugar cookies...I love you, and I love the life we're building in Sugar Creek. I don't want to be anywhere else. I don't want to be *with* anyone else." He grinned. "I want to put down *roots* with you."

"I love you too," I whispered. "And I'm sorry I didn't trust that."

"So what happens now?" Rex asked, his hands finding mine. "Do we go home and pretend this never happened?"

"We go home," I agreed. "But we don't pretend it never happened. We learn from it. We promise to talk to each other about the big stuff, even when it's scary or complicated."

Rex nodded solemnly. "Deal. No more secret job interviews. No more protecting you from my doubts."

"And no more jumping to conclusions or making comparisons to past relationships," I added. "We're us, not me and Craig or you and whoever came before."

"We're us," Rex repeated, smiling. "I like the sound of that."

As we walked back toward the parking garage, hand in hand, I felt a lightness I hadn't experienced in days. The crisis with Rex had forced me to examine what I really wanted and what I was willing to fight for. And Craig's reappearance had shown me how far I'd come from the woman who'd once contorted herself to fit into someone else's dreams.

"Oh crap," I said when we arrived on the parking level where I'd left Della's car.

"What? Rex asked, his eyes filled with concern.

"Um, yeah, what kind of car does Della drive again? I was in such a hurry that I forgot where I parked. And...uh, what kind of car I was driving."

He laughed as he took the key fob from my hand, held it high in the air, and pressed the button repeatedly until we heard the horn beeping.

"So," Rex said as we reached Della's car, our fingers intertwined, "how was dinner with your ex?"

"Illuminating," I replied, leaning against the driver's side door. "It reminded me of all the reasons I left Chicago in the first place. And all the reasons I'm grateful to be building a life with someone who actually treats me as an equal partner."

"Someone devastatingly handsome and charming?" Rex suggested with a grin.

"Why yes!" I smiled.

"Someone who's loved by animals?" he grinned.

"Yes..." My heart was practically pounding out of my chest.

"Someone who knows how to hit number ten on your bucket list?" he whispered in my ear, kissing his way down my jawline, and pulling me tighter against him. "Twice in one night?"

"Yes," I answered breathlessly, "someone exactly like that." He closed the distance between us and pressed his lean, hard body against mine, kissing me so intensely he took my breath away.

When we came up for air, Rex laughed, the sound echoing in the parking garage. "Good to know."

I drove Rex to his truck on level six, and we talked on the phone the whole drive back to Sugar Creek.

We talked through all the events of the past few days — Rex's anxiety about the job interview, my hurt at being excluded, the relief we both felt at clearing the air. By the time we reached town, it felt like we'd not only resolved our conflict but emerged stronger for having worked through it.

"Your place or mine?" Rex asked as we approached the decision point where our routes home diverged.

"Mine," I said without hesitation. "I want to show you something."

Ten minutes later, we were climbing the stairs to my apartment above the bakery. I could hear the familiar sounds of Sugar Creek settling into evening: distant laughter from the bar down the street, the soft murmur of conversations as people walked past, the gentle hum of the streetlights flickering on.

"What did you want to show me?" Rex asked as I unlocked my door.

Instead of answering, I led him to the window in my living room, and opened it enough so we could climb through to the tiny Juliet balcony, where a perfect view of Main Street stretched out below us like a jewel.

"I just figured out I could open this window yesterday," I grinned. "Nice view, isn't it?"

The hardware store's sign glowed softly in the evening light, the trees on the square were filled with twinkling lights, and if you stood on your tippy toes on the far left side of the balcony, you could see Lake Sugar.

"This," I said, gesturing to the scene below. "I wanted to show you this. What we've built here. What we're part of."

Rex moved to stand behind me, his arms encircling my waist as we looked out over our town. "It's beautiful," he said softly.

"It's home," I corrected. "And I choose it. I choose this place, this community, this life we're building together. I choose you."

"Even if it means turning down opportunities elsewhere?" Rex asked, and I could hear the echo of his own choice in the question.

"Especially then," I said firmly. "Some things are worth more than opportunities, Rex. Some things are worth staying for."

Rex's arms tightened around me. "I couldn't agree more."

We stood there in comfortable silence, watching as Sugar Creek prepared for night. A few blocks away, I could see lights still on in the veterinary clinic where Rex had built his practice. Below us, Maddy Cakes waited for tomorrow's batch of fresh pastries and the customers who had become like family.

Rex's arms to face him. "What if we start looking for a house together this weekend? A place that's just... ours."

My smile was radiant. "I'd love that. A real home, not just somewhere we crash between work obligations."

"With a porch where we can sit in the evenings and wave at neighbors walking by," he added.

"And a kitchen big enough for both of us to cook in without bumping into each other," I continued, warming to the vision.

"With a big yard with a fence for the dogs," he grinned.

"*Very* Sugar Creek of us," I teased.

"The best kind of life," Rex replied, kissing me softly.

As we headed back inside, already making plans and dreaming about the future, I felt a profound sense of contentment settle over me. This was what partnership, what a *relationship*, really looked like. Two people choosing each other while remaining fully themselves, building something together that honored both their individual dreams and their shared vision.

For the first time, I was creating my own life and not just allowing myself to be an afterthought in somebody else's. Since I'd arrived in Sugar Creek, I'd knocked half the items off my bucket list. I'd finally achieved my dream of owning a bakery. I felt an overwhelming sense of belonging in a place that had always felt like home. I'd stood up to

Craig when he tried to steamroll me once again. And I'd stood up for what I wanted–what I needed–in my relationship with Rex.

I felt...proud.

And I knew Gram would be proud of me too.

My phone buzzed with a text from Lacy: *Did you find him? Do I need to bail you out of airport jail?*

I quickly typed back: *Found him. We're good. Very good.*

Her response was immediate: *Thank God. I was already planning your jailbreak. See you tomorrow at the bakery for a full debrief.*

"Everything okay?" Rex asked, noticing my smile.

"Everything's perfect," I said, and for the first time in my adult life, I actually meant it.